THE LOST BOYS OF
EVERYWHEN

THE LOST BOYS OF
EVERYWHEN

MAX THOMPSON
WITH K.A. THOMPSON

The Wick Books Reading Order

The Emperor of San Francisco
The Wick Chronicles, Book One

Ozoo
The Wick Chronicles, Book Two

Forked
The Wick Chronicles, Book Three

*

The Space Between Whens
Wick After Dark, Book One

The Blessings of Saint Wick
Wick After Dark, Book Two

*

The Whens of Wick
Return of the Wick Chronicles, Book One

The Book of Hyrum
Return of the Wick Chronicles, Book Two

Jump
Return of the Wick Chronicles Book Three

The King of Saint Francis
Return of the Wick Chronicles, Book Four

*

Waiting to Inhale
Wick Shorts, Book One

No Matter the When
Wick Shorts, Book Two

THE LOST BOYS OF
EVERYWHEN

A WICK NOVEL

1

"Why is there a disembodied head on the dining room table?" Aisha tossed her bag onto the breakfast bar and set her hands on her hips, head tilted a touch as she considered the lifeless face. "Should we search the apartment for the body?"

"There's no blood on the table." Will set the grocery bags he'd carried up the stairs next to her purse. "None on the floor. No drag marks across the living room. I suspect we're only dealing with a wayward head."

You're both surprisingly calm about finding a head on the table.

"Well, we do have Charlie," Aisha mused.

Fourteen-year-old Charles Blackshear, Charlie to his parents and Chucky to his classmates, was neither a psychopath nor a sociopath, but he tended to leave a wake of destruction behind him. He disassembled toys on a whim, often unable to put things back together, and as he eased into adolescence his curiosities about the way things worked had extended to an expensive video monitor, a brand-new vacuum cleaner, an antique pocket watch, and a table-top hologram simulator he'd been left alone with in Will's office at Ozoo Enterprises.

It was not a stretch to assume that he was responsible for the lifeless head currently occupying the foot of the table. It was also not a given; his siblings were almost as guilty in the let's-break-crap-for-fun department. Alex disassembled the entire shower stall in her bathroom, searching for a wayward creak that turned out to be her brother's bed on the other side of the wall. And Rhys took apart...everything. The difference between him and the others was his ability to reassemble the things which he'd taken apart.

Footsteps lumbered in the stretch between our apartment and Oz and Drew's. Those feet were a size and a half bigger than Charlie's and moved with purpose. I turned just as Rhys entered, his arms wrapped around a bright red storage case that was as big around as he was. At fifteen, he was as tall as his father, thin but not skinny, and the muscles in his forearms pressed against taut skin as he set the case on a chair near the head of the table.

"Good, you've met Horatio." He grunted, standing upright. "I invited him to stay for a while. I hope it's all right. He doesn't eat much."

Aisha turned to Will. "All right, so it's not Charlie we need to worry about."

"Friend from school?" Will asked.

"He's this year's cybernetics challenge project."

Aisha touched a finger to the head's dark hair. "So, where's the rest of him? Is he a gender-neutral drone or does he have—"

"Jesus, Mom," Rhys sighed. "It's a head. Just a head. There's no body so no...junk."

"Just curious."

Amused, Will asked, "What's the challenge?"

Rhys fished his phone from his front pocket, and then reached to the back of the head, fumbling for a switch. As the eyes slowly opened, he said, "We've been going over artificial intelligence, the laws surrounding it, why there are limits. That kind of thing. There are no laws about the structural appearance of androids and robots, yet no one has pushed to create one that looks fully human."

"Well, personal 'bots are a thing," Aisha mused. "They look

pretty damned human. You have to get *awfully* close to see that they're not."

With another sigh, Rhys went on. "Those function on a near-humanoid level, but there are quirks. Little things that make it evident that they are not, in fact, human." He tapped at his phone's screen, and the head's lips curled upward. "A smile, for example. We can make a drone smile, make its lips move and mimic speech, but it always looks a little off."

"That is creepy," she agreed.

"You've seen a personal 'bot?" Rhys pressed. "Did it smile normally?"

She wasn't looking at his face.

"Hush, Wick," she said after Will repeated what I'd said. "I knew someone who had two, but I never saw them powered up."

"Two?" Rhys scrunched his nose. "Why would anyone need two?"

"Male and female—"

"The challenge," Will reminded them.

George Denton's cybernetics challenge for the year seemed simple enough: figure out what the issues were with the drone's face, and make its smile appear natural. He'd run the annual challenge since the school opened ten years earlier, but no one had come up with a satisfactory solution.

"I've been listening to everyone plot and plan out how they expect to make their drone heads smile, but I think they're on the wrong track. They're focused on the code and the order of executable commands. I don't think that's the problem. I think it's anatomical."

As Aisha put the groceries away, Rhys worked at peeling off the drone's face, exposing its metal and wire skull. There were a surprising number of blinking red and yellow lights, tiny flashing indicators that were buried deep yet were also evident to anyone who peeked beyond the disturbing eye sockets and empty nasal cavity.

He set the face on the table, careful to not break any wired connections, and then tapped at his phone again. Several of the wires flexed, and he pointed at them.

"Right there. These are standard conductive wires, and they don't have much in the way of elastic or constriction capabilities. There also aren't enough of them to create a structure that will mimic facial muscles. Without that, it can't smile naturally."

Will bent over to examine it closer. "Interesting."

"Compounding the issue is that people have different smiles, depending on their degree of happiness or amusement. A big, shit-eating grin is not the same as a sad, forced smile. You smile differently at a lame joke than you do when the dog does something funny. So even if I figured out how to make it smile and look normal for one thing, it won't for another."

"Were there parameters regarding the depth in which you need to go for this challenge? Do you need to create a single, simple smile, or a range of complexities?"

Rhys only needed to make Horatio smile, and make it look natural. He wanted more, however. He wanted to make Horatio react appropriately to stimuli, both laughing and frowning.

"Do the challenge first," Will suggested. "The rest you can accomplish on your own."

"Can I use Ozoo resources?" he asked, referring to the mega-tech company his father had co-founded with Drew.

Will nodded. "As long as you're not impeding others' work. Perhaps ask Drew for workspace—"

Rhys patted the top of the storage case. "He's already lent me tools and a few thousand flex cables and wires."

"Lent."

"I'm giving the tools back. The wires, probably not."

Will picked the face up, as careful of the wires as Rhys had been. "What you propose isn't cost-free, not if you take it beyond the challenge."

"I know. But I can get a lot of supplies from school and I think I can cover the rest. I've saved a lot of my—"

"Challenge first," Will repeated. "But aside from that? After school tomorrow go to Ozoo and ask Hyrum for an expense card. This is worthy of the investment."

"You just want the patent," Aisha snorted.

"If you accomplish this," Will said to Rhys, "the resulting patent would be yours. But yes, I want Ozoo to have first crack at it."

"AI laws—"

"Don't apply off world. And a drone that looks fully human would do well on the Mars colony and outlying stations."

"The future is in your hands," Aisha said with mock gravity. "Go forth and improve mankind. But take it to your bedroom, because I am not looking at that damned thing during dinner."

~

She looked at that damned thing during dinner.

Horatio was carefully placed on the breakfast bar, his face securely adhered to his skeletal structure, eyes closed. She sighed when Rhys set him there—he'd worked on replacing a critical power source up until she growled that the table needed to be set—but didn't complain about his presence.

Horatio was given gender because he looked too real for anyone to continue referring to him as 'it.' Rhys allowed that once he began working on him after the challenge, after he'd been coded for conversation, Horatio could decide for himself what he was. "If we give him a body, we'll let him choose. He might not care, but if he does…"

"He'd be one ugly woman," Charlie said. "Can you soften his face?"

Alex scrunched her nose. "He's kind of androgynous. I don't think it will matter."

It was possible to give Horatio a range of appearances, but Will reminded them of horses and carts and the order in which things go, and then turned to Isaac to ask if he was participating in the challenge.

"Not allowed," Isaac said, sounding disappointed. "Since it's my dad's challenge, no one wants it to look like I have an inside track."

"You wouldn't cheat," Alex said.

"I know. They know. But it's nice that they're pretending I have a snowball's chance in hell of winning."

"There are, like, three kids who have a chance," Charlie pointed out. "And one of those only has a chance because he might get lucky and *his* dad will help him. Seems to me that coming from a hundred years in the future would disqualify him, especially with a dad who works in robotics and engineering."

It was no more or less fair, Will pointed out, than allowing any student to participate. Blackshear Academy was home to students who came from a two-hundred-year range in time. Rhys had an advantage over his classmates born in this When simply because he had his father's intellect and years of his personal instruction; there would always be someone who had a step up, no matter where one stood on the ladder of time.

Isaac, Rhys's best friend, wouldn't be born for over two hundred years; Will wouldn't be born for nearly one hundred seventy. It was complicated and confusing, and we'd given up trying to keep the timelines pure. Whatever happened, happened, and experience suggested it didn't matter. If they altered something, it simply adjusted the old timeline behind them, the present remained largely unaffected, and one could still jump forward and nothing there would have changed.

A small number of Academy students were related, picked from their respective spots on the timeline by Liam Finnegan, the ancestor and descendant they had in common. Isaac was unrelated, as far as anyone knew, to another student. It also meant that unlike everyone else, he was free to engage socially beyond close friendships without examining his genealogy.

I jumped onto the breakfast bar and sat next to Horatio.

You dating anyone, Isaac?

"What?" His eyebrows scrunched together when Rhys, laughing, translated for him. "Where did that come from?"

It occurred to me. You can hook up with just about any of your classmates. So who are you sucking face with?

"Oh my god, Wick. You know better. No one."

"But you want to," Alex teased. "You *love* Dharma Michlovich."

"When I found out she was future-forward, I asked her if she had a gift, and what it was, that's it. I'm not interested."

"Uh huh. It was more like, 'Hey, show me what you can do.'"

Closing his eyes, Isaac sighed heavily. "My dad comes home when?"

Will glanced at a watch he wasn't wearing. "Four days."

"Jesus."

2

I'd given up my nightly stroll through the building, checking every bedroom to make sure children who should be asleep actually were and that those sleeping were free from nightmares. There were too many of them now; Will and Aisha had three teenagers, and often had a fourth—usually Isaac—sleeping over. Oz and Drew had three boys, Zed and Sophia had three boys and a girl, Jay had a little one, and there were the adults, too.

I often checked in on old King Eli, because he was alone and someone needed to be sure he was all right. Every now and then I checked on King Jax and Queen Aubrey, but they had each other and if one couldn't sleep, they had the other to annoy. I checked on Hyrum, the Queen's brother, because, well, he was Hyrum and I needed to see him as much as he needed to feel my whiskers tickling his chin every night.

Mostly, I stayed in Will and Aisha's apartment, usually curled up on the window seat in their bedroom. From there I could hear everyone in the apartment, and only woke someone if Rhys's dog, Thor, needed to go to the rooftop lawn to pee, or if he couldn't wait that long, to the balcony one floor down.

Eleven-year-old Thor was—after they had discussed Horatio's head and how involved they wanted Rhys to become—the topic they discussed in bed that night. He'd reached his senior years, but Rhys still needed him as much as he had when he was a newly minted and very hopeful four-year-old. Thor was his nighttime confidant, seventy pounds of unconditional love that the fifteen-year-old couldn't bear to lose.

"He's arthritic," Aisha pointed out. "I can see him struggle to get off the floor sometimes. It feels too soon for him to move like an old man."

"Trait of the breed," Will sighed.

"I know, and I know we talked about this years ago, and I know we said Rhys would learn that it's all part of life, but—"

"But this is Thor. He deserves better and he deserves more."

Everyone feels like that about their pets.

Will lifted his head to look at me. "I know."

But you also know you can do something about it.

"I am aware of that, as well. Cheat the system, as it were."

"Translate." Aisha sat up so that she could see me, too. "What's Wick want?"

Look, Thor tells me things. He's not in a lot of pain, just a little achy now and then. But take Thor to Will's birth When and dunk him in a tank. Let Mass turn the clock back for him.

"That'll be one hell of a post-surgical bath," she mused after Will repeated my notions. The tank, one used for surgery in the future but could also be dialed in for rejuvenation purposes, was filled with thick goo and nanobots, and the gel had to be cleaned off once the patient was pulled from the tank.

With people, it was easy.

With all of Thor's fur, it would be work.

Trim his dangly fur bits before he goes in. He won't mind if you tell him why.

"Well?" she asked, nudging Will. "Is it feasible?"

"Entirely. We could have him treated for the arthritis here, but there?"

"Eliminate it, and also give him a few more years."

You can give him a lot of years. Double at least. Do it for me if not him. He's my buddy and I'm not done letting him chase me up and down the stairs.

I had no doubt that Will was about to launch into a lecture on the ethics of not interfering with the natural life cycle and probably physics and playing with time, along with pulling statistics about my 500-year life length versus Thor's probable 15 out of his ass, but a clinking sound from the kitchen diverted his attention.

It's Isaac. He's been out there a while.

I followed Will from the bedroom to the kitchen, where Isaac was attempting to put ice into a glass one cube at a time, quietly.

"Can't sleep?" Will asked, making him jump.

"Jesus. Did I wake you up? I was trying to be quiet."

"No. And you weren't loud."

"Yeah, no, I can't sleep," Isaac admitted. He sucked in a deep breath. "I keep feeling like I need to call Odie. I even reached for the phone once. And I don't know why because it's not like I *can* call him."

Odie—James—was Isaac's stepfather, though he hadn't been married to George when Isaac was born. James was also Aisha's ex-husband and Jay's father. The family tree was more like a knotted vine, and I tried to not think about it too hard. James had screamed like a little girl when he learned about the realities of the Blackshear family being able to move through time, and he probably screamed more when George confessed that he was from the same future as Will. He had no choice to do anything other than accept it, not if he wanted to remain in Jay's life, and eventually settled there to be with a woman he'd fallen in love with.

She'd been out of his life for years, but he'd remained. There were other men and women he'd been involved with, people he found more interesting than his birth-When contemporaries.

James was, to be nice, a bit of a man-whore.

Jay made sure that Isaac had a relationship with the man he called Odie, or Other Daddy. He carted his little brother—who was not actually related to him, but he wasn't about to let a little DNA get in the way—along on most of his visits, but they hadn't been there for several months. Isaac rarely asked someone to take him through a portal, but he was on the precipice of doing just that when Will sat across the table from him and mused that he was heading in that direction this week. "Perhaps it would be a good time for you to visit James."

"He's probably busy."

"He won't be too busy to make time for you." Will leaned

back in his chair, folding his arms. I saw what Isaac likely didn't, a quick, dark flash in Will's eyes that held warning if James was unable to see him. It had happened more than once, times when Jay had taken him forward without warning his father they were coming, and James was either halfway across the world or busy, and once, not even on the planet.

Isaac understood it wasn't personal, but his frontal lobes were still cooking, so of course it was personal.

His shrug told Will as much.

"We'll take Rhys. If James isn't home, you two can find other things to do. Borrow jet packs from the lab and tour the city."

Or go to Bounce.

Bounce was an antigravity playground where one could float, engage in sports, play tag, or do anything they could imagine, as long as they kept their clothes on. He and Rhys had been there a dozen times with the other kids, but he scrunched his nose at the idea.

"That place makes me barf. Jet packs would be cool. How come we don't have those now? It's possible, right?"

Will nodded. "Possible, but someone else needs to invent them first."

"But I've seen—"

"Not commercially viable, user-friendly packs," Will said. "What exists now are systems that have come and gone dozens of times over the last four hundred years. Someone needs to work out the logistics of fuel, power, heat—"

Stop him or he'll explain it in super great detail and you need to sleep at some point.

"Are you suggesting that I'm verbose, Wick?"

I'm not suggesting anything, Will.

Isaac reached across the table to pet me. "I wish I understood you."

"Trust me," Will said as he got up, "some wishes are better left unfulfilled."

3

Thor understood—in a very basic, *I'll do anything to make my Boy happy* way—what Will wanted him to do. He tolerated the severe haircut, his beautiful golden fur trimmed down to less than an inch long, and he promised he would be, as always, a good boy.

"Good boy! Good boy good boy good boy!"

He says he'll eat the treat Mass is holding if Rhys gives it to him.

"You know it will make you sleepy, right?" Rhys asked him.

"Good boy!"

He knows. We played hard all morning and thinks a nap would be nice.

"Don't read into things he says, Wick," Rhys warned me. "I want to know what he's saying."

That. He said that. You know I hear his intentions, right? Not necessarily the words. It's not the same way you understand me.

Rhys understood the words that rode out of my mind on the breath of each meow; if he could hear Thor's words, he would hear an endless stream of *good boy*! and nothing else. There was another layer peeled away between his mind and mine; I heard his words the way the world heard my meowing, but his intentions slipped into my brain as surely as my words slipped into Rhys's and Will's.

"It won't hurt," Rhys promised his dog. "Okay? When you wake up, you'll be wet and maybe a little tired, but nothing will hurt."

"Good boy."

He wants the treat now.

"Good boy?"

Sorry, dude, you only get one. Maybe when you wake up, we'll talk them into going somewhere we can get meaty treats.

Will had to drag Rhys out of the room; neither wanted to leave until Thor was asleep, floating in the tank, but more than staying, Will wanted Rhys gone before Thor was lifted onto the exam table to have that long tube shoved down his throat, before the respirator was attached to it. He'd seen a person floating in a surgical tank; not even a year earlier Isaac had ruptured a disk in his spine and spent half a day under anesthesia, centered weightlessly in orange surgical goo. Rhys stayed with his friend, waiting in a battered blue comfy chair placed carefully on the right side of a bright DO NOT CROSS line on the surgical room floor.

But this was different. This was Thor, and he'd only consented because Rhys wanted him to.

"Just a few hours," Will said as we made our way down the hall to the elevator. "After Isaac is done visiting James, we'll pick up Thor and go to dinner. What would you like to do in the meantime?"

Rhys didn't miss a beat. "See a drone. A humanoid drone. One I can actually talk to."

~

Cash Blackshear practically leaped from his chair to greet Will and Rhys. He extended his hand before he was even out from behind his desk, but it was Rhys he went to first. I'd never met him, but he knew who I was without introduction, and after he'd greeted Rhys, he held his hand up to my face so that I could sniff, and asked before tickling me just under my chin.

"The forever cat," he said lightly. "Stories abound about you, Wick, but we're never sure what's true and what Uncle Finn is teasing us with."

Tell me who I live with right now. I'm still here, right?

Oh. Wait. I died in this When. End of the world and all that.

Cash was Will's cousin and current CEO of Ozoo Enterprises. He had followed Finn's career path, lived outside his When for a few years when no one was sure if the world would end or not, and returned when Finn found a way to keep a planet-killing meteor from doing just that.

"How come we've never met?" Rhys asked Will.

"I left this When before Cash was born," Will said. "Neither he nor his siblings knew me as they grew up."

"Oh, but we had the stories," Cash said, brightly. "And with two—no, three—Finns running around here now?"

"He lies," Will said.

That made Cash laugh. "Doesn't matter. He's entertaining." He turned back to Rhys. "I understand you're interested in android technology."

Rhys nodded. "AI isn't exactly legal in our When and I was just curious. Like, how advanced are they? And what do they look like? And—"

Cash touched a bright light on the edge of his desk. "Brent, can you come in here?"

There was no answer, but it didn't seem as if he expected one.

"If I recall correctly," Cash said, "there are humanoid drones in your When."

"Sex 'bots," Rhys sighed.

"Personal robots," Will corrected.

"Same thing. I don't need to see their junk or anything, I just wanted to see how real they look, and how advanced the communication skills have become. Like, how well can they think for—"

Brent arrived, knocking on the door frame before entering. He was tall and trim, with blond hair and dark eyes; he was in need of a shave, and was dressed in black jeans and a maroon sweatshirt. He could have walked out of the Ozoo lab two hundred years in the past and fit in just fine with every other mechanical and chemical engineer there.

"You called?" he said.

Cash nodded. "This is Rhys, my younger cousin. He's interested in cybernetics and robotics, and would very much like to meet an android. I didn't think it would be difficult to arrange."

"Indeed."

He sounded like Will, and it made Rhys exhale a tiny, amused breath through his nose.

When Brent said nothing else, Rhys shifted from one foot to the other, confused. "Um. Yeah, I would like to meet one. Maybe talk to it. Or him. Or her. I don't know what the pronouns are here. I'm just curious because in the When we come from—"

"What would you like to know?" Brent asked.

"Like, how close to human have androids become? Are they more like the drones we have? Those are shaped like humans but they're obviously *not* human. And how autonomous are they? Like, do they power down at the end of the day wherever they are, or go home to some apartment. Do they eat? Do they have friends? Feelings? Sex? I just kind of want to know everything."

"Sex," Brent repeated with a chuckle.

"Well, I mean, I wouldn't ask that if it's over the line but I kinda want to know if they do and if it's by choice instead of on command like the personal 'bots at home. It's not like I want the horny details or anything."

"Good, because you wouldn't get them. But I can tell you that androids are autonomous, have friends, feelings, are self-aware, and do have their own residences, just like anyone else."

"Yeah, but—"

Brent held his hand out, gesturing for Rhys to take it, as if he wanted to shake hands.

"We feel human. Act human. We can eat, have sex, work, pay taxes, engage in hobbies and sports, do nearly everything a human can do."

Rhys' eyes went wide. "Holy shit, you're—"

"Not human. But perhaps the next best thing, and you'll probably see the prototypes for me in your lifetime."

~

Will sat with his fingers pressed to the bridge of his nose, whether trying to stave off a headache or to avoid listening to the barrage of teenaged chatter bubbling between Rhys and Isaac while we sat at an outside table at *Sof y Z's*, I wasn't sure. The tortilla chips went untouched in their enthusiasm, Rhys because he'd spent most of the day with Brent, and Isaac because he'd had James's undivided attention for several hours.

I gave up trying to follow their conversation two minutes in. It was a stream of two different topics at the same time, and while they were able to follow each other, I began to feel the pulsing of Will's headache and decided my time was better spent watching a pigeon that had come far too close to the table for my comfort.

It stood on the pavement between the table and the bay water, staring at us, waiting for someone to take pity on its thieving little soul and toss a chip or two its way.

I don't trust pigeons.

Normally, Thor was enough to scare the fluffy pests away, but he was curled up near Rhys's feet in a post-surgical haze. The little flying rats could have stomped up to him and pecked his shiny black nose without waking him, and I wasn't about to rouse him, not as tired as he was.

I opened my mouth to ask Will to scare it off, lest it call to its feathery pigeon gang to swoop in with the intent of taking off with my tiny self, but he sighed and said, "Rhys. You inquired about his body hair. You asked if he had pubic hair."

Rhys gave a half shrug. "He said he was open to anything. I just wanted to figure out if he'd still be taken for human if he didn't have clothes on." He looked at Isaac. "He's got *everything*. Like, little freckles, a tiny scar on his hand, and he even has a fake tooth."

"Aren't all his teeth fake?" Isaac wondered.

"Well, yeah, but this is like an obvious dental crown. You'd have to crack him open to know he's not human."

I'm surprised you didn't ask if you could do that.

"That would have been rude," Rhys said.

"He eats?" Isaac asked. "Where does it go? The food, I mean."

"He's kinda like Quinn with food," Rhys said, referring to

his friend in the simulated world of Saint Francis. "When he eats, the food is digested by internal nanobots, and eliminated pretty much the way you or I would."

"He shits," Isaac guessed.

"He shits."

Didn't we have this conversation ten years ago, with Shivan? Drew was just as fascinated by it.

"We did," Will said. "Though Andrew never spent hours asking Shivan to do things like smiling and laughing, or sneering and winking."

"Hey. That was research. I wanted to see how his face moved. I got a lot of information from that."

You asked him to snort, dude. Like he had a wad of boogers he needed to loosen.

Brent hadn't hesitated. Everything Rhys asked, he answered or demonstrated, which made me several kinds of glad that he hadn't actually asked Brent to strip.

You people, naked?

It's disturbing.

"It helped me figure out some things I want to try with Horatio's head." Rhys finally reached for a chip and scooped an absurd amount of salsa onto it. "I can do a lot of it at home but it would help to use your office workspace, Dad."

Will agreed, but I kind of wondered if he might regret that later.

4

Horatio's head centered on a long, narrow metal table was no less disturbing than it was when resting on the dining room table. The pseudo flesh at the base of his neck fanned across the shiny silver surface, creating tiny wrinkles that puckered uncomfortably; I wasn't the only one who noticed, given that Alex kept trying to smooth them out.

Rhys crouched, looking at Horatio's head from its own eye-level. "I'd trim that if I knew for sure I was allowed. Just leave it."

"It's a freaking skin skirt," she grumbled.

"Fake skin. It's an approximation of a freaking skin skirt."

"And that helps so much."

"Fine. You trim it and see what George says when he gets here." He glanced up at the clock over Will's office door. "That'll be in about five minutes, so get to it."

With a finely honed teenaged sigh, Alex pulled her hand away. "It's just creepy, that's all."

Isaac stood at the bay windows, Thor near his feet, a hand pressed to the glass. He waited for a bright streak cutting across the night sky, the light that streamed behind Elysium's shuttles as they left and returned to Earth. His focus was directed toward Marin County, where the final shuttle of the day would land, and with it, his father.

"Dad won't care. Cut it if you want. The extra skin is only there because of the way the head was removed from the body, and the body doesn't exist anymore."

"Gross," Charlie muttered.

"What's gross about it? It was disassembled for its spare parts. It's not human."

"But it *looks* human," Charlie said.

"If it looked human," Rhys countered, "I wouldn't be trying to make it smile."

Rhys had added more hair-thin, flexible cables than he could count, soldered new relays into place, changed how Horatio's eyes moved, made his nose crinkle, and programmed—he hoped—a responsive sense of humor into the database.

What he couldn't do but had wanted, was to give Horatio a voice. He'd managed to craft a sense of hearing, but there hadn't been enough time to construct a voice box. "If he smiles, being able to laugh seems like the next logical step," he told Will when asked why it was important.

Alex had more to say about Horatio's creepy skin skirt, but Isaac sucked in a tight breath and took a step back. "They're landing now." He turned around. "Man, I really wanted to be there. Waiting sucks."

"Security and all that crap," Rhys reminded him.

"I know. At least your dad is there. He said he'd jump him here. Do you know if he meant, like, right away and right here or just in the building, or—"

He was cut off by a quick flash of static in the air; Will and George appeared in the center of the room before Isaac was able to turn all the way around. Will's hand was on George's neck—contact was the only way to bring him along on a jump—but once there he dropped his hand away and stepped back so that Isaac could leap at his father.

Isaac, on the other hand, stiffened and gave his father a bare nod. "Hey, Dad."

Rhys snorted. "Freaking hoser. No one cares if you squeal like Hyrum at Christmas. If you don't, I'll do it for you."

Isaac zoomed the dozen steps toward his father. They grabbed each other in a hard, tight hug, and stayed there until I was uncomfortable.

Should we turn a hose on them?

"Wick," Will said under his breath.

Thor jumped up to follow Isaac. "*Good boy! Good boy!*"

Wait your turn, bro. They missed each other.

"They're making fun of me, aren't they?" George asked as he and Isaac parted.

"For once, no," Rhys said. "Thor wants to say hi and be petted, and Wick told him to be patient. I'm guessing. I still don't understand Thor."

George bent over and gave Thor what he wanted, a two-handed, thorough rubbing of his cheeks and neck, all while murmuring what a good boy he was and that he'd missed his goofy grin while he was gone.

"The cats won't be anywhere near as happy to see me," he said as he stood up.

His cats had stayed with the old King, Eli, in his downstairs apartment. Eli was the Chosen One, as far as Bucky and Frog were concerned. They'd first stayed with him when George was stuck in his home When following a catastrophic accident that kept him away for half a year, and he'd only reluctantly returned them when George and Isaac settled into an apartment and were ready for them.

Every year since, Eli cared for the cats while George and Isaac were away, and even Isaac admitted they seemed to prefer the old man.

"They ignored me when I went to see them this morning," Isaac said. "I even offered tuna, like *real* tuna, but they wouldn't take it until Eli put it in their dishes. Someday we're gonna have to give up and just let them live there."

"You'd be heartbroken," George said, but Isaac was already shaking his head.

"They're senior kitties now, Dad. They should get what they want."

"If it helps," Rhys grunted as he bent over to turn Horatio's head off, "Grandpa Eli has to head for New York tomorrow, anyway."

George tilted his head a touch as he looked at the lifeless, rubbery-plastic face. "No specifics, but how's it going?"

"Good so far." Rhys lifted it by the hair and settled it into its travel case. "How much modification am I allowed? I have ideas but I'm not sure where the line is."

"Anything short of using a completely different head. Add to it, remove things, whatever you think it requires to meet the challenge criteria. Worst case, you don't win."

"I want to win," Rhys said lightly. "I want to crush the competition. I have hopes of making at least one of the others cry."

"Then make the son of a bitch smile. Do that, and you'll have done what no other Academy student has in the last ten years."

5

Just a day later, we were back in Will's work space, Horatio's head on the table, a cart loaded with tools off to one side, a lifeless and headless drone body propped up nearby, while Finn stood staring out the window at the fog-shrouded Golden Gate Bridge.

Will's father was known to be a bit scattered and easily distracted, but there was nearly always a point to his inward musings and he ended up where he'd intended to be from the outset. But this time, there seemed to be no rhyme or reason to why he wandered away from the table to the window, his hands in his pockets, to fixate on the bridge towers poking out from a blanket of fog.

Rhys wasn't bothered by it and Alex snorted with amusement. They went back to the task at hand, preparing Horatio for an upgrade; Rhys did the work while Alex hovered and fetched the tools he needed. They worked quietly for an hour, during which Finn barely moved, and the pulsing sound of Rhys's plasma-soldering pen nearly lulled me into a comfortable cat nap on my bookshelf perch. I was just drifting off when Charlie bounced into the room bearing a fist-sized metal container, with Will a few steps behind.

He tossed the container on the table and started, loudly, "Hey, Grandpa! Grandma said to tell you—"

"Don't bother," Alex said. "He can't hear you."

With a sigh, Charlie asked, "Is he on Mars, or did he go, like, to Jupiter?"

"And for how long?" Will added.

"About an hour. We were talking about AI and speculating about how one day androids like Brent will become indistinguishable from humans. Like, what it would take."

"Very specifically," Will said. "What was said that pulled him into himself?"

Rhys gave a light shrug. "I dunno. I think I said something about DNA. Like, DNA is the building block for everything, sort of, but did it have to be a living being sort of thing? What's the cybernetic or universal equivalent of DNA? He started to answer, but, then. Well, you know. You've seen it happen."

Finn had opened his mouth to share whatever musing he had regarding the possibilities of android DNA, but never made a sound. Instead, his eyes seemingly unfocused, and he wandered to the window, where'd he been since. It was nothing new to Will; Finn had been distracted his entire life. What was relatively new to Will was the knowledge that he could easily pull his father out of himself. By gently setting his hand on Finn's neck, he could silently whisper to his father that it was time to pack up his toys and come home; Finn would blink a few times, and be back.

For now, he wanted to let Finn soak in whatever mental gymnastics he was engaged.

"But Grandma—" Charlie started.

"She understands him. If you're worried, call or send her a text and tell her he's standing on a rock somewhere left of Mars. She knows what that means."

"Fine." Charlie dropped onto the sofa under the shelf I was lounging upon, letting out a pretended, exaggerated sigh.

They work you too hard. Expecting you to deliver messages and all. It must be rough.

"Cat, I don't know what you said, but bite me anyway."

Trying to still be of help, Alex worked at prying the top off the metal container. "Dad, can you help with the drone body? I don't think I can lift it to set it on the table."

Rhys was perfectly capable of moving the drone from its spot near the wall to the table, but couldn't maneuver it onto the table without help, and he didn't trust anyone else with Horatio's head. Will, on the other hand, was able to easily lift the two-hundred fifty-pound headless humanoid and set it gently onto the table, resting on its back.

After she had the container open, Alex reached for a towel nearby, and set it over the drone's groin.

"Really, Alex?" Rhys snorted. "It's not like you've never seen one before."

"I don't want anyone's junk in my face," she said. "Why did you have to use a gendered drone? Why not one of the others?"

"Because this is the one Drew said I could use. Charlie already took it apart."

"You know someone has fu—"

Will cleared his throat.

"It was a sex 'bot, Dad," she went on. "Why else would it have gender? Someone has done some really nasty things to it."

"And that offends you?"

She wasn't offended, just a bit creeped out, and mostly wanted to know if the head came off before, after, or during whatever last activities it had engaged in.

"I removed its head yesterday," Will said. "When Rhys is done with the challenge, he'll put it back."

"I will?" Rhys asked, though he sounded more amused by Alex than the idea that he had more work ahead of him.

"I presumed you intended to replicate your work with Horatio's head on the drone's."

Rhys nodded. "All right, that's fair. And by then hopefully I can streamline the process. I already see changes I can make. Can you lift the torso a few inches so I can snap the cervical spine into place?"

Will grabbed the drone by its hands and pulled its torso off the table while Alex held Horatio's skin flap out of Rhys's way. It took effort to get the head into place, but when he did there was a satisfying click as it connected; he held the head steady as Will pulled the drone into a sitting position, and kept it there while Rhys finished making all the connections.

Half an hour later Horatio almost looked like a real boy.

Finn still hadn't moved.

"Don't use the skin glue until you're done," Will said, pointing at the container. "It's difficult to remove once it sets. I suggest only gluing it down in a few spots so you can remove the head later."

Rhys was close to being done, but agreed to wait until the next day. Charlie reminded them that the rest of the family was waiting at Union Square, and Grandma had just texted that it was time to kick Finn off his rock.

Will set his hand on Finn's neck, and waited for his father to hear him. It took nearly a minute, but Finn blinked a few times and then turned to Will.

"DNA, Will. What if it's all DNA?"

6

I rode on Rhys's shoulder as he made his way across Union Square. We'd jumped from Will's office to Finn's underground lab, and the moment the elevator doors slid open he spotted young Eli near the Christmas tree with Hyrum. As he did every year, Hyrum stood with his mouth hanging open, his head tilted all the way back, and little Eli had braced himself against Hyrum's back to keep him from falling over.

He had both hands pressed just below Hyrum's shoulder blades, feet planted firmly; to anyone else it looked as if he were trying to push his great uncle over. When Hyrum began to bounce gently on his toes in excitement, Rhys sped up, hoping to spare the eleven-year-old from the strain of keeping him upright.

If Hyrum had a clue how hard Eli worked to keep him in place, he would have stopped gawking at the tree. The reality was that he probably had forgotten Eli was there, absorbed in the enormity of the Union Square Christmas tree, and the notion that in just a few weeks, Santa was coming.

He was in his fifties, but he still believed and no one wanted to take that away from him.

"I got him," Rhys whispered to Eli. He put one hand between Hyrum's shoulders, holding him in place. "Good job."

"He's gonna go over someday."

"But not today, thanks to you."

I stretched to get closer to Hyrum's head. *Is it prettier this year? It looks like there are more lights.*

"Uh huh. It's more sparkly." He finally lifted his head. "I think it's the same size but it feels bigger."

It's the same tree every year, dude. But maybe they added extra lights or a few inches to the base.

"You think so? Would Will know?"

Probably.

Without even acknowledging Rhys, Hyrum trotted off in the direction Will was headed, the bakery on the corner of the Square, where a good chunk of the family clustered at two tables. Eli watched until Hyrum flung himself at Will, and then looked to the top of the tree, though without Hyrum's penchant for leaning back too far.

"Tomorrow's Santa Day," Eli said. "Are you gonna go?"

"How else will he know what I want?"

"C'mon," Eli grunted.

"Your brothers still believe," Rhys reminded him. "So does Hyrum. We're not ruining this for them."

"I know, but..."

"It's fun, Eli. Stop thinking about knowing who Santa really is and start enjoying how excited Hyrum and the younger kids get. Half my fun used to be getting you so excited that you damn near wet yourself."

Still looking up, Eli nodded.

He stood there nearly as long as Hyrum did, quiet, and Rhys waited until they were the only ones near the tree. "What's bugging you?"

Eli glanced at Rhys but continued looking up. "The city is sick, Rhys. It wants to die, but we won't let it. I know you can hear it, too."

"Sometimes. What do you hear?"

With a sigh, Eli turned, and gestured to the building across the Square, the one where Isaac and George lived. "It's not just what I hear. It's what I see. The colors are changing. They're not steady anymore. Every building—" he put splayed fingers together and alternated extending and smashing them together, making a *woosh-woosh-woosh* sound "—does like this with the light around them and places I used to see maybe three or four shades of three or four colors, I see dozens."

"Dozens," Rhys repeated. "I'm not seeing that."

He sees more colors than you do. He sees like a bird.

"It just wants to be allowed to go," Eli said. "But it doesn't know how."

"It will, in a few years. You've been to my dad's birth When, you know how much it changes. The next time each building is too old to rebuild, they'll be torn down. Something new goes up."

"But there won't be time to get better between," Eli said. "Besides, how do you tell an entire city it needs to be patient? That it will die in little bits. I can hear it but I can't speak to it."

Maybe we need to prove it. Get Jax to tear down something old and then wait to replace it.

"Maybe," Rhys allowed.

I didn't see Eli roll his eyes but I practically heard it happen. "So I'm supposed tell Grandpa that the city says it's sick and he needs to knock down some buildings so it knows it'll get what it wants?"

"Well, when you say it like that..."

He'll believe you. Anyone else, probably not. But he knows what you can do, bro. He knows what all of you can do. He'll take you seriously.

The King would take him seriously, of that I had no doubt. Eli and Rhys shared similar gifts, though Eli was just coming in to some of his and didn't always understand what he could do or what he saw. But Jax would believe that the boy with unnaturally violet eyes saw the changes in every color the sounds of the city made, and heard the city cry out.

"What happens if the city doesn't get to change?" Eli asked.

Rhys didn't have an answer, and I didn't want to say what I thought it would be.

It had only been a couple hundred years since the last earthquake that nearly leveled it all. Maybe that was a warning.

~

Jax stood pressed up against the edge of the balcony, watching. To anyone else he looked lost in thought, but Will waited patiently because there was a purpose to his quiet and barely blinking gaze. The King's head turned slowly as he took in the sight of the buildings that surrounded Union Square, and when he was done, he let out a sigh.

"I don't see the colors half as well as Eli does," he finally said. "But he's right. The cadence has changed and it's not because the people in those buildings are doing something different."

"Rhys feels it, too," Will reminded him.

"And the cat thinks the earth will literally move if we do nothing."

I'm guessing.

"I can't bring this before the council. There's no way to tell them that we need to begin tearing this city down to let it die and then become reborn. I'd lose—"

"I know," Will said. "No one can learn of this family's gifts."

Just tell them it's time to change the city charter. Stop requiring everything to be preserved to match the twenty first century. People have clamored for a contemporary look for years now.

"That would fly," Jax said.

"The key is determining how long the real estate needs to lie dormant before it can heal. And will the city survive a piece-meal approach?"

Once you roll back that law, people are going to start knocking shit over just to knock it over. They like shiny new things.

"When did he start swearing?" Jax asked Will.

"It's been years."

"And your kid," Jax went on without really listening to Will's answer. "He has his toes right up against the AI line. If I understand him correctly, he's uncomfortably close to having a drone of the same level that instigated the ban in the first place."

"Visually, perhaps. He's years away from being able to create a self-aware, fully functioning android."

Jax snorted. "Years. He could do it in a few months if he stumbled across the right data."

That data was not easily accessible. Rhys would need to recreate it, and that, Will argued, would surely take him well into adulthood. The odds were greater that he would grow bored before the end of the school year. Will intended to allow his pursuit of a more human-like drone to be used off world and would not allow Rhys to step over that legal line.

"I control his research funds, after all."

Damn, I wish I could laugh. He has a grandfather with deep pockets, and you know Finn will put science first.

"Fine," Jax said. "But why is he pursuing this over other things? The drones we currently use are more than sufficient. Andrew saw to that."

Drew was comfortable with technology and his interests were firmly rooted in taking existing things and making them better. Drones and robots had been commonly used for centuries, as had computers. He improved function in immense strides, turning high-heat systems into cool-running tools; where the government had once been on the precipice of the greatest leaps in computation ever made, only to have everything go up in a wall of flames, Drew made it work. He redesigned drones to near-android state, which became the workforce of the space station Elysium—which went from an abandoned, dormant orb in the sky to a fully functional entity because of his work with low-temperature computer systems.

Jax didn't say it, but the implication was that everything Drew had done, Rhys was capable of eclipsing, and would unless restrained.

He only needed to be restrained because of a long-standing law against artificial intelligence. Drew placed his work right up against that legal line, but at 15 Rhys might inadvertently step over it.

"Mars colonists are no longer simply people we placed there," Will reminded Jax. "There have been four generations of humans born there who are, truly, Martian. They have far fewer qualms about the advancement of AI and have made it clear they would like drones that appear more like themselves."

"Sex 'bots not enough?" Jax snickered.

"Personal robots are not an export item," Will said.

You should let him try. No one said that if he created an android that it has to be made public.

"You expect him to keep quiet?" Jax mused. "He's a teenager, that's not—"

Fair? It's as fair as trusting him to keep quiet about time travel. About being able to stop time. About reading minds and shooting electricity from his fingertips, telekinesis and probably levitating.

"He doesn't levitate."

Not yet. But you never know. Rhys has gifts he doesn't even know about.

"Wick is not wrong," Will said. "We trust our children to remain silent about this family's plethora of gifts, and about our ability to move through time and space. Rhys is mature enough to understand that if he succeeds, the news of his accomplishments may never go beyond the walls of Ozoo."

Jax grunted, and then asked when Rhys would present Horatio's head in the school challenge.

"Next week. He has a few hours of work left, but he believes he'll be ready by then."

"I want to be there when he does. Figure out a way to make it seem plausible. Not that I'm checking up on what those kids are up to, but that I'm there to support them all."

7

Jax's insistence on attending the challenge presentation—held at the end of the Blackshear Academy Science Fair, which meant we were all there all day because, for Bast knows why, *all* of the Blackshear kids entered, which made me a little salty but my irritation was lessened when Jonathan's battery experiment exploded—caused a flurry of last-minute changes of location and security. It was normally held in a lecture hall at the school but had been moved to a spacious conference room in the Westin Hotel, literally a three-minute walk from the royal house.

Following the general science fair events (Jonathan clearly did not win, but he wasn't terribly upset by it, and was happy for Isaac, who did win) we entered a side room to find dozens of chairs lined up in neat rows, and a long table set up on the far side of the room. There were three heads on the table, all covered with dark cloth, and one occupied chair at the left end of the table, also covered with a dark cloth. A few dozen people milled about the room; some were parents, some were media, and many—more than necessary—were members of the Royal Guard.

"Expect this to become a standing room only event," Will said to Jax as they made their way to the front. "The guard will limit the number of audience members, but they have made an allowance for overflow to observe from the back."

"Exit protocol?"

Will gestured toward a double door beyond the display table, flanked by uniformed guards. "After congratulating the participants, you'll leave through those doors. The guard commander will be waiting to escort you through the hallways, and you'll exit the hotel from the door through which you arrived."

"She's waiting in the hall? I thought she'd want to see this."

Will nodded. "She'll be here momentarily, but will slip out once the event has concluded."

It's not like Isaac is even competing in this part. If he was, she'd have handed your security to someone else, like she did for the rest of the fair.

Vicat, no official last name, was Isaac's aunt and newly commissioned head of the Royal Guard. It was the first promotion she had accepted since becoming combat training supervisor thirty years earlier, and she leaped ahead of a dozen other names on the list.

There was no grumbling, no cries of favoritism; Vicat had earned the position with literal blood, sweat, tears, and experience. She'd saved the lives of royal family members more than once; she'd been trusted as Rhys's personal guard until he was four years old and only left the position because he viewed her more as a friend than a guard. She was still Cat Lady to Hyrum and was now a family friend, but to the guard she was as formidable a commander as they'd ever had.

Aisha and Aubrey were already in the room, flanked by family. The first two rows of seating on the left side were reserved for them; most of the kids had already found their seats, but Oz, Drew, Jay, and Navi stood nearby, talking excitedly with Finn and Jo.

"Zed and Sophia?" Jax asked. "Their kids are here, where are they?"

"Hallway behind the doors," Will said. "Zed is giving last minute instructions to the competitors and Sophia is there for support. George is with them."

"Is he upset that we've basically upended his program?" Jax asked. "He never intended for it to be…this."

"On the contrary, he's elated. Your presence will draw more students to the challenge next year."

"Meaning I turned this into an obligation just by being here."

"Indeed."

He sat quietly through the beginning of his new obligation, as George opened it with a few remarks about the student cybernetics and engineering program and those who had chosen to participate. He explained that they would present one at a time, and after each presentation their project head would be re-covered as to not distract from the next student; it was possible that there would be no victor in the end.

There had never been a winner; no one had succeeded in making Horatio smile naturally.

Kid on the far right looks like he expects to win. Smug little s-o-b.

"Wick," Will whispered.

Well, he does. Kid in the middle wants to throw up.

George began with Smug Boy, who—as directed—informed the audience about his approach to Horatio's smile. There was an incredible amount of coding to be done, but he was sure he'd found the answer, which revolved around specific parameters of movement. He found the existing code lacking, and because of it Horatio never had a chance of managing more than a tight smile that felt more like a grimace. With a flourish, he whipped the covering off his version of Horatio's head, and powered it up.

There was no question, his Horatio smiled. The lips rose as expected, but his expression remained dull and lifeless because the lips were the only thing that moved.

Hyrum didn't notice that the eyes were blank; he wiggled in his seat, hands to his mouth, and said a bit too loud, "It's smiling! Look! That's a smile! He smiles like my daddy did!"

Smug Boy took that as a bit of a victory, though George didn't give him a hint one way other the other regarding his opinion. Instead, George tapped notes into a tablet, and then took a half dozen pictures from various angles.

Hyrum's enthusiasm for each of the students never waned. He clapped eagerly for the second presenter; her code-enhanced Horatio managed a tight grin, but it was lopsided, and again, the eyes did not match the smile.

He giggled loudly when the third head erupted in a mass of smoke that poured from its nostrils and mouth when powered up. The boy standing just behind it shrugged and said, "Yeah, well, I guess giving it the three-alarm chili for lunch was a bad idea."

Still, George took his notes and photos, giving no indication that this expensive piece of technology was now useless, and Hyrum offered his assurances that the chili was probably worth the smoke, on account of that means it was super tasty.

None of the students took Hyrum's chatter as an offense; they knew him. He had been their playground supervisor when they were small children and new to the Academy. Hyrum had made them feel safe then, and their affection for him was greater than the potential irritation his outbursts might cause.

When George was ready, he nodded to Rhys, and asked him to uncover his project and explain his reasoning behind his choices. With a deep breath, Rhys whisked the covering off, revealing the full drone, seated with its hands on its knees, eyes closed. There was a dull murmuring through the audience, and I heard one person whisper, "Is that cheating?"

George heard it, too, and answered before Rhys could. "No, this is not cheating. I did not place limits on their modifications. Let's hear your reasons why, Rhys."

Rhys glanced at George and then Will before addressing the crowd. "Well, I worked on just the head for a bit. Instead of making huge changes to the coding, I worked on its facial anatomy." He bent over and peeled a section of the artificial skin away from its face, revealing thousands of tiny flex-wires and blinking lights. "One of the problems I saw was that Horatio could technically smile, but his cheeks didn't move the way a human's does, and his eyes didn't crinkle at the corners. Adding to the code wasn't going to change its anatomy, and I thought it needed anatomy structured closer to human. Like, the equivalent of muscles and tendons and stuff."

He set the flap down and smoothed it out, tucking the seam under Horatio's shirt collar. "The other problem I saw was that people have a bunch of different smiles, and it would only look natural in the right setting. That's when I worked on code, and got it as close to real as I could…but even that didn't look right. And it occurred to me that no one would look natural if they were just a head on a table. The angle would always be wrong, because the head couldn't tilt back the way a little kid does when they look up at you and smile, or tilt when you find something amusing. So, I borrowed a body, and gave Horatio some added dimensions."

He flipped the switch at the base of Horatio's head, and then grabbed his computer tablet. With a few taps on the screen, Horatio stood, and with another tap, he slipped his hands into his pants pockets, thumbs hanging out.

"He can't speak, but he can respond to certain things." Rhys looked at Alex, and asked her to compliment him.

"Horatio, you look handsome today," she said.

His eyes brows lifted just a touch, as if caught by surprise, and then he grinned. His cheeks rose, eyes crinkled, and Horatio looked quite pleased.

"Dude," Charlie said when Rhys nodded toward him, "your fly is down."

Horatio's eyes opened wide and his hand went to his mouth, and then his expression settled into amusement.

George stopped taking notes and stepped closer to examine the drone.

"What else can he do?"

Isaac leaned in his seat to see past his father. "Horatio, why did the teddy bear turn down dessert? Because she was stuffed!"

Horatio's lips turned up in an I'm-tolerating-the-toddler joke way, lips pressed together, eyes crinkled at the corners.

"Can he laugh?" someone behind us asked.

Rhys shook his head. "Not yet. I haven't given him any vocal abilities, but that's a possibility later, if I get to keep working on him."

The other challengers left their Horatio heads behind and swarmed Rhys's, wanting a closer look. Smug Boy was nearly nose to nose with it, and he ran a finger across Horatio's lips and chin. When he stepped back, he said to Rhys, "Yeah, I think someone finally won this thing. Your Horatio is *awesome*."

Horatio was pleased enough to raise both hands in the air, tilting his head back, and he bounced on his toes once.

"Don't let him fall over!" Hyrum called out. "I fell over once like that and it really hurt!"

George brushed the kids away and took several pictures of Horatio, and when he was done, he stood to the side, skimming through his notes.

"Come on," Smug Boy finally said, "He did it. We all know he did it. This thing smiles like a farting baby."

I needed a new name for him. He no longer seemed so smug.

"You think you can do more with him?" George asked Rhys.

"I know I can. I ran out of time, but I'm sure I can give him a voice, and the ability to carry on conversations. He has the programming. I mean, most of it. It stops short of giving him the ability to make decisions beyond speaking, sitting, standing, and the like. He can ask questions and parse logic from the answers, but he can't, you know, act on his own behalf."

"And you're sure about that?"

Rhys tapped out another command. "Horatio, how are you today?"

Horatio lifted his hands to chest height, and began signing, using Universal Sign Language. "I am well. Well. Well. Well."

"A few hiccups," Rhys said. "But it's a start."

George took a step closer. "All right, Horatio, if it was a beauty contest, I suppose you'd win."

Horatio's lips curled; he seemed amused by the notion.

George tossed the tablet onto the table and turned to face the audience. "Emperor. Your Majesty," he said, "it looks like your son and nephew has done it. For the first time in ten years, Horatio's head has a smile, and we have a victor."

Under his breath, despite his smile, Jax murmured, "And we have a problem."

~

"I'll need a new challenge," George pseudo-whined over pizza and beer. "What else can I torture the little monsters with?"

"Jet packs," Rhys answered. "Uncle Jax gets the first one after they figure it out. He's wanted one as long as I can remember."

Jax could step through a portal and play with a jet pack in Will's birth When anytime he wanted. He lamented that there was still no commercially available personal system, and while the military had plenty to choose from, no one was going to let him play with one of those.

"I'll ban you from the challenge if I do that," George warned. "You already know how they work."

"Maybe. But I might not be there next year."

The chatter that swirled around us, adults and children talking over each other, dropped to near nothing. The only people unsurprised were Zed, Will and Aisha; Alex and Charlie were as flummoxed as George.

"He's chewed through the curriculum already," Zed offered. "His choice, but it might be time for him to move on and accept the scholarship UC is dangling in front of him."

"He's fifteen," Jax said.

"I am aware," Will said. "Which is why we're giving him the choice and time to make the decision."

Drew leaned forward to see Rhys past Will. "What about dating? That might be hard in college."

"It's hard *now*," Rhys argued. "I never really know if someone likes me for me or because I'm, well, me. The family name carries some weight."

"Jenna likes you," Alex said, teasing. "She doesn't care about who you are."

"And she's only thirteen," Rhys countered. "Besides, I don't think she does. Not really. And even if she did...*thirteen*."

Will stopped the potential torrent of teasing and pointed them all toward the arcade at the back of Piazzo's. Hyrum bounced in his seat, waiting for an invitation to join them, nearly squealing when Rhys turned and asked him what was taking him so long. If he stayed there, he was going to be stuck with old people.

"He understands Hyrum is our age, doesn't he?" George asked Will.

"What he understands is that his uncle is one of his best friends, and therefore not old. Hyrum, however..."

"He's been holding back lately," Jax mused. "Why?"

Aubrey set her hand on his arm. "Because, sweetheart, Rhys has surpassed the age when kids start pulling away from him. From what Red has told me, all of our older nephews and nieces drifted away when they hit their early teens. He might not realize it, but he's protecting himself from it."

"The kids would never—"

"He knows," she said. "But he also can't control what he's feeling. He feels as if he's an intrusion, and doesn't want to upset anyone."

"He, Rhys, and Isaac are still the three amigos," Aisha said. "I'll make sure Rhys understands how Hyrum is likely feeling. They would never intentionally exclude him, but a reminder might be in order."

My teeth are in service. In case someone needs to be nipped at.

"We don't bite the kids," Will said, sighing.

I suppose you save that for Aisha.

Oddly enough, he didn't translate that.

8

The rock upon which Finn stood was likely a good twenty steps past Mars, and we left him alone to assemble whatever mental puzzle pieces bounced around in his head. Instead of standing at the window in Will's office, he sat in a chair facing it, his elbows on his knees, and to anyone else wandering in he looked as if he were transfixed by the bay and the people playing on the beach.

Hyrum glanced up from his spot on the floor every now and then, checking for the gentle rise and fall of Finn's back, just to be sure. He was sketching on a massive piece of paper that had been carefully removed from a thick pad gifted to him by Jay, using treasured colored pencils that prompted him to ask Aisha and Rhys to stop him if he put one anywhere near his mouth.

He didn't mind ruining his crayons or craft-store pencils by chewing and gnawing on them, but these were the type that Jay used for work; they were expensive and Hyrum didn't want to risk breaking one before he had the chance to use it up. With these, he was deliberate in his drawing. The people he drew were not the stick figures of his crayon world, but fully featured, with attention paid to eyes and lashes, ears and hair trimmed around them. He had listened to Jay's prompts on scale and proportion, and he asked Rhys for reminders as they both worked at their projects.

Today he wanted to sketch the drone Rhys was tinkering with, so Rhys and Aisha pulled it from the table and settled it on the floor where Hyrum could better see. Rhys acquiesced to Hyrum's initial discomfort—"no one wants to see his wiener, Rhys"—and slipped a nanosuit onto the drone. There was no opening of the drone's head or chest cavity today; instead of poking around at hardware he had already spent nearly a hundred hours working on, Rhys attached wires to ports at the base of the skull, and sat leaning against the sofa with a computer in his lap, adding to the drone's base programming.

Aisha was there to help with the math. While Rhys benefitted from her teaching him higher concepts from the time he left grade school and could rattle off equations and answers without blinking, he lacked her confidence when it came to complicated equations. Today, he did not want to second guess himself. She sat on the sofa with her own computer and worked on grading her students' tests, pausing when Rhys had questions.

He'd worried about imposing on her time because he knew she had just finished a round of high-level exams and had students whose futures hung on the results of those tests, but she swore that multitasking was to her benefit and something she was used to.

"These same tests were graded with three toddlers swirling around me," she reminded him. "It's honestly harder with total quiet."

"What'd you do when Jay was a baby?" Hyrum asked. "Borrow a couple more kids?"

"I should have. But I did the next best thing. I bundled him up in his stroller and headed for a park just behind the apartment building. There was a nice set of benches near the playground and I sat there to work and watch kids run around."

"Jay ran around when he was a baby?"

"Well. He slept a lot then. When he was a toddler, I spent less time working and more time trying to keep him out of trouble."

"Was that the playground with the big pile of sand he wanted to climb?" Rhys asked. "He said it was like a mountain. Not that he'd exaggerate."

It was, to a toddler, an insurmountable heap. To an adult, it was a several-feet-tall hazard inexplicably replenished every few months. No one was sure why it was there to begin with, and she had—along with a dozen other parents—petitioned the city to remove it before someone was hurt, but for the entire time she lived there, the pile of sand remained and no one who worked for the city could explain it.

"Originally, it was meant to refill the playground's surface. Someone kept adding onto the pile, though. Kids plowed into it on purpose, and we were terrified someone was going to kill themselves. When Jay was four, I think, some teenager on a bike sped toward it, probably thinking he would ride right over it... and plowed his front wheel all the way into its side. Soft sand, stupid kids."

Hyrum sat up sharply. "Oh no. Was his bike okay?"

She wasn't sure, but it had gone in past the front fork, with only an inch or two of the wheel still showing.

Hyrum crinkled his nose. "It was probably okay, then. You can get a new fork. Those are easy."

"That's a pretty important part of the bike," Aisha said.

"I know. But if you take the stem apart you can pull it right out. Take the handle bars off first, though. If you don't, it's just harder."

"I will take your word for it."

He'd taken his fork off; one of the things Will insisted on, as Rhys and the twins began riding and were old enough to take care of their own bicycles, was that they learn how to maintain them. Hyrum learned right along with them on his own bike, reasoning that he'd had it for a long time but only knew how to change the tires and the chain; it had been a gift from Santa, his first big present, and he wanted to take the best care of it.

"Yeah, we probably need to check all the bikes," Rhys said. "It's been a while since we redid the brakes and cables and stuff."

"Look really close at Charlie's bike," Hyrum said. "It rolled down the stairs at Union Square and when it fell over the top tube went *bang* against the hand rail."

"And that's bad," Aisha prompted.

"Could be catastrophic failure," Rhys said.

"I don't think the cat had anything to do with it." Hyrum bit at his bottom lip as he considered it. "But there might be a crack. And if it cracks, he needs a new bike."

I think Aisha was about to proclaim that if he needed a new one, he was paying for it himself because that seems like a Mom thing to say, but Rhys tapped a key on his computer and the drone's nanosuit shifted and became jeans and a t-shirt. Hyrum giggled and scooted closer, running his fingers over the drone's leg.

"Put a hood on him! You can make him look like anyone! Like the time we did that and made it look like Shivan!"

"Do you even remember that?" Aisha asked Rhys.

He nodded. "When Drew went to Elysium and wound up floating outside the station. Dad jumped Shivan into space to help save him. That was a brilliant idea."

"It was Hyrum's idea," she pointed out.

"Only kinda." Hyrum was more interested in the drone laying on the floor in front of him. "Oh! Let's make him look like a cat!"

He jumped up and ran for Will's desk. In a cabinet just behind it, there was a stash of nanosuits, including the cowl he wanted.

"Uncle Jax thinks humanoid drones are disturbing?" Rhys chuckled. "Wait until this thing walks in the door."

Spoilers.

They did not take the drone home. But they did turn its head into a nightmare-inducing replica of future-Jo's cat, Luxor, mimicking his bright-white fur and piercing blue eyes, and Hyrum captured a lengthy video to share with his AI-loathing brother-in-law. The sight of it made Aisha erupt in laughter, made worse when Finn finally stood and turned, uttering, "What the actual hell?" when the drone turned to look at him.

"See what happens when you leave for Mars?" Rhys mused. "The cats take over. Say hello to your new feline overlord."

~

The air swirling around the balcony that night had a bite to it, the kind that whispered to people that they should enjoy it now, because in an hour or two, fog would unfurl across the city like a cold, wet blanket. This had the feel of not being able to see ten feet ahead, and those who chose to brave the frigid balcony with Will and Jax had bundled against it.

Will wore his Wick shirt, giving me a nice, body-heated pouch to lounge in while they sipped scotch and ignored the noise on the other side of the door.

"So," he asked Finn as he poured a splash of the scotch into a glass for his father, "how far from Mars were you today? Rhys thinks you may have bounded across the galaxy this time."

"It's not where I was. *When.* Liam and I have been discussing his travels. We're of the mind that he's crossed timelines on multiple occasions without realizing it."

Liam Finnegan was simply another version of Finn from a When far removed from our own. He could have been in the line ahead of Finn by three or four, but he also could have been a thousand Finns ahead. We knew for sure of one time he had hopped from one timeline to another, when he stayed in the past to make sure Jax's parents made it home from the future—a future that assured Queen Donna's survival, which created a new line— and then found his way back.

Will had no doubt that Liam had managed to line hop more than once. He was the only Finn that Will didn't trust implicitly, and the only one he never referred to as his father. Still, there was fondness, and Will was interested in the things Liam did, especially in his work.

"And which aspect of his travels are you focusing on?"

"None. All. It's more trying to pull the strands apart to see how he's doing it. He hasn't utilized null space in centuries—"

"Unnecessary with the portals," Will said.

"—yet I cannot conceive of a way to do it without bouncing off null space. A redirect once there might make it possible and even plannable, but without it?"

"You once had no idea how to manage any sort of time travel without it. Given that he's so much older, he has a jump on that."

Jax sighed. "Is it important? You have the portals. You have transporters. Will has the damned jump bracelet. You have any conceivable point in time, anywhere on this planet, to play on."

"It's a puzzle," Finn answered, as if Jax should know. "I don't have all the pieces, and I want them."

"So ask Liam," Will said.

"Ask Liam." Finn snorted. "That sounds a lot like asking you how you came up with the bracelet before I even nailed down the transporter."

"You already knew how the transporter should work, Dad. You'd done it, basically."

"Not without the transponders. Yes, let me jam one into your brain, and I could have moved you from point A to point B in a short burst to a designated point. That was a failsafe with the machine. I needed to know how to do it without. You're awfully stingy with the answers. And before you say it, I don't care about being first. I care about understanding it."

Show him the code. All of it.

"He's seen the code, Wick."

Finn set his glass aside and leaned forward, elbows on knees. "No, the cat is right. Let me see it again. Spend time with it. If I can understand how you utilize the jump bracelet, perhaps I can utilize the transporters for time travel without the need for the portals. Without the need for the tunnel."

Construction on the tunnel would not begin until after Will's birth. Using it required a transponder embedded in one's brain; step into a portal and be instantly moved from one point in time, to the tunnel, and then into another When. It gave Finn pause to know that he had created it yet had not fundamentally created a transporter at the same time. He transported people, and yet, did not. He'd later created a unit based on the gate Will had once used to send a young Finn from our When back to his own, one that held a massive meteor in place before shoving it off into space, but there was a hiccup in his understanding exactly how and why it functioned as he'd hoped.

The gates had been manufactured with a high-speed projectile system that embedded multiple transponders into the meteor; he knew of no other way to move the massive space rock. Yet Will understood it, fundamentally, and had used the same data to create the bracelet that required no transponder. It could still read information output by an individual's embedded transponder, but it mostly operated by tactile input.

There was nothing left to hide; Will agreed to open the

files to his father's perusal. "Rhys will be in my office all week tinkering with the drone. If you don't mind his inquisitive company, feel free to take ownership of the computers in the workspace."

"He's determined to create a fully functioning android, isn't he?" Jax asked with a bit of a sigh.

"Lines will not be crossed," Will said.

"He might cross those lines before he realizes what he's done."

So have him work somewhere else. Somewhen else.

"If he works in my birth When, he'll have unwanted access to all the data he seeks," Will pointed out. "This is something he needs for himself, to do largely on his own."

Saint Francis. Their access to data is controlled, isn't it? But he can work there. There's the lab and equipment—

"Saint Francis," Will repeated.

"Technically," Jax started.

"Technically Saint Francis lies within a government two hundred years in the future. Its residents yield to your rule by choice because they see Finn as their creator and he lives under your rule, but the simulator's location is under the purvey of a democratic socialist government."

"One that doesn't know it exists," Finn pointed out. "And if they did? No one would care. AI is not illegal there. Controlled but perfectly legal."

Shivan is Prince Regent. Ask him. If he says yes, then Rhys has freedom to explore. And he might come up with something that makes everyone happy.

"You understand this," Finn said, as much to himself as to Rhys. "The code. The math. All of it."

"In an abstract way," Rhys responded. "What I've seen of it. I mean, I get the math. And I can see how point A leads to point B, then on to C through Z. I'm not one hundred percent sure how Dad accounted for the exchange in matter but I'm leaning toward it being a mechanical solution rather than just math. Somehow, he got the jump bracelet to shift matter between Whens to avoid losing any."

Loss of matter meant, theoretically, creating a black hole.

One does not want a black hole on earth.

So I'm told.

Hyrum glanced up from the book he was reading. "Are there fractions? I bet there are. That means there are minuses and Will probably had to make them pluses so that it's not all wrong."

Hyrum hated fractions. His refusal to consider them beyond what he needed to know for baking purposes had resulted in a few spectacular tantrums that caused Aubrey to fold her arms and quietly order him to go to his room. She never yelled, but the bare spark of simmering anger was enough to propel him from his chair to his room, where he often fell asleep.

She never allowed him to nap through dinner, however. That was a given; his mother had withheld meals as a punishment for behaviors he could not control, and Aubrey refused to add onto that misery. If he was asleep, she woke him gently, he apologized, and that was the end of it.

Rhys had witnessed dozens of those tantrums. He understood

how to deflect Hyrum's frustrations, and when presented with the possibility of a quarter of something, or three-fourths, he simply explained things using decimals instead. Point-two-five. Point-seven-five. He never argued minuses; he instead found a way to assure that Hyrum was calm.

"No fractions in this code," Rhys told him. "It's more like a language, one that uses a lot of math instead of words."

"Will told me once that it's like baking cookies. You need the right amount of flour, so you have to add a little extra to make sure you have enough when you send the cookies to somewhere else." He paused to consider. "I bet they bake along the way."

Distracted, Finn asked, "What kind of cookies?"

"Probably chocolate chip. So maybe you need enough chips, too. Extra, just in case."

We all knew the look that passed over Finn's face. It meant that in a few seconds, he would be gone. The question was whether he would remain in place, or absently cross the room to stare out the window. Rhys snorted when Finn set his tablet on the coffee table, and when he slowly rose to cross the room, he and Hyrum turned their attention to the materials they'd been reading.

Hyrum fell into a story about a young boy sent to school in space, where he was expected to learn things that would save the universe from giant ant-like creatures. This was the sort of story he preferred—space as a backdrop, where there was always a happy ending in which the world gained a new hero. He enjoyed books with magic, stories with dragons and treasures, but his first love in literature was space.

Rhys returned to long lines of code, his finger gliding across the tablet screen as he scrolled along. He didn't have to completely understand it because the data would settle to the back of his brain and simmer until he needed it. This was his happy place as much as Hyrum's was in a good outer space romp; the world had secrets, and he wanted to know them all.

When Rhys's alarm went off, Finn was still somewhere near Mars. He and Hyrum left the room quietly to get lunch—burgers and shakes at Gunders, with a small plain, no-bread, chopped-up burger for me—and he was still there when we returned an hour later. Rhys knew he could bring his grandfather out of it, but he didn't see a point to that. Instead, he left a note reminding Finn where we'd be, gathered up his tools, and opened the portal to Saint Francis. Horatio's head and nano-suit cloaked body waited there on a table in the lab; Quinn and Shivan were probably already there poking around under Will's supervision. If not for kingly duties, Jax would have been there as well, though his interests were more aligned with preventing Rhys from breaking AI laws.

The drone was already functional, so much so that it was closer to being an android than not. Rhys had replaced the main processing units and given it the ability to speak. It could compute faster than the drones Ozoo sent to Elysium, understood a few steps beyond basic commands, and only required a few missing pieces before he began tinkering with the operating system.

"Are Charlie and Alex coming?" Hyrum asked as the portal closed behind them in Saint Francis. "Did you bring a towel? You'll need a towel if Alex is coming, on account of she doesn't want to see his wiener."

There were plenty of towels in the lab, but Rhys's siblings would not be there. "They have school," he explained. "Exams are next week and they don't want to miss all the last-minute info. Besides, Horatio is in a nanosuit. Alex wouldn't wind up being offended by his junk."

"Wait. How come you're not in school?"

Rhys had taken his exams. He was on an early break, giving him time to ponder his next educational step. Hyrum thought he would miss all his friends if he left school, but then flipped on his own opinion and told Rhys he should go to college. He could meet new friends and still have fun with his old ones in the afternoon.

"Or," Rhys said as he pushed the lab door open, "I could just do what I always do. Study, then tinker with shit. I've never really hung out with a bunch of people. Just you and Isaac."

Hyrum stopped just inside the door. "But don't you have friends?"

"Yeah. You and Isaac. I have a few friends at school, but we don't really hang after."

"Well, maybe you should. Friends are fun. That's why I go for bike rides all the time. I get to see my friends and I'm not working when I'm riding. Sometimes I run into Ash and we get burgers or he gets an egg salad sandwich on account of it's his favorite, or sometimes I stop and help Mrs. Mewler pick up trash outside her store, or I stop and talk to Mr. Picardo while he waits for his daughter to come get him. You need more friends, Rhys."

"Friends your own age." Will was seated at the table near the little kitchen. Shivan and Quinn were with him, and there were coffee and cookies, which made Hyrum skip past Rhys to grab one before they were gone. "You have a lifetime of adults ahead of you."

"I know."

Quinn jumped up to help Rhys with his tools. "They don't get it."

"Oh, I get it," Will said. "But I've been in the situation of having no friends my own age, Rhys. If you remain at the Academy—"

"I know, Dad. But this situation isn't the same. I'd still be in school, and the people I'd meet wouldn't be that much older. You were stuck without school at all. There's a big difference there. Grandma is a terrific teacher, but you didn't have any social structure. I will, either way."

You had friends, Will. You just had to wait for Jax to grow up.

"I still don't get that," Hyrum said around a bite of cookie. "He's older than you."

When Will met Jax, he was fifteen and Jax was six, hanging from a support post on the Bay Bridge. It took two years of Will's life, popping back and forth between Whens, skipping chunks of Jax's childhood, for them to catch up to each other. By the time Will left home at 17 to live in this When, Jax was 18.

Deflecting, Rhys reached for a cookie. "Who made these? Are they real or simulated?"

"Real," Quinn said.

"Yeah, that doesn't tell me anything. I've seen you drink lubricant."

"Your grandmother made them," Will said. He pointed to the fridge and added, "Aubrey sent lasagna. Just heat it up when you're hungry."

"You're not staying?"

"For a bit. I have shelter business to attend to and a date with my wife. Which means I'm counting on you two to not get lost in your work and to get home at a reasonable time."

I'll make sure they don't stay late. I'll need food and I'll bite someone if I have to.

"Well, there we go," Rhys said. "We'll be home by eight, because His Majesty can't eat lasagna."

10

An hour later, Rhys had installed a secondary processing chip, one programmed to a base program that he could, if needed, use to disable the drone remotely. He wanted everything to be self-contained, with no need for integration into another computer system, bypassing an opportunity for multiple drones to access a major system for their own amusement or agenda.

He was aware of the potential of drones becoming self-aware to the degree that they could figure that out on their own, but he wasn't going to make it easy. After sealing the pseudo-skin and slipping the nano-suit back onto the drone, he asked Will if it was still all right to move onto the next step: loading Quinn's programming into the drone. Creating the programming to craft a new individual could take months; stuffing Quinn into the drone's computer would take a minute.

It had been done once before; a decade earlier, when Drew was stuck floating in space following a shuttle explosion, Shivan's program was transferred to the closest available drone and then jumped into space to help him. He'd felt as if he'd been stuffed into a box, looking out at the world through a window; Rhys's additions meant that—theoretically—Quinn would feel no different in the drone than he did in the simulator. If it worked, Quinn would be able to leave Saint Francis and wander San Francisco. If it did not, Rhys could simply transfer him back to the simulator's computer.

"And if the transfer fails?" Shivan asked.

"I'll create a save point just before we move him," Rhys said. If something goes wrong, we restore him to that point."

"You have the right of refusal," Will reminded Shivan.

"And you have the right of demand." Shivan waved his hand before Will could protest. "I know you wouldn't, but we can't pretend this is my choice. It's Quinn's. We've discussed it at length…he wants to experience your world, and if not now, then when he reaches majority age. Which is merely weeks away."

"You're sure?" Will asked Quinn.

"Absolutely. Just, well, what happens to my body here when I'm transferred? Does it stay? Or maybe crumble, like I was returning to earth?"

Shivan knew the answer to that; his wife had watched him literally fall to pieces when Will transferred his program. She warned him against it; close your eyes, go outside, anything other than witness your son return to the vast pool of nanobots. Because of that, Shivan excused himself to wait in one of the offices, his back to the door to avoid the temptation of the narrow window beside it. Someone would get him when the drone was fully activated.

"It's not like he won't exist anymore," Rhys mumbled as the door closed behind Shivan.

"But it would feel as if he were watching his son die," Will said. "When someone here dies, their bodies are carried to the orchards, where they return to the earth, so to speak. I cannot fathom having to stand here and be witness to my child's body falling apart, leaving a pool of it on the ground, and then watching as it's absorbed back into the simulator."

"But—"

"You're applying logic to this. He's protecting himself against the pain of knowing that one day, he will return to the pool, and after that, so will his children."

Think how you'd feel if you had to watch Thor disappear. Or me. Just that chance that something would go wrong would eat at you, don't you think?

"Dad stuff," Quinn mused. "Come on, let's get rolling so he's not stuck in there brooding about all of this. I know he doesn't want me to do it, so let's get it done and spare him the anxiety."

"Won't take long." Rhys reached under the edge of the table where the nano-suit clad drone waited, and activated the computer keyboard. The sides of the table lifted and the red-lit keyboard slid out, clicking into place. He tapped a few keys, glanced at the drone again, making sure the suit's head cowl was attached to the torso, and then looked at Quinn. "Last chance to back out."

"Let's go."

It took longer to exhale than it did to transfer all of Quinn into the drone. A second after Rhys tapped the last key, Quinn's simulated body broke apart in microscopic pieces, raining to the floor, where everything disappeared like water sucked into a sponge. A second after that, the nano-suit activated and the drone became Quinn, right down to the tiny freckle under his right eye.

The drone's chest heaved with its first breath, and its eyes fluttered open.

Rhys leaned over the keyboard, his eyes narrowing as he inspected the places where the suit might gap. "Well? Are we here yet?"

Quinn cleared his throat, testing, and then sat up. "That was the freakiest thing I've ever felt. It...tingled."

"Were you aware of the transfer process?" Will motioned to Hyrum to get Shivan.

"It was like falling asleep in one room and waking up in another because Dad carried you to bed." Carefully, he slid off the table, feet hitting the floor with a thud. "But the falling apart thing? That was like a whole-body...well...it tingled."

Shivan bolted across the room. "Well? Are you all right? Do you feel okay?"

Quinn took a moment to assess. "I feel a bit heavy, I think. And everything has distance." His hand went to a spot at his jawline near his ear, and he double-tapped there with his finger. "That's better."

"Interesting," Rhys said. "You recalibrated without having been told how. Like it was intuitive."

"Explain," Will said.

Self-recalibration was part of the new programming; Rhys assumed that there might be a few incompatibilities between the drone and Quinn's program, so he added parameters that would allow adjustments based on what Quinn wanted. He thought vision might be a minor issue, along with speech quirks related to syntax. Adding self-calibration gave Quinn the ability to bring himself to the forefront, ahead of the drone's operating programming.

"Like a doctor making himself feel better!" Hyrum blurted.

"Speaking of feeling." Rhys reached a hand toward Quinn. "How's your sensation? Can you feel, physically?"

Instead of shaking Rhys's hand, Quinn slapped at it. "Yeah, I felt that. Normally, too. It felt like it's supposed to feel." His hand went to his stomach. "Can I eat? Because I feel hungry. Like, really hungry."

"You can eat. All the same cues should be there."

"Did you fix the butt thing?" Hyrum asked. "So that when he eats it doesn't all squirt out?"

Quinn's eyes widened. "What? You didn't warn me about that!"

Hyrum's squealing laughter stopped Rhys from answering and made Will sigh.

"All right." Will took a step back. "Reheat the lasagna and feed Quinn. And for today, stick to the simulator to give him the opportunity to adjust. We can introduce him to San Francisco tomorrow afternoon."

"Your birth When?" Rhys asked.

"That seems most prudent."

The first proof that the cowl over the drone's head functioned well was the look of disappointment on Quinn's face. He wanted to leave the simulator now, not wait. But he also knew better than to argue with a man who could stop him from ever setting foot into a portal; he sucked it up, headed for the refrigerator to get the lasagna, and Will left. Shivan lingered for only a few minutes, long enough to ask them to head for the house before wandering off to explore.

While the lasagna was in the flash cooker, Hyrum poked around the small pantry, looking for something I could eat. He reminded them twice that there were things in the lasagna that were bad for kitties and grumbled when he couldn't find something suitable for me.

I'm fine. I ate breakfast.

Hyrum was not fine. If they were eating, I was eating. If I wasn't, he wasn't. When Hyrum's back was turned to him, Rhys quietly pulled out his phone and tapped on the screen. "Check the middle shelf to the back, probably on the right side," Rhys said to him as he slid the phone back into his pocket.

"I looked there already."

"Grandpa always keeps food for Wick there. Okay, well, most of the time. If there isn't anything, we can scramble an egg or something. You'll eat an egg, right, Wick?"

Put some cheese in it, and sure.

With a heavy sigh, Hyrum stood on his tiptoes and shoved his arm as far into the pantry as it would go. He flopped his hand around, feeling for anything he might have missed, and then grinned when his fingers slid across a small, round, metal can. He held it up as if it were a prize, wiggling it in his hand. "Cat food! And it's his favorite beefy gooshy food!"

Thank you for looking again. I'll enjoy this more than an egg.

Happy, he headed for the bathroom to wash any pantry dust off his hands. Quinn waited until the door closed and then asked, "Okay, how'd you do that?"

"Grandpa installed a program onto my phone. I can connect to the lab outside of the time shift and someone there is always listening for the alert."

Alternately, you can just shout if you need help. He added that to the sim program when all the kids started visiting here.

He did not want to shout with Hyrum there. It was not an emergency, and it would have frightened Hyrum anyway.

Before digging into the lasagna—which, by the way, was enough for six adults but not two with absurdly high metabolisms and a teenaged hologram stuffed into a drone—Quinn hesitated. "What happens if I eat this? I can usually eat real food, but this isn't my body."

"You can eat," Rhys assured him. "Your stomach pouch is lined with nanobots, and they'll do most of the digestion. In a few hours, you'll get a signal telling you to eliminate anything extraneous. Food, liquid—anything."

"What the hell else do you think I'm eating?"

"Right now? Nothing. But once I refine the sensors, you'll be able to taste something to determine if it's poison. Or just rotten. You could get a job as the King's taste-tester. If he had one, anyway."

He has one.

"Oh, come on, Wick."

Not for at home. But if they eat out? Or at an event? Before that plate gets in front of him, someone else has already eaten some. Or something has. It's kind of a drone, about the size of a loaf of bread. One of the guards takes batch samples of the food and feeds it to the drone, and tests for things that could harm the King or Queen.

"Seriously," Rhys said. "I didn't know that. Has anything ever been found?"

Allergens, no poison. It found mango in a dessert, back when Marco couldn't have any.

Marco, Zed's oldest, used to swell up like a balloon when given mango. You'd think that would keep him from trying it, but he loved it and kept sneaking bites.

"Ah, yeah. They finally had Mass take him forward to cure him of the allergy."

"You do that a lot?" Quinn asked. "Jump through time just for a doctor's visit?"

"Personally, no. But throughout the family? Oh, yeah. It's just easier. Break a bone, go to my dad's birth When, hop in a tank, and it's fixed in a few hours. My mom had ovarian cancer— Mass found it on a simple exam, shoved her in, and it was gone before dinner time."

Jax had brain cancer. He was in a tank at the same time, but his took a few days.

"Aren't there pills for that?"

"Yeah, but then the disease and treatment become part of the public record. If we go there, it's private. No one had to know that he had the same cancer that killed his mom."

In this When. They went back and saved her when you were little. It created a new timeline, but at least she's out there somewhen now. Alive.

"So he can't go see her," Quinn mused.

"Not until we find a way to move between timelines. We're lucky to move around in this one as it is."

"But it's a secret," Hyrum reminded him. "Only a few people can do it. I can't go anywhere unless I'm with you or Will or Drew."

I can take you anywhen.

"I know. But we still have to get permission. Just like if Eli wanted to go, or his brothers. Aisha could take us, but she hasn't on account of I never asked her to. Do you think that hurts her feelings? Should I ask her?"

Rhys was sure her feelings were not hurt. After all, she had a job to worry about and kids to deal with; it likely never crossed her mind that someone else was doing all the fun things with Hyrum.

"Speaking of moms." Rhys got up and headed for the sink, ready to wash his dishes. "We need to get moving, so we can go see yours and then decide what else we're going to do."

~

After presenting ourselves to Lani—she was impressed that she could barely tell the difference between drone-Quinn and not-drone-Quinn, but more than that, she was relieved he was all right—we walked to Ocean Beach. Quinn thought there was a good chance that Jeff, a dragon I had created from a wish, was there flying over the water. He'd been a baby dragon then, just 20 feet tall with shiny, obsidian-black flesh, but now he was grown and there was no telling what color he was.

He'd learned to change his scales on a whim. He interchanged between green, gold, blue, and most impressively, ruby red. That was his favorite skin; we appealed to his ego by pointing out that he shimmered like red diamonds in the sun, gloriously, and it was that skin he wore as we made our way across the Great

Highway to the sand. He soared overhead, dipping a wing to acknowledge our presence. On the beach looking up at him was Fluffy, my other wish-creation.

Fluffy was as tall as a Clydesdale, perhaps a bit more. He'd come to life as a ginger tabby cat, but had also learned to change. Most of the time he wandered Saint Francis as a multicolored feline, each strand of fur a different bright color, but today he was stark white. He looked like Luxor, Jo's cat and my best feline friend; even his eyes were the same startling blue.

Hyrum broke away and ran to the beach, calling out Fluffy's name in one long breath. He landed against the giant cat with a thud and wrapped his arms around him as far as he could, which was not much. When he was ready, he took a step back and waved at Jeff, who was not there for our amusement; he was at work, keeping tabs on his own creations, and guarding the city.

Might as well find a place to plop down. Hyrum and Fluffy are going to play for the next hour.

"It's a shame Fluffy can't leave here." Quinn left out a tiny oof as he sat on the sand. "He's happiest with Hyrum. We try to play with him, but…he's just brighter when Hy is around."

"That would go over well in San Francisco. A giant cat with swords for claws and teeth to match."

"They'd get used to him, don't you think?"

Rhys didn't want to tell him someone would probably hurt Fluffy; fear makes people stupid sometimes, and scared people often lash out. Instead, he just grunted, "Maybe."

Fluffy is marketable.

"Marketable," Rhys repeated.

Fluffy: the feline nuclear option.

"Yeah, and then people would start exposing their cats to radiation. And then sue when all they got was a cancer-riddled cat, not…gigantikitty."

"It's louder there, right?" Quinn asked. "Maybe he wouldn't be happier. I wonder if we would. Saint Frank is quiet, by design, I think. The worst noise we get is when the sprites band together and scream like feral cats. And that's gross enough because I'm fairly sure it's mating behavior."

The people of Saint Francis could be acclimated to the noise if leaving the simulator en masse was ever made possible. Rhys reminded Quinn of the fillers that populated the city before he was born: Shedu guards, the man-shaped tools Tobias used to control the elves and the outliers who helped them. Bring those back, add some air traffic, and they'd get used to it.

Quinn gave a light shrug. "Not that they'll ever get to leave. My dad and I may be the only ones who ever get a chance to see what life outside this place is like."

"Someday," Rhys sighed. "I mean, I know AI isn't illegal in my dad's birth When. That's the obvious destination for anyone who wants to peek outside. And when Oz becomes queen, she might be more open to letting you wander around in my When."

"And how many of us will be alive then?"

That gave Rhys pause. "All of you," he finally said. "You don't *have* to die. You can live as long as you want, just...wish for it, I guess."

"There are only two of us with that power, and one of them is technically forbidden from it. Hagar and Tobias. The rest of us are blocked from the information that would allow it to happen."

You dad might have access. He's the Prince Regent.

"He's never said he has any special access to anything other than the computer he uses to communicate with the Emperor. And it's not even the idea of living forever. It's the idea that all we have, all we'll *ever* have, is this. Work as a fisherman or wheat thrasher. Maybe working in the orchards. Teacher. Brewer. We don't have options, and almost everything we have in the arts is handed down from outside."

But you have things we don't. Dragons and Fluffy. You never have to worry about where your food will come from or if you'll have a place to live.

"We don't have *purpose*, Wick. We were created for human entertainment and if not for a hiccup along the way when Tobias turned to the dark, we'd still be nothing but entertainment. We'd exist to humor people who landed here by accident, and nothing more."

I didn't point out that Tobias's "hiccup" was intentional, written into the program. It was true; the original purpose of the simulator was to occupy the attention of someone who attempted to use the portals as a permanent way out of life, or if they tried to go far into a future that might never exist. We'd discovered Finn's creation when Drew, learning to control his passage through portals, had a stray thought that seeing life 1,000 years from now would be awesome. The portal detected the thought and pushed us into Saint Francis to save us from the possibility of exiting into nothingness.

Waiting for us at the portal exit was Shivan. He was fifteen years old and declared himself to be the last of the Blackshears; in under an hour, we eased from abject skepticism to belief, that this was the future and he was training to lead a war against the dark wizard, Tobias, who held the elves as slaves. He had the backing of the outliers, was gathering an army, and would soon march into a battle that would bring freedom and peace to Saint Francis.

There was nothing, initially, to tell us that we had stepped into a world of make believe, but even after Will was certain of it, we stayed to fight. It didn't matter if we were involved in a complicated game; Oz had demons she needed to face, and fighting gave her that chance. It wasn't until we were near the end that we understood that the people with whom we fought knew who and what they were, but to them it was very real and had we walked away, they would have continued to live under Tobias's oppressive, dictatorial thumb.

Yet, Quinn was also right. The people of Saint Francis had won their right to exist; Finn agreed to keep the simulator running and left them to their lives, but he hadn't given them *more*. And if Quinn was proof, they wanted more.

"Create your purpose," Rhys said. "There's never been anything to stop the elves from making art, or inventing new jobs, or even from expanding their footprint from the village to the city. Open shops and restaurants. Colleges. Hospitals."

"But the data—"

"Ask for more. Your dad is Prince Regent. All he has to do is ask. If you don't have access to data, it's because my grandfather hasn't considered it. And that shouldn't surprise anyone."

With a sigh, Quinn agreed. "Hard to see things here when you're stuck on another planet."

"And the whole dying, not dying thing? Maybe it'll take time, but you'll have a choice. That's on my agenda, anyway. If I have any say, someday you'll have all the information you want, and you'll be able to leave here."

Talk to Drew. If anyone is willing to make that happen, it's him.

Saint Francis was Finn's creation, but it was built upon the bones of a nanobot dynasty that Drew had—or would in his lifetime—pieced together.

Rhys knew the code for the program; if anyone was going to pick it apart to make it grow, to give its citizens freedom to move beyond its borders, it was him.

And that was going to piss off the King.

11

He tripped twice on the walk home. The first time he landed with a loud thud, clutching his chest as he rolled onto his back. "I can barely breathe," he wheezed. "Why? Why can't I—?"

Rhys crouched next to him. "You just knocked the air out of yourself. It'll be fine. Just relax and you'll be able to get a good breath in a few seconds."

"But why?" He carefully pushed himself up. "I've fallen on my face before. I've never had this happen."

"You've never had lungs before. The drone has pseudo-lungs, and when you fell it expelled all the oxygen and alerted your systems that sometime was wrong. It's scary but when you relax, you can breathe."

"I have lungs!"

"You have an approximation of lungs. I don't think you can force all the air out because the nanobots just regroup and provide you with more. The drone isn't programmed for that."

"Well. It should be."

The second time he tripped, Hyrum caught the back of his shirt and kept him from going over. No one said anything, they just kept walking; Rhys and Hyrum slowed when Quinn did, and said nothing when it seemed as if he wanted to stop. By the time we reached his home, he was shuffling, and dropped into a garden chair near the door.

"I feel the weight of this body," he admitted when Rhys asked if he was all right. "Why is it so heavy?"

"Gravity."

Quinn's hand went to his chest. "I can feel my heart pounding. I've never felt that before. That wasn't even a long walk, but I'm tired. Why am I tired? This isn't even my body."

"Do you need a few days to get used to it? We don't have to explore tomorrow. We can do it anytime."

He wanted to go in the morning. There was nothing more that he wanted than to see life outside Saint Francis; if he was tired, he was tired. Hyrum assured him they could find places to sit and rest, and he knew the best place for a cheeseburger in Will's birth When. They could have burgers and milkshakes, even onion rings if Quinn thought he could eat all that without throwing up.

"Is that a challenge?" Quinn asked.

Don't try to outeat Hyrum or Rhys. They have stomachs that reach all the way to their toes. You really will throw up.

"Then it is a challenge," he said. "This could be fun.

~

"We'll start midmorning, when things tend to be a bit quieter," Will said when Quinn admitted the idea of the noise of San Francisco worried him. "I have business to conduct, so the four of you can wander near Union Square until I'm done."

Five. I'm going with them. Business is boring and they might discover some shenanigans to get into.

"No shenanigans. Hyrum is in charge, so whatever impulses you have, he gets final say."

Hyrum's eyes went wide. "Me? But I—"

"You're the adult."

"But—"

Rhys snorted. "You're not a teenaged hornball, Hy. The rest of us are easily distracted by whatever pretty girl walks by."

"Speak for yourself," Isaac grunted.

"All right. Some of us are more distracted by shiny metal objects, but the point is the same. Keep us from drooling over the girls we see and keep Isaac from running into the street because he saw a cyber-puppy zooming through an intersection."

"Indeed," Will said. "When I'm done, we'll meet on the Square."

"What if something bad happens?" Hyrum asked.

"Call me. And if you're more than a few minutes late getting to the Square, I can track Rhys with his transponder." He slipped his wallet from his back pocket and pulled out a shiny gold card. "This works in any When. Use it for food and drinks, and if you like—" his eyes flicked toward Quinn "—souvenirs. Your parents have been amazingly tolerant of this project. Perhaps gifts to thank them."

"Any When?" Rhys asked as Will handed it over. "Like, three hundred years ago?"

He nodded. "Any point in time from the advent of metallic credit cards going forward. So, presumably, four hundred years or so. It's attached to an account in my name, but I've added each of you as authorized for use."

You added them all four hundred years ago.

"I've had a busy morning," Will sighed.

"I'll pay you back if I buy anything," Hyrum said. "But mostly I'll probably just buy lunch."

"I do not expect remuneration. Consider this a gratuity, if you will, for helping Rhys with his project."

"I don't know what that means, but okay."

Sweet. I'm getting that sports car I've always wanted.

Will sighed. "Get a license first, Wick. If you can convince the MVD to give you one, I'll buy you a car."

Oh, well. Not if there are strings attached.

How about the car and a chauffeur?

"Can we rent jet packs?" Rhys asked.

Will nodded. "I suggest you head for the launch pad near the Embarcadero and rent from there. It will be...easier."

There was an instructional rental kiosk near *Sof y Z's*; over the last 10 years Will had taken his kids there at least 4 times a year, and the owners knew him and knew Rhys. More importantly, they knew Hyrum and would not press him to join in. Instead, Hyrum would set up where he had a long sightline. He had the choice of recording their flight or simply observing, and if he wanted, someone would bring him a cup of hot chocolate, extra chocolate with no whipped cream, because he always got whipped cream on his nose and it embarrassed him.

Judging from the look on Quinn's face when we exited the portal in Will's birth When, he needed the time it took to walk from Union Square to the Embarcadero to adjust to his new surroundings. It wasn't loud, exactly, but the Square was bustling with tourists and shoppers. Cars zipped overhead and down the streets. There was a persistent whine, an urban soundtrack that Quinn expected yet wasn't quite prepared to hear.

Compared to our When, it was loud.

Three steps out, he stopped, surprised by a woman doing a fast jog-walk cutting right in front of him. Rhys urged him forward, poking at his back until we were in the center of the Square, where he could get a good look around.

"That's where Dad grew up." Rhys pointed at the eight-story building directly across the Square. "Hell, it's where we live now. Looks different, but basically, the same. And that—" he turned to gesture at the elevator behind us on the far side "—is where the lab is. It's actually under the Square, but that's where you go in."

In Saint Francis, the lab entry was a dilapidated single room shack with a poorly lit staircase leading down to the first level. Quinn knew it well and twitched in that direction. The lab was quiet; the lab was safe. Will set a hand on his shoulder and quietly said, "Give yourself a moment. This will quickly sound no worse than Jeff and Scooter chasing the small dragons over the village as they learn to hunt."

Quinn's eyes darted back and forth, trying to follow people hurrying past. "Will they notice? Me?"

"Look at them. Not one has turned in your direction. There is nothing out of the ordinary about your presence here."

And there are androids here, anyway. No one cares.

"So I'm allowed here, but not there," Quinn said. "Why do I exist more for this When then that one?"

"Because of one old law that has yet to be rewritten." He leaned to see past Quinn. "Buddy system. No one wanders alone, all right? And again…listen to Hyrum."

As Will walked away, the others turned to Hyrum. "All right, fearless leader," Rhys said. "Straight to the jet packs, or shopping for stuff Quinn can give his mom? Food? Booze?"

Hyrum straightened his shoulders. "We should go where Will thinks we're going. Jetpacks. But if you see a good store on the way, it would be okay to go inside. On account of he said Quinn should get presents, so we're still doing what he said."

There was only one store that made Quinn pause; he wanted to stop and stare in the window of a jewelry store, fascinated by all the glittering things laid out on display. He mused that his mother would enjoy seeing all of that but wasn't sure she wanted to own any of it. There was a necklace he was drawn to, a thin gold chain with a ruby charm shaped like a wave, and he gave it real consideration.

"Will didn't give a price cap, right?" Isaac asked, amused.

Quinn had no clue about money and the price of things. "Is it a lot?"

Hyrum pressed his nose against the glass. "That's more than I make all year at Ozoo."

"But is that a lot?" Quinn pressed.

In unison, all three answered, "That's a lot."

Will would not have blinked. Rhys knew that but agreed they could find something reasonable. He knew Lani; she had as much awareness of money as did Quinn but would be happier with something the average tourist might buy on a whim. He suggested renting the jetpacks, and then after we could hit up Pier 39, where there was a seemingly endless supply of souvenirs to choose from.

As we neared the Embarcadero, Hyrum began looking for a spot where he and I could wait. He wanted to take pictures and video of Quinn's first flight, something the teen could show his parents; he knew where he wanted to wait but he also wanted a backup spot in case someone else was lingering there.

"Right there by the fountains," he said. "I can see you take off and you can fly close enough that I can get video. Just don't go too fast or you'll be all streaky on the pictures and you might smack right into a building."

A collision had not occurred to Quinn. He began to slow, and completely stopped when we were ten feet from the kiosk. Before Rhys began the rental process Quinn insisted on reading every rule posted, including each cautionary clause and warnings regarding faulty equipment.

"Maximum weight four hundred pounds or one hundred eighty-one kilos," he read aloud. "How much do I weigh? I don't know that. What happens if I'm four hundred five pounds?"

Daphne, the owner of the jet packs, leaned over the counter. "Hon, if you weigh two hundred, it'll be a surprise."

The weight of the drone. Do you know how much he really weighs?

"He's solid muscle," Rhys said. "He might be over two-forty, but he's for sure not over two-seventy-five."

"But what if I am?" Quinn pressed.

Daphne jutted her thumb toward a scale off to the right. "Step on, let's see."

Carefully, Quinn stepped onto the platform, and she read the numbers that popped up on her data screen. "Two-sixty. No problem."

"Still." Quinn crossed his arms over his stomach. "I've never done anything like this, Rhys. If I wreck, all your work—"

"Your program will transfer back to the sim," Rhys said. "You're in no danger."

"Ah. Droid." Daphne was not surprised. "I have a data-based instructional program if you have a synth port. We can plug that in, and in a few seconds, you'll know everything you need. You'll even feel experienced."

He wasn't convinced. If he plowed headfirst into a building, his life might be spared but the drone body in which he was encased would be destroyed. It was not replaceable, and—

"It's replaceable," Rhys assured him

"And we're insured," Daphne said.

Hyrum stepped onto the scale. "Do I weigh enough? Quinn, will you feel better if I go, too? I'll go if it will make you feel better. I watch Rhys and Charlie and Alex do this a lot. They never had an accident. So I'll do it to make you feel better."

"You weigh enough," Daphne said, not pointing out that the average six-year-old was big enough. Hyrum was small for an adult; he barely reached five feet tall and celebrated every pound gained. But he was making a point, assuming a risk over something he was terrified to try, so no one said anything about how small he really was.

When he stepped off the scale, I climbed down Rhys's shoulder and his leg, and stepped on.

How about me?

"Wick, there are no packs tiny enough for you," Daphne said. "But for the record, you're four-point-seven pounds."

Ah, man. I lost weight. I was almost six a few weeks ago.

I get all the foods at lunch today.

"He's ridden with me before," Rhys said, tugging on the front pocket of his sweatshirt. "My aunt makes these because we haul him around everywhere—"

Daphne was aware.

"No." Quinn sucked in a deep breath. "I'll do it. Rhys, do I have a data port? Can I learn that way?"

"Magnetic," Rhys answered. "Just behind your left ear."

Daphne held the data dongle to the rigid spot behind Quinn's ear, and true to her word, the information transferred in under ten seconds. It took another two for him to process it all, and by the time he blinked, he was ready to go.

"You can still go," Rhys said to Hyrum. "If you want to try it, I'll stick close enough to hold your hand. Wick will be fine waiting here."

Hyrum twitched toward Daphne, but I could feel it. He did not want to strap a jet pack onto his back, and especially did not want to fly. This would not have been his first flight; he'd been brave enough once, many years ago, with Oz and Drew. He'd even enjoyed it, but once on the ground witnessed someone else lose control.

They were caught by a safety net and were fine, but he couldn't shake the image from his head.

Wick does not want to wait here alone. Wick wants to sit by the fountain and offer snarky commentary about what the harness does to your junk, and how goofy you all look up there. It's no fun to snark alone. Do you mind, Hyrum?

Hyrum reached down to scoop me up. "I better stay with him. And I want to take pictures, I really do."

Can Quinn throw up? I asked Hyrum as we made our way to the fountain. *I bet he throws up.*

"If he does, I hope it's not when he's over us. Oh! Maybe he'll do it when he's really close to Rhys and Isaac, and they'll start slapping it away, and then it'll splatter *everywhere!*"

Remind me to introduce you to the art of Jackson Pollack.

"Jay showed him to me! But Aubrey won't let me paint my room like that even though I want to."

She won't stop you. I suspect she thinks you'd get tired of it pretty quick.

"Maybe. But it would be really fun to do."

You have fun with the other art Jay teaches you, right?

"Lots of fun. I'm never gonna be as good as him but he says it doesn't matter as long as it's fun. Oh! Maybe I'll show him the pictures and he can draw Rhys and Isaac and Quinn flying."

If Quinn barfs, you know Jay will.

12

Flush with excitement, Quinn ran toward us as fast as the weight of the drone's body allowed, shouting Hyrum's name. He hoped there were pictures, and please let there be video. Without it, his brother and sister would never believe him, and he especially wanted to witness older brother Darville's jealousy.

"I got lots of both," Hyrum assured him. "Mostly video. But Rhys knows how to get pictures out of that."

He even captured the moment you screamed like a little girl.

"I did not!" He turned to Rhys. "Did I?"

"Little bit, yeah. But to be fair, if you're not screaming, you're not having fun."

They contemplated another round, because why not, but Quinn also wanted to find gifts for his parents. All three teenagers engaged in a nonstop stream of chatter as we made our way down the Embarcadero, which made me worry about Hyrum feeling left out. He walked a few steps behind them, hands in his pockets, while I rode on his shoulder. He could hear everything but couldn't really participate.

I rubbed my face against his ear.

They're not ignoring you on purpose. Teenaged boys—

"They're excited, Wick. It's okay. I want them to be happy on account of they don't get to have fun like that a lot and it's Quinn's first time here."

Quinn acts like a real boy.

"He is a real boy. Wick, you've known him since he was almost a baby."

I mean that no one here can see that he's a computer program running inside a drone, covered in a nanosuit. All they see is a teenager, and he looks like one.

Hyrum scrunched his nose as he considered it. "His hair could be better. And he stomps. But I bet that's on account of the drone. It's heavy."

Rhys can code better hair for him. And teach him to step lighter.

When we reached the entry for Pier 39, Hyrum sped up so that he could get ahead, then turned and asked, "Rhys, can you give Quinn better hair?"

Quinn's hand went to his head. "What's wrong with my hair?"

"It's not *wrong,*" Rhys started.

"But it looks like a toupee," Isaac finished. "A good toupee, but still."

Quinn ran his fingers through his hair, then reached out to touch Rhys's. To his credit, Rhys didn't flinch or act as if it was weird; he was as curious as Quinn, and watched in amazement as Quinn registered the difference, and then changed the texture of his hair. It softened and laid flatter, except for one wild patch near his ear that stuck out.

"Awesome," Rhys muttered.

Isaac snorted. "Mornings would be so much easier if we could all do that. Think away the bed head, change clothes on a whim, anything."

Change eye color, skin color, and gender, too.

"Maybe someday Finn will give me access to all the data that would let me do that," Quinn mused, as if it weren't an ongoing wish.

Or maybe you'll decide to stay like this and can do it anyway.

"But the drone has boy parts," Hyrum reminded me. "Rhys needs to make a girl drone to stuff him into."

"I don't want to be stuffed into a girl drone," Quinn said with a sigh.

"At least not the way Hyrum means," Isaac said.

The look Rhys gave him was a warning: don't corrupt Hyrum. But Hyrum clamped his hands over his mouth and giggled. "I know what that means. Kissing things."

Do you have a girlfriend? I asked Quinn, counting on Rhys to translate.

"Not right now. I was going out with a girl called Vanya last year, but she was super religious and I knew going in that she wanted to join the Order."

"The Order?" Isaac asked.

"Religious group that worships Rhys's grandfather. He's the Creator and they spend a couple years learning everything they can about him."

"He's not happy about it," Rhys added.

That's what you get when you give your creations freedom of choice.

"Finn as God." Isaac snorted. "Nope, I don't see it."

"Yeah, it's hard to see someone as a religious figurehead when you've been crop dusted by the dude during a family dinner." Quinn scrunched his nose. "There's another reason I want access to the data that will let me change things. Sometimes I'd like to not have a sense of smell."

Do you have one now? Just curious.

He inhaled deeply. "This place smells like popcorn and fish."

Hyrum bounced on his toes. "Oh! We gotta get popcorn! We can toss it to the birds and make them dive for it, and people love that!"

"They do?" Quinn asked.

"No," Rhys said, laughing. "But it's funny sometimes, and we get yelled at by the guards when we do it."

"So...we have to do it. No guards, right?"

There were no guards trailing us in this When. I almost told Rhys not to do it; most of the people around us were tourists and it wasn't fair to upset them on their vacations, but if that was the Big Bad Trouble they wanted to get into, I wasn't going to press them into considering anything worse.

Hyrum plucked me off his shoulder and held me close. "I won't let the pigeons get near you. I promise."

We shopped first; Quinn bought trinkets and brightly colored coffee mugs for his parents and siblings, a backpack to carry it all, and then they bought a giant bag of popcorn, dropping kernels on the boardwalk as we made our way back to the Embarcadero.

There were no guards trailing us, but as we learned, there were security officers, and halfway through we were stopped, the popcorn confiscated, and Hyrum was directed to "take his kids and leave."

Don't argue with him. He's just doing his job. Please don't be upset.

But Hyrum wasn't upset. He giggled again and skipped his way out, counting on the others to follow. When we reached the end of the boardwalk, he spun on his feet and turned to them. "He thought I was your daddy! That hasn't happened since Rhys was a little boy!"

"How could he presume that?" Quinn wondered out loud. "You're not old—"

"Yes, I am! I'm old enough to be Rhys's daddy. I'm even old enough to be yours! You're only two years older than him. Oh! I'm old enough to be a *grandpa*!"

"That old?" Isaac asked.

"Jax is two years older than me and he's a grandpa. And Will had Rhys when he was almost forty-five, so he's old enough to be a grandpa, too. But he's gonna live to be almost two hundred, so maybe it's not the same."

"Two hundred," Isaac said, quietly surprised.

"Yeah, well, hold onto your hat," Rhys said. "Your dad is from the same When. You were born there. You'll probably live that long, too. I might. Wick is already around five hundred, so he'll probably still be around. As long as nothing shitty happens, we're here for a long time."

"Except me," Hyrum said. "I might live to one hundred. That would be nice."

Rhys slipped his arm around Hyrum's shoulder. "Dude, trust me, we'll do anything and everything to make sure you live as long as we do."

We headed for *Sofy Z's*, contemplating our lifespans, while ignoring the fact that one of us, unless someone unplugged a computer, might never die.

~

Quinn had never seen a menu. He squinted as he perused the tiny type on the laminated paper—Rhys opted for printed menus over the floating digital one that rose from the center of the table with the flick of a switch—flipping it over several times, a scowl slowly etching its way onto his face. I watched from my towel-covered highchair; the others knew what they wanted before we reached the restaurant, but Quinn had no idea.

"Too many things," he muttered.

He was not unacquainted with the concept of eating somewhere other than home. There were small cafes on the outskirts of the elf village in Saint Francis, but the choices were limited to three or four things, usually stews or sandwiches. He'd never heard of ethnic cuisine, had no idea what Mexican food was, and was especially confused over the notion of 'authentic Tex-Mex.' How could it be from both Texas and Mexico? He'd taken classes in geography; Mexico and Texas touched, but what did Texas do to the food to make it theirs? Did they have a reason to claim it? Why couldn't it just be Mexican food?

"Enchiladas," Rhys finally said, a sigh riding on his breath. "Trust me, you'll like them. Just order them mild."

"Mild? As opposed to severe?"

"Spicy!" Hyrum beamed. "I like them spicy. But no one else will like you later, on account of all the farting."

Quinn looked confused. "Do I fart?" he asked Rhys. "I mean, I know what I do at home, but in the drone?"

Rhys nodded. "Your system is designed to digest. Part of that produces gas, and it has to come out somehow."

"Usually when your friends are trapped in a tiny room with no functional windows," Isaac groaned.

They ordered beef enchiladas, and the Wick Special for me. That tasty treat landed on the menu not long after Will began frequenting the café when he visited this When; it was a small unseasoned steak cooked to medium rare and chopped into tiny bites. Originally meant for just me, it became popular with parents of small children and those who ate on the patio with their pets.

I was allowed inside, something unexpected but very much appreciated. The owners knew in which When I resided, and my proximity to their founder. It helped that Will was known here as the Emperor; he carted me around, and if he wanted to eat here, I was welcome as well.

To be fair, my presence was rarely an issue. As long as I remained in the highchair, seated on a towel, no one complained.

Well, I complained, but only half seriously. Steak went a long way into making me suffer the indignities of a highchair in a grumbling sort of quiet.

Still, we dined on the patio, because it was a beautiful day and Quinn wanted to watch people as they went by. The noise startled him less and people were interesting, though he was surprised to look past Rhys to see King Jackson and his Queen, Aubrey, approaching. They walked hand in hand, and she leaned into him, laughing, paying little attention to everyone swirling around them.

"Shit," Quinn swore under his breath. "What's he going to do when he sees me? Will he make you take me home?"

Rhys turned in his seat to look. "What are they doing here? But yeah, no, he can't make you go or do anything. Dad brought you here, and it's totally legal."

"Maybe they won't notice us," Isaac offered, but then Hyrum jumped to his feet, waving his arms over his head as he called out his sister's name.

They noticed us.

"How come you're here?" Hyrum's excitement over seeing them helped to push Quinn's annoyance aside. "Did you come to play with the jet packs? Rhys and Isaac and Quinn already did that and they had lots of fun."

Jax grumbled that Aubrey wouldn't let him, but she set a hand on his arm and said to Hyrum, "We're meeting Will for lunch, sweetheart."

"Oh. We're meeting him, too, but we decided to go ahead and get our food on account of we wanted to."

"Dad's running late," Rhys explained.

"Quinn's never seen a menu!" Hyrum blurted.

"No restaurants in Saint Francis?" Jax asked. "I never noticed that. Plenty of storefronts, and I know I saw at least one sandwich shop."

The one store he'd entered was a re-creation of an athletic shoe store, bereft of customers or employees. There were shoes on display, treadmills lining the back, and posters on the wall, but it was clearly not operational. He'd hoped those stores would have been taken over in the years since he named Quinn's father as Prince Regent, but the elves were reluctant to move beyond the village, and the outliers were content with what they already had.

He'd suggested they have lots of babies, but there were few born in any given year.

Unless Finn added to the digital population, Saint Francis would not grow.

"A few places with *pre-fixe* menus," Rhys explained. "Usually the same thing every day. It's great if you love stew or chicken sandwiches."

"Or spaghetti," Quinn added. "Krisf's spouse sells spaghetti and garlic bread."

"Yet you've never had Mexican," Isaac said.

"We're not exactly diverse."

Aubrey didn't agree. "Sweetheart, I've spent enough time there to know your village is quite diverse."

He didn't understand.

"You're racially complex," Rhys explained.

"Well, no. I didn't mean it like that. I just meant…it feels like we're all alike. No one has the ambition to really crank out a solid business plan and then implement it. It's like we get up in the morning, go to work and school, come home, and just kind of exist. Sometimes it's like I'm the only one who wants more."

"You're like your old man," Jax said. "He wanted more. He got more. It wasn't all that long ago that your life would have been nothing but scrambling to survive during the day and basic imprisonment at night."

"I know. Life sucked under Tobias. But there was a lot more before him, right? Until he snapped and tried to take over the world, there were factories and stores, and people made things. Did things. Went over the bridge and saw other people."

"You could do that now," Jax said.

"People go. They don't come back."

Aubrey was horrified. "But, why?"

Quinn shrugged. "Who knows? Kilfin goes to Sausalito and comes back. He thinks others try to go beyond and get lost."

That wasn't supposed to happen, and Jax knew it. Finn had added to the program to allow the people of Saint Francis to travel as far as they wanted. He'd populated Sausalito to Sacramento at the very least, and there was no reason for someone to get lost.

"Maybe they find something more fun and just forget about going home," Hyrum said.

"Possibly. But I wish they'd think about the rest of us left behind, wondering and worrying." Quinn glanced up as the server brought baskets of chips and bowls brimming with red salsa, stopping to thank her. "It's like they just jumped off the bridge without anyone else noticing. And they might as well have. They're just...gone."

Aubrey bent over and kissed the top of his head. "They're not gone. As Hyrum would say, they've gone on an adventure. Sometimes those take a while, even years."

"Aubrey went on an adventure," Hyrum said. "She left when I was just a little boy but then I went on my own adventure when I was forty and I found her, but then she made me take a bath so I'm not sure who wins that one."

"How long?" Quinn asked.

"I left home when I was fourteen," she answered, gently. "Hyrum was six. Sometimes, the adventure takes a very long time."

Just as gently, Jax added, "And sometimes, you never go back because what you find is what you needed. Those people aren't gone, Quinn. They either haven't turned around to go home yet, or they've made their home somewhere else. Finn wouldn't create a world without happy endings."

"But he did." Quinn's thoughts were interrupted by Will's arrival, and he let it go.

Will was not alone. He apologized for being late; he'd dashed home to get Aisha, reasoning that she would want to join them and feared her wrath if he hadn't.

They opted for a table inside. Will told Rhys that after they were done eating, they could wander and he would send a message when it was time to leave. He took Quinn's gift-laden backpack for safekeeping and ducked inside where the beer and tacos lived.

Quinn and Isaac wanted to rent jet packs one more time; Isaac pointed out that it might be Quinn's last chance, and he still hadn't experienced going so fast and hard that the safety nets were activated. Rhys thought it was unfair to Hyrum and argued for something they could all do, but it was rendered moot when Quinn tasted the enchiladas and decided a single plate would not be enough.

By the time they were done eating, no one wanted to move.

Instead, they pulled out their computer tablets. Rhys slid his phone across the table to Quinn since he didn't have one, and they decided to read. Or, in Quinn's case, to research Will, certain he would find embarrassing pictures to torment him with. Their loud chatter eased to a dull roar, and then quiet. Rhys engrossed himself in a paper his grandfather had written while creating the portals, Isaac searched for information on friends he had in this When, and Quinn fell down a rabbit hole lined with stories of the Emperor. There was little available data on William Blackshear, other than the date of his birth and a few mentions of his achievements in the martial arts.

There was a plethora of historical information on the Emperor, the man who served as King Jackson's right hand, the man who came as close to ending homelessness in Pacifica as was possible. He learned about the generous shelter program, the Emperor's Playground, which provided day care and education for families in need, and his work in raising the basic income entitlement alongside a comprehensive food program. He also learned about a paternity suit filed against the Emperor before

Rhys was born, a charge levied against him by a young woman named Dallas Engle.

"Say, what?" Rhys turned his tablet off. "Dad has another kid out there?"

No, he does not. And you might not want to pursue this.

"Nah, it says the suit was unsuccessful. But listen to this. 'When pressed to reveal the history of his past intimate encounters, the Emperor stated, clearly, a single name. Aisha Salazar Blackshear.'"

"Dude. Just his own wife?" Isaac asked. "Like, ever?"

"Apparently," Quinn said, still skimming the article.

"Then how?" Rhys asked. "If mom is the only woman he's been with, how can this other one even *think* she could get way with suing him?"

It's complicated, and you need to let it go.

They would not let it go.

"Looks like there was a paternity test done right there in the courtroom and it caused a fuckton of confusion. Turns out the bio-father had been dead longer than she'd been pregnant. How the hell?"

Rhys shrugged. "Artificial means, I guess. Who's the daddy?"

Quinn looked up. "George Matthew Denton."

Isaac stood up so fast and hard that his chair skittered back and fell over. "*My* dad? I have a sibling out there?"

No. No, you don't. Would you just listen to me?

"Wick says you don't," Rhys told him. "Sit down. That means it was probably you. You don't really know anything about your bio-mom, right? This must be her."

"Are there pictures of her?"

Quinn turned the tablet so Isaac could see. "A few."

He picked up his chair and sat down carefully, his gaze fixated on a photo of Will seated at one table in the courtroom and Dallas Engle seated at the other. He looked for slivers of himself in her, shrugging when he could find no resemblance. In a near whisper, he said, "This has to be a mistake. My dad's not dead."

"Nope," Rhys agreed.

He looked up, and his face was flushed red. "How? I mean, forget the fact that my dad is *solidly* gay. How?"

"Well," Rhys said, "when a boy jacks off into a test tube—"

"Fuck you."

"Come on. Your dad obviously wanted a kid and used a surrogate."

"A surrogate who didn't know he was the father? Surrogates know whose kid they're carrying."

"Your dad has never told you about your mother?" Quinn asked.

"No. I mean—" The red in his face deepened. "I don't know. I've always just been glad that Dad's here. He's alive. I don't know why. I never asked because it all feels delicate and I don't want to rock the boat."

George nearly died for real twelve years earlier, and Rhys remembered. He saved George's life by stopping time, giving Will the chance to jump his sliced-in-half body to an emergency surgical tank 200 years in the future. His recovery took half a year, during which Isaac lived with Will and Aisha, sharing a room with Rhys.

He remembered staying with them for a long time, but not why.

"Fucking eidetic memory," he grumbled, not quite serious.

"It's not eidetic," Rhys said. "Just...really good. Maybe almost eidetic. And not the point."

"The point is I have a mother out there. And what if the test was wrong?"

Hyrum. Go get Will.

"Don't get dad," Rhys sighed.

Go. Isaac's about to lose it and he deserves answers. I shouldn't be the one to give them.

Hyrum ignored Rhys's protests and scrambled to get Will from the dining room. By the time they came outside, Isaac was near tears. He didn't give Will a chance to say anything, but looked up and asked, "Are you my father?"

Will spoke as if his word needed air. "Isaac."

Hyrum tapped Quinn's shoulder. "I want dessert. Come on. We'll get some inside."

"After eating all that?"

"Please? I don't want to go alone." He refrained from mentioning his sister or brother-in-law, who were probably elbow-deep into chips and salsa, and probably a margarita or three. "The churros are really good."

Will took Quinn's vacated seat. "Isaac," he repeated. "No, I am not your father. Why would you ask?"

Rhys slid the phone toward him.

This feels like something that's been building up in him. Tread carefully.

"Hm. I'd almost forgotten about this. Still…your father is your father. Have you ever asked him about your birth?"

Isaac shrugged. "I asked him if I had a mom. He said no, and sounded sad. So I dropped it. And Odie says that I have two dads, so I don't need a mom, even though he's not really my dad. I just—"

"You found the article, and it brought up every question you didn't know you had."

"Even more. It says Dad was dead."

"He was living in this When," Will explained. "There were circumstances that required a death certificate be issued for him. When he returned, he was given new identification."

He avoided the entire story, how George had once taken a swing at the King, and then later pointed an antique gun at Will while attempting to flee with an unwilling seventeen-year-old Jay. He was banished instead of executed as a favor to Will, and later was allowed to return because of Isaac. Will painted a picture of a man living outside his own When, needing to get home, not one of a man so desperate to be right that he nearly killed someone while trying to kidnap his stepson.

"But how could she not know? You're pregnant, you know who the father is, right?"

Careful.

He waited a beat before answering. "She truly believed she was carrying my clone," he finally said. "It's messy and complicated, but the short version is that there existed a group here intent on recreating the Emperor of San Francisco. They used your father to obtain a sample of my DNA, but instead he gave them his own."

Isaac's face scrunched in confusion. "Why?"

"Because he wanted a child of his own. There was no reason for him to expect that Dallas Engle would find a way to another When. His intention was to wait until she was nearly full term, spring the news on them, and then fight for custody."

Isaac was horrified. "What the hell? He could have hired someone."

"He could have. But in doing this, he also ended the threat of physical harm in their quest to clone me. There was a domino effect, Isaac. He effectively ended the Cult of the Emperor and brought Liam into my life. You were, truly, his reward for what he'd done."

Don't forget the part where you gave him a boat load of money to fight for custody.

"You paid for the custody fight?" Rhys asked.

"It was a loan and I was repaid. And that's not the point."

"The point is that my own mother didn't want me enough to win that fight," Isaac said, sadly. "I mean, I love my dad and my life with him, but if I could have also had a mom?"

Gently, Will said, "It is so much more complicated than that. She was incredibly young and had not truly wanted to be a part of the cult."

"She didn't want me at all then."

Don't lie, either.

"I am unaware of her feelings on the matter, but I gather she understood she was not prepared for parenthood."

Rhys grunted. "And the freaking cult probably turned away when they found out you weren't a new Emperor. She would have been alone. At least with your dad, she knew you'd have family."

"Wait." He looked up, eyes brimming. "She thought she was having a clone. Is that what I am? A clone? My dad's clone?"

"He does not view you as a clone." Will spoke gently. "You are his son, period."

I stepped across the table and sat directly in front of Isaac, counting on Rhys to translate.

I've never known someone to want something as much as he wanted you. He didn't just want to be a father. He wanted to be your father. I think even if you'd been Will's clone, he would have fought for you.

"Would you have fought him for me?" he asked Will.

"I would have, yes."

"But Aisha..."

"She would have been beside me through everything."

"Dude." Rhys tossed a balled-up napkin at him. "They all fought for you. Does it matter how you got here? You're here. Your dad, Odie, my parents, *and* Jay all have your back. *Everyone* wanted you. They still do."

"Except my mom."

"Stop thinking like that. She was a host. She was never going to be anyone's mom."

"But—"

"You don't have her DNA. Like, at all."

You're not helping.

Will talked over me. "It is an unfortunate fact, Isaac. And I am sorry this is how you found out."

"I need to go home. Can you take me? I just need to go."

Rhys stood. "There's a portal across the street. I'll take him and then come right back."

Will wanted to be the one to escort Isaac home, presumably to have this discussion with George. But Isaac wanted Rhys to take him, and said he'd have his dad call later. He got up, but paused at the end of the table.

"Is it stupid if I kind of wish you had been my dad? Not that I don't want mine. But, yeah. You know."

"It's not stupid," Will said. "There have been many times when I've thought the same."

"You know, before my dad went to Elysium, he asked where I wanted to live if something happened. You or Jay. I didn't think Jay's feelings would be hurt, if I...well."

He watched Rhys and Isaac wander down the Embarcadero. Rhys slung his arm around Isaac's shoulder, pulling him close, the same way he did for his little brother when he was feeling out of sorts.

Think he'll be okay?

Will hoped so, but he understood the pain of wanting a mother and not having her there.

Yours wanted you. There's a difference.

"Indeed. But pain is pain, and right now Isaac is deeply wounded."

13

Will had one more stop before heading home, bypassing our When to a day several decades into the past. He left us on the Embarcadero near Pier 39 with the same caveat: Hyrum is in charge. Whatever you want to do, if he says no, you don't do it. As Will headed down the street toward Ghirardelli Square, Rhys pointed at a door across the street and suggested we chill in there.

Hyrum squinted. "Dick's. No. That's a bar, Rhys. You can't go in there."

"It's better than a bar." He prodded Hyrum's shoulder, and started making his way across the street. "Trust me."

"I said no!" Hyrum jogged a few steps to catch up. "Your daddy said—"

He'd already opened the door and Quinn went inside. "I promise, if you don't like it, we'll leave."

Hyrum stopped three steps in. His mouth hung open and he blinked, taking in all the brightly colored lights and cherry-red and white checkered tiled walls. Across the side wall there was a long, highly polished wood bar with red and black stools, and on the other side there were booths with bright red bench seats. Rhys gestured to a booth in the center, and they piled in.

"Soda bar," he explained to Quinn. "Dad told me about it but I've never been. I thought Hyrum might like it."

Hyrum focused on the menu board above the bar. "That's a lot of soda, Rhys."

"Lots of different kinds of root beer, too. But if you want to try something different...Dad says the cherry cola is pretty good."

Hyrum turned to look at Rhys. "Will doesn't like soda."

"But my mom does. They come here for the cherry colas and fry baskets."

No one was the least bit hungry, but they still ordered a giant basket of fries and large cherry colas. Rhys apologized because there was nothing tasty for me, but I was still stuffed from lunch and didn't mind.

"What is it your dad does here?" Quinn asked. "I understand having business in the When he comes from, but why here?"

Rhys gave a half shrug. "For all I know he's checking up on teenage Uncle Jax. Or dealing with investments. I know he's got a ton of banking things spread out over time. He probably has to show up once in a while to keep things moving forward."

Or he just wanted to give you guys some extra time outside of Saint Francis and he headed for the aquatic park to watch swimmers and kids playing in the sand.

"Then we should go do something after this," Rhys said. "Coit Tower? Watch the ferries?"

"Ride one!" Hyrum bounced in his seat. "I love the ferries!"

"So does Isaac," Rhys mused. "Even though he barfs over the side every time."

"Oh. I don't want to hurt his feelings if we go without him."

"I don't understand him," Quinn said. "He exists. Why does it matter how he got here? He lives and he has freedom to simply be."

Complicated feelings are complicated.

"He's never had a mother and he wants one. Finding out the woman who carried him didn't want him? Never wanted him? It hurts. A lot."

"You'd be sad if your mom didn't want you, too," Hyrum pointed out. "My daddy didn't want me and I was sad all the time."

"But he kept you," Quinn said.

"Sometimes I wished he didn't. He was mean, Quinn. People who don't want you are really mean to you."

But then you set his hair on fire, and got even.

Quinn barked out a laugh. "You set your dad's hair on fire?"

"I didn't mean to! And I put it out really fast. But he was

really mad about it." Hyrum giggled. "He never did bad things to my sisters again, though. And there was a tiny piece on his head where his hair never grew back all the way."

"You can do electricity," Quinn mused. "What else? Fire? Do you know?"

Hyrum could discharge electricity in seemingly endless ways. He could also absorb it and had often called himself a 'sparky sponge.' I'd seen him shoot ropes of light from his fingertips, send balls of light drifting across a room, and in a protected arena, he sent sheets of power in every direction from his entire body.

Will thought there might be more that Hyrum could do, but he'd spent the first 42 years of his life working to suppress those gifts, and wasn't willing to explore to find things hidden deep down. The important thing, Will noted, was that the gifts he knew about had kept him alive during the two years he wandered across Midlam to Pacifica; on cold nights he heated rocks to place in his sleeping bag, and when he was stranded in a winter cabin, he kept rocks in a fireplace hot, refusing to use fire "on account of I'm not allowed and my mom woulda been mad."

He had control over the gifts he knew about, and when Rhys began showing signs of similar abilities—sparks dancing on his fingertips—it was Hyrum who taught him to control them.

Rhys was a spectrum of gifts. Everything Hyrum could do, he could do. Sparks, electricity, light and power. But he'd also inherited Will's ability to hear someone's thoughts with a simple touch; he could place a finger against someone's head and send them into a deep slumber. He had Jax and Oz's synesthesia, but where they didn't know life without the color of sound, Rhys was able to turn it on and off on a whim. He could stop time, picking and choosing who was and wasn't affected. He had Zed's gift of sniffing out emotions and feelings, and was growing into Aubrey's empathy.

He also had Will's physique and the abnormal level of strength that came with it. He ran warm, inhaled food at Hyrum-like levels, and was—as his brother Jay said—"stupid smart."

What he hadn't looked for inside himself were the gifts his brother and sister had. Charlie was a human torch; where

Rhys handled power and electricity, Charlie handled heat and fire. Alex existed on the other side of the coin; she played with ice and could freeze with a touch. No one doubted that Rhys had those gifts buried inside, but he left them untouched, leaving them for his siblings.

"My brothers and sisters can do things, too," Hyrum explained. "But we never talked about it when I was little. Daddy would have been mad if he knew they could do things."

"He was upset about you?" Quinn asked.

"Daddy didn't like me, even before he knew." He said it simply; it was a fact, something that no longer bothered him. "Mom made them hide it from him. She would have made me, too, if I knew what she meant when she said not to do things."

"And your sister? She doesn't mind?"

"Aubrey loves me just like I am."

"To be fair," Rhys said, "his mom does, too. But she hid her kids' gifts to keep his dad from killing everyone."

"Killing." Quinn sounded as if he didn't believe it.

"Daddy was a dick," Hyrum said solemnly.

It was a topic they could have expounded on for an hour, and they might have, but as we left Dick's, Rhys spotted a car at the intersection ahead, parked at an odd angle at the side of the road. We were in an era where traffic was allowed downtown, but this car had clearly veered off the magnetic track, and its owner stood helplessly in front of it, hands on hips as he assessed the situation.

"We should help," Rhys said as his pace quickened.

The car's owner realized they were headed his way, and he smiled. There was something familiar about that smile and I could almost hear the laugh that likely went along with it. But I'd never met him; I spent little time in this When, and while my memories from this decade were often spotty, people usually stirred something inside me if I'd met them.

He was dressed in white; a crisp dress shirt, tailored slacks, and dress shoes. His dark skin popped from the contrast, and his gold wedding ring twinkled in the sunlight. Rhys slowed to a trot as he neared, and called out "Need help?" from fifteen feet away.

"My wife" —he gestured to the car— "is on her phone searching for a mechanic. But thank you."

"I'm pretty good with cars," Rhys said. "Why spend the money if I can get you going for free? What happened?"

"What happened." His voice was deep, and there was a hint of a British accent. "I was about to make the turn, there was horrendous clicking, a snap, and here we are."

"Click and a snap. Got it." Rhys approached the front-end access panel. "Can I at least take a look?"

He nodded.

Rhys lifted the panel and leaned in close. His head went halfway in as he searched for anything out of ordinary, and a few seconds later he said, "Yeah, I see it. The magnetic regulator decoupled from the control panel. That's an easy fix."

He pulled his head out and turned to Hyrum. "You know where the repair kit is? Same as on my dad's car?"

"I got it!" I rode on his shoulder as he skittered to the other side of the car. The repair kit was right where he hoped, and he skipped back with it dangling from his fingers. "What else can I do?"

"We passed a shop about halfway up the block. I think it was a drug store." He plucked me from Hyrum's shoulder and placed me on Quinn's. "Would you mind going and getting some bottles of water? One for each of us. And maybe some hard candy. I have a feeling my mouth will taste funky after sticking my head in there for a few minutes."

"Son, I could have gone for that," the owner said, watching Hyrum scramble away. "That's the least I could do."

Rhys picked through an assortment of wires in the kit. "He would want to help, and this is a one-person job. This way, he feels useful, and we'll probably want water soon, anyway. But you might want to tell your wife to hold off on that call until we see how easy this goes."

He found the wire he wanted and held it up. "Should go pretty easy. I'm going to use a slightly heavier wire than the one that broke. It doesn't look like the original and seems pretty thin for the amount of force it goes under."

It was not the original, the man explained. He'd had it replaced a year earlier, and was unaware that it was substandard.

"Izzy," he said as he leaned in the open rear door, "I believe this young man will get us up and going soon. And remind me to have a word with Darrel about the quality of his work."

He took a step back to give her space to exit the car. "Rhys, your 'word' will be nothing more than finding a new mechanic."

Rhys pulled out from the hatch and turned. "What? Oh. Oh! Your name is Rhys. So's mine."

"Is it?" She smiled at him, warmly. "What a coincidence!"

He went back to work. "I mean, it's not an uncommon name or anything. But still, kinda funny."

The smile came to me. I jumped from Quinn's shoulder to Rhys's back, flexing my claws to make sure he listened.

Stop fixing the car.

He kept working.

Seriously, stop. You can't do this.

"What a beautiful kitten," Izzy said. "Is he friendly? Would he mind a cuddle or two?"

"Anything to literally get him off my back," Rhys snorted.

I admit, she smelled good. She was gentle and nuzzled her face against the top of my head, murmuring that I was wonderful and how lucky Rhys was to have me.

Yeah, he totally is. But he needs to stop.

With a grunt, he yanked on the wire, listening to the magnets realigning. It was too late to stop him; the repair took under five minutes, and Hyrum was on his way back, loaded down with water and candy.

"One day," Izzy whispered against my head, "I'll get a kitten just like you. I forgot how soft you can be."

Yeah, well, now you have the chance. Unlike ten minutes ago.

She handed me back to Rhys after he closed the access panel. As Hyrum passed the water bottles around, she reached up for one last pet, and asked, "How old are you, Rhys? I think I have a daughter your age."

"Ah..."

The elder Rhys laughed loudly. "Leave the boy alone. She's barely thirteen. He's too old for her, and we shouldn't punish his generosity by forcing him to meet our irritable and hormonal teenager."

"Tsk. She's not irritable."

"Fine. Irritating."

That made Rhys laugh. "I have a little sister. I get it. But, you're done. The wire's attached and the magnets are back in position. Just be a little careful for the first five minutes or so in case they need to realign again. Sometimes being on the track pulls the wire a little tighter and it'll click all the way in."

We waited as he powered the car up and carefully pulled away. Hyrum dug through the bag of candy for the piece he wanted, asking if he missed anything.

"Just Wick bitching about something. I couldn't really hear what with my head down near the motor."

I was telling you to stop. You shouldn't have fixed their car.

"I was not leaving them stranded, Wick."

We're in the past. Your mom just turned thirteen.

"And?"

His name was Rhys.

"And?" he pressed.

What was your grandmother's name?

Irritated, he sighed, "Ismeldra. Why?"

What'd your grandfather call her? Did your mom ever tell you?

He shrugged. "Izzy." The lightbulb went off. "Izzy!"

"Did you just meet your grandparents?" Quinn asked. "Your mother's parents?"

"I mean, probably. What are the odds of another Rhys and Izzy? Freaking cool."

Not cool, Rhys.

He ignored me. There was a ferry to catch, and he honestly didn't want to hear anything other than how wonderful it was he spent time, even if it was under fifteen minutes, with the grandparents he'd never known.

~

"Damn. Rush hour."

Quinn squinted, though it was not especially bright out. The fog was rolling in and the sky was cloudy, but he squinted anyway as he looked at the long line of people waiting to buy tickets for the next ferry. "No one is rushing."

They stood still in their sprint to get home. Quinn grasped that, and he understood that there were people living beyond San Francisco, but he hadn't considered that those same people would travel to work here. "They don't have work where they live? Why come all this way when they could work there?"

"Depends on the job, I guess," Rhys said. "Like, if someone specializes in business finance but they live across the bay in, say, Concord, they'll work here because San Francisco is a major banking hub."

"There are no banks there? It seems far to go for working."

"It's not far, not really. Not much further than if you went from your village to the Bay Bridge. They just go by boat."

Make his head explode. Tell him about Kansas and how some people commute from there.

"But *why*?" Quinn pressed.

"Why did you want to leave Saint Francis to come here?"

Think of it as having the best of both. You live in Saint Francis but spend most of your day in San Francisco. Work here, but go home to where your family is.

"So it's quieter there?"

Rhys shrugged. "Some places are. San Francisco is pretty quiet compared to other major cities, mostly because it's a historical artifact and hasn't changed much in a few hundred years."

Oh, let's take him somewhere. Chicago right now would be a good place. Lots of tall buildings with glass and things flying around them.

San Francisco was, intentionally, maintained to resemble the city of four hundred years past. Aging structures requiring destruction were replaced with something appearing identical. Internally, construction was modern; externally, someone from 2030 could be plucked from there and dropped here, and they wouldn't feel lost.

"Places are just different," Hyrum said. "Not better or anything."

"Yet still worth seeing." Rhys checked his watch. "Let's just hang around until it's time to meet my dad, and we can ask him. He'll probably say no, but it doesn't hurt to ask. Hy, you okay with skipping the ferry ride?"

He scrunched his nose. "Yeah. Too many people. Are there more people here than at home? It feels like it."

"I think it just seems like it because so many people got off work around the same time. I don't think the population numbers are higher right now."

Cars on the road might make it seem worse. That'll change in about a year.

"What happens in a year?" Rhys asked.

The lone royal offspring will ride an antique bicycle with substandard brakes down California, where there's cross traffic. And a very young Emperor will rat him out. After that...the King banned traffic downtown.

"Seriously? Uncle Jax is the reason why?"

Ask your dad about it. It was a wild ride.

In a few days, I'd wish he asked.

~

New York City. Paris. London. Tokyo.

Rhys listed every major city he could think of, hoping that Will wound bend to his whims and take them somewhere Quinn could see modern architecture and feel the electricity of a well populated area. And Will twitched in that direction; he wanted to take them, but he also wanted to hold to their original agreement. A few hours in San Francisco. That was it.

"I don't have permission from Quinn's parents to take him anywhere other than here. If we leave San Francisco and something happens, his program might not make it back to Saint Francis. Give me time to put together a backup, and find out if Shivan will allow it."

"So, no," Quinn sighed.

"I'm not saying no. I'm saying later, if they give consent. I'll discuss this with Shivan when we take Quinn home, and if he's amenable, we can go next week."

Rhys turned to Quinn. "That's a yes. He doesn't do that whole, 'well, maybe' thing when it really means no."

"You know it's my mom you have to convince," Quinn said. "She'll say I'm too young and it's too dangerous."

Remind her that when she was younger than you, she fought in the war against Tobias and his Shedu guards. She was fighting a ticked-off Shedu when a tornado ripped through Golden Gate Park, and she held onto a tree with her bare hands. That was dangerous, and not everyone survived. Going to New York is just a trip.

"A tornado? Really?"

Your parents were brave teens, Quinn. I wouldn't worry about them freaking out over a field trip to a big city.

"Indeed," Will said. "And you have a bigger worry to face right now. Your presence is requested at dinner tonight, by the Queen herself."

14

We used the portal across from the Ferry Building, and within two seconds Will had his hand on Rhys, who in turn had hands on Quinn and Hyrum, and we jumped directly to the landing near the balcony of the royal house. For those two seconds, Quinn was breaking the law simply by existing, and he was sure he continued to violate the laws that Jax supported.

"This building," Will said, referring to the royal home, "is sovereign land, so to speak. If the King chooses to invite you here, you're free from any legal repercussions."

"Which means Aunt Aubrey told him to get his shorts out of a wad and let it go tonight," Rhys said.

"No leaving the premises. Quinn is fine inside, but one step outside and he's technically in the wrong."

"For simply existing," Quinn grumbled.

"Jax did not write the law," Will said.

"How about the balcony?" Rhys asked. "Are we allowed out there? He can at least see Union Square from there, and all the holiday decorations."

Will nodded, and then left to report to Jax and Aubrey that we had returned. I was torn; I wanted to run to the living room to hear what they were talking about because I was certain Jax would go off on AI and how this was six kinds of wrong, and Aubrey would stare at him with that "Who broke you?" look.

She might even say it out loud.

Instead, when Thor trotted up and whined to go out, I went onto the balcony with Rhys. He held me close and his grip tightened just a bit, knowing that I'd rather hide under a chair where the pigeons would not see me. He encouraged Quinn to get close to the railing to take in the view, but stayed back a bit for my comfort.

There were skaters on the ice rink, tiny people scrambling like ants, and the Christmas tree popped with thousands of tiny, brightly colored lights. Other decorations hung from lamp posts around the Square, pine wreaths wrapped in ribbons and light, and everything twinkled.

"This is what Christmas looks like." It was not a question, and he did not seem impressed. "Why?"

"Jesus's birthday!" Hyrum beamed. "But we get presents instead. Well, maybe he does, too. I dunno how they do birthdays in Heaven."

"It's like the Festival of Saint Francis," Rhys said. "It's a reason to celebrate. We decorate, find fun things to do, and exchange gifts. Though the gifts are optional. Not everyone does that."

"And Santa comes!" Hyrum blurted.

He was familiar with Santa. In Saint Francis, the counterpart was Hagar, a very-much-alive wizard given credit for sneaking into the elves' homes where he left a hand-crafted toy for each child and beer for the adults. Rhys and I both knew that Hagar simply allowed his name to be used, and the toys were made by the parents. Quinn was sensitive enough to not tell Hyrum that he didn't believe there was a Santa, just as there was no gift-giving Hagar.

"I just didn't know you did all this," he said, gesturing to the Square. "Maybe we need lights. It's pretty. I think the little ones would like it."

"Big ones, too!" Hyrum said. "I can't wait to decorate the tree this year. Jax let me buy a really tall one that has twinkling stuff all over, and it's so tall it touches the ceiling."

"You bring a tree inside?"

"Artificial," Rhys explained. "Some people use a real tree, but those are expensive and only last a few weeks."

And Thor won't pee on a fake tree.

"Good boy!"

Well, you might try to, if we ever have a real tree.

"Good boy." He tilted his head a bit. *"Good boy?"*

Sure. I bet Quinn would like to see the roof. He might even scoop up after you.

Quinn did not scoop after Thor. He circled the open space, commenting on the tent of lights, the lawn, the firepit, and the see-through barrier that lined the human-waist-high walls. The scattering of toys across the lawn amused him—he'd forgotten there were smaller children in the family—and expressed regret over being too big for the swing set on the far side of the grass.

Hyrum, on the other hand, was not, so he hopped on and began kicking his legs back and forth.

"Remember the one my brother built? It rocked back and forth like crazy, but we had so much fun on it."

"I remember when it cracked," Rhys said, laughing. "Darville had damn near gone level on his swing, and when that noise exploded? He freaking spun in the air getting away from it."

"It made for good firewood," Quinn said.

Simulated imitation firewood, crafted by the finest elves in Saint Francis.

You have to say that with your little finger stuck out.

"And you would know that because you dine with royalty every day?" Quinn snorted. "Wait. How formal will dinner be? I know they're fairly casual when they have dinner with my parents, but what do they do in the pretend castle?"

"It's no different. Just behave the same way you would if they were having fried chicken at your place."

"Are you even hungry? I feel like we've spent the day eating."

Hyrum and Rhys had high metabolisms, and were always hungry. It didn't matter what Aubrey was making; they would scarf it down and sniff around for any leftovers that weren't slated to be taken to the guards' lounge downstairs. If Quinn had no more room for food, he hid it well and was excited when he saw that the menu for dinner was homemade pizza.

"You've never had pizza?" Jax asked as he took his chair.

"I have, a couple times when Rhys brought it."

"But it wasn't fresh," Rhys added. "By the time I got it to Saint Francis it was kinda cold."

Aubrey, in the kitchen to pull the first ones out of the oven, asked the same thing she did anytime she fed someone for the first time. "Any allergies, sweetie? I don't want to make you sick."

Jax turned his head to look at her, then looked at Quinn. Rhys snickered, and Will calmly turned to her and said, "He's not human, Aubrey. You could feed him scraps of metal and he'd be fine."

"I can digest metal?" Quinn seemed surprised. "That wouldn't damage my system?"

"You could at home," Rhys answered. "The nanobots would digest for you. But don't try it in the drone. Something might get plugged up."

It was Will Quinn turned to. "Wait. What do you mean, 'he's not human.' I'm human."

Jax answered. "You're a computer program hitching a ride inside a human-shaped drone. Looking human doesn't make you human."

"Besides, you're part elf," Rhys said.

"And elves are human," Quinn insisted. "I don't care what your fantasy stories and cookie manufacturers say. We're human. We always have been."

"You're a computer-generated approximation of human," Jax said.

"Maybe. But that doesn't change the basics. We're human. Finn made us to be human."

Will tried to intervene. "My father did, indeed, create the elves as a branch of humanity. There is nothing in their programming to thwart that belief. Yet, they also understand that they are components of a larger computer simulation."

"And your people?" Quinn pressed. "A whole lot of you know you're human yet believe in God and an afterlife, and all of that is part of a larger community. This is no different."

"Except I can go unplug the computer, and Saint Francis is gone," Jax said.

There was a loud bang as Aubrey slammed the oven door shut. "Jax!"

"I didn't say I would."

"And that would not erase their existence," Will said. "It would simply shut the program down until the computer was plugged back in. None of their experiences would be lost."

"Doesn't change the fact that they are just lines of code," Jax grunted.

Quinn's face pinched. "Look, I know you don't like me—"

"What? Jax was genuinely surprised. "I like you. I'm quite fond of you. I've known you since you were, what, six years old?"

"Then...why?"

"I won't pretend you're something you're not, Quinn. You might feel human, but you're not. And I don't like it, but your very existence is illegal right now."

"You don't like it, but you won't do anything about it? Why not? Because I'm a hunk of machinery not worth the time and effort?"

Jax held up a hand to stop him before he got rolling. "I won't do anything about it because we have very good reasons for the ban on AI, and it's simply not the right time to pursue changes to the law. But no, I don't see you as a hunk of machinery. You're not human but you *are* a person. A person who is not in the time period to which he belongs."

"To be fair," Will said, "neither am I."

"And you're human. There's no law against a time-traveling human to exist here, and god, don't ever let it be known or the council might pursue that."

Quinn sighed. "So you're okay with my life, just not...here."

"Pretty much."

Rhys nudged him with his elbow. "You don't exist yet. You're from my dad's birth When, not mine. That's why we started off there today. You having rights here is like expecting someone from the nineteenth or twentieth century to have the same rights as someone from now. Plop me in nineteen-forty, and I'd have, like, nothing."

"Why?"

Rhys held his arm out. "Skin. Racism was abundant, and I would have been less than."

"Less than what?"

"Less than anyone white."

"It's not personal," Jax said. "It's just not your time."

"So I'm stuck in Saint Francis, with no hope of finding something in my life with more meaning."

"No. Your own When is fully welcoming of alternative forms of life. You really can't fight for rights in a When that isn't your own."

"Besides, dude," Rhys said, "I need time to figure out how to bring you into the real world without the drone. Someday you'll be able to walk out of the simulator without it, and live wherever you want."

It wasn't life outside of Saint Francis he wanted. It was choice. It was having a higher purpose, and access to the information that allowed him to become whatever he wanted. A large part of what he wanted was to grow opportunities in Saint Francis, but he didn't see a way to do that without access to, as he was calling it now, the Real World.

"Information is limited," he reminded them.

Will leaned back, folding his arms as he pondered Quinn's unspoken request. "I'll speak to my father," he finally said. "If I frame your request as a desire to step into Hagar's shoes, he'll likely honor it. Once you have access to the same database as Hagar, I believe you'll find it sufficient for the time being."

"You think I should become a wizard."

"I think you should have access to all the information he has. Whether you choose to pursue magic is up to you."

"Magic," Rhys snorted.

"As the elves call it, yes."

"And you're okay with that?" Quinn asked Jax. "You're the King. You can overturn that."

Jax shrugged. "I'm King of Saint Francis in name only. If Finn is willing and your parents are agreeable, it's none of my business." He glanced up as Aubrey set the first pizza on the table. "Go forth and learn, Pinocchio. When the When is right, you'll be a real boy."

~

We stepped through the portal into Saint Francis, into darkness punctuated with a starlit sky, the aroma of wood smoke wafting in the air. The village fire had been stoked and there were a dozen elves perched on halved tree trunks circling the fire, and none of them did more than glance in our direction.

I rode on Hyrum's shoulder; his arms were loaded with pizza, as were Rhys's, and Quinn carried the gifts he'd purchased for his family.

He hesitated. Home was just to his right, twenty feet away; the garden gate was open and there were drinks on the patio table, which meant his parents were waiting for him. I don't think he was ready to be home, yet at the same time the sight of the familiar fire was comforting. These were people who loved him, people who believed in their humanity as much as he did. People who would embrace him if Finn consented to his becoming Hagar's apprentice.

"Am I wrong?" he asked Rhys. "I feel human. I look human. Am I not?"

"Here, you are," Rhys said. "But Uncle Jax is also right. You're a person, regardless."

"If I get access to the higher data, do you think I'll understand his side?"

Rhys nodded. "I think you'll understand not only his side, but the side of the computers that caused the ban in the first place."

True AI had been attempted hundreds of times over the last few centuries, always disconnected when the computers and drones endeavored to, as one on-site observer said following the last major attempt, stray from their lane. It was during the reign of Queen Wyatt; a series of highly programmed computers—like, Quinn, stuffed into drone bodies—were given the parameters of a possible war situation, deciding that the greatest threat to the world was not the war itself, but the people running the war.

Their deduction was not to shut down all weaponry; their decision was to activate it. All of it. The computers came to the conclusion that the planet was better off without people, and initiated the sequence that would have ended life on earth.

"It was just a simulation," Rhys explained. "Not even as advanced as this one. But it was enough to put an end to it. I think what Uncle Jax worries about is that if people learn about your existence, they won't be happy. In our When, you'd be in danger. And with that...any hope that AI can move beyond its failures fizzles."

"But your temporal history," Quinn said. "Oz is the one who will start lifting the bans, right?"

"If she becomes Queen within the next few years, sure. If we were riding along in the same historical boat, though, she would already be the queen."

"I may not live long enough to see it happen, then," Quinn said, finally walking toward the house.

"You can live as long as you want to," Rhys said.

"If Finn says yes."

"Rhys will make it happen," Hyrum chimed in. "He's smart. He figured out how to put you into the drone, right? And you can go outside, you just have to go to where Will was born."

"With an escort," he grumbled.

"I'll figure it out," Rhys said. "It might take a dozen years, but I'll figure it out."

Quinn wanted more than being able to leave the simulator on his own. He wanted a purpose.

Rhys was sure he could figure that out, too. "For now, if Hagar takes you as apprentice, work your ass off. Become a wizard of light, and by the time you can do that, I'll have figured out how you can leave here, come back, and be anything you want."

"Just like that," Quinn snorted.

"Maybe." Rhys set the pizzas on the garden table. "Look, one thing I think you probably need to know. A big reason Uncle Jax isn't going to bust his balls to change anything is the family. He's not going to do anything that even hints about the existence of the portals. All the questions that would come up if people knew about you? It's risky."

"There are other humanoid-presenting drones."

"But not like you. Not yet. He'll allow things to progress,

but only on a timeline he's comfortable with. One that doesn't risk exposing a huge secret."

"So the Blackshears are the only people who ever get to use the portals?"

It wouldn't always be like that; after their development in the not-too-distant future, the world would know. But the world, as much as they needed the portals, would not be given open access. There was global grumbling that morphed into shouting and threats of war, but Finn held fast and would not share the data.

"You open it up to everyone, and who knows the fallout? We're just now exploring how making changes in the past affects the now. Like, what changes just slide into now, and which create new timelines. Time might not be a closed loop. Yet it might have millions of loops, or strings, or hell, some damned laser show effect. So it's a secret, and you might lead people to it."

"I get it. Kind of," he sighed. "Don't take this the wrong way, but you look tired. Get me out of the drone and then go home. You need sleep."

Quinn sat in a garden chair and waited as Rhys pulled a computer from his backpack, and as he tapped his fingers on the keyboard. There was a hum, a pop, and the drone went— for lack of a better term—limp. Another hum, and Quinn's body reformed with nanobots, standing next to the now-silent drone.

"We'll do this again," Rhys promised.

"But maybe not for a bit. I need time, too. I need to process."

We left the drone seated in the chair; Quinn said he would take it into the house later, but even if he didn't, it was safe where it was. The elves might gather around it and look, but no one would touch it, not without Shivan's permission.

We headed for the portal and home. Rhys wanted to take a few days off from thinking about the drone and the things he could do to turn the ideas in his head into a fully functioning android, as well as figuring out a way to turn Quinn's simulated body into something that could survive outside Saint Francis. There were other things to look forward to: Thanksgiving, Aubrey and Jax's birthdays, and then Christmas.

"I can take a break until after New Year, right?" he asked Hyrum, not expecting an answer.

He could have, but...real life and all that.

15

He came out of his bedroom at 2 am, hair sticking up in all directions, and he shuffled the way old men do. Will was stretched out on the sofa, tablet in hand, not surprised to see his son in the middle of the night; neither slept easily and often spent quiet hours together while the rest of the family was in bed.

Will sat up and set the tablet aside, making room for Rhys on the sofa. "Can't sleep at all, or something woke you up?"

"Both, I guess." Rhys dropped onto the sofa. "I think I dozed. Never really got to sleep, though. I did something today, something maybe I shouldn't have."

Will waited.

"When you took us backwards, we ran into this couple having car trouble," he explained. "It was a pretty simple fix, I mean, just a wired coupling that needed to be replaced. And I did a pretty good job of it, but I told him to make sure he had it checked out because it was for sure a temp fix."

"And you're worried that you should have left it alone. Possibly. But we're operating on the principle that we don't really change—"

Rhys cut him off. "It was mom's parents. I didn't realize it at first. He told me his first name and I just thought, you know, coincidence. He told me his wife's name and I didn't even clue into it until Wick said something after. But it was too much of a coincidence for him to be Rhys, her to be Izzy, and they mentioned a daughter who'd recently turned thirteen."

Will sucked in a deep breath, and slowly exhaled.

"That When...that was the year she turned thirteen, right?"

"The year they dropped her at her aunt's for an extended visit," Will said.

"And if I hadn't come along, he would have figured out the repair on his own, but he also would have used the wrong wire. And then headed home to Vegas."

Will didn't need the entire story. Rhys Simms and Izzy Salazar left San Francisco for Las Vegas, just made it to the city, when their magnets failed and they rolled off the street. It was a jarring, horrific wreck, taking out a small playground and several trees.

Aisha stayed in San Francisco with her aunt.

"If I saved their lives, what does that mean for the rest of mom's life? She won't stay here, she won't meet you—"

"And it won't change anything for you, or your mother. Not in this When."

"New timeline."

"Perhaps. The possibility exists that something else causes that accident and you changed nothing."

Rhys couldn't stand that idea, either. "That's part of what I'm chewing on. That no matter what I did, they still died."

You could go back and stop yourself from helping. It's been less than twenty-four hours. Just chase after yourself and keep us from walking all the way down that street. You'd believe you if you said you needed to head in a different direction.

"And then for sure let them die? I can't do that, Wick."

"Worst case, you've created a new timeline, Rhys. It's all right."

"Do I tell mom?"

Will glanced at the bedroom door. "I'll handle that."

"How upset will she be, you think? I mean—" his phone pinged "—Isaac." He read the text and sighed. "He can't sleep, either, and his dad just got called into work. Can he come over?"

Will nodded, and got up. "I'll walk across the Square and meet him at the door. And before he can protest, tell him it's not an offer. I don't want him wandering out there alone this late."

~

They sat together at the kitchen table while Will did what had become the Blackshear family late-night insomnia tradition: he made hot chocolate. They kept their voices low to avoid waking Aisha or the twins, but Will had sharp hearing and didn't miss a word while he stood near the stove and stirred.

"He said it never occurred to him to mention how I was born, since I never asked about my mother," Isaac said when Rhys asked if they'd talked. "He didn't think it mattered, the only thing that mattered was that I was born and he wanted me. He doesn't seem to think it even matters that *she* didn't want me."

"Why not?"

"Because she was kinda trapped into having me. If she hadn't done it, I would have developed in an artificial womb and would be alive either way. But he doesn't understand that I still want to know about her and I always have."

"It's not enough to just exist," Rhys said. "I get that. I really do."

"Yeah, but you have your parents. You know them, and you know they both wanted you."

Rhys explained what he'd done after taking Isaac home. "So you feel like crap because of your birth mom. I feel like crap because maybe I should have let two people die, and because I didn't, I probably won't exist in the next When. Quinn feels like crap because he has the potential to exist, and can't."

Aren't you a little young for an existential crisis?

"Fuck," Isaac groaned. "That means I won't exist next go-round, either. Hell, Jay might not."

Rhys turned in his chair. "Dad? Should I go back and change it?"

He brought three mugs of hot chocolate to the table and sat own. "There's no need. The worst case is a new timeline, and it doesn't affect you here."

"But—"

"You'll never know about it, Rhys. I died in every timeline ahead of this one, and I don't feel that."

"But at least you know you existed. And you will again."

"Also," Isaac chimed in, "your mom wanted you. She will again. Over and over for infinity."

Will couldn't argue that. There was nothing easy he could say to make either of them feel better. I knew he'd kept tabs on Dallas Engle and could, theoretically, arrange for Isaac to meet her. But there was nothing he could do to ease Rhys's realization that he might be a biological one-off, along with his siblings.

In the next When, he might not meet Aisha at all.

PART TWO

16

"Let's go on an adventure."

Hyrum bounced his butt on Rhys's bed, and when Rhys's eyes didn't open, he did it again. And again. After the fifth bounce, Rhys groaned, but didn't snap at Hyrum to knock it off, though his half-opening of one eye pretty much told me he wanted to.

"Why?" Rhys croaked.

"Because you're mopey and an adventure always makes you feel better."

He opened both eyes all the way. "You're using the generic 'you,' I take it."

"I don't know what that means, but okay. Let's go do fun stuff today and maybe even get into a little bit of trouble."

"What about work? Don't you have to work?"

Hyrum grinned. "I'm gonna play hooky on account of it's not an adventure if you take a real day off."

With an exaggerated sigh, Rhys sat up. He'd been mopey for three days, and Hyrum had enough of it; Rhys grasped that. He also knew that Hyrum's idea of an adventure was riding the cable cars while standing on the outside rail and then getting ice cream before having lunch, or taking the ferry to Sausalito to get cupcakes at the place with the pink to-go boxes, because Oz had done that at six years old all by herself, so of course it *had* to be an adventure.

Today he wanted to ride his bike to the shops in the Haight. Aubrey's birthday was coming up, and he wanted to look for a nice present to give her. "I don't gotta buy it today but I want to know what I want to get her. And maybe Christmas, too. Oh, and I want to stop at Wheelies on account of they got some pegs for my back wheel and they're gonna put them on for me. I'd do it but it means taking apart the back wheel and Denny said I should have someone else do it."

"Pegs," Rhys grumbled.

"Pegs! Then if you want you can stand on them while I pedal."

He wanted them because they sparkled in sunlight and lit up in the dark; taking a passenger wasn't something he'd considered until after he paid for the pegs and his friend Denny—a bicycle taxi driver—pointed out that they were designed to hold the weight of a grown man.

I rode in the front basket, one Drew had designed to keep me safe in case of an accident. Rhys jogged alongside the bike, begging Hyrum to not go too fast, not unless he wanted to see Rhys hork his breakfast onto the green bike lane. We headed for the bike shop and left his fifteen-year-old bright red bike there while we wandered in and out of stores, happy enough that no one had to see Rhys's partially digested oatmeal and eggs.

This felt a long way from Hyrum's first Christmas here, when Oz and Drew took him shopping and he was almost too shy to speak to sales clerks and cashiers. Now he wandered the stores eagerly and didn't hesitate to find someone to answer his onslaught of questions. "If she doesn't like it, can she bring it back? Oh, can someone else bring it back for her? Sometimes she's really busy and needs to get someone else to run errands. Oh! What if it doesn't fit? She's about this tall—" he raised his hand to six inches over his head "—and she weighs—"

"Nope, don't say it," Rhys warned. "They know who she is. Everyone probably has a ball park figure in their head."

He placed two gifts on hold after assurances that he could change his mind later, one of them a t-shirt the clerk seemed hesitant to sell to him.

"She sure didn't think Aubrey would like that," Hyrum muttered as we left the store. "It's funny! She likes funny."

"She'll like it," Rhys assured him.

Sure, what's not to like? A bright purple shirt with bright metallic gold letters proclaiming, 'The Queen is Not Amused.' We're all going to get a laugh out of that.

"When Oz is Queen, I'll get her one, too!"

Oz will show up to state dinners in it, you know that, right?

They'd seen photos of our future queen in her bright red tuxedo and high-top sneakers, and the idea made them laugh.

"You feel better yet?" Hyrum asked.

With a short nod, Rhys exhaled loudly. "Getting there. It'd be better if I could quiet all the noise in my head. I feel fine, Hy, it's just a lot of jabbering in there right now."

"Who's jabbering?"

"Who's not?" His brain swirled with ideas on how to deal with Quinn, and what the next steps in creating a self-sustained body for him might be. He worried about Isaac and his deeply seated feelings of abandonment from a mother he'd never known and now never existed in the way he hoped, while he also grappled with the reality that he was his father's clone. He'd also spent hours poring over Finn's data on portal creation, the mistakes he thought he'd made when designing the first egg-shaped time machine and later the portals themselves, and what he'd done to correct that.

"There are things in his notes that he just doesn't seem to *see*," Rhys said as we headed back for the bike shop. "All those years working on transporters with Drew's dad? Grandpa already had every bit of data he needed. He was transporting with the portals, just not as efficiently as he does with the actual transporter. Now he's chewing on time as a whole, whether it's linear or not, if it's a closed loop and if not, how it really works. He thought he had it down, until Liam Finnegan proved he could hop a timeline."

"I don't know what all that means, but old me says time is spaghetti."

You're not supposed to have that conversation with him.

"I wasn't supposed to meet him at all," Hyrum said, chuckling.

"Your future will be whatever it will be," Rhys quoted his father. "Protect what you can, but you have to live your life."

Hyrum tilted his head a touch as he considered it. "I wish there was an old you to go talk to."

"Someday I'll be the old me, trying to decide if I want to share any secrets with the next me."

Might as well. Your dad went back and told himself everything.

"Everything."

Well, the highlights. Though young Emperor was mostly interested in all the sex he might have someday.

Hyrum pressed his hands to his mouth and giggled.

The young emperor was nineteen, so...

"He did that after he came up with the jump bracelet, right?" Rhys asked.

Changing the subject. Fine. And yes. He took a portal and made it so tiny it fit on his wrist. Don't ask me how. I slept through his monologs explaining it.

"As one would."

Now see, right there, you sound just like him. Look like him, too.

"I guess. I'm the darker, more sophisticated version."

I once told your mom she was like hot chocolate.

"Damn, dude, you didn't. You don't compare people to food."

I've heard your mom call your dad a tasty snack, you know.

"Just...no."

I know better now, by the way. But you totally are. You look like them both, and you have both of their brains.

"You should give those back," Hyrum said. "They might need them."

For half a second, I thought he was serious, but then he laughed loudly and started running toward the bike shop.

~

The safest place to learn how to carry a passenger, Hyrum declared, was the Embarcadero. It was flat and there were no cars other than taxis and delivery vans, and if we were lucky, we might even run into Denny. As a bicycle cab operator, Denny was a font of helpful tidbits on bike maintenance and repair, and Hyrum thought that if he had trouble steering or balancing with Rhys on the back, Denny could help.

On the other hand, Hyrum and Rhys's guards were not as enthusiastic. Usually trailing behind to give them a sense of privacy, the guards edged closer, and Graden, Hyrum's head guard and somewhat-friend, pulled his airbike close to issue a warning.

"This isn't a good idea, Hy." He did not forbid their intentions, but he made it clear he didn't like it. "You won't have complete control over the bike, and you might fall. You both might fall."

Straddling the bike, Hyrum popped his thumb against the little bell on his handlebar. "I fell outta bed last week but no one said I shouldn't sleep anymore. We'll be careful. I can't learn if we don't practice, right?"

Graden's jaw twitched as he clamped his teeth together. "Helmets," he said after a moment. "Cinch them up a bit and make sure they don't move on your heads. And please don't leave this area until we're all sure—"

"Just up and down the Embarcadero," Rhys said. "We won't ride, like, down the hairy part of Van Ness. Or the wiggle down Lombardo."

Hyrum perked up. "But that would be fun!"

He rode up and down steep streets often, but never with one hundred fifty pounds of teenager resting on the backside of his bicycle. I wasn't sure if he fully knew about Jax's high speed ride down California Street on an antique bike when he was sixteen, but I was certain he didn't know the details. There was traffic then, personal cars and vans zipping along, and cross traffic to complicate things.

It was the first time Will interfered with time. He watched as Jax rocketed down California, then as the lights changed and a cargo van sped through an intersection at the same time Jax entered it.

The young Emperor knew that Jax was not supposed to die at 16, but he witnessed the brutal demise of the boy who should have grown up to be King; everything in the Old Mint told him Jax was not supposed to die. Every recorded When was specific regarding Jax's survival, so he slipped through a portal and set into motion things to keep Jax from colliding with that van.

Hyrum probably didn't know about it and Graden positively did not know. Rhys might, but I wasn't going to ask him in front of Hyrum. An explanation would ensue, and Hyrum might be inadvertently convinced to never ride again. That bike was his great joy. The consequences for taking that joy from him would be steep, no matter who the perpetrator was.

There was no argument; Graden would not forbid them the ride, though he was within his right to traverse that gray area between allowing them normal lives and preventing a tragedy. With anyone other than Hyrum, he would hide in the shadows, unseen until needed, but he followed Hyrum openly, usually on an airbike. Other guards pedaled acoustic bicycles, looking like tourists who'd rented for the day, but no one could keep up with Hyrum unless he wanted them to. Hence, Graden followed on an airbike, something that could match his speed up the steep slopes of San Francisco.

My ear twitched at the sound of another airbike. Vicat, head of the guard, pulled up next to Graden.

"Cat lady!" Hyrum blurted.

"Hyrum!" She was not offended; he'd called her that from the beginning, and she enjoyed it. "What's the plan today, men? Ride and then go eat until you explode?"

"We're having an adventure!" Hyrum gushed.

"So. Ride and then go eat, right?"

Rhys snorted. "It's like you know us. We'll be careful. He had rear pegs put on his bike and just wants to try them out. I doubt we'll get up to any speed where I can't leap off if I need to."

On the other hand, I'll be stuck in the basket. Doomed.

"No hills, all right?"

Hyrum nodded, and Rhys said, "Flats, but maybe a small uphill. There's no way he can pedal hard enough to get us up a steep one."

"Flats," she repeated.

They both nodded.

And I think they meant it.

~

Fifteen years of cranking up San Francisco streets turned Rhys's declaration into failed supposition. After half an hour of learning how to balance with a passenger, Hyrum wanted to tackle a short hill. He turned away from the outskirts and headed for the center of the city, easily pedaling up the first incline he encountered.

"I'm skinny but I got strong legs!" he shouted over his shoulder.

He turned onto another flat street, turned again to go up a hill, and after half an hour I was turned around enough that I was no longer sure where we were, and I don't think Rhys was certain, either. Unlike Hyrum, who cycled every street in the city center regularly, Rhys mostly jogged on the main ones, the long traffic-free stretches that surrounded downtown. When he ventured out on his own bike, he skirted the tourist areas and avoided the long up and down streets that were laid out in an undulating grid. Still, he was comfortable enough to hold a conversation with Hyrum, and never asked if we should turn around and go back to the relative safety of the Embarcadero.

"Where ya wanna go after this?" Hyrum called out. "After food, I mean. We should go get pizza at Sean's."

"Sean doesn't work there anymore. He's got his shop now."

"Yeah, but he owns it. His grandpa gave Piazzo's to him. So now it's Sean's place!"

"All right. Sure, let's get pizza. And maybe after that we can ride to Ozoo for a few minutes. I need to pick up a data file from Grandpa."

"But I'm playing hooky!"

Rhys assured him he could wait outside on the playground. But he needed that file; his brain was overrun with all the things he'd been reading about the portal tunnel and the egg-shaped time machine Finn initially used to travel through time, but there were things he felt were missing and wanted to read it before bed.

The notion of pizza stuck in Hyrum's head. And Piazzo's was behind us, at Fisherman's Wharf. He made a u-turn in the intersection and started rolling down the street, pedaling just as hard as he had going up.

"Hy!" Rhys shouted. "Hill!"

"I forgot. I'll take the next turn. It's only three blocks."

"Well, slow down!"

We did not slow down.

"Hy!" Rhys shouted. "We need to stop!"

Gently, Hyrum squeezed the brake levers. Then squeezed harder. There was a snap, the levers went all the way to the bar and he shouted, "I can't stop! Rhys! They're broken!"

I felt the weight shift from the basket; Rhys pulled back, sticking his back end further out, hoping to give Hyrum room to do the same and slow the bike a bit. The air filled with the hum of two air bikes accelerating; Graden matched Hyrum's speed on one side and Vicat was on the other. She reached out, yelling at Rhys to grab her hand, while Graden yelled that he was going to get in front of the bike and use his own speed to slow us down and stop.

"I don't know how!" Hyrum shouted.

We picked up speed. I felt the wheels wobble and the basket began twitching along with the front end of the bike. Both Hyrum and Rhys were mumbling but most of what they said was lost to the panic of feeling the heat rolling off Graden's air bike in front of us, and I squeezed my eyes shut as Rhys said, "Holy shit, we need that pile—"

"—of sand my mom—"

We landed with a jolt and a thud, tiny airbags deploying to keep me centered and safe in the basket. I heard the muffled sound of bodies hitting the ground followed by Hyrum's groan when he stopped rolling, and then a string of expletives coming from Rhys.

I couldn't see anything. I was held in the center of the basket by the rapidly deflating airbags, surrounded by darkness and the smell of moist dirt. Hyrum called out my name and the bike began to move backward in jerky movements that vibrated up through my toe beans and made my ears twitch. Hyrum pleaded with Rhys to pull harder. "We gotta get him outta there! He probably can't breathe!"

Out of where?

The bike jerked again, moved an inch, and with one more yank, it popped free. I squinted against the sudden sunlight. The air was considerably warmer than it had been, and there were few clouds. No fog. Inhaling felt different, as if I'd taken a deep breath with my face pressed close to the roaring fireplace, and my mouth went uncomfortably dry.

"Oh no. He's panting!" Hyrum moaned. "That's bad, Rhys, that's really bad."

I'm fine.

"He did that once on a bike ride on account of I didn't know he needed water. He needs water! He needs water right now!"

Rhys opened the top of the basket, and carefully picked me up. "You're all right, right? Are you hurt?"

Nothing hurts. Dry mouth is all. Are you two okay?

"Rhys, we gotta get him water!"

Dude, I'm fine.

"Water." The voice was soft and feminine, the hand clutching a bottle of water was brown and I knew if I rubbed my head against it, a comforting mix of cool and warm. "Are you boys all right? I swear, if they don't get rid of that damned pile of dirt—"

In unison, we looked at her.

Just go with it. Hyrum, don't say anything yet. She's not who you think she is.

Rhys accepted the water bottle. "Thanks. Yeah, I think we're okay."

"Your cat." She nodded toward the park benched behind us. "It might be shock. Come sit down and give him something to drink."

He carried me over, leaving Hyrum to pull the bike the rest of the way out of the massive pile of sand. I hadn't lied; I was fine. But when he poured water into his cupped hand, I realized how thirsty I was and lapped up as much as I could, as fast as I could. I was too busy drinking to notice that Hyrum dragged the bike behind him, shoulders slumped, but when he sat on the bench, I looked up and saw the tears.

"Is he okay?" Hyrum's voice cracked.

"Yeah, he's fine. What's wrong?"

"It's broken, Rhys. My bike is all busted up and I don't think it can be fixed."

The woman helped to right the bike, leaning on its kickstand. "Maybe that can be straightened out," she said. "It's bent a little, but not cracked in half."

"No, it's ruined," Hyrum sobbed.

"Top tube," Rhys explained. "The structural integrity of the frame is compromised."

She said she was sorry, but looked at Hyrum as if there was no way it could matter as much as he seemed to think.

"Santa is gonna be so mad at me, Rhys. I was supposed to take care of it. What's he gonna think?"

"Santa?" she asked.

"It was the first big present he ever gave me when I went to live with my sister. I promised I would take care of it."

"You did," Rhys said. "You've taken the best care of it for literally my entire life. Santa won't be mad, Hyrum. I promise."

Her mouthed formed, "Ah," but she didn't say it. "Your... friend? Rhys? Your friend is right. Santa doesn't get upset about these things."

"He's my uncle," Rhys explained.

Hyrum blinked, and began looking around. "Where are we?"

I'm surprised you haven't asked who she is.

"She looks like your mom." He heard me, yet didn't. "What happened? Where are we?"

Las Vegas.

She sat next to Hyrum on the bench, reaching over to push a wayward strand of hair over his ear. "Are you sure you're all right? Does anything on your head hurt?"

"I think he meant specifically," Rhys said. "We don't live here, just visiting. And we've never been exactly here."

"Ah. Fine. You're in Freemont Park, just north of the Strip. Is there anyone I can call for you?"

Rhys tapped his pockets, searching for his phone. "I'll call my dad."

"He's here. In Vegas."

"San Francisco." I don't think he wanted to lie any more than he had to. "I mean, we can shuttle back, but I'll call him and let him know what happened."

Her eyebrow twitched upward, just a tiny bit. "You're here without a parent."

Rhys gestured to Hyrum. "I have adult supervision."

His adult supervisor looked down and noticed a rip in his bright neon jeans, and blood that had stained the frayed edges of that rip. "I'm bleeding, Rhys! That's lots of blood!"

Rhys picked at the rip, and looked at Hyrum's knee. "It's just a scrape, Hy. Pour some water on it to get the dirt off, but it's fine."

Hyrum would not take the water bottle. "That's for Wick. We have to keep that for Wick on account of it might take *hours* to get hold of your daddy."

"Hours," the woman repeated. "It's too hot for you to sit out here and wait."

"We'll find somewhere safe," Rhys said. "And if it looks like contacting him will take too long, we'll just shuttle back. We have options."

"Absolutely not." She stood, arms folded. "You're not going anywhere until you speak with a parent. Come on. My apartment is just over there. You can get cleaned up and call him from there."

"But—"

"Sweetheart, do I look like a serial killer? I promise, you're safe with me."

She's your mom, dude. Or will be.

"Wait, really?" Hyrum sputtered. "I just thought—"

"Really. I won't hurt you. I just want to help."

Rhys stood up. "But are you safe with us? That's what you should ask yourself. You're inviting a couple of randos into your home."

She tilted her head as she considered him. "There's something about you. I'm not sure what it is yet, but my gut says you're both harmless and probably quite nice. I'll take my chances."

We had no idea how we went from careening down a street in San Francisco to plowing into a sand pile in Las Vegas, but there were two certainties: we'd jumped a When, and landed right in front of Aisha Salazar Okuda.

~

Her apartment felt familiar. I'd never been in it, but it was filled with furniture and things she'd taken when she followed ex-husband James to San Francisco. It was large and had an open floor plan; one wall was lined with windows that faced the park we'd just left and another had floor to ceiling shelves, loaded with photos, artwork, and ceramics.

In another When, in a few more years, her shelves would also be heavy with printed books, one of Will's few indulgences. Now, though, it was the framed photographs that stood out, and drew Hyrum's immediate attention.

He carefully rested his broken bike against the wall by the door, and then zoned in on a picture of an unhappy toddler, one that Will would eventually, unintentionally, discover, exposing a carefully guarded Okuda secret.

"Who's this?" he asked, pointing to—but not touching—the photo. "She's super cute."

"Jaime," she answered. "That was taken about a year ago. And no, she was not happy about having to wear the dress, in case you're wondering why she looks like she wants the photographer to spontaneously combust."

His eyebrows knotted together.

"Burst into flames," Rhys explained. "It's just a saying."

"But who is she?"

"Ah. My daughter."

Don't ask, Hyrum. We'll explain later.

Wait. Unless Rhys doesn't know.

He rubbed a finger across my head, right between my ears. "I know, buddy."

"Is he still doing all right?" Aisha asked. She headed into the kitchen, which was separated from the rest of the room by a long, wide island. "I can give him water, but I'm not sure I have any cat-friendly food."

More water would be nice.

"He ate not too long ago," Rhys said, truthfully. "I think he'd welcome something to drink, though."

"I can feed the two of you, if you're hungry." She filled a bowl with water and set it on the island, patting it in invitation to me. The island, not the bowl. "It might just be peanut butter sandwiches, but I can feed you."

Hyrum turned away from the pictures, sharply. His mouth dropped open, horrified, and was probably about to beg for anything other than peanut butter—worms and dirt or cold, wet sand from the playground—when Rhys suggested something else.

"Look, you've been nice enough to help us. Can I buy lunch for you as thanks? There's got to be someplace that delivers good pizza."

"Pepperoni?" Hyrum asked hopefully.

She snickered. "So, not a fan of peanut butter."

"More like a huge fan of pizza," Rhys said at the same time Hyrum blurted, "Peanut butter can suck my—"

"Dude, no." Rhys laughed, but held up a hand to stop him. "Yeah, no, he hates peanut butter. Like...hates it a lot."

"Well, you eat it every day for two years and see how you like it. Every day all day long, nothing but stupid, *stupid* peanut butter. Two pieces of sticky white bread that got squished in my backpack with *peanut butter* and not even jam or jelly, or... pickles. Not even pickles!"

"Now why would you do that?" she asked.

"On account of I was walking to find the queen, and my mom said that was safe to eat. But I got some fruit sometimes, and bought some chips, too. And one time a pastor I met at a rest area gave me some ham sandwiches and cookies. But it was so much peanut butter, all the time, and now I hate it and might barf if I smell it."

She nodded as if that made perfect sense. "Did you find the queen?"

He nodded, and Rhys quietly said, "He calls his sister the queen, just so you know."

Oh, this is going to be fun.

Aisha leaned her elbows on the island, bending to look at me. "You remind me of a cat I used to know. I don't imagine he's with us anymore, but he talked quite a bit, too. And funny enough, he actually lived with a queen."

Ask them my name. I want to see the look on your face.

"You mean Wick?" Rhys asked. "He's named for the royal Wick. Kinda. But he's still alive."

"Really now. I just assumed. He must be...well, very old by now."

Five hundred years, give or take.

Order the pizza, dude. Get her off the subject of me.

He had his phone in hand, poking at the screen as he connected to the local internet. Aisha directed him to a place just down the road; he ordered 3 large pizzas, one with just cheese so that I could have a few bites, one with everything except anchovies and mushrooms for her, and pepperoni for Hyrum.

"Hungry much?" she asked him, amused.

"You haven't seen us eat. There might be leftovers, but not much."

He's not kidding. They'll be hungry again in three hours.

While we waited for lunch to arrive, Aisha found sweatpants for them both to change into while she tossed their sand-stained jeans into the washing machine. Rhys helped Hyrum clean the scrape on his knee and then covered it with a bright red bandage peppered with tiny puppy faces, and reminded him to wash his hands before the pizza arrived.

It was a slice of normal; this woman was younger and had no clue who we were, but she felt like our Aisha. She was warm and personable, and her need to help was innate. Her need to talk was also the same, and she peppered them with questions while they ate.

How old are you? What grade in school? Siblings? Sports?

Rhys patiently answered everything without giving away too much. 'I'm fifteen and kinda having to figure out what I want to do about school. Younger brother and sister, older half-brother. No real time for sports but I train in karate and would like it more if our old instructor came back.'

She latched onto school. "What's to figure out?"

"Without bragging? Eh. Basically, do I want to stay in high school where my friends are, or do I want to move on and go to college. I've kinda finished...everything."

"Ah. Intellectual prodigy."

"Not really. Just interested in everything and I like to read about it all."

"Everything as in literally everything? Or are your interests more specific?"

Hand Rhys a book and he'd read it, no matter the subject. But his current interests were—obviously—cybernetics and artificial life, and he wanted to also learn more about nanotechnology.

"Heavy stuff," she noted. "Do you enjoy the math side of all that?"

"I freaking *love* math. I get that from my mom, I think. I

mean, my dad is good at it, but she's brilliant. And she relates it so well. A class of a hundred usually bored college students sit up and pay attention when she's in front of them. And when they get it, and the little lightbulbs go off over their heads? Man, she is so damned *proud* of them."

"She teaches."

He nodded. "Tenured professor, teaches mostly advanced calculus, but every semester she also takes on a remedial class to get those kids up to speed so they can at least meet their graduation requirements."

"Those are my favorite classes," she said. "I also teach math, but to high school students. Getting them over the '*oh my god this is math*' hump makes it worth it."

"Do you make them do fractions?" Hyrum asked.

"Of course."

"Well, that's just mean."

She wasn't sure if he was kidding or not.

"Fractions are just minuses and I can already do minuses, and—"

"Hyrum." Rhys reach across the island and tapped his arm to make sure he had his attention. "No one is asking you to do fractions, okay? We're just talking. We can change the subject if you're worried about it."

"Well, first there was peanut butter and now maybe fractions. So."

"No worries." Rhys looked at Aisha. "It's a touchy subject."

"I got a new one," Hyrum said. "How come you don't have a Christmas tree? We got ours already. There's nothing on it yet but I get to start decorating soon."

"Dude, it's still November," Rhys reminded him.

"We'll put ours up next week," Aisha said. "My daughter is visiting her dad's parents this week, and we'll do it when she gets back."

Again, Hyrum was confused, but he listened to the little voice reminding him to not say anything.

"How old is she?" Rhys asked.

"Four going on forty," she sighed.

That made him chuckle. "Is she in the 'why' phase? My younger cousins drove me nuts with 'why' all the time."

She sighed. "'Why' and a whole host of other things. No one prepares you for how stubbornly independent toddlers can be."

"They know who they are," Rhys said, carefully. "If I learned anything from having the cousins around, it's that when they tell you who they are, just listen. They might not have the words, but they know."

That gave her pause. "That's oddly apt and very astute."

He gave a light shrug. "They're also little assholes. Except me, I was a wonderful toddler and never gave my parents any trouble at all."

"Except when you took things apart," Hyrum said. "You took everything apart. Even your daddy's computer. You didn't do it as much as Charlie, but you still did it a lot."

He wanted to know how the laptop system worked. While Aisha worked in her home office, grading papers, Rhys spread a sheet across the living room floor, grabbed the laptop off the end table, and quietly pulled it apart. He set each piece on the sheet in the order he'd taken them out, until all that was left was the case and keyboard, and he was about to pull that apart when she came out of the office.

She stopped at the edge of the carpet, and with a sigh asked, "What are you doing?"

"Looking at the guts."

"Well," she said as she stepped over the corner edge of the sheet, "put it back together when you're done."

"No one got mad," Rhys said. "I mean, I think I got it back together, but if I didn't no one ever said so. Looking back, I'm surprised she wasn't yelling at me all the time, but she seemed pretty cool with it and always asked me to clean up after myself. That was it. Just, you know, put things back together and clean up the mess."

Jay says she never got mad when he colored on the walls, either.

Hyrum did me the favor of repeating that.

"Jay is my older brother," Rhys explained. "He used to

draw and paint on walls and floors, until she bought him a ton of paper."

"And he teaches me how to draw now, too," Hyrum beamed. "Sometimes I use crayons but he gave me some really nice pencils, but I only use those when someone else is with me so they can tell me not to eat them."

"You eat the pencils."

"I don't mean to. My sister says she's not mad about it but she worries I'll get splinters. But I don't want to eat Jay's pencils on account of they're real artist pencils and he trusts me to be careful."

"Your family sounds very patient," she said.

"Yeah, we got lucky," Rhys mused. "I know that. And—"

He was cut off by a knock on the door. Annoyed by the intrusion, Aisha slid off her stool, gesturing for them to put their trash away and to close the boxes, and then went to the door. She yanked it open roughly, wanting the person on the other side to be clear about how not happy she was.

Her words gave it away.

"What the actual fuck? What are you doing here? No, I don't really care why. But what the hell?"

He took a half step back, and his voice came out as breath. "Aisha?"

"No, really, what the—? How did you even find me?"

Hyrum stepped around the island, clutching his hands to his chest. "Will! You found us!"

Rhys scrambled out of the kitchen. "Hyrum, no," he hissed. "That's not...him."

The Emperor looked past Aisha. "I'm sorry. Truly. I had no idea you lived here."

"Then?" she prompted.

"I received an alert that my bank card had been used at this location. I apologize for the intrusion, but—"

She didn't want to listen. While we stood there uncomfortably, she erupted. How could he accuse her of theft? How would she even get hold of his card number, much less the card itself? "What do you think I did? Swiped it when you weren't looking ten years ago and just held onto it all this time? And then used it on *pizza*? What the hell, Emperor."

"I didn't think—"

"It was me," Rhys said. "I'm sorry. My dad gave me the card for travel needs and I thought it was all right to use."

"Rhys. It was. It is." He turned back to Aisha. "Again, I am sorry."

"Oh, bullshit. Get in here. What the hell is going on?" She spun to look at Rhys. "Did you set me up? Was all this just to get him here?"

"What? No. He and I have never met."

"And yet you know him."

"We're kinda related."

The Emperor entered the apartment and didn't flinch when she slammed the door. He crossed to get closer to Rhys, and stopped just short of being close enough to touch. "I never thought I would meet you," he said, softly. "Your father told me about you, but to be honest, I never thought—"

Rhys knew his father had visited his nineteen-year-old self, but didn't know that his existence had been shared. "So you two know each other?" he asked, tongue in cheek.

The Emperor nodded. "We were friends."

"Friends?" she snapped. "*Friends*? Emperor, you broke my heart. You broke *me*. Don't tell me you're just here to see the kid who co-opted your credit card."

"All right, we were more than friends," he said to Rhys before turning to her. "Aisha, I *am* sorry. Deeply. I came here hoping that the card had been used by his father, to reconnect with him. But for what I did...I cannot begin to apologize."

Hyrum began bouncing on his toes, his t-shirt wound through his fingers as he clutched it tightly. "Rhys, we're in trouble, right? Bad trouble? What did we do?"

"Nothing," the Emperor answered. "You're not in trouble. Rhys had permission to use the bank card. May I ask, who are you?"

"Hyrum," he said softly.

"My uncle," Rhys added.

It took a beat for Hyrum's name to register with the Emperor, and he deliberately did not ask how he'd become Rhys's uncle. Instead, he asked what they were doing in Las Vegas.

"We took a wrong turn somewhere," Rhys said "To be honest, I'm not sure how we got here. One minute we were riding down a street at home, the next we were here. The oddest part...no portals were involved."

"No portals," the Emperor repeated, while Aisha blurted, "What?"

She stomped across the floor "Spill it. Tell me the truth."

"I have told you the truth," Rhys said. "I left some things out, but I swear, we're from San Francisco and we'll get out of your hair as soon as we can figure out a way home."

She practically growled. "Take. The fucking. Shuttle."

He flinched at her anger, but addressed the Emperor instead. "It's a little more complicated than that. It's not just that there wasn't a portal. We may have jumped a timeline. If we try to get home with a portal, the only thing that will happen is that we pop out into the right When, but one where you only know me because you met me here. Otherwise, I don't exist here. I really screwed something up, I don't know what, and it's biting me in the ass."

"Will someone speak in plain English?" Aisha demanded.

"I don't know how to explain it without giving too much away."

The Emperor nodded. "I think that ship sailed, Rhys. But I will try to help you get home."

"Say the truth, Rhys." Hyrum's voice wavered. "Jesus would say to tell the truth."

"I am."

"No, all the truth." He turned to Aisha. "We're from a different When. Sometimes we go through a portal to visit other Whens, but this time we just kinda went *pop* and wound up in this When, before you stop being mad at Will."

"Will," she repeated.

She doesn't know his name, dude.

"Oh no! I forgot! I'm sorry, I didn't mean to."

"It's all right, Hyrum," the Emperor said. "My given name is William. Apparently in their When I'm using it again."

Flustered, she sputtered, "English, goddammit. What the hell is a When? And how did I never know your name? I thought your parents were just odd little ducks that named their kid 'Emperor.'"

Eggshells, dude. Walk on a few.

Rhys sat on one of the island stools. "A When is a period of time," he explained. "Kind of like a generation. My current When is about thirty years in the future. I won't even be born for fifteen years. Hyrum exists as another person in this When, but he's, like, twenty-eight or twenty-nine and living in North Carolina with his parents."

She got close to him and growled, "Tell me the goddamned truth."

"He is," the Emperor said. "Please. Sit and listen. It might be best if we start from the beginning."

Or just start from the day you left her on Union Square. Show her why.

"How much do you know about that?" he asked Rhys.

"Some. But, yeah, show her what you can do. And then we'll show her what we can do. She'll either believe us or she'll call the police. Maybe both."

He's the Emperor. The police aren't going to do anything.

That was enough to distract him for a moment. "Wick, how are you possible? How are you still here?"

We'll get to that.

He sat at the corner of the island and gestured for her to take the stool on the other side. "First, I owe you an explanation for that day on Union Square."

"Well, no shit, sunshine. Do you understand how badly that hurt? And how confusing it was? You jogged toward me, all smiles. I thought you were happy to see me. No, *thrilled* to see me. And then…fuck you."

"I was. Both happy and thrilled. I saw you on the Square and it was like the proverbial ray of sunshine breaking through the clouds to highlight the woman of my dreams. I had decided what I wanted for my birthday and as I ran up the steps, I was certain I would ask you. I wanted to."

"Then?" She folded her arms, and her jawline twitched as she ground her teeth together. "And it better be good."

"You began telling me all the things that had run through your head that morning. All those wonderful, happy things that if they'd been possible would have resulted in the future I longed for. I believe I wanted them as much as, if not more than, you. When I realized that, I also realized how impossible it was, and if I went through with anything it would have destroyed your future."

"My future. How dare you—"

"Your child," he said. "What I wanted from you? A simple, single kiss. That's all. But I then understood I could never stop with that, and even if I learned to control the cascade of events that happen when I touch someone, I'd rob you of a future that included a child who deserved to be born."

"My daughter—"

He held his hand out to her. "Please. Just set your hand on mine. It's the only way I can show you what happens."

Her hand twitched, but she didn't lift it. "You don't touch. Ever. You know, I used to take that personally, but after seeing you on the news all these years, I know you don't touch *anyone*."

"Because of this." He moved his hand toward her half an inch more. "I won't hurt you."

With an exaggerated sigh and a look at Rhys that would have, if he were a typical teenager, made him want to run, she set her hand on the Emperor's and waited.

Her eyes darted as she listened to the words slipping into her head, as she saw the things swirling in his own head. His eyes closed, and Rhys was so focused on them that he didn't see Hyrum sink into a squat, his hands pressed to the sides of his head. I jumped down and went to him, patting his leg with my paw.

It's all right. They'll be okay.

I meant it, too.

But then she let go of his hand, and slapped him across his face.

18

I didn't know laundry could sound angry.

A quarter second after the crack of her palm against his cheek vibrated in the air, the washing machine sang a pretty song alerting that the jeans were ready to be shoved into the dryer. She stomped off, leaving the Emperor to massage his now-red left cheek, Hyrum crying on the floor, and Rhys wide-eyed and unsure how to respond.

"I deserved that," the Emperor said simply.

You really didn't, bro.

At the sound of the dryer door slamming, Rhys reached for his phone and began scrolling. "I'm finding the next shuttle," he said when she came back. "As soon as our pants are dry, we'll leave."

"Rhys." She returned to the stool she'd been on, but refused to look at the Emperor. "You're welcome to stay as long as you need to. Keep trying to get hold of your dad."

"I can't." He set the phone down again, not gently, and clenched his jaw a few times before going on. "You were listening, I know you were. He showed you. None of this is made up for our entertainment. My parents are waiting thirty years from now and have no idea what happened to us. We're not lying. And I'm feeling desperate."

"Party trick," she murmured. "What he did is a party trick."

He picked the phone up again and flicked through his photos. "Here. The pictures I didn't want to show you. Jax and Aubrey. Oz and Drew. My dad and me."

Reluctantly, she looked. It was obvious that the photos were of her old friends. She had no clue what Oz looked like, nor Drew, but Will had not changed much and there he was with his fifteen-year-old son. Rhys was in his karate uniform and drenched in sweat, mouthguard hanging from his lips. She studied the pictures, eyebrows knotted together, then handed the phone back.

"Filters," she sighed. "You can make anyone look old—"

"Stop."

"He's not your father."

"Not yet."

Dude. Hyrum.

He was still crouched low, hands on his head, and sparks danced across his knuckles and fingers. Rhys scrambled from the stool and went to him, sliding on his knees as he reached out to wrap his arms around Hyrum. "It's okay, Hy. We'll find a way home, I promise."

"We're gonna miss Aubrey's birthday and Jax's birthday and Christmas." His voice was muffled against his knees. "Santa won't be able to find us. And then we'll miss Disneyland. Everyone's gonna be sad, Rhys. My mom."

His voice broke at the thought of his elderly mother enduring the news that he was missing.

"I'll get us home. I just have to figure out how to use a portal to cross the timeline, that's all."

Hyrum sniffed, and dropped his hands. "How?"

"Well, for starters, I have most of my grandpa's files on my phone. And I know the Emperor has access to some pretty beefy computers, if he's willing to help us."

"I am," the Emperor said.

"See? Come on, who's the smartest person you know? He's got a big brain. He can help."

"You're smarter," Hyrum sniffed.

"He's experienced," Rhys said. "That matters."

"I have to pee." He rolled to his side and onto his knees, and got up. "I don't care if I have wet pants. If we need to go now, I'll wear wet pants."

Aisha lifted Rhys's phone and looked at the picture of him and Will. "Explain the sparks," she said without looking up.

"Why? What's the point? You don't believe in any of it."

"Humor me." She looked up again. "Convince me."

Rhys held out his right hand, palm side up, and watched her face as thin strands of light lifted from his skin. They swayed as if there were a breeze, then twirled around each other until he held a tiny tree of light. Then as quickly as he'd formed it, he clamped his fingers over it and snuffed it out.

"Fascinating," the Emperor uttered.

"He reads minds and has a few other neat tricks," Rhys explained with a nod toward the Emperor. "Hyrum absorbs and expels power. Aunt Aubrey is an empath, a true empath. I can do all those and more. The problem is that no one taught him—" another nod to the Emperor "—how to control his gifts, so he lives in fear of invading other peoples' minds."

"Among other things," he said.

"I can teach you," Rhys told him. "I mean, my dad learned. Oz helped him."

"Oz. She's a little girl, Rhys."

"She's a middle-aged mom now. But back then she was eighteen and my dad had just realized he wasn't going to die after all. I don't know the whole story, but the gist? She let him practice on her. He learned to close off a window in his mind to protect his thoughts, and to keep from hearing anyone else's."

"And he taught you."

"I was born knowing how. But give me a couple minutes and access to your brain, and you'll know how, too. It's not something I can articulate, but I can share it."

Keep talking. She's starting to believe you.

Or at least believes you think you're telling the truth.

Oddly, the Emperor seemed reluctant. "Until today, I have not been touched since I left home. I was seventeen."

Aubrey did, once.

"Really?" Rhys asked. "Aunt Aubrey? When? What did she hear?"

She'd set her hand on his cheek and he was too distracted to stop her. "She learned who I was and why I was here. Who she is to me. And swore to never tell."

"All right, I'll bite," Aisha said. "Who is she to you?"

"No," Rhys said. "There's no reason you need to know that."

She was hurt. I saw it in her eyes, just long enough that I was sure she blinked to hide it.

Do you want her to believe you? Ask about her daughter. Ask how George feels about things.

Confused, the Emperor raised an eyebrow, a silent "What?" to Rhys.

"What about George?" Hyrum asked as he returned. "Is he here? He's smart, too, maybe he'll help."

"How do you know George?" Aisha asked.

I stomped across the island and sat in front of her. *He's a pain in your asterisk. He loves your kid but will do anything and everything to stop what you know is going to happen. And someday you're going to tackle his ass into a whole other century, you'll wish him dead...and then he'll become a close friend.*

"Wick," the Emperor sighed.

I looked over my shoulder at him. *Buckle up. I know your feelings are hurt because your Wick doesn't seem like he remembers you, but he will. His memories will be spotty for a while, but he'll get most of them back. And I promise, he'll always be your Major.*

"You remember me," he murmured.

He has a secondary transponder. Remove the primary and then turn that on. That's how I got my memories back. Finn activated the secondary just before he was going to send me through the portal.

"I have a vague notion about that. Rhys's father...wait, you were there, weren't you? The night he appeared in my apartment, and then helped me to sleep."

"Please tell me you're not talking to the cat," Aisha said.

"I'm talking to the cat," he answered without looking at her.

Translate for me, I said to Rhys.

Your name is Aisha Salazar Okuda. You have one child, designated female at birth, named Jaime. But Jaime has announced he's really Jimmy, and you're struggling with that, but you accept it. Your ex-husband is James, and you're on good terms even though you think he's a slut. Your favorite color is purple, you like beer, and I am very upset that forty years later you still won't tell me the story of Jax's fountain of vomit.

"Fountain of vomit?" Hyrum asked.

Well, I would tell you if I knew.

She might have, too, but her eyes filled with tears and I don't think she could speak.

19

It turns out, making hot chocolate has the potential to sound just as angry as laundry. Amidst the banging of a pot against the stovetop and the slamming of the refrigerator door, Rhys sat in the living room with the Emperor, close enough that their knees touched. Hyrum sprawled out on the floor with a stack of comic books Aisha pulled from the hall closet—gifts to Jaime from James, already tattered and worn from sticky toddler fingers—and he allowed himself to get lost in the story of a blind superhero.

"So, every time I use the card, my dad gets notified?" Rhys asked him.

"The Emperor in any When is notified. Use is expected, but the notification helps to keep track of money going out."

Do you get told when money comes in?

"I do. Last year a substantial amount was deposited and I can only assume that I had traveled here from another When."

"You wander around and talk to yourself, don't you? I mean...you could pop forward and ask yourself how we got home?"

He adhered to the principle of not traveling outside his known lifespan, and stuck to his father's requirement that he not go home. He would travel into the past to see himself, but rarely forward.

"I have gone forward to a certain extent, certainly, but typically to solve a problem that should not exist."

"Well, that's me and Hyrum being here, right?"

Don't ask him to do that. Don't fix his future to a specific point.

"Meaning?" Rhys asked me.

I looked toward the kitchen. *He doesn't need to know how this plays out...and if it doesn't swing your way, there's no getting that back, I don't think.*

"Things can be changed, Wick. Hell, that's why we're here. Something changed and I think it's my fault."

"Explain," the Emperor said.

Rhys gave him the short version: wanting to do nothing more than help a stranded driver and get him and his wife back on the road. It hadn't crossed his mind that he was in a When other than his own and needed to leave things alone. All he saw was someone who needed help he was capable of giving.

"It wasn't until they'd left that Wick explained why he kept telling me to stop."

You weren't listening.

"They were my grandparents. On my mom's side. And they mentioned having thirteen-year-old daughter. I've been chewing on it ever since. Her parents died when she was thirteen, in a wreck caused by a malfunction in their magnetic drive. Because of that, she moved to San Francisco to live with her aunt, went to school there, and met my dad. By fixing their car, what did I screw up?"

"And yet she *did* attend school in San Francisco, where she met Aubrey and by extension, me."

"Yeah, I get that now. But I was chewing on it, and the fact that they lived? It probably caused a new timeline."

"I don't believe—"

"We know that's what happens. Make a major change too far from when it first happens, and it splits off. I mean, it doesn't split if you change something because it wasn't supposed to happen in the first place, but saving lives comes with a cost."

"You know this, how?"

"I'm not sure I can tell you."

I am. Pretty soon you're getting a visit from yourself and Jax. They're going to take Queen Donna to the future to be cured. And then that timeline splits off.

"The queen does not die."

Aisha brought the hot chocolate into the living room, balancing mugs on a cookie sheet. "Say what? What's wrong with the queen?"

Rhys stood and reached to help her with the mugs.

"She's ill," the Emperor said, sadly. "And unfortunately, the symptoms went unrecognized until it was too late. She has less than six months left...it will destroy King Eli."

"But not if she's taken to your birth When. Mass, Brian Massimo, will be there and he'll fix everything wrong. She's only doomed if she stays here."

"Tell me more." The Emperor nodded his thanks when Aisha handed him a mug. "As much as you know."

Rhys did not have enough details to share; he'd been a small child when his father and uncle decided that the data in the Old Mint didn't matter as much as they'd believed, and they were going to save the Queen. He couldn't tell the Emperor about the days they spent in Will's birth When, waiting with a young King Eli as his wife floated in a surgical tank. He didn't know how they found their way home, or how we knew the timeline had split because Liam Finnegan—an adjacent future version of the Emperor's father—stayed and chronicled the lives of the royal family.

But I was there, and I remembered.

Let Rhys teach you how to control your mind, and then listen when he shows you how to craft a box in your brain where you can store all the extraneous memories. After that...we can try to mind meld like a couple of old Vulcans, and I'll show you everything you don't yet know.

~

He needed time.

Rhys quietly, carefully fed him the instructions on closing off his thoughts to others, and how to not listen when in physical contact with someone else. It took longer to construct the box, because his brain was mostly done cooking and he was resistant to change. Oz created one on the fly when Will shared the memories of his life, but she was eighteen and still malleable.

While he was at it, Rhys shared as much as he could, the future history of the Blackshears from the viewpoint of a fifteen-year-old. He lacked the majority of the important things, though, but that could wait. I had a feeling we'd have time.

While he sat quietly on the sofa and sifted through the highlights, trying to shove things into the box, Rhys and Hyrum ran to the diner downstairs to grab cheeseburgers, fries, and shakes for everyone, and Aisha sat at the kitchen island with her phone, ordering cat food, a litter box, and litter for delivery.

We were not leaving that night. She only believed a fraction of the things she'd been told and shown, but she listened to that little voice in the back of her head and it suggested she would have regrets if Rhys and Hyrum left. She had no idea why she trusted them or even why she'd had the original impulse to take them home. I watched her poke at the screen on her phone and wondered why she hadn't asked one particular question, because it surely had to have occurred to her.

Who is Rhys's mother?

She saw the picture of him with Will. She saw pictures with obviously older Jax and Aubrey. Rhys had not shown any of himself with his mother; many of the photos on his phone, she'd taken, or one of his siblings had when she wasn't around.

Remind me to tell Rhys to take more pictures of his mom. Someday he'll regret not having enough of them to look at.

She glanced up. "I don't speak Wickian. Sorry."

Wickian.

I'll remember that.

"Go check on the Emperor of Suck. Make sure he's breathing, because I haven't heard him move in fifteen minutes."

He doesn't suck. You're just still upset.

"Still don't understand. I hope you like beef and chicken, because that's all they seem to have for delivery." She set the phone down, and I scooted closer. It was not the same phone Aisha of the future used, but it was similar and I recognized the note icon. I touched my nose to it, hoping she would understand and help navigate to the part where I could type something.

"Great. Cat snot on my phone." She started to pull it away, but then noticed I'd managed to get the note-taking program open. On the chance that I'd done it intentionally, she clicked on the keyboard icon, and set the phone in front of me. "Fine. Let's see what you can do."

I was slow, but tapped my nose against the screen well enough to butcher, *'Food ok. H no suck. H luv. U.'*

"Oh, my god," she murmured.

'I slow.'

"Wick, who cares? This is...oh my god."

'Tey say true.th. Us futre. Lost here.'

Her hand went to her mouth, and her eyes filled. I waited for her to speak again, but she struggled against the flood of feelings washing over her, so I went back to the phone.

'U. Mom.'

"I know, but Jaime—"

'Rhys mom. Wil b.'

"I'm his mother?"

'Wil be.'

She looked at the closed door, and then toward the living room where the Emperor sat, still, barely breathing. "What does Rhys need, Wick? How can I help him?"

'Comp.u.ters. Hi sped. 2or3.'

"Anything else?"

'Tools. Take aprt. Wire. Pt 2gether agin.'

"I'll make a call. I know someone who can get his hands on high end equipment, but it might not come free."

'Wil. Rich.'

He probably didn't want her to know that last bit, but honestly, I didn't care. She believed me, she bought food for me, and in half an hour I'd be able to pee without balancing on the seat of the toilet.

~

Around a bite of cheeseburger, Rhys managed to sigh and say at the same time, "Wick wants you to know that he can actually spell, but phone keypads are tiny and his nose is not. So."

She was impressed nonetheless, as one would be when the cat finds a way to text with the human.

You need to invent a translator that works with my transponder. Then I could talk to anyone.

"Oh, hell no," Rhys snorted.

Think about it. The looks on peoples' faces when I'm riding in your Wick shirt, telling them how beautiful they are and to get the fork out of my way.

"And that's exactly why I won't do it."

Killjoy.

Aisha might have been in favor of it. "When you translate what he says, are you doing it verbatim, or just giving context?"

"Verbatim, usually," he answered.

"I change the bad words," Hyrum offered.

The Emperor grinned. "As did I, when I was a child. He learned to swear before I did, and taught me more than my parents were happy with."

Aisha poked a french fry in his direction. "You had a horrible potty mouth. So bad that drunk Aubrey wrote up a list of forbidden words."

"She still has it," Hyrum said. "And she wiggles her pointy finger at Wick when she knows he says things off it. One time, she made him go to my room."

Sterling punishment there. She sent me to a giant room with a comfortable bed and a massive TV. I had a nice nap and watched one of Jax's favorite space shows after.

"TV," Aisha repeated.

"Broadcast and narrowcast entertainment and news," Rhys explained. "In Florida, it's called 'television,' or 'TV' for short. But it's become so well-known because of Hyrum that it's kinda taken over in San Francisco and is winding through Pacifica."

"Next stop, Midlam?" she teased.

"Midlam is part of Pacifica now. So, sure."

The Emperor wanted to know more; as far as he knew, the two countries didn't merge until Oz became queen and Drew was Midlam's king. He hadn't gone through that part of the box in his brain and was unaware of the grittier details of the war between Florida and Midlam that spurred Jax into absorbing Pacifica's closest ally in order to protect them.

He was poised to ask and then carry out a lengthy political conversation while the table was cleared, but there was a knock on the door. Aisha jumped up to answer it; Rhys leaned over and whispered in Hyrum's ear, presumably to remind him that if it was someone they knew, to stay quiet about it. They would not know us.

Hyrum's inner teenager came out, and he rolled his eyes.

George Denton stepped in, arms loaded down with laptop computers, a roll of thin wire, and a backpack. "As requested, three of the best portable systems I've got. But I still want to know what you need them for. Are you getting into something nefarious, and if you are, can I play, too?"

He set them on the island, only then noticing the Emperor. His eyes went dark, nostrils flared, and he turned to Aisha with, "What the hell?"

The Emperor stood. "I know you, don't I? You seem familiar."

"How can the two of you know each other?" Aisha pushed the door closed, cutting off George's quick avenue of escape, and it was clear he wanted to run. "Business?"

"School." George nearly growled. "We were in grade school together."

It still hadn't formed in the Emperor's mind, but Aisha's belief suddenly flared. "Not possible. The Emperor is not...from here."

George didn't take his eyes off him. "Yeah, no kidding."

"No. Emperor, how?"

He was still trying to place George.

"Second grade." George stepped closer. "The pool. High school. The dojo. Hell, fucking *preschool* when you read my goddamned mind and nearly destroyed me."

It clicked.

"George Denton."

Rhys scrambled to get between them. "If it helps, in my

When, you're really good friends."

"There will be a blizzard in hell before that happens," George seethed.

When he took another half step, Rhys set his hand on George's chest. "I saved your life when I was three years old. You were basically cut in half in an explosion. He rushed to help. If he hadn't jumped you forward two hundred years, you'd have been dead within a minute. And your son would have lived with us."

At that, he stepped back. "What? My what?"

"I'm not from this When," Rhys said. "We're stuck here, and he's trying to help. I just want you to get past hating each other and get to tolerating each other, so Hyrum and I can go home. And don't tell me you don't believe it, because you've been yanked through time, too. You know the portals exist."

He gave a slight nod, listening.

"I'm thirty-ish years in the future. You have a son, Isaac. He's my best friend and you trust his life to my dad. Any time you travel, he stays with us. If you work late, he comes over to do homework or just have dinner. Hell, you just went to Elysium and before you left, you asked Isaac who he wanted to live with if something happened, us or Jay, and he chose us. You were okay with that."

"Jay."

"Jaime." Aisha's voice was soft. "It happens, George. Whether you like it or not, it happens."

Breath coming quick, he pivoted. "I don't like it for Jaime. The results—"

"He had my dad," Rhys interrupted. "He had access to the future. He didn't have his surgery here, he had it there. In a tank. And I know that matters to you. You want to fight it because you're worried it's a mistake he'll never recover from, but if you could take him there, you'd consent."

"Because she could change her mind. There, she could have a do-over."

"He won't. But the point is, my dad took him. And now Jay has access of his own, and can get there if he needs to."

"And your dad is the Emperor."

Rhys nodded. "William Blackshear. Emperor is just a made-up title. He doesn't care for it much."

"And you told Aisha this?" George asked the Emperor.

"Some. She remains unconvinced."

"A few minutes with Wick swayed me a bit," she said. "But screw you, that doesn't mean I'm anywhere near ready to forgive you."

"I understand."

Reluctantly, George clicked into acceptance. "There's a story here," he guessed, looking at Rhys. "You can tell me later. What is it you need with the computers? I know my way around them, maybe I can help."

Rhys held his phone up. "I have all the code for the portals here. But I need a series of high-speed processors to wade through it, and then figure out how to take a city-sized system down to portable sized. After that, I use it to jump a timeline. Simple stuff."

"Simple. Well, I enjoy a good challenge." He slid a computer across the island to Rhys, and sat on one of the stools. "Now, tell me how you're going to manage a portable sized particle accelerator, because I don't think you're going anywhere without one."

20

They were only partway through the portal code at three in the morning. Aisha reluctantly went to bed at one, and Hyrum was curled up on an inflatable mattress in the living room, sleeping in fits. Rhys, George, and the Emperor sat at the kitchen table, faces bathed in the light of their respective monitors as they went over the code line by line.

They needed to speed up. I'd seen the code; it would take them years to get through it at the pace they were going.

I lounged at the table's center. I napped now and then, waiting for one of them to jump up and shout "Eureka," but then they would have woken Aisha and none of them wanted that.

George needed sleep, but he was more interested in the things Rhys had loaded onto his computer. He stared at the screen, bleary-eyed, exhausted yet excited to be trusted with data he would never be able to ethically use on his own. He was simultaneously looking at the future while examining a part of his history, and the enormity of that didn't escape him.

"How tempting it must be for your grandfather to build this in your When," he mused, glancing at Rhys. "And how difficult it is to save the discovery for his future self. I'm not sure I would be able to."

"I guess he's more vested in the reasons he created it in the first place."

"I would pop through the closest portal and at least tell myself, I think."

Will nodded. "Before I left, he was adamant about protecting the progression of time. I wonder if he feels the same now."

"How comfortable are you with knowing something important in your future?" Rhys asked the Emperor.

"I've learned quite a bit today and am no worse for it."

"Yeah, but this one would rob you of discovery. And doing something your dad never could."

What, like send a bowling ball through a transporter without turning it inside out?

"Yeah, well, that," Rhys snorted. "But this is something bigger. You're probably working on it now, anyway. But I have all the data for it. The code, the math, everything."

The Emperor leaned back in his chair. "Something big that I'm already working on. It's certainly not the motorcycle, which I hope I've finished by then. I doubt it's finding a way to get my father home without using a portal."

Yeah, you can take his asterisk through one when he gets here. He won't need the egg thingy. He'll need you, though, because he stuck his transponder between his man boobs and then broke it.

"Wick's right about that. I know he told you to never use a portal to go any further forward than the day you left, but you can. Once he's here and has most of his memory back, you can send him home using a portal."

"Hm." He did not seem convinced.

"The future beyond that point exists," Rhys said. "I've been there. As long as you know it's there, you can go. He just didn't want you trying to get to where you thought his current When was, in case the world ended before he expected."

And we now know that's a pretty uncomfortable trip. When it ends, I mean. Let's not do it again.

"Personal transport device," the Emperor realized. "It works?"

Rhys spun his computer so that the Emperor could see the code. "I've always wondered how it worked, but he said I didn't need to know yet. I didn't realize I'd grabbed this when Grandpa told me I could have the rest of the data."

George leaned over to get a look, and they sat still, reading, for half an hour before the Emperor finally breathed out, "Incredible."

"Am I reading this correctly?" George asked. "It still uses the existing portal structure as well as a transporter?"

"Kinda," Rhys answered. "The portals use transporter tech on a super basic level. The jump bracelet can function away from the portal tunnel infrastructure because it contains its own, well, tiny particle accelerator."

"Impossible."

The Emperor nodded. "Your mental image of a particle accelerator is not what my father created for the portals. You're picturing the older, building-sized apparatus that politicians have been certain would rip the world apart. What my father created is a very small unit that runs in a thin line atop the tunnel itself."

"And because of that, the portals are essentially projected upward," Rhys added. "The state of flux means they're accessible in any When where San Francisco exists. Well, the part of the city where the tunnel is in the future, anyway."

Meaning we can't go tour Pangea?

"I don't know. I mean, geographically that area probably exists. But it's not worth the risk."

"'Null sp,'" George read out loud. "What is that?"

"Null space," Rhys said. "It's, I dunno, kind of the cushion between Whens. It's what Grandpa used to move through time. He launched from here, bounced off null space, and redirected to the When he wanted to visit. Once the portal tunnel was finished, he didn't need to use it anymore."

George pointed at the screen. "Yet this seems to use it."

"And that's what I need to figure out."

The Emperor understood it. This was his work, albeit a bit further on. "This is the same principle as the original time machine. It skims instead of bounces, reducing the risk of getting stuck."

"You can get stuck," George muttered.

"Grandpa got stuck for four hundred years."

So did I. I'd have waved at him there, but...slow motion and all that.

"You were there." George seemed uncertain. "With his grandfather."

No. I was there by myself because of an idiot teenager. It took the same four hundred years for me to get unstuck, but then

I landed in the early twentieth century. Right before a freaking earthquake.

I might as well have slapped the Emperor as hard as Aisha had. He told Rhys to keep reading; there was a dedicated transporter built in and he hadn't gotten that far in his own research. He needed a break, and left the table to sit on the sofa in the living room.

I followed him. I was useless on the table but I could be a sounding board if he needed one.

You looked in the box, didn't you?

"Indeed." He sounded sad. "And yet, what I see is incomplete. It's comprised of stories and not memories."

That's all Rhys knows. The stories. But I'm okay, you know. And in our timeline, I went back and rescued myself so that the next me didn't have to wait sixty years for Finn to find me.

"The next Wick—Seven?—is living with Hyrum in the future?"

Only until you're born. I'm not sure who he'll live with between Hyrum and then, but maybe someone will skip ahead and take him to tiny you. He'll be Major all over again.

"Does he know that?"

Seven? He knows. He's having an awesome life now, Will. And now that you know, you can jump back and get him. Bring cheese wrapped in foil. But maybe wait until your Wick has his memories back.

"Wait? I'd like to go right now."

Time it right and it won't matter. You could go now, or you could go in fifty years. You'll still get to him right after he lands.

"I could stop the whole thing."

Wait until little Eli is fifteen. If I'm going to exist in the next When of this timeline, the whole idiot teenager thing has to happen, and I have to be launched into null space for no reason other than I think that's how I learned to speak to you. At least, Drew and Jo need to breed a few cats to launch. Otherwise, I won't be born.

Hyrum rolled over. "I met Seven lots of times. He's really, really happy and loves Lux."

Your mom's future cat, I explained.

"He's your best friend, Wick," Hyrum said.

That made the Emperor smile. "You have a friend."

"He's got lots of friends. Like Lux. Thor is his best dog friend. Will and Drew are his best grownup friends."

You're a grownup.

He giggled. "Not all the time. But Will was your friend first." He rolled off the mattress and sat next to us on the sofa. "I keep wanting to call you Will. I know you're the Emperor here, but…"

"I would prefer it if you called me by name, Hyrum. I miss it."

"Then you need to tell Jax and everyone else what your name is."

"I would, had my father not explicitly told me to use 'Emperor' instead."

Finn wasn't always right. In fact, he messed up an awful lot. Tell Jax your name. And tell him who you are. He's going to find out eventually.

"Eventually. During my lingering pre-death days, I presume."

You're not dying this time around. For all we know, you'll still be alive on the day that you're born. So you might as well be honest with Jax and everyone else, and they'll be of more help when Finn shows up with no clue who he is.

"One thing at a time. We need to get you home first." Slapping his hands on his legs, he stood. "Back to bed, Hyrum. Whether he likes it or not, Rhys will join you in a few minutes."

"Where are you going to sleep?"

He gestured to the sofa. "I'll rest here."

Hyrum slid back onto the mattress. "What about George?"

"I live across the hall, Hyrum," George said. "Blackshear is right, we need to rest or we're going to make some stupid mistakes."

He offered real beds for anyone who wanted one, but Hyrum worried Aisha would get up and no one would be there, which was rude. Rhys wasn't leaving Hyrum, and Will reminded them that sleep for him was rare, so he planned on stretching out on the sofa to sift through more data.

"Yeah, you just don't want to be the only one here when she wakes up," Rhys said. "Just talk to her, cripes."

"We'll have those discussions when and if she chooses to."

"You get a say."

"No, I truly do not. I'm the one asking forgiveness, Rhys. I don't get to dictate the time it takes to achieve that."

She was forty-three in our When.

"You really want to wait that long?" Rhys pressed.

He didn't, but he would.

The wheels were already spinning in Rhys's head.

21

I woke to the aroma of coffee and hot chocolate, and the Emperor at the table with Aisha. His attention was concentrated on his tablet—reading the news, I guessed, or possibly unclassified state documents forwarded by the prince's staff, as was typical morning reading fare—and hers was directed to whatever liquid was in the mug she cupped between her hands. Hyrum was splayed out across the mattress, which explained why Rhys was now on the sofa with a computer perched across his knees.

Despite the tension clinging to everything like static, it felt like normal life.

Normal meant jumping on the table and plopping down between them. I was immediately rewarded with a soft head rub, several blinks ahead of my expectations.

"Good morning, Wick," she said. "What's your plan for the day?"

World domination. But, absent that, providing purrs for anyone who needs it.

"You'll be busy," she guessed. "What about you, Emperor? What are we doing to get these boys home?"

He set the tablet down. "Math. And if you're willing, we'll need you to cross check if not outright do it for us. It will be a considerable endeavor."

"I'll text George and ask him to bring over a white board."

George did not have a white board; he had a clear board, which thrilled Hyrum. "It's like in the movies!" he gushed, gripping the front of his t-shirt. "Will the letters be blue? I hope the letters will be blue. That's what they are in the movies when the mad scientists are writing out their plans. But sometimes it's the good guys and they're trying to make medicines or space ships."

"He and Drew watch a lot of twentieth and twenty-first century cinema," Rhys explained. "Like, an absurd amount. So much so that he and Wick can quote old movies. With context."

I'm still in search of a Felicia I can say 'bye' to.

Letters and numbers written on the board could be any color Hyrum chose. The first half hour was lost to letting him play with it; he scribbled pictures in every color he could find on the pen, convinced Rhys to smash his face on the board while he traced it from the other side, and then stopped suddenly when it occurred to him that he wasn't letting anyone else play with it, and that was selfish.

"It's okay," Rhys said. "All I would do is math and this is more fun. But now I'm thinking that when we get home, we need to ask Santa for one. We could do these big pictures, and then digitize them so we'd have them forever."

Hyrum frowned as he considered it. "Nuh. I bet it's expensive. We shouldn't be greedy. Santa has a lot of people he gives presents to so we shouldn't ask for things that cost a lot of money."

Then ask Will. He has a lot of money.

Hyrum snickered. "So do I, Wick. I don't spend a lot of my pay. I bet I could buy one for myself."

"Yeah, well, I'm asking for one," Rhys said. "Some of us don't have jobs that pay out the ass."

Under her breath, Aisha said, "And now I'm wondering what constitutes a lot of money."

Not finding the curiosity inappropriate, Hyrum said, "Drew says I make about the same as a professor that has ten of yours."

"Ten of yours," she repeated. "Ten of your what?"

"Tenure," Rhys said.

"Sweety, that's not a lot."

"But I don't have to pay rent or buy food even though I keep saying to Aubrey, 'I should buy some groceries on account of I'm not a little kid,' and she keeps saying, 'Save your money, Hy. You might need it someday.' So I say, 'But I'll just get yours when you die,' And she goes"—he sucked in a long breath and then let it out through pursed lips— "and that makes me laugh." He scrunched his nose as he thought about it, and snorted. "Well, I think Oz and Zed get it, but it's still funny to make her huff like that."

Don't be so sure. Oz and Zed had trust funds. I bet she leaves you a little something. I bet she leaves me a little something.

"We're getting off track," Rhys said. "One point is that we both want one of these and if Santa doesn't bring one, we can buy it. And the other point...we need to get to work. I have calculations that need retooling for our problems, plus I need to make a list of the materials I need to make a jump—"

He was cut off by a sound much like a squeaky door rising from nothingness to irritation in under a second, followed by a bright light. Rhys and the Emperor took steps toward it, just past the kitchen island, while Hyrum ducked behind the clear board, hiding where he could see everything.

There was a tender pop—so slight I might have been the only one who could hear it—and then standing right next to the island were two men, dressed identically in dark blue, form-fitting flight suits. Both had metal bands on their wrists, and their suits were adorned with glowing metallic piping in thin lines down the front. They looked as confused as we were, as if they'd landed in the wrong room at the wrong time, but after two or three seconds of adjustment, the closest one clicked on Rhys.

"Rhys Blackshear." It was not a question. "You don't belong here."

Rhys took a step back while the Emperor took one forward. "Come with us."

The Emperor remained remarkably calm. George backed away, not out of fear but understanding he needed to let the Emperor handle this, though if necessary he could spring forward and choke a bitch. Aisha had just begun to get her wits about her and headed for Rhys.

"He's not going anywhere with you," the Emperor said. "Who—"

They ignored him. "You need to come with us." The close dude cocked his head to the right, a heavy twitch, and then reached to his jaw to scratch at it. "Static."

Rhys squeaked out, "What? Why?"

"You're out of synch and not supposed to be here." Close Dude—that was now his name in my head; Close Dude and Far Boy—seemed confused that Rhys was not comprehending any of this. He reached out a hand and said, "You must leave."

It was the hand reaching out that flipped a switch in Aisha. She stomped toward him, finger jabbing in his direction, and stopped next to the Emperor because he was not going to let her get closer. "Touch my son and I will break your arm off at the shoulder and then beat your ass half to death with it."

"Son?" Far Boy uttered. He cocked his head, too.

"He does not belong here," Close Dude repeated.

They need a new script.

The Emperor held up a hand. "What exactly do you want with him?"

"We need to remove him from this—"

"Who the fuck *are* you?" Aisha seethed.

Robotically, overlayed with a sense of confusion, Far Boy said, "Guardians. Of time. Rhys Blackshear is displaced, and we're to take him—"

"Again," Aisha said, "your arm, my bloody weapon. This is my son. You will not touch him. You will not take a step closer to him. You're not taking him *anywhere* without some kind of... time warrant. Or whatever the hell it is."

Close Dude's shroud of confusion thickened. "He's your son."

"Are you *high*? How many times do I need to repeat it? He's my son. I will not allow—"

"Proof," Far Boy said. His jaw itched as well.

"Do you have DNA profiling capabilities?" The Emperor sounded calm, but I recognized the look. If they took another step toward Rhys, they were dead guardians. "Settle the matter before we become violent. And we *will* resort to violence if you cannot provide the means for this and continue to insist that he's leaving with you."

"This is your home," Close Dude said, mostly to himself, while Far Boy stepped around the island. He pulled a small, rectangular card from under his sleeve, tapped on it, and then held it toward Aisha.

"Each of you touch a corner. It will draw a small drop of blood and we can analyze."

She took it first and then passed it to the Emperor. When Rhys had it, he hesitated. "This is total bullshit, you know that, don't you? Since when are there time cops? How does that even work? Someone finds a way to travel in time and you just follow and arrest them? Why?"

Close Boy opened his mouth, but then closed it when Aisha twitched toward him.

"We're not cops," Far Boy said, taking the card from him. He slipped it into the space between two of the metal piping strips on his torso and tapped the back. Five seconds and an odd whirring sound later, he pulled it off and glanced at it, then handed it to Close Dude. "The DNA matches. Yet, it also proves this is Rhys Blackshear. He must come—"

Aisha got within a foot of him, and practically growled. "The only thing he *must* do is listen to us. His parents. And right now that happens to be math, cleaning up any mess he left in the bathroom, and then science homework. So unless you have that warrant, get the hell out of my apartment. You do *not* have my consent to be here."

Far Boy touched his index finger to a spot at the junction of his jaw and ear lobe. "We'll leave."

With the same pop, they were gone.

"What the hell?" Aisha breathed out.

George began slamming computer lids closed and shoved the rest into his backpack. "You know they're coming back. Once they verify that he's definitely the person they're looking for, they'll come back."

"Indeed." The Emperor grabbed his own backpack and looked at Aisha. "If you're coming with us, get a bag with a change of clothes, some identification, your phone, and any medications you'll need. But don't feel obligated."

"Hell, yes, I'm going." She darted to her bedroom.

Neither Rhys nor Hyrum knew what to do. We had nothing to gather, other than shoes and socks.

"Where are we going?" Hyrum asked as he slipped his socks on.

"San Francisco," the Emperor said. "I can protect you there."

"That's the first place they'll look," George warned. "You need somewhere off the radar, so to speak."

Denver.

"Denver, Wick?" the Emperor asked.

There's a safe house there, right? And most of it is under ground, undetectable. There's food and water, clothes, computers, and even a litter box for me.

"There is, indeed."

"That's not a safe house, though," Rhys said. "I mean, we go there a lot. It's just a place to stay when we feel like having some time to actually play outside, but people know about it."

It's a safe house in this When.

"All right. It's under an hour away. My car is just outside."

"My car," George said. "Emperor, you can't take yours. Leave it parked here, we'll take mine. And don't argue. I'm damn well going to help get them home even if I do think you're a raging asshole."

"George."

"Will. Those people travel through time. You know they do. We might have an hour, but we might only have a minute. Protect your future son, grab your shit, and let's go."

Aisha jogged from the back of the apartment, bag in hand. "He's right. Especially about the time travel. We might not even have enough time to get to the car, let alone go anywhere."

Hyrum stared at the clear board longingly, understanding he wouldn't be able to play with it again. "Do the thing, Rhys," he said. "Make a bubble."

He nodded, and told everyone to get in close. "I can hold us in one moment of time," he explained. "I shouldn't hold it for too long, but I can keep it long enough to get us to the car and on our way. Who's driving?"

"Will," George said.

"Watch for birds," Rhys warned him. "They'll hang in midair, and if you hit one, there will be damage."

They all had questions. George especially had a dozen things at the tip of his tongue; instead of asking, he opened the door and held it as we filtered out, and was as silent as Aisha until we were in his blue luxury air van. He sat in the middle seat, directing Aisha to the front; Hyrum and Rhys sat next to him, and the bags went onto the rear seat.

Everything around us begged to have an explanation. Her neighbor was outside, trapped in mid-step. Cars hung above the transit lanes; pedestrians were locked into place on the sidewalk. On the playground, a young boy on the swings hung in the air, his mouth wide open with glee, and behind him his father stood with arms out, the engine of his flight.

There was no sound, except for our breathing.

Las Vegas was near one hundred degrees, and the world was frozen.

22

A minute and a half after the Emperor hit the accelerator, Rhys flicked his middle fingers away from the palms of his hands, and the birds began to fly. Another car zipped past; Will pushed the van higher, away from the traffic lanes, causing Aisha to gasp loudly and George to laugh.

Will glanced at her. "Problem?"

"It's a van," George said. "It can be used as a shuttle. We don't need to hover over the magnets."

"Well, *you* knew that," she said. "How the hell does he know that?"

"I have driven a van before," Will said.

"And you." She turned in her seat. "What the hell was that? What did you do?"

Rhys gave a light shrug. "I stopped time."

"You stopped time."

"It's one of his things!" Hyrum beamed. "He can do lots of things. Jax thinks that someday he's going to float off the balcony but so far he hasn't done that. I want to be there when he does, on account of someone's gonna shout and maybe even pee a little."

This particular gift did not seem to phase Will or George.

"How long have you been able to do that?" Will asked, glancing over his shoulder.

"I dunno. I might have been four or five."

Three. You were three years old when you stopped time to save Sophia. That was the first time that we know of.

"Sophia?" Will slapped at the dash, activating the dummy driver. "Sophia Lopez? You saved her life?"

Sophia Blackshear now.

"Yeah, I kinda did," Rhys said. "I mean, you were running toward her and I think you were going to grab her and pull her out of the way, but I just kinda...knew. So I stopped time, you grabbed her, and I started it again slowly enough that the truck landed without, you know...crashing."

"Who?" Aisha asked.

"My aunt. Zed's wife. There was a truck..."

Will turned back around. "Sophia Lopez, the daughter of Texas Governor Robert Lopez. In every timeline of which I am aware, she dies young."

And you plan on being there to stop it this time.

"Indeed. My intention is to find a way to prevent her from being in the area. Everything I know about Zed suggests that his life will be much better if she remains in it."

Zed was there. Old man Zed, I mean. He showed up hoping to stop it, too.

"Zed thought he could stop it," Will said, mostly to himself.

Well. Mostly. He had a darker agenda, too. But you're right. He needs her in his life. Everyone needs her in his life.

"How do you know so much about it?" George asked. "Don't tell me you memorized all of history before coming here. You were just a kid."

"Seventeen," Will said. "But no, I didn't memorize all of history. I have access to volumes of information contained at the Old Mint in San Francisco. Most of that data pertains to the attempts to stop the meteor headed for earth, but there are banks of data dedicated to the history of the Blackshear family."

"Ego project or relevant?" George asked.

With a chuckle, Will said, "Both."

"Not all the data there is right," Rhys said. "It's skewed to the When that you're in. And even then, you don't have all the variables, so what you expect might not happen."

"Such as?" Will pressed.

"You. If you take what you know now, and do something with it, you'll live to see forty-three and beyond."

"What the hell does that mean?" George asked.

Aisha turned in her seat. "Emperor?"

The little spot near the back of his jaw twitched; he was not happy, and ground his teeth together as he decided whether to toss the rest of the truth out.

"I have an expiration date," he said.

"We all do," Aisha pressed. "Spill it."

"I'd rather not."

He grew up on stories about the Emperor of San Francisco. And his end was always the same—a few weeks before his forty-third birthday, he dies.

George and Aisha focused on me, absorbing what Rhys repeated, and she told me to go on.

He also knew the story about the young Prince who decided to climb the Bay Bridge. Six-year-old Prince Jackson got stuck, and none of the people standing there gawking at him had the guts to follow him up to save him. But then this kid showed up out of nowhere, scrambled up and carefully grabbed him. By then the Queen was there, followed by the King, so he held the prince close to him and carried him to his parents. King Eli asked his name but the only thing the teenager said was, "Emperor."

"Wait." Aisha frowned. "You're younger than Jax. How were you a teenager?"

"Time travel," Will said simply.

The thing is, until he went home and told his dad what he'd done, he didn't know that he really was the Emperor. His dad realized it and broke down, sobbing so hard he nearly threw up. Because he finally understood that his son was the Emperor, and the Emperor died at forty-two.

"But *you* don't have to," Rhys stressed. "In the When before mine, the Emperor died because Wick went into the portal to see if the world was still there. Wick didn't come back, so he lost his anchor. But in my When? He went instead of Wick. With Wick alive, he still had his anchor."

It's creepier than that. He went in, and got stuck because there was no exit. There are probably hundreds of versions of me stuck in portals throughout time. Zed is the one who realized that Will was stuck in there, because he could smell his fear from the outside.

Oz finally reached in and pulled us out. But it was tricky because we weren't exactly solid all the time.

"Us?" Will asked.

Well, yeah. Once Zed smelled him and knew he was alive, I didn't want him waiting there alone. I knew it might be a while. So I stepped in to keep him company. I'm awesome like that.

Will's voice softened. "Indeed, Wick."

"The point," Rhys said. "He survived. And if you don't know what your dad did after that to move the meteor off its track, I'll give you the data I have. All you need to do is to take that information to him, and the sooner you do it, the sooner he can have the gates built. And maybe this time he'll have the light bulb moment where he understands that he already built a freaking transporter, and he doesn't have to start from scratch again. Because holy hell, he's spent my entire life trying to get it right and only recently revealed it."

"My understanding is that he used it to push a bomb through to end the war. You would have been around ten years old. Perhaps eight?"

"That was in another When," Rhys said. "In ours, that war ended differently, and a lot sooner. But he did use a prototype to send some EMF explosives through to Florida in a later conflict. In the initial test runs, everything Grandpa sent through was coming out the other end inverted, so they purposely created the bombs to turn inside out, releasing millions of mosquito-drone-driven EMF explosives. It wiped out most of the electrical grid in Florida."

Aisha turned back, looking out the windshield. "I am lost, and I think I want to hear the whole story. Start with being a teenager when Jax was six, and get me up to speed."

The rest of the short flight was dedicated to repeating

everything I'd said, but with bigger words and a few more details. By the time we landed in the old red barn attached to the cabin atop the safe house, he'd told her about discovering he was the Emperor, and the two years of bouncing around, waiting for Jax to catch up in age, before he left his birth When for the past.

This time, she believed all of it.

23

As far as I knew, the Denver safe house had been used for its intended purpose only once, during Midlam's war with Florida. After Red's quiet warning of Levi Munson's intention to assassinate Prince Andrew of Midlam, Will fled with Oz, Zed, and Drew, and we landed in Denver. There was a small cabin on the surface, a cozy, one-bedroom vacation home, but underneath was a massive structure designed to withstand the brutal forces of war. It was largely undetectable, with shielded tunnels that extruded several miles out. Some were used for storage, but mainly, they were escape venues.

In the years since my initial visit, when the tunnels were breached and Oz was kidnapped as the headliner in Levi's sick agenda, it had been decommissioned as a safe house and was now used as a family getaway. The royal children were brought here several times a year, mostly for the opportunity to play outside, to enjoy the large meadows and woods that surrounded the cabin, and occasionally Will brought them for physical training.

It was easier to convince a temperamental ten-year-old to run hard through the woods, pretending to be a soldier or superhero, than it was to prod them into jogging endless laps around Union Square. Outside the cabin, Will felt comfortable letting the kids see the spectrum of his martial arts talents; outside the royal home, he would not demonstrate how to run up a wall and then backflip nor was he willing to punch the crown princess in the face.

It was in the clearing between the cabin and the woods where he honed Oz's fighting proficiencies, teaching her new skills for self-defense, while giving her the strength to withstand the brutality of her days under Levi Munson's thumb.

Now we fled there with the same intent—protect family—but the sense of urgency this time was comparatively abated; Will maneuvered the van into the large red barn, but no one ran from the garage to get inside. It was like every other recreational visit. They filed out one by one, grabbing bags, without a hint that someone was after us.

Rhys and Hyrum knew the underground space well, and after the Emperor lowered George's van into the garage, they headed inside first. George slung his backpack over his shoulder and followed, though at a more age-appropriate pace, and I traveled on Will's shoulder as he escorted Aisha in.

My first time there, Will stood in the main room's center, pointing out where everything was using old clock terminology. Twelve o'clock, kitchen. One o'clock, living area. Two o'clock, gym. Three o'clock, entry to the dorm.

Like then, all I wanted was the litterbox.

"We have approximately two minutes until the sensors report our presence," Will called out from the security center. "Rhys, Hyrum, I need you here when the system activates."

They came out from the dorm. "How come?" Hyrum asked. "Can't you just tell it we're supposed to be here?"

He could have. One simple code input with the keyboard nestled on the ledge under one of the large monitors would have been enough to alert the King's security that Will had intentionally entered the safe house. He wanted to trip the alarm; he knew what would happen: the screen would turn itself on, he would be confronted by the guard on duty, and then turned over to the King.

While he waited, he turned on the secondary computer to access the security protocols.

"I'm activating a protective shield," he said when I asked what he was doing. "It won't affect the cabin above us, but should block any sensor sweeps down here."

It won't keep anyone out, though. They can still get in.

"If they know how, yes."

Two minutes after our arrival, the monitor flickered. Five seconds later we saw a young T'Neeka Soto, currently head of the household detail, soon to be head of the royal guard. Without speaking, she noted Will's presence, sighed, and flipped the switch that alerted the King.

"Stand by," Rhys read on the screen. "Stand by for what?"

Will stood a bit straighter, hands clasped behind his back. When the screen flickered again, he waited long enough for King Eli to note each person on his own screen, and then gave a short bow. "Your Majesty."

"Emperor. What's in Denver that I don't know about?" He squinted. "You took Wick?"

Hyrum pumped his fists in the air, bouncing on his toes. "Eli! Eli! Eli!"

He had the King's attention. "I am. And who are you?"

Hyrum dropped his hands and grabbed onto the front of his t-shirt, though he wasn't upset. "I'm Hyrum. Oh! I forgot! You don't know me yet!"

"Yet." He let a smile tug at the corners of his mouth. "Hyrum, that was the most enthusiastic greeting I believe I've ever had. Thank you." His attention shifted to Rhys. "And you?"

"Rhys Blackshear. And no, you haven't met me yet, either. This is George Denton—" he gestured to his left "—and this is—"

"Aisha Salazar," Eli said. "I remember you. The one who turned the Emperor stupid."

"Sir," Will sighed.

"Well, I'm not wrong. She showed up and you transformed from a thoughtful, efficient, introspective young man into a… teenager. All right. Explain why you're in the safe house. I presume it's not for recreation."

Will gave him the short version.

"You'll have a son," Eli mused. "As touch phobic as you are, you'll eventually manage that. Huh."

"I am not phobic, sir. I—"

"I know why, Emperor."

"Sir?"

Rhys nudged him with his elbow. "Surprise. He's known you since you were, like, five or six. He's friends with your dad."

He looked at Eli. "He also likes to snoop in the Old Mint and read data packets he's not supposed to. He knows a lot more than you realize."

"Guilty," Eli said. "But I know nothing about you, not from anything I've read there. Everything I know says you're not possible."

"In my When, the Emperor didn't die," Rhys said, gently. "Short version, my grandfather saves the world two hundred years in the future, Wick doesn't die, so he doesn't die. So, if you all take the info he now knows and do something with it, this one won't die, either. You'll celebrate, you'll adopt him, you'll adopt Hyrum, and trust me, you'll enjoy every bit of that."

He didn't seem surprised with the idea that he would adopt an adult Emperor. But Hyrum gave him pause. "And who am I to you, Hyrum?" he asked.

Hyrum beamed. "You're my daddy who loves me."

Eli smiled. "I have no doubt. Perhaps the better question should have been, 'How did we come to know each other?'"

Will answered. "Hyrum is one of Aubrey's younger brothers. He is also a topic in need of serious discussion when I return. In his When, you adopt him at forty-two, but it shouldn't wait. As soon as we find a way to send these two home, we *must* intervene and remove him from his parents."

"And piss off Levi Munson at the same time? I'll enjoy that."

"My daddy was mean," Hyrum said. "Really mean. He took all my toys and threw them away on account of I was twenty and he said I was too old, and he did...things...and then threw me out the bedroom window, and he yells all the time and makes my mom cry, and he even makes my sisters—"

"I am so sorry, Hyrum," Eli said. "If I could change that for you, I would. But I promise, we'll change that for *him*."

"I set Daddy's hair on fire once."

Visibly, Eli tried to not laugh.

"But I put it out before it really hurt him."

Eli wanted to know what Rhys needed. There was little he did not have immediate access to, though most of what he needed was available in the tunnel storage, including tools and computers. There was a cabinet loaded with laptops in stacks of ten; there were small tools and large tools, and if he dug deep enough, tools that would allow him to drill and then dig a substantial hole under the house.

The only things Eli wasn't sure about—he had an inventory list in front of him—were the components needed to mimic a miniature particle accelerator and the thin metal bands Rhys needed to create a jump bracelet.

"Strip down a door if you have to," Eli said. "There are access doors within the tunnels. If necessary, remove one and cut it up."

"Sure," Rhys snorted. "I'll just use my handy dandy pocket knife to slice it to ribbons. We'll use any leftovers to weave into baskets and—"

Will leaned toward him and whispered, "Your King, Rhys."

"King what? He's my grandpa...oh."

Eli was not offended, and laughed. "I look forward to meeting you, Rhys. You, too, Hyrum. I have a feeling life will be so much more interesting with you in it."

He let go of his shirt. "I won't set your hair on fire. I promise. I love you and wouldn't do that."

Eli inched closer to his monitor. "When I sign off, I'll go talk to Aubrey. And when this one gets home—" he pointed to Will "—we'll go get you. Nothing will stop me. I swear to you, I will be the daddy who loves you."

Don't forget to tell him I'm not his Wick and someone needs to go feed him.

"No one will forget to feed the cat at home, Wick," Will sighed.

Eli tilted his head. "Eh. You can talk to Wick. I suspected as much when you were younger but I was never certain."

"Coulda asked," Rhys said.

"I imagine there are a million things I could ask. That doesn't mean he would answer. You know how he is."

Amused, he reminded Will to get in touch if we needed anything, and the monitor went dark.

"You know, you can take the stick out of your ass when

you're around him," Rhys said. "He doesn't like being treated like the King unless there's someone else around."

"I am someone else." He headed for the living area, where George was pulling computers from his backpack. "I am not family."

"You're his great, great, great grandson. You're family, and he knows it."

Jax and Aubrey don't, so…

"That stick is fused into place," George said. "It's been there since he was in pre-school, at least. He might have been born with it."

"Does it hurt?" Hyrum asked Will.

"What?"

"I bet Doctor Brian could take it out for you. I had a really big splinter in my hand and he took that out and it didn't even hurt. Your butt might hurt on account of it's your butt, and butt stuff hurts, but you should still do it before something bad happens."

"I don't have—"

Aisha laughed. "Yeah, you kinda do. Don't worry, Hyrum. Once this is over, we'll make him see a doctor."

Rhys's eyes lit up.

In his mind, that meant she intended to keep seeing Will.

I could have told him the truth, but it seemed mean.

24

I'd explored the house before; I'd run up and down the tunnels with Oz and Drew, and later with Rhys, Alex, and Charlie. Fine, I rode my hover cart with Rhys and the twins, mostly because I am old and the main tunnel is several miles long, and the cart is approximately 6,000 times more fun than running. I knew every inch of the underground living space and most of the cabin above.

I'd only poked my head into the storage tunnel, however, and when Will took me with him to look for supplies, I was stunned at the depth of the tunnel and the number of things packed floor to ceiling. He carried an inventory map on his tablet as he made his way down the aisle; the tunnel was a good twenty feet across with the aisle taking up only five feet. Each stacked item—everything in multiples—took up roughly four feet of floor space, half hoisted onto high shelves, leaving me to wonder out loud how one was expected to fetch heavy, high things without falling and breaking a significant body part.

Will gestured to a space next to a tall pantry, where a forklift waited. On that forklift was a cherry picker, and he assured me it was enough to move anything in the tunnel. "The hard part is finding exactly what you're looking for, beyond the food stores. Replacement saucepans? That might take a while."

He was looking for a spare monitor, one Rhys could utilize as a computer display or a touch screen. He needed to display an insane amount of math, and thought it would be easier for everyone if it was on a single, large display. Will volunteered to get one out of storage, assuring Rhys that it would be big enough.

I don't remember ever seeing a really big one here. Well, inside. Why am I this far into storage? It's creepy in here.

"There is nothing in this tunnel that can hurt you," he said. "I'd be surprised if you found even a tiny bug."

Well, that I would play with.

"And consume."

No, I don't eat them. Mostly I poke at them until someone notices. The idea is for someone to scoop it up and take it outside.

He paused to consider it. "Truly, I don't recall ever seeing you eat a bug."

I probably have. But I don't want to think about it.

"A cat consuming a bug would not be unheard of, Wick. It's normal."

And reminds me of the before times. No thank you.

Halfway down the tunnel were three monitors, lined up one in front of the other, and each was eighty inches across. I was about to ask how he thought he was carrying that thing by himself when he tapped a finger to the tablet in hand, and the first one slowly rolled forward.

It followed us out and past the kitchen, stopping in the living room.

"Big enough?" he asked Rhys.

There are two more, if not.

"This should do it."

Are you sure? These people are old and might need the others so you can use really big type that's easier to read.

Hyrum giggled. "I'm the only old one here, Wick. Except you."

"He gets snarkier as he ages, doesn't he?" Will asked, not expecting an answer. He went about plugging it in, and then stepped aside so that Rhys could wire the laptop to it. A few minutes later, the monitor filled with data from Will's future jump bracelet.

"Fascinating," he murmured.

"This is preliminary stuff," Rhys said.

"This is years beyond my current status. Hardly preliminary."

George stood nearby, his head tilted as he took it in, line by line. "Explain what I'm looking at."

There were sections. One addressed time travel and utilizing transponders embedded in someone's brain. One addressed transporters. Others addressed emergency movement to prevent a person from jumping into the center of a rock or where another person stood. It was missing something, but I couldn't place my paw on it.

"A portable portal," George mused. "With a transporter."

"Well, to be fair, the portals actually are transporters, but... you gotta know my grandpa to understand why he doesn't think so."

Will understood. "Because they only move someone through time. He doesn't consider that to be the same as moving someone through space. They exit the portal in the same geographic location they enter."

Did he turn anyone inside out during testing?

Aisha grunted, "Ew," while Will shook his head.

"I don't specifically recall the early testing phases as I was all of two or three years old, but one might assume I would have been told if that had happened. As far as I know, the only mishaps involved multiple tunnel failures. It simply didn't work in the earliest days."

George wanted to see the data independent of the jump bracelet. Rhys had the code for the transporter and the portals; if George could examine each part, he thought he would be able to better assist in creating a model Rhys could use to bridge the timelines.

While he perused that information, Will turned to Rhys. "I need to ask. Are you anchored to Hyrum, and is he anchored to you? That will determine how much time we have."

"Anchor?" Aisha asked.

"Time's a little bitch," Rhys explained. "If you spend too much time in a When other than your own, it tries to force you back. If you have someone you're tethered to, like this acute emotional connection, they can anchor you into place. My dad was anchored to Wick until he formed a tether to my mom. George was anchored to his brother until he met James."

"What happens if you lose your anchor?"

"You get sick. Like, super sick. You age quickly, you're nauseated all the time, and you can begin losing touch with reality. Eventually your body just breaks down, and you die. That can take anywhere from a couple weeks to several months. I'm not sure why."

George needs to keep that in mind.

"I do? Why?"

Because if you keep being a little bitch, you're going to lose your anchor and it'll make you do things that you'll regret. Our George was lucky. Aisha tackled him through a portal to his birth When, so he lived. But if you aren't so lucky, you'll die.

"Do I want to know?" he asked Rhys.

"Wick knows more than I do. I'm not sure what he's talking about."

"He's talking about my death. Come on, Wick, spill it."

It's simple. Stay out of Aisha and James's way when it comes to making the big decisions for their kid. Support it. Help them.

"I already said I wouldn't get in the way, if they can take him to the future."

She jumped on that, jabbing her pointy finger in his direction. "Him. See? You used that so easily."

"Yeah? And? Have you noticed that you don't?"

"I'm *trying*. Goddammit, they handed me a baby and congratulated me on my daughter's birth. My brain is still trying to correct that."

"So's mine."

She flinched. "All right, that's fair. And I know, it hasn't been that long."

He grunted, and went back to reading the code. She turned around and started for the door leading to the dorm and the bathrooms, and shot Will a look that clearly said, *'This is your fault.'*

He probably thought so, too.

I thought the blame belonged with Will's mother—she knew he could control his gifts but never told him—but no one asked me.

~

Will pulled an extra laptop from storage and set it up for Hyrum to watch TV. There was a moment of panic—I don't know how to watch TV on this. I watch TV on a TV and this isn't a TV! How come there's no TV here?—that Rhys gently dialed back by creating links to Hyrum's favorite things and placing them on the screen; after that, Hyrum fell into whatever show had caught his attention while Rhys and George worked quietly in the living room.

I perched on the chair behind Rhys and watched for a bit as he pulled bits and pieces from one of George's computers. It felt random, like he was five years old again, taking apart his father's computer just to see what was inside, but this time he knew what he was digging for and he had to force himself to slow down and not just rip it apart. Tiny screws went into little drink cups lined up on the coffee table, and other small parts were set aside, just in case he needed them.

For this, I was useless. I jumped down, careful to not bother him, and went to the table where Aisha and Will sat. She held a coffee mug between her hands, looking like it was morning at home and she just wanted five more minutes to wake up. It didn't smell like coffee, though, so I worked my way up to her, and pushed my head over the rim to get a good look and a deep sniff.

"Not for kitties." She rubbed her fingers between my ears, gently pushing me back. "I'm pretty sure you can't have chocolate."

Ah. Cocoa. Does Hyrum know there's cocoa? He loves hot chocolate.

"He does," Will answered. "He had some when you were napping."

Good.

What are we talking about? Anything juicy?

"I'm trying to wrap my brain around the concept of anchors," she said. "I understand needing someone but I don't understand how a tracking invention like time could interfere with your well-being."

No one really understood. He thought it helped to separate the construct of how we keep track of minutes, hours, and days from the existence of everything; there was time on a clock, and the time of existence and eternity. They were the same, but...not.

Old Hyrum says time is spaghetti. Each noodle is a When, but you jumble them together and get time itself. Without the sauce.

"Interesting," Will murmured.

But then you once said it was string cheese. Finn thinks it's salt. So who knows.

"Are you sure you heard correctly, or were you simply hungry when that discussion took place?"

I'm always hungry. Now, our Hyrum likes the idea he saw on an old TV show. It's about this guy who travels through time and space in a British police box. He's the Doctor and says time isn't linear. It's a big ball of wibbly wobbly timey whimey stuff.

"Who?" Aisah asked.

Exactly.

"Doctor Who," Will said. "Another one of Jax's passion diversions."

Jax watches it? I thought he was all about the space ships and the dude with the pointy ears. He thinks you're that guy, you know.

Sighing heavily, he grumbled, "I am not Spock."

You have that book. Jax gave it to you. But the guy who wrote it figured out he really is Spock, so...yeah.

"I remember that," Aisha said. "He wanted to watch every episode of every version of Star Trek and guessed it would take him fifteen to twenty years at the rate he was going. Every now and then I think about it and wonder why we haven't advanced that much. We're what, a hundred years past when it was supposed to take place?"

"I think we'd be there, if not for world wars and civil wars, not to mention the age of anti-intellectualism. The early twenty first century cost us at least a century of development. Now we're in deep space, but without drive capabilities and without real-time communications."

"Hell of a leap of faith, taking off for deep space knowing you'll never come home."

At some point, those ships would turn around and head

home, but the originating crews would be long dead and their descendants would likely never step foot on the planet. They would live out their lives on those ships, and Will wasn't certain that any type of earth-normative culture would be maintained on those ships after a century or so.

"So they might never return," she said.

"We'll likely never know. It wouldn't happen in our lifetime."

That you know of.

"You're aware of something, Wick?"

Well, travel to Mars is down to a couple weeks. We have real time coms with them. Drew's brother makes the hop three times a year. When he first started going there, the trip was months long.

"Carter? Please tell me he grows up to be less…himself."

Eh. He's arrogant but basically a decent person. That doesn't erase a lot of the things he's done. And trust me, he's done too much and a lot of it unforgiveable. Like, prison-time-deserved unforgiveable.

"I am not surprised."

Aisha set her mug down. "Wait. You two started gossiping and threw me off track. I was going to ask about Wick being your anchor. How? And why not send you with another person?"

"Your anchor needs to be someone with whom you have a significant connection," he explained. "There was no one else for me. When my father realized that I was going to leave home…he took Wick back and left him with Eli. Jax was just a baby." He sat back in his chair, eyebrows knotted. "He took Wick to Eli. Why am I just now understanding? Of course they knew each other."

Aisha went in a different direction. "How is Wick that old? I thought the record for a housecat was somewhere around thirty-five to forty years."

Joke's on you. I'm somewhere around five hundred.

She could not hide her disbelief. "Hon, I believe you're old, but come on."

"Part of that was null space?" Will asked. "I wasn't sure you were serious."

From across the room, Rhys said, "He's not kidding. But don't ask him details unless you want your heart broken."

"Well now I *have* to know," Aisha sputtered.

The short version? Tiny, tiny me in a tiny, tiny time machine, stuck in null space at the same time for the same duration as Finn. Four hundred years. I landed in nineteen hundred six, just before the big earthquake, and survived by the skin of my teeth until Finn found me in the mid-sixties. The rest you know.

He peeked into the brain box, then told Aisha the story.

She scooped me up and held me close, and for the next minute her tears soaked the fur between my ears.

I'd probably still be there, if Rhys hadn't called out, "Hey, Dad, do you have the code for the transponders? I—" He sucked in a deep breath. "I'm sorry. Just habit."

"It's fine. I don't mind. And yes, I have it."

Just how much memory do those freaking phones have?

He didn't need to answer; I knew he could literally carry every book written in the last five centuries on his phone. I knew he made a habit of keeping copies of his work data accessible, including all the specs for the antique motorcycle he was restoring. I just wanted to poke the bear, but he said, seriously, "It's on my tablet, Wick."

He handed it over and added, "Passcode is my mother's birthday."

Despite the King's permission to destroy a door inside the safe house, Rhys did not wish to spend hours cutting one into metal strips. He didn't think they were thin enough, nor pliable enough, but if he could find something in the house or in storage, all he needed to create a functioning jump bracelet was a few more wires and a sensor that could connect the bracelet to his transponder.

"It'll be clunky and I'll have to strap a flex keyboard to my forearm, but with a sensor I can make it work."

"Why the keyboard?" Will asked.

"The chances of having the right stuff to create an input screen on whatever I use as the bracelet are slim to none."

He needed a biometric sensor. Taking one from the security system wouldn't work; he couldn't force that into reading data from the transponder in his brain. There was one in his phone, but Will nixed the idea that any of them should cannibalize their phones; if they were separated somehow, they'd need them.

Hyrum looked up from the TV. "What about my watch? It does body things."

Rhys looked pained and stopped short of cringing. "Hy, you spent a lot on that watch. You love it."

"Would it work?"

Sighing, Rhys nodded.

"Then you can have it." He got up, pulling the watch off as he crossed the room. "I can get another one. I only like it so much because it's like a walkie-talkie, too, but I still have my phone. It's okay. I'll buy a new one and won't even ask Santa."

Dude, you have to take it. If you're really worried, I haven't spent much of my allowance this year and I'll buy him a new one.

"Your cat gets an allowance," Aisha mused as Rhys took the watch from Hyrum.

George snort-laughed. "You've been exposed to this craziness, and that's what surprises you?"

I asked Will for one when Rhys was a baby, I think. I don't have any other way to get money.

"And what does a cat need money for?"

Christmas and birthday presents. I said I'd buy my own toys, too, but he said that's his job.

"Dad deposits a lump sum into an account for Wick every year," Rhys said. He didn't look up; he was busy pulling the watch apart. "It's just easier than giving him money every time he needs it. Mostly because he won't ask."

"He even has a bank card!" Hyrum squealed. "Sometimes we help him shop online but sometimes he does it his own self."

I think they were more impressed by that than the humming and lights that popped on when Rhys pressed the sensor to his skin and turned the jump unit on.

All he needed was something to use as the bracelet itself, and George solved that by cracking open the printer near the security station. He pulled out a two-inch-wide ribbon with wires running through it, and asked Rhys if that would work. Because if it did, we at least had the first step in getting home, as crudely constructed as it was.

He jumped from his seat, thrilled. The ribbon would work; after dinner they could start testing it, going into the tunnels to jump back and forth. They were all happy, everyone except Aisha, who looked at him with a longing I hadn't seen since the time Rhys's mom dropped her hot fudge sundae on the floor.

~

There was math.
There was coding.
There was more math.
The post-dinner testing kept getting delayed by all the checks and balances Will insisted on before allowing anyone to strap on the jump device—it could hardly be called a bracelet—to move from one part of a tunnel to another. There was also disagreement over who should make the first attempt; Rhys wanted to because it was his creation and he needed it to work with his transponder. Will wanted to because he didn't want to risk Rhys's life, and brushed aside the notion that Rhys needed Will in order to get home, with the unspoken reminder that if it didn't work, Rhys and Hyrum needed him to simply get by in a new When. Aisha had no transponder, but no one would have let her regardless, because she had a small child. When Hyrum offered, they all blurted out "No!" in unison, despite his lack of a transponder. It didn't fit on me.

George volunteered, but had no transponder. He'd been escorted from his birth When to this one; he was not offered a transponder intentionally, none of the rescued people were. Finn realized that a large number might regret their choice to flee the end of everything, and they might try to return.

It would be a long time before he conceived St. Francis, a refuge for forward-time-jumpers.

So. What then?

Will dug to the bottom of his well-worn backpack, and pulled out a long, narrow metal case. He held it up to show them, and then asked George if he was serious. In the container were three spare transponders, intended for Zed and Drew, but if Rhys was positive that they could jump forward, he could replace those.

You carry them around?

"I never know if or when it might be necessary, Wick. If something occurs and I need to take the children and run, I want them on hand. So, typically, I have them. Not always, but usually."

Fair enough.

"You're giving me access to the portals, and to home." He turned to Rhys. "Your George. Does he have one?"

Rhys shook his head. "He relies on one of us to take him back and forth."

But he was offered one, after Will was sure he really was a changed person.

"He turned it down?" George asked.

George is less convinced that he's become a better man than everyone else is.

Will found that puzzling. "Why deny him access at all, if you knew the future existed?"

Because for a while there, he was dangerous. Someone needed to keep track of which When he was in, just in case. But it's possible now to track people through the portals, so…I'm not sure.

This George didn't think he was any decent sort of person, but he wanted to see how the jump device worked. Moreover, he was convinced that it would; getting access to the portals and birth When was less attractive than being part of the creation of tech that allowed someone to move through space. The time aspect was not the most exciting part of this; he just wanted to jump.

He didn't flinch at the size of the needle required to implant the transponder. George perched on a stool near the dining table and sat still, not blinking, barely breathing, as Will plunged it into a soft spot behind his ear.

When he was done, Will swabbed alcohol over the puncture and then sighed, "Now we wait. It will take a few hours to partially integrate, and you're going to have a headache while that happens."

"How bad of a headache?"

Reaching into the case for a pain patch, Will answered, "Significant enough that you'll need this. But it's not intolerable."

"Is that why I don't have one?" Hyrum asked Rhys. "Because it hurts?"

It was not the only reason, but Rhys nodded. "It hurts, like, a lot. I don't remember getting mine but I think that's because I was sedated."

"How old were you?" Aisha asked.

"Two?" he guessed. "I was old enough to walk and talk. I was still in diapers. So probably two."

"What the hell?" George fumbled with the pain patch. "Why would anyone give a toddler access to time travel?"

Will answered. "The eldest of the royal offspring are given one as a method of escape. Oz's was implanted at roughly the same age because she often accompanied us on shorter trips, and it was a bit of insurance in case something happened to either Jax or me. All she needed was to find a portal, head through it, and think 'home.'"

"And how easy is finding a portal?" Aisha asked. "Are they out in the open? Behind closed doors?"

The portals ran along the portal tunnel, which circled five miles of San Francisco two hundred years in the future. They extruded upward throughout time, and were always in the same location.

"The portals are invisible," Will said, "although they emit a subtle hum. If you don't know exactly where they are, if you listen closely, you can find them."

They have the hum for Oz.

"Indeed. Sound was added for Jax and Oz, to accommodate their synesthesia. Where I can only find them by the sound, they can also see the sound emitted, and find them that way."

"They see sound," George muttered.

Hyrum bounced on his toes. "So can Rhys! If you whistle he can tell you what color it is. He can even tell you what color your whole body is on account of it makes noise all the time."

"Something we don't tell anyone but family," Rhys reminded him. "It's a secret, okay? No one needs to know that Uncle Jax or Oz can do that."

"We're all family, right?"

George snorted. "Most of you."

That made Hyrum frown. "You're family. You're Isaac's daddy and Isaac is like our little brother. Except he's older than Rhys."

"Hm." George moved from the stool to a chair, leaning his elbows on the table. The headache had begun, but the pain patch had not yet worked its magic. "I've never so much as kissed a woman, nor do I want to, and you people think I'm going to father a child?"

Cloning.

It's a thing.

Hyrum grabbed the front of his shirt. "I could do that? Have a baby without doing kissing things?"

"Yeah, it's possible," Rhys said. "You'd be a good dad."

He sighed and let go of his shirt. "I'd be a good daddy for babies. But not for bigger kids. I think Drew and I talked about it once. He said I'd be a good daddy, too, but...babies grow up and get smarter and stuff."

"You'd still be a *great* dad," Rhys insisted.

"Maybe. I'll just wait until you have babies, and then I can be their uncle, too, and we can have fun when you're busy doing grown up stuff."

George rubbed his forehead. "And your kids?" he asked Rhys. "Will they get this thing stabbed into their heads?"

"Probably. But not because they're oldest. Maybe if it's a safety thing, like it was for Oz. I'd probably wait until they were old enough to consent."

Like Zed was. He was sixteen or seventeen. Before that, he didn't want one. He still didn't want one, but there was a war and things change.

"If he and I become friends," George said, "hell yes, things change."

"Go lie down for a bit," Will said. "Rest until the medication kicks in."

He waved it off, swearing he was fine. Rhys turned back to the jump device. Hyrum went back to the TV. Aisha and Will sat together at the table, awkwardly silent, until she breathed out, "Please tell me there's booze in this place. Because right now, I need a good stiff drink."

~

There was booze.

Will knew there was booze; he headed into the storage tunnel and came back with a bottle in hand.

"How?" he asked me. "This is Chambrizi. It doesn't exist yet."

Eli. I told you, he doesn't play by the rules. He's visited your birth When. I bet he's got bottles all over the place.

As he poured out four glasses, he mused, "One day I would like to get to know that side of the King."

And one day everyone will wish that you don't refer to him as 'the Old King' to avoid using his name in front of Oz. Just so you know. She probably picked her first kid's name once she and Drew decided they were going to get married when they grew up.

"So noted. But isn't that a decision they make when she's twelve or thirteen?"

"What?" Aisha reached for the glass he offered. "They decide that young?"

The joke is that it's an arranged marriage and they handled the details themselves. But, yes. They specifically decided to be good friends to each other with the intent of getting married someday.

"That seems clinical," George said.

They fell in love along the way. So much so that Drew didn't blink at walking from here to Kansas to save her from Levi Munson.

The Chambrizi, Aisha declared, was liquid heaven. George melted into nostalgia and declared that this alone was reason to go home for a visit, even if he avoided his family. It was not new to Hyrum, who liked it but preferred Drew's cinnamon whiskey; he took a sip and asked why Rhys didn't get any.

"He's fifteen?" Aisha sputtered.

"Will lets him have a small glass sometimes, if he wants."

Rhys shook his head. "He does not want, not right now. He wants a clear head for testing the jump device."

Aisha felt no such compulsion, and shot hers back, then refilled her glass. "Yes, I know, sip it and enjoy. I'll do that with this one."

She and George sipped for enjoyment through four glasses.

Halfway through his third, George declared the headache gone and wondered out loud how long it would now be before the transponder was active. If he was going to risk scattering his atoms all over the safe house, it should be before the Chambrizi wore off. Drunk on heaven would be a nice way to go, he declared. If the worst happened, no one should feel bad because he knew the risks and embraced them, and he'd already had an amazing life.

"Also, I'm an asshole. There's no missing that. A few people probably think I deserve it."

Aisha did not disagree, but pointed out, "You have people who love you, and people who are going to love you. Asshole or not."

"So I should be forgiven."

"Everyone deserves forgiveness." With a sigh, she looked at Will. "Except maybe you. You destroyed me, Emperor. You stood there and let me go on and on and on about a future you didn't want, and then just—" she snapped her fingers "—ran away."

"I did want—"

"Oh, fuck off. If you'd really wanted it, you would have stayed. You'd have explained. You could have *trusted* me, Emperor. I trusted you enough to bare my truths, but could you extend the same courtesy? No, you blurted out the thing you knew would hurt me most, and ran off like a scared little boy."

He sucked in a deep breath, but didn't respond.

"You could have told me, you know. It might have taken time to fucking *believe* you, but you could have explained all your weird and quirky behaviors. You could have trusted me. Trusted Jax. Trusted Aubrey. For fuck's sake, Emperor, we *respected* your right to not be touched. You could have at least respected us enough to be honest."

"He was a child," George said.

"Oh, you can fuck off, too. You weren't there. You weren't deceived and lied to. You weren't left standing on Union Square crying so hard you couldn't stand. You weren't the one Yolo had to scoop up like melted ice cream and then lead home. Don't defend him."

"Yolanda was there?"

"She showed up. I don't know why. You think I'm angry with him? Ask her how she feels. Then sit back and listen to the fireworks."

Hyrum.

Will and Rhys both turned to see. Hyrum had crouched low, and his hands were plastered to the sides of his head. He gasped for breath as tears rolled from his eyes, and he was beginning to slowly rock on the balls of his feet.

Rhys got up and went to him, crouching beside him. "Hy." He reached out to rub Hyrum's arm. "What hurts? Your body or your feelings?"

"Tummy," he sobbed. "They're supposed to love each other, Rhys. Why don't they love each other? I want them to be happy, not mad."

"I know," Rhys whispered.

Will sat on the floor next to Hyrum. "I'm sorry. No one meant to upset you."

"But you love her, right?"

Carefully, "I deserve her anger, Hyrum. Everything she's said is correct. I am guilty of inflicting considerable emotional pain, and I cannot fix that as easily as I did it."

"But if you say sorry—"

"That's not enough."

Rhys gently pulled Hyrum's hands from his head, and eased him back until he was sitting on the floor. Whispering to only Hyrum, he said, "I want the same thing, you know. I want them together, in this When, because if they don't? I won't be born. Neither will Alex and Charlie. But what I want is selfish."

"Sometimes it's okay to be selfish. Father Dan said that to me."

"Remember what Father Dan said about hurting someone and apologizing?"

Hyrum almost grabbed onto his shirt, but wrapped his arms across his chest instead. "He said that sorry is just a start. If you want forgiveness you gotta have a perfect action of contraband."

"Act of contrition," Rhys said. "I think in this case, it means the Emperor is going to have to do some actual work for her to get past being angry and reach the point of forgiveness."

"You gotta be born, Rhys," he said, still crying. "They're gonna go get me and I'm gonna need you on account of Drew and Oz will grow up."

The Emperor didn't understand that, but I did. When Hyrum arrived in San Francisco, Drew became his champion and his best friend. He treated Hyrum like an adult and demanded that everyone else did, too. He and Oz took Hyrum on dates, they played with him, and made sure he felt every bit their equal.

But, despite being married adults, they had more growing up to do. Drew took the mantles of Ozoo while Oz dove into creating the Wastelands amusement park, and as their work flourished, their time diminished. Drew still had movie nights with Hyrum and took breaks with him at work, but it was not the same and it only compounded when they began having children.

Rhys needed Hyrum as much as Hyrum needed Rhys. He helped raise Rhys; they were best friends. He couldn't see a happy future for the Hyrum of this When without him.

Will needs something to fight for.

"I have—" He thought he had something, but I knew he didn't quite realize how much.

I'm going to show you.

Shave my belly, big boy. You're going to take a walk through my brain, and learn a few things.

"Shave you."

Exactly. We've always wondered if you could touch my thoughts the way you do with people, and we've wondered if we could trade chunks of memories. My fur has always been in the way. So tonight you're going to shave me, and we're going to see if I can show you the highlights. Maybe even some lowlights. When you're done, maybe then you'll see the Great Big Why of what they want.

25

You're buying me dinner after, right?

Flat on my back on the table, arms and legs flopped to the side, my upside-down view was of the Emperor's crotch. He had a pulse razor in hand and its tiny, whining buzz reverberated in my ears, a stinging sensation that almost made me call the whole thing off.

I wanted to know, though. Will could touch anyone and hear their thoughts; he touched me and there was nothing. For him, that was a good thing. I was warm and comforting when he needed me to be, and he could cuddle me close and not worry about what lurid thoughts ran through his head. Once the fur grew back, he could have that, but for now, I wanted to know if it was possible.

Be gentle with me. It's my first time.

"It doesn't hurt, Wick," Hyrum said. "After he found me when I was looking for the Queen and she made me take a bath on account of I was really dirty, Will showed me the razor and used it on his arm, and then he helped me shave and it didn't hurt at all. It kinda tickled."

I remember. You said you'd made people soup.

It was less than the tickle Hyrum suggested, but the razor felt warm sliding over my skin. As promised, it was painless, and the Emperor finished shaving my belly in four quick strips. Gently, he blew on me, getting stray hairs out of the way, checking to be sure I was truly fur free. Instead of immediately putting his hand on me, though, he took great care in cleaning off the razor and putting it back in its case, then poking at me to get me to roll over so he could clean off the towel.

Aisha nudged him out of the way and said she'd get it. "Just take the cat into the living room and do what you need to do."

He's going to molest my useless nipples, that's what.

"Wick, right now, I cannot recall why I wished so deeply that you remembered me and spoke to me more often."

Yeah, well, one day this thought will come back to you at three in the morning when the lights are off and you don't want suggestions for a better and brighter tomorrow.

"I'm not sure I want to know what that means."

"Horny details," Rhys sighed.

I wound up on my back again, this time stretched out on the Emperor's legs with my back feet planted against his stomach. "You can still change your mind," he said, careful to keep his fingers off my bare skin. "I am not entitled—"

Put your hand on me, bro.

He set his hand on my skin and closed his eyes, listening for something, anything, and he ignored Rhys and Hyrum's snickers. I felt my breathing settle into a slow cadence and closed my eyes, too. There was something, a sliver stirring deep in my brain, one that became bigger, teasing, and with the flash of a bright light, a door opened and every memory I had access to jumped up, split in two, and half ran into the light.

He already had the memories given to him by Rhys's father just before his 20th birthday; he wanted the things I knew that happened after. I let him know he was free to explore and witness anything in my mind, but he carefully avoided things between others that were clearly private. Anything I saw behind Jax and Aubrey's closed doors, he turned away from. He rejoiced at my memories of the royal offspring, but gave their adult relationships the same respect.

I felt him hesitate at the memory of pulling a tiny and lifeless Oz from the water at Fisherman's wharf, and equally felt his determination and resolve to change the outcome of her adventure to Sausalito. He imagined his own grief at losing her and the joy of reclaiming her, and amusement at her quest to find cupcakes. He paused equally at the memory of entering the safe house with Drew, finding Zed out cold on the floor, Oz gone.

He became overwhelmed at the idea of Oz being taken under his watch, and under his feet he felt the steps taken as he walked across Colorado to Kansas with Drew and Zed. He saw the moment he admitted to Drew who they were to each other; he rejoiced at the sight of a battered and broken Oz struggling to her feet, just so she could punch Levi Munson right in the throat.

He bubbled with joy over the memory of Aisha arriving at his 43rd birthday party, amused at his own anxiety when she approached him. He hung on the moment of his first kiss, standing in the center of the dance floor with her. I felt his near ecstasy when she dropped to one knee to propose to him, the pressure of when we discovered St. Francis, fighting to help free the residents from Tobias's grasp.

It didn't escape me that he was not terribly upset about being stuck in the portal; instead, he found himself awash in warmth as he felt me climbing his body. In a flash, he heard me relate the story of Us while we waited for Oz to reach in and grab him, and he felt his own overwhelming relief at the realization that while we were stuck, his father went home, and saved the world using Drew's suggestions.

He ran through as much of what I had to show him as he could. When he'd seen the highlights, he turned back and focused on Aisha. I made sure he saw the laughter, the way she looked at him, heard how gentle they were with one another when the lights were out and all they wanted was to talk. He felt the bemused pain of her attempts to cook for her family; he felt the pat of little hands on his legs, tiny voices calling out, "Daddy, daddy."

Almost as an afterthought, I took him to San Francisco in 1906, where a tiny me had fallen from null space. I called myself Seven then, and I had no idea how I was there or why, but he had cheese and I wanted it desperately. I broke his heart when I made him leave me behind, reasoning that the sixty years I fended for myself needed to happen; he was elated when I snuck through a portal later, dragging Lux with me, to arrive moments he and I had left. I brought Seven home, because there was no reason to put him through the nightmare of my early life.

It took an hour, but he took everything I had to give him.

When he took his hands off me, I felt drained and he was quiet. After a beat, I flipped over and sat on his lap; his eyes were filled with tears, and while he looked at me, he didn't quite see me.

It's not fixed, Will. Everything bad, you can change or avoid. You can stop Levi's assault on Chicago, which means Oz won't be taken from the safe house. She won't be brutalized. And you should stop that because it was never supposed to happen. Hyrum will never have to walk across Midlam on his own. You can rescue him now. He's already been through too much, things you can't undo, but you can save him from more.

Quietly, Will spoke to no one in particular, filling in some of the details. Hyrum stood nearby, crying softly; Aisha stood behind him with her arms wrapped around his shoulders, nuzzling the top of his head. Rhys sat in a chair opposite the sofa, quiet. George listened as Will explained what he could, his eyes flicking in Hyrum's direction every few seconds.

"Are you all right?" he finally asked Hyrum.

"Everything was my daddy's fault," he whimpered. "Maybe not Aisha being mad, but lots of the other things. He ruined everything. All the time."

"He can't hurt you now," Rhys said. "He's been gone longer than I've been alive."

Hyrum nodded. "He was killed."

"I know he was in prison when it happened. I just don't know how."

Will knew what I'd shown him: after Levi's trial, he was held in a Kansas prison while awaiting transportation to a Canadian Lockdown. He was found one morning hanging by his ankles, sliced up from pubic bone to his jaw, his blood a massive pool on the floor. The presumption—because he'd been their puppet—was assassination by Russian operatives to cover the connection between Florida and Russia, and it was left at that.

Hyrum sniffed and wiped the tears off his face. "But that's not true. It wasn't Russians."

"Who else could it have been?" Rhys asked. "I mean, it makes sense."

"It was David. He said so."

David Munson, Hyrum's slightly older brother, lingered in a Royal Guard holding center for five years before the declaration of his death, for the crime of trying to blast Red Munson's shuttle out of the sky. He'd never exactly admitted it, but when offered release and probation by the King, he declined and asked Jax to keep him right where he was.

"He asked to stay in jail," Rhys said.

"On account of he paid someone to sneak into the prison and kill our daddy," Hyrum said. "David said he should stay in jail because that's a big, big sin and he deserves it. But he also said there are people who are still mad that Daddy is dead and they kinda think he did it, so if he got to go home, they'd kill him, too. Or his family."

"Why?" Rhys was incredulous. "What was the point?"

"David did it on account of what Daddy did to Oz. When he found out he got super mad, Rhys. Red says he's mad at himself on account of he didn't understand what Daddy did to Aubrey and me and maybe our sisters, too, but when he found out that Daddy tried to do bad things to Oz, too, he decided he'd rather go to Hell than let Daddy live anymore."

Aisha was still holding him. Her voice was very soft as she asked, "What did he do, Hyrum?"

"He punished me. Like he punished Aubrey and our sisters. He was going to punish Elle, too, and she was just a little girl and I got really, really mad and set his hair on fire. Then he never did anything to my sisters, just to me. But that was okay if he left them alone."

"No, dude," Rhys said, "it was not okay."

"Mom said, 'there's a price to pay for everything, Hyrum.' That was my price for setting his hair on fire. But she said it about getting in trouble for stealing cookies so maybe I got it wrong. I said it to myself when he threw me out the window, though."

Aisha let go and moved to where she could see him. Her eyes were red, and she was angry again. "He threw you out a window?"

"A few times," he admitted. "But there was a thingy across the patio and it caught me. I don't remember what it's called. It's supposed to give you shade when you sit outside."

She reached for his face, cupping it in her hands. "Sweety, if that man were right here, right now, I would kill him for you. And I would enjoy it."

George cleared his throat. "No, you wouldn't. Trust me, that sticks with you."

She turned to him, confused. He shrugged and gestured to Will. "Ask him. That's what he saw in my head and why he scared the absolute fuck out of me when we were little. He saw the memory of me killing my sister."

"What the hell?" she sputtered. Will just looked confused.

"I know your sister," Rhys said. "I've known her my whole life. She was even my personal guard for a while, until we got so close that she had to stop."

George shook his head. "Not my sister. Not possible."

"I know her, too," Hyrum said. "She's Vicat. But I call her Cat Lady on account of...cat."

"Her name was Ja—"

Rhys held up his hand to stop him. "Call her by her real name and she will hurt you. She goes by Vicat."

"And I have no memory of her death," Will said. "She slipped in the bathtub and hit her head, but you were nowhere near her."

It was a messed-up story, and George listened carefully while I filled in the gaps. He'd teased his two-year-old sister as she took a bath, from across the room. She stood, slipped, and hit her head on the tub's edge; after she was taken out on a stretcher, he never saw her again.

His parents told him she was dead; they blamed him.

They left her at the hospital, presuming she would die. When she didn't, when time spent in a surgical tank repaired her injuries, they ignored the calls to come get her. She wound up in her aunt's care, raised with foster children, told that she had been given up because her brother was violent.

You reunited when Will dragged her to their birth When. I mean, she didn't want to, but Will was the Emperor so she had to follow his orders. Now you're pretty tight, and she's a good aunt to Isaac. Your son, not your brother.

He looked like I'd punched him in the face and then taken all his cookies.

"All these years," he murmured. "Emperor, I tried to kill you. I was terrified that you would spill my worst secret. I got you into that body bag and taped it shut, and then pushed you into the pool..."

"I remember."

"If not for Kathleen Rosey...God, I hated her for getting the teacher, then having to stand there and watch her rescue your sorry ass. And I might have tried it again, but you left school—and for what? I thought you had a horrific secret to hold over me, when in truth the real monsters were at home."

"He tried to KILL you?" Aisha blurted.

"Tried to." Will shrugged it off. "He was clearly unsuccessful. We were seven years old, so a grudge is not necessary. And I believe I turned the tables later, in the dojang." He looked at George. "You ran from the dojo, crying, too afraid to spar with me. And while it amused me and I admit, I have cherished that memory, I always wondered why you never returned. You were talented. More than most, I think."

George found another school to train him in marital arts, and began competing. I knew from our George that he became quite proficient and had competed at the international level, but before I could say anything Aisha stopped him.

"What the hell. How is it possible that I know two people from the future and they're both important in my life? And wait—is that why you're so protective of Jaime? Because of your sister?"

He nodded.

Will squinted, trying to access that part of the memories I'd given him. He saw George on Union Square, antique gun in one hand, Jay's wrist held tight in the other. "There's no point in getting in Jaime's way," he said. "If what Rhys says is true, I'll be able to find Brian Massimo and take him forward to get the care he needs."

Rhys bounced in his chair, grabbing for his phone. He pulled up a photo of Jay with Navi and their new baby, holding it where they could see. "He's, like, eighteen years older than I am, but he's a really good big brother and I know he's going to be an amazing dad."

"Rhys," Hyrum hissed.

"Screw it. I want them to see what can happen. This is what can happen. The Emperor takes him forward, and he gets the life he already knows he wants. I don't care if he's just four years old right now. He knows who he is."

She took the phone from him, gazing at the picture. "How is this even possible? Fatherhood, I mean. Did they—?"

"I was not privy to the details of conception," Rhys said. "I assume it was the usual way."

"Surgery two hundred years from now assures he will be one hundred percent biologically male," Will said. "That includes fertility."

A look of defiance crossed her face when she handed the phone back to Rhys. "I'm taking that as a promise. No matter how pissed off I am, whether I get over it or not, it's a promise."

I jumped to the coffee table and sat in front of George, counting on Rhys to translate.

Your job now is not just to stay out of their way, but to not pull all the crap our George did. No forcing your way into getting third parent status unless James and Aisha ask that of you. No forcing Jay into dresses for staged photos. No sarcastic corrections of the pronouns you want. I know you thought you were getting a daughter when you married James, but that was never his to offer. There's no point in waiting until you reach the same point our George has, not when Jay can feel like himself before puberty.

He had no objections; until now those were rooted in the permanence of the procedures Jay would be required to endure in their own When. "Take him forward to get it done, and if he changes his mind in a few years, it can be undone."

"Does that ever happen?" she asked.

"Rarely," Will answered. "In any When, it's rare."

"But it does happen."

"Does it matter?" Rhys asked. "This is your kid, and this is his mental and physical well-being. If he knows you've got his back, he'll be all the better for it."

Hyrum was confused. "Jay used to be a girl? Does Jesus know? How does that even work?"

"I'm pretty sure Jesus is okay with it, Hy. God gave surgeons talent and brains for a reason. I'll explain the rest later." He got up, reaching for the jump device. "I'm going to set up in the tunnel next to storage. Whenever you're ready."

Hyrum and Will followed him.

"You want me to stay out of your way?" George said to Aisha as he got up. "Stop fucking my husband."

26

"Well, that could have gone better." Rhys helped George remove the jump device, sighing when the last strap was undone. "But you didn't die, so."

"You didn't warn me I'd wind up naked."

"I swear, I didn't know."

I knew there was something missing from that code. You have to account for layers. Will had to do that after seeing both of his parents literally run around the Wastelands without clothes when they helped test the first bracelet.

Will was unbothered by George's nudity, but Aisha was amused and George noticed. As he pulled his pants back on, he asked, "All right, straight woman. If I leaned that way, would I be...acceptable?"

"If I knew nothing about you other than what I just saw? I'd hit it."

"Oh my god," Rhys groaned.

Hyrum was equally horrified, but for other reasons. "You'd hit it? Why would you hit it? It hurts when someone hits your wiener, Aisha. It hurts a lot."

"That's not—"

"She means sex, Hy." Rhys headed for the door. "She thinks she'd have sex with him, under other circumstances."

"Oh. Ew."

I think she wanted to defend herself, and George was laughing out loud at the both the idea of her saying she'd nail him and Rhys's revulsion, but Will stepped between them and suggested they all go to bed. *We could get a fresh start in the morning, after coffee and reconstituted donuts.*

"Seriously? Reconstituted? Is that even a thing?"

"It sounded funny in my brain. Go to bed."

You're not sleeping tonight, are you? You're going to stay up to stick that clothing code in.

"I am. I'll also look for any errors that might account for the limited range in which George was able to jump."

It might not be an error in the code. Could be user error. If he hit the command to jump three feet further to the left, he would have wound up embedded in the wall if not for the safety protocols.

"Did your Emperor have limitation issues in his initial testing?"

No. He just needed eye bleach after his parents started playing with it.

"Understandable." He sat on the sofa and pulled one of the computers onto his lap. "You should get some sleep, too, Wick. As much as I would enjoy your company, rest is your better option tonight."

I almost said no; he'd gone so long without his own Wick remembering him that I wanted to stay awake and talk to him, to remind him that it was temporary.

But then I realized Aisha would sleep, and I had things to say to her.

~

I can't put my paw on someone and hear their thoughts the way the Emperor can; trust me, I've tried. The closest I can come is trying when he's also touching them, speaking silently. Then, I can hear and make myself heard. But when they're asleep, just entering a dream, I can snuggle close, place a paw on their head, and slip in. We discovered this when Will was a small boy, on a rare night of relaxed slumber. It was an accident; I'd cuddled next to him, curled up on his pillow, and found myself immersed in the nightmare of his childhood.

I visited his dreams often, because it was often the only way he could express his crushing loneliness and frustration about being the odd boy out. He swallowed his pain whole; I learned to sit back and witness as he worked through the trauma of his day. I learned when to speak up and when to be silent. Eventually, I learned how to direct him to a spot inside his own head, where we could sit and talk.

As an adult, he always found me near a bench at Crissy Field, where we had a panoramic view of the Golden Gate Bridge. Usually he waited there for me, feeling my paw pressing against his forehead, but often I nudged him to it. It was that spot I nudged Aisha to, and waited on the ground in front of the bench until she realized where she was.

At first, she didn't see me. She was taken in by the twilight view and how the bay practically glowed as the sun set, keenly aware of how loud the silence was. There were no other people there; it was just her, staring out at the water, and me, waiting near her feet.

Hey. Down here.

She twitched and finally looked down. "Wick?"

I'll leave if this is creepy. I should have asked for consent first, but I didn't want Will to know I was going to try this.

"No, don't leave. How? How are you doing this?"

Kind of the same way Will can listen. I'm limited to slipping into your dreams, but it's a way we can talk, if you want. You'll hear a lot of meowing but the words should also slip through.

She patted her lap, inviting me up. "Of course I want to. I admit, I've been a little jealous of how you carry on conversations with the boys. The moment I admitted to myself they really were speaking with you, I wanted this."

I hope you still will after this.

"Why wouldn't I?"

Because I want permission to show him the aftermath. I want him to see what happened when he left you behind on Union Square. And I want to show you his aftermath, what I saw when he got home.

"How can you show him, Wick? You weren't there."

I stood on her legs and touched her face, giving her a glimpse of that day on the Square. Will, Jay, and I sat on a planter off to the side, watching; Jay had been grappling with a hiccup in his relationship with Navi and thought seeing it would somehow help, and Will was there because of him.

We didn't intentionally spy on you. Well, Will and I didn't. Jay was totally on board with invading your privacy.

"I was one hot mess, wasn't I?"

He was glad that your friend was there to help you. That was one thing he hadn't considered. The fallout. I think he knew you'd be mad, but not...destroyed.

"And why do you want me to see him after that? What would it matter?"

Because he was broken, too. He was never quite the same after that.

"Then maybe he shouldn't have done it."

He should have. And he would do it again. He would do it knowing that you might never forgive him, because no matter what a previous Emperor says, there's always the chance that you'd rather he choked on his own spit than speak to him again.

"Because of my son."

The potential of your son. Knowing that if you didn't go off and have him, there might never be even a chance for Rhys, much less Alex and Charlie. Knowing that you were both so young, the odds were not with you, but age might change that. And knowing what Jay would become.

"He knows what my son will become."

In an abstract sort of way. He knows the world needs Jay.

"Why? What does he do?"

Again, I only showed her a flash. It was enough for her to get the idea: Jay's work, hanging in the Museum of Modern Art—both in San Francisco and New York.

In our When, right now, his career is gaining traction. He's earned a global reputation. The world needs gentle art, Aisha. And his is glowing with gentleness. People are comforted by the things he paints, and he makes them laugh and cry, sometimes at the same time.

Do you want to see what Will did after he left you?

I couldn't show her how he ran. He'd taken off on foot, running until he couldn't anymore, but I was able to show her how he broke down in the shower after. He curled up on the shower floor, crying so hard he nearly threw up, staying there until the water ran cold and he was shivering. When he was able to drag himself up, he went to bed and stayed there for days.

There was nothing I could do but bear witness.

"Fine, he felt bad. So?"

All right. Maybe you need to see something else.

Before she could protest, she was at his 43rd birthday party, looking at life through my eyes. She heard the words, saw the first dance and their first kiss; in a blink she watched herself give birth to Rhys, and saw Will's tears. They slow danced in the living room with a toddler clinging to his legs, and each held a baby on a hip. Will, up all night with sick kids, cleaning up after them, urging her to go back to bed because it didn't make sense for her to be up when he wasn't going to sleep anyway.

I let her see Will in the safe house with Oz and Drew, and later when we found her in Chicago. She saw the agony on his face as he stood there to witness the exam after. The moment Will admitted to Drew who they were to each other. How he took care of the royal offspring, guarding them even after they were too old to touch.

I fed her as many things as I could, as quickly as I could. I wanted her to see the man he was and could become, not the teenager she was still angry with.

But last, I left her see the look on his face as he approached her on Union Square. He was overjoyed at the sight of her. There was no mistaking that; the young Emperor radiated and it was clearly aimed right at her.

For the first time, she really saw his face. As she spilled the things she'd been contemplating, her promises to be patient and wait until he was able to reach out and truly be with her, there was a clear point when the realities punched him right in the face. His joy slipped away and became confusion, anger, sorrow, and then acceptance. She saw the moment when he realized he had to walk away from her, possibly forever.

Still, there was longing in his eyes. I needed her to see that.

He loved you. He still does.

"And he thought he was going to die," she whispered.

It was certainly a possibility. He knew the Emperor before him had lived, but my Will? He met his Aisha with the absolute certainty that he wouldn't live to see forty-three. He was just not willing to subject her to that loss.

"I understand it, Wick, I really do. But that doesn't change the fact that he should have trusted me. I was owed the truth, as much of it as he could have admitted. And maybe that's the issue. He didn't trust me and I'm not sure I can believe that he does now."

That's fair.

I just wanted you to see. And to talk to you. I never get to do that, just talk to other people.

"You could sneak into their dreams, too."

I do, sometimes, but usually quietly and only if I think they need something.

"And what did I need, Wick?"

This was about what I needed. Once in a while, a guy has to be a little selfish.

"Somehow I think you're the opposite of selfish."

You haven't seen me around steak and shrimp. But I hope you will, someday. Even if it takes until his forty-third birthday.

27

At 5 a.m., I found Will sitting on a weight bench in the gym, a heavy metal plate clutched to his chest. Surprisingly, he was shirtless, and I watched from the doorway, catching glimpses of the tattoos my Emperor had removed just prior to his wedding. I hadn't forgotten about them, but it had been so long that they no longer looked right.

I heard her creep up behind me, and meowed a hello. I didn't want her to worry about startling me, but more than that, I wanted Will to know she was there. Scaring me just meant turning me into a temporary ball of floof; scaring him meant he could lose his grip on that plate and send it slamming into his chin.

He was useless to us with a fifty-pound weight embedded in his head.

He stopped halfway through a crunch and quickly sat up, setting the weight aside. "My apologies. I assumed I could do this quietly and not wake anyone."

She waved it off. "You're quiet. My brain is not. I just couldn't sleep."

"I'm sorry. I know how frustrating that is."

"I know." She gestured for him to scoot over, and sat next to him on the bench. "Look, I know you heard what George said to me before we went into the tunnel."

"It's none of my business."

"Still. You must think I'm horrible."

"Aisha. You're single. You have the right to be with whomever you choose."

"He's *married*, Will."

He nodded. "And that is his problem, and his infidelity. Given your history and the child you have together, it's also understandable. I imagine there must be some comfort in that sort of close relationship."

"It's still wrong. I know he's married, which makes me just as complicit. I mean, it's over, but still."

He waited a beat. "Do you want me to be offended or upset about it?"

She waited another. "Honestly, I don't know. Maybe?"

"That day," he said, carefully. "Because of Rhys's father, I knew that you would leave and eventually meet James and fall in love. I knew you would have a child with him. Until I was standing there right in front of you, a large part of me refused to honor that, despite an equal certainty that I wanted it for you. It was a life I could not give you, and in time…you would resent that. But more importantly, I wanted you to have that relationship and everything it implied. So no, I will not judge you for having feelings for the father of your son, even if the marriage did not work."

"I told you that I would wait as long as it took, but I knew it would happen. We would have a family one day. That's what did it, right? You went through with it because you knew I desperately wanted at least one child."

He nodded. "I could have been less abrupt. Less harsh."

She began to cry, softly. "But then I just couldn't shut up. I broke your heart before you broke mine, didn't I?"

"I broke my own heart, Aisha. The comfort came in knowing that in time, the world would have your son. Comfort came in understanding that Jay brings immeasurable joy to that Emperor's life, and is no less his son than Rhys. There was also this niggling fragment bubbling in the back of my brain, his suggestion that the world *needed* this child. I don't know why, but I trusted the information. I could not—would not—deprive you of the joy of being his mother, nor whatever it is he will gift the world."

Uh. I showed her why. My bad.

"All of it?" he asked.

Jay's artistic talent. A glimpse of his successes.

"And the rest? Do I know all of it now?"

I think so. George going off the rails? Trying to kidnap Jay, almost shooting you? She tackled his asterisk through a portal and took him home where he almost died but then didn't and went on to insert himself into the whole Cult of the Emperor thing, resulting in Isaac? Between my Will and my memories, I think you have it all.

He sighed, and after a moment of consideration, held his hand out to her in silent invitation.

"George," she breathed out when Will was done. "How could he be that cruel? I know he can be hard around the edges, but he loves Jaime. I've never doubted that."

Jay understands him. Or did. He realized that George is always afraid. He's afraid of living and he's afraid of the guilt that consumed him for all the years he thought he'd killed his sister. He felt like an imposter in his own life. Your George seems different, closer to how ours is now.

"Our future cannot be the same," Will mused.

You know too much. But this is a new timeline, so I doubt it matters. Except to Rhys.

"But why?" she asked. "What happens here has no bearing on him, not after he gets home."

He wants to exist.

I get that, you know. I don't like the idea that there are other Whens coming up behind us, and after the next one, I probably won't be born. It's one thing if you don't know about the layers of time. But when you do, you hate the idea of missing any of them.

"A When without Wick?" Will asked. "No, I don't like that notion, either."

It gets worse. Eventually, there will come a When in which the whole save-the-world thing is settled before you're even born, because Finn will get everything he needs from the Old Mint, and he'll have the gates built before they're needed. He might not even get around to the time machine or the tunnel. You two will never meet in that When.

Aisha's voice cracked. "Never?"

Sucks to think about, doesn't it?

"I suggest we don't," Will said, getting up. "Let's focus on the issue at hand. Getting Hyrum and Rhys home...and I hear him in the living room, approaching."

Aisha brushed tears from her face, but not before Rhys bounded in. If he noticed she was crying, he didn't say anything, instead drawn to Will's shirtless torso.

"Holy hell! I knew you'd had tattoos but I've never seen them. This is awesome!"

"You've never seen them?"

Rhys stepped closer, unashamedly inspecting the large tattoo that covered the Emperor's chest and stomach. "Yeah, no. Not even pictures. Dad had them removed before I was born."

"Why?"

Rhys shrugged. "Mom didn't like them. And Grandma made him get rid of the portraits. I dunno why."

Because of your mom. Jo said that no one wants to see their in-laws while they're getting busy.

Oh, look at that. This Emperor blushes.

"Cat, I will shave the rest of you."

Rhys snorted. "Leave each other alone. I had an idea. I think I know how to fix the jump device. It means taking apart one of the main system computers, but we need the faster processor and larger power source. It'll also mean having less of a bracelet and more of a computer strapped on, but then we can all jump together as long as we're touching."

That meant losing either communications or security; between the two Will preferred to lose communications. "I cannot give that permission without consent of the King," he said. "If we cut either, the royal guard will descend on this house, calling attention to our presence."

Rhys shrugged. "So wake the old man up, and ask."

~

"Take everything apart, if necessary," Eli said. "You still have a phone with a direct connection to my desk. That's your communications. If you need the second system, then sacrifice security and head for my office."

"San Francisco is probably the first place they're looking for us," Rhys said.

"Son, if those guardians can pick out the needle that is you in the haystack of Pacifica, here or there doesn't matter. The royal house is as safe as it gets, and if there's any question, we'll hide you in the war room."

That piqued Rhys's interest. "There's a war room? Where?"

Will placed a hand on his shoulder. "Not unless and until it's necessary."

When the screen blinked and went dark, George reached over and yanked on Rhys's hair, causing him to yelp. "It's going in the car, kid. If they're using DNA sniffers, we want something to throw them off a bit. I'll set the auto controls and send it home. Maybe they'll follow."

"Nuh." Hyrum shook his head. "What if Aisha's baby comes home early and they scare him? No, you gotta send it to San Francisco, on account of they'll find it there and see there's nothing in it, and think that you sent it on purpose and that we went someplace else."

"You could send it somewhere different," Rhys suggested. "Hell, Florida. Park it in the Munson's driveway."

"But I'm there!" Hyrum blurted. "Young me!"

"I don't think they'd hurt you, Hy."

"But I might hurt *them*, and I don't want to hurt anyone."

"Okay, okay. It doesn't have to be Florida. It can be anywhere. Send it to Canada."

"I'd like to get my car back at some point," George said.

Will told him to send the car to San Francisco, parked along the street in front of the royal house. "Hide it in plain sight. If nothing else, it will give the guards a clear line of sight to the guardians."

George nodded. "Rhys, don't start destroying those computers until I get back. I can transfer the security protocols to our tablets. At least then we'll still have full control and eyes on the outside."

"How do you even know how to do that?"

He gave a half shrug. "I wrote the programs for that system. I know all the backdoors. It won't take long to clone it, then you can destroy the whole thing to your heart's content."

Hyrum bounced on his toes. "Can we do sparky things and melt it?" He snapped his fingers, causing sparks to fly. "It might go *whoosh*. Or *boom*. That would be funny."

He knew there would be no melting of the computers or the monitors, but the idea amused him. Instead, Rhys handed him a screw driver and told him he could help take the back panels off the casing around the power sources, but to be careful he didn't touch the wires inside.

"Why? On account of it'll shock me? That won't hurt."

"Because you might inadvertently redirect electricity and blow up my future parents, and then we'd all feel bad."

"Maybe you would." He pretended to consider it, still amused. "I don't think they would blow up. They'd just get cooked. Would that smell like barbeque? I bet it smells like barbeque."

"Ugh. Dude."

"Let's not test it, all right?" Aisha said.

"Okay." Hyrum snorted. "I already know what cooking people smells like, anyway. Sometimes when I work at Alcatraz the cremating thing is on. It usually stinks but for a few minutes in the middle, it smells like meat. And then you hear a *squeeee* noise, and then a clunk and water, and you go open the machine and there's a shiny stone."

Aisha was grossed out, but Will was intrigued. "There should be no extruding aroma."

"The equipment is old," Rhys said. "Some of the seals aren't the best. Also…he's teasing."

It took George only a few minutes to clone the security programming, and then they went to work. While Rhys and Hyrum pulled everything apart, Aisha worked on the math, accounting for the increased power going into the bigger processing unit. George showed Will how to use his tablet to monitor security, and I stood on the kitchen table, watching and waiting, because there was nothing else for me to do.

~

We went back to the tunnel to test the improved device. Will had tested the additions to the code he'd made while everyone else slept and he had no reservations about letting Rhys strap it on—the pocket-sized power source hung from his belt, the keyboard was strapped to his forearm, and the sensors affixed to his wrist with the salvaged printer cable—and we watched quietly while he jumped to different points in the tunnel. Hyrum giggled under his breath when Rhys jumped to a spot near the door and then tripped over one of the go-bags Will had insisted on placing in various spots around the house, but he otherwise didn't make a sound.

I admit, I would have laughed, too, if I could laugh.

He wasn't hurt. It was funny.

He went all the way to the far end of the tunnel, over four miles, and back, and then specific distances between. He was confident he could get anywhere he had a map for, but when he attempted to jump outside, nothing happened. There was no hum, no waver in his appearance; he remained in place.

"I don't get it. I should be able to get through the walls."

"Perhaps your transponder senses natural rock where you're attempting to materialize."

"It should just move me a little to the left or right. There's something else." He squinted, looking overhead, and I knew that look. He'd engaged his synesthesia, searching for the visible proof of a sound he wasn't aware he could hear. "Security net jacked up a notch."

In tandem, Will and George flipped their tablets over. With a swipe of his fingers across the screen, Will closed the tunnel door, and additional floor lights turned on. They both stood silently, staring at their screens, until George pointed to a spot on his and whispered, "Here."

Just as quietly, Will said, "They're in the cabin, moving toward the pantry."

"Pantry," Aisha said.

"They know where the entry to the safe house is, then.

Everyone grab a bag, and start toward the center of the tunnel, third access hatch. The ladder is painted yellow."

"We're running," Rhys said.

"If necessary." He kept his eyes on the screen as we walked, watching as they pried the locked panel from the back of the pantry. When it was open, he switched the camera view to the central area of the safe house, where the stored staircase began unfolding from the wall.

We stopped near the ladder, huddled around Will and George, watching as three men in the same metallic-piped blue clothing as before made their way in. They searched the kitchen and the dorm, walked the perimeter looking for other doors, and then gathered in the living room.

"Same guys as before," Rhys whispered. "They brought help. That new one doesn't look confused the way they were. He's definitely in charge."

"We need to leave," Will said.

That's when Hyrum let out a tiny whine. He was barefoot, and knew it was cold outside.

"Ramp up the heat a little," Rhys said. "I will, too, once we're outside. We can keep everyone warm." He pointed at George and told him to go first, then Aisha, and then Will.

"I will not leave you in this tunnel alone" Will insisted.

"No choice. Those rungs are metal, and if Hyrum is going to turn on the juice to get warm, they'll be too hot for any of you to touch. I'll send him up before me. I can take the heat without getting hurt."

You can be burned.

"Not likely if I ramp up some juice, too."

Will did not argue; no one wanted to leave Hyrum in the tunnel alone. They climbed the ladder and slipped outside. Will reached down to take me from Rhys, and then crouched near the hatch as Hyrum climbed out, and then Rhys. Will took their bags as they rose from the darkness, slinging both over his shoulder, and he took George's bag while he fumbled with his tablet.

Anyone else would have dropped them. Will had four bags slung over his shoulders, and he didn't bat an eye.

Steam rose from the ground around Hyrum's feet, but he said he wasn't cold and we should just do what we needed to do. Rhys fumbled with the keyboard, tapping coordinates to King Eli's office, but before he finished, the air around us crackled. Rhys stopped typing, and before us stood the guardian he'd decided was the boss.

Boss dude was annoyed.

"Rhys." He sounded exasperated. "Please. You just need—"

"Fuck that." He thrust his hands out, fingers flicking from his palms, and I felt the bubble swell around us. "Take that, time cop."

He wanted time to finish tapping the coordinates in. The bubble was supposed to give him that. But the guardian looked up, sighed audibly, and then stepped into it.

"You can't use that on me. And I'm not a cop. You—"

I heard the sparks lift from Hyrum's hand before I saw them. He'd worked up a ball of light, and before the guardian could finish his sentence, he threw it. The ball elongated, still connected to his fingers, and he used it to punch the guardian right in the throat.

He flung back, through the bubble, flat on his back, snow skittering in puffs around his feet and calves.

"Hands on me," Rhys barked. Without questioning, they reached toward him, fingers on his skin, and he slammed his thumb onto the keyboard. The bubble collapsed, I blinked, and we were standing in the woods on snow covered ground, twenty miles from only Bast knew where.

28

"It's fine. It's fine. It's fine." Rhys held his arm up to inspect the cables connecting the keyboard to the bracelet, and the cables plugged into the power source. "I just didn't get to input those last few—"

Where's George?

"He let go," Aisha said. "That son of a bitch."

Hyrum began bouncing on his toes. "But they're gonna get him! What are they gonna do to him?"

Rhys's concern was that he hit the keyboard before George could touch him, but Will shook his head. "He specifically did not reach for anyone. He intended to stay behind."

"That son of a bitch," Aisha repeated.

"No. He provided a diversion. They'll need to deal with him before following us. Any residual material we left behind will dissipate before they can lock onto it, if he can capture their attention."

Heat rolled off Hyrum in a wave.

"He's fine, Hy," Rhys said. "They don't want him. Worst case, he'll have to walk back to the cabin above the safe house and wait. He's got food and water there, and a comfortable enough bed. He'll be fine. Once we get to San Francisco, we can ask for someone to go get him."

"Promise?"

With a sigh, he lowered his arm. "I can't promise. But that's what makes sense."

"George is annoyingly resourceful," Aisha said.

He has his tablet, right? That means he still has access to the security alarms.

"Indeed," Will said, "he does. He can call for help. He'll be fine, Hyrum."

"Will we?"

Will gestured to the go bags, which contained everything we needed for several days. There was food, clothing, shelter, and water. None of it would likely fit Hyrum, though.

He could keep himself warm for a short time, but I had followed him across the country during winter, and knew he needed protection as much as anyone. Then, he'd kept warm at night by heating rocks and placing them in his sleeping bag, but I also recalled the gratitude he'd felt when gifted a warm jacket and thermal underwear by the angel who shadowed him.

Fine, the angel was Drew, but he hadn't known that.

Hyrum needed socks and shoes and a jacket; if he kept using his innate source of heat, the resulting hunger would be insatiable.

The snow was only an inch deep, with patches of dirt around the tree trunks. Fifteen feet behind us, there was a clearing rimmed by carefully split logs, and it felt familiar. It was a neglected campsite, one that hadn't been used in years, and might not have been for another thirteen had we not come upon it.

We're twenty miles from the safe house.

I camped here with Will, Oz, Zed, and Drew once. I'm pretty sure Will and Jax camped here when they were teenagers.

"God, is this the death march campsite?" Rhys groaned. "Emperor, let me tell you something. Teenagers don't need to slap heavy backpacks on and then trudge through the woods for twenty miles. And we *really* don't need to walk back the next morning. Just...remember that."

Will wasn't looking at him; he was fixated on a spot far ahead of us. "All that fresh air is good for you. And we should head off in that direction. There's a shelter roughly half a mile up. You'll be able to recharge the power supply for the jump device."

"Motorcycles?" Rhys asked. "I know you have a bunch around here."

He nodded. "There are four stored there, but don't get excited. There's no fuel on site."

"You could convert those to electric, you know."

"Or we could stand here and freeze to death," Aisha said. "Argue about the toys later."

Will took the lead and we followed. Hyrum leaned toward Rhys and whispered, "Well, she sounds like your mom, anyway."

"All moms sound the same. Clean your room. Stop picking on your brother. Oh my god don't eat that, it came out of your nose. Jesus H. Christ, leave that diaper on!"

"I can hear you," she called out. She spun in her heels, walking backward. "I say that a lot, Jesus H. Christ. Ever wonder what the H stands for?"

Rhys shrugged, but Hyrum blurted, "Hucking!"

"Hucking."

"That's what Joe said and Joe doesn't lie to me."

"Well, then. All right." She turned back around and jogged a few steps to catch up to Will, who had picked up speed.

Hyrum wasn't done. "He's my little brother but he's way bigger than me. Everyone is way bigger than me. My niece, Bree, is as big as you."

"Tall," Rhys corrected.

"Big. Tall. Same difference."

"Hon," Aisha said, "if you tell a woman she's big, you're going to hurt her feelings."

"Why?"

"She'll think you mean fat," Rhys explained.

"What's wrong with fat?"

"Nothing, but..." Aisha trailed off, looking up at the mountain ahead. "Tell me we're not walking up that thing."

"We are not," Will said. "We're going inside of it. There's heat and water, and a power supply sufficient to recharge phones and the like."

"Socks and shoes, I hope," Hyrum grumbled.

Will doubted there were any clothing items on site. At best, there were a few blankets. For the most part the shelter was stocked with tools and electrical equipment, but it was secure and there were hidden cameras where we could get a view of anything outside.

"What about the safe house?" Rhys asked. "Can we get a peek there? See if George is still there?"

"If he's made his way back into the house, yes. I wouldn't count on that, though."

"You think they took him?" It was not really a question.

"I think he needs more time to get there. However, it's possible."

Rhys was less certain. After all, the guardians were looking for him, not George. There was no reason to hold him because he hadn't done anything wrong.

"Harboring a fugitive?" Aisha guessed. "How do time laws work? Surely, we're in some deep shit here."

That was the issue; there were no laws regarding time travel. As far as anyone in this or our home When knew, it didn't exist. There was no reason to legislate something people regarded as a trick of fiction.

"Even in my birth When," Will said, "there are no laws forbidding it. For us, it's a tool, it was a way to save as many lives as possible."

"But eventually it will become regulated," Aisha said. "Those men are proof. If they've enacted laws against it, they'll use it to find people and hold them accountable to rules they aren't even aware of."

"By that logic, they would have wanted me, as well," Will said. "And George. We are Other When, and don't belong here."

"Other When," Rhys snickered.

"Who started the whole 'When' thing?" Aisha asked. "Why not just say 'from another timeline?'"

"Because we are within the same timeline, with Rhys and Hyrum being the exception. We don't move from one place to another, we navigate within one small period of time. Not someplace, but somewhen."

"Grandpa just wanted to sound cool." Rhys trotted ahead of them. We'd arrived at the base of the mountain that rose from the ground in a steep, rocky slope, and he stood nearly toe-to-wall with it. "I've never been in here. I know there's an access plate. Where is it?"

Will reached past him, running his fingers over rough rock, and when he found the right spot, he pressed hard. A small piece popped open, revealing a number pad behind it. "The code is the Queen's name, converted to digits."

Rhys tapped out DONNA, using the old alpha-numeric keypad method. There was a quiet hum, creaking, and then doorway slid open, revealing a darkened entry.

"Turn on the lights," Hyrum hissed.

He refused to step inside.

"Hyrum, there's nothing past this door that can harm you. The lights will come on when the door closes behind us."

He shook his head. "No."

"You're not afraid of the dark," Rhys said.

"I am of *that* dark."

Do sparky things. Make your own light.

"Oh. Yeah. I can do that." He held his hands out, palms up, and let tendrils of light seep upward. He formed a fist-sized ball that hovered over his palm, and satisfied that he'd be able to see, told them that we could go in.

It wasn't bright enough to light up the room, but it eased his fears. And then as promised, when the door slid closed, the lights came on.

Compared to the safe house, this was grim. Dark gray walls lined with dust-covered work tables felt closed in. To the left of where we stood was a heavy, industrial cage where the motorcycles were stored, and to the right was a door leading into a small storage room. While Rhys explored, looking for blankets or anything else they could use, Will searched for the climate controls.

A minute later, heat blew from floor level vents, and within five, Aisha stopped shivering.

The air smelled like old, cooked dust and industrial rubber. I hoped we wouldn't stay long.

"No clothes," Rhys reported when he came out of the storage room. "There are a couple of old blankets, but they smell worse than they look. I wouldn't use them."

Aisha offered to rub Hyrum's feet for warmth, but he shook his head. "I'm not cold. I just don't like walking around without shoes on account of rocks and sticks hurt. This is okay."

"Just don't try to heat the floor, Hy," Rhys said. "It might not be rated for high temps and can crack. And then the rock surrounding the place…"

"You can do that?" Aisha asked. "Heat things around you?"

"I can make them asplody, if I get it hot enough. Sometimes Rhys and I go down into the lab where his daddy built this special room with really thick windows, and I can let all the sparky things out. It gets really, really hot in there. And I glow."

"You glow."

There were no chairs, so they sat on the floor in a circle. Will played with his tablet, searching for an outside signal; while they dug into their go bags for shoes, Hyrum and Rhys explained the underground playground Will had once constructed to test Hyrum's gifts. He did more than glow; from where we watched on the other side of the glass, it looked as if he were about to go nuclear.

"They wanted to peek at my brain while I did sparky things," he explained. "I said okay because I wanted to see the pictures after. It was really pretty, with lots of red and yellow and even big black spots."

"Image representation," Rhys said. "Your brain is not red and yellow."

"Duh. But I had fun until Drew asked me a lot of questions about kissing things. That just made me mad."

"Kissing things."

"Sex," Rhys said. "And we respect his choice to never do that, all right?"

She understood, and then shifted the attention to him. "And what about you? What choices of yours are we respecting?"

Hyrum snickered. "He wants to do kissing things but he can't find a girlfriend."

"I could if I wanted. I just don't have time for a real social life. Between school and karate and trying to work on the drone… it wouldn't be fair to someone else."

Without looking up, Will said, "Make time. If not for a romantic relationship, then time for close friends. Trust me on this."

"You have friends."

"Now. But when I was your age, my life was studying and karate, and not much else."

"Bullshit," Rhys said. "When you were my age, you were surfing through portals every day, keeping track of Uncle Jax. You had the time. You just chose to use it that way instead of crawling out of your comfort zone and speaking to people."

He considered it. "All right, that's fair. But you understand my point."

"I do. And I have friends. I socialize. Just not…like that. Isaac and Hyrum understand when my nose is buried in books or I'm engrossed in the innards of a drone. They'll help, too. But when I take time to go out and do stuff, they're the ones I'd rather hang with."

In a stage whisper, Hyrum said to Aisha, "He's lying. He wants a girlfriend."

"Or boyfriend?" she mused.

"I've never met another guy that has made me think that's the direction I lean. On the other hand, I've met plenty of girls who do. Not that I wouldn't be open to anything if the time and person were right. You never know."

"Like James?" Hyrum asked. "He likes boys and girls."

"That's an understatement," Aisha snorted. "Sometimes, he even likes them at the same time."

"I don't know what that means," Hyrum said.

Before Aisha could answer, Rhys said, "It means he's had crushes on more than one person at a time, and they've been men and women."

"Oh. Like when Charlie liked Genie and Monica and didn't know who to ask on a date, but instead one is a boy? He shoulda made up his mind on account of they both got boyfriends before he could think about it. But then he decided he liked another girl but she got mad because he wore a skirt to school and it was just like the one she had on but he looked better in it."

Somehow, Aisha followed his train of thought. "Charlie likes skirts?"

"He's fairly fluid," Rhys said. "Heteroflexible, I guess. No questions about gender, but he's also very fluid when it comes to expression. Always has been."

"My mom says Charlie is an angel that Jesus sent to teach her patience about having an open mind." He gave up on finding shoes. "But she also says the same thing about me sometimes."

"That seems...mean."

"Oddly, no," Rhys said. "You'll get to meet her someday. She's totally the victim of growing up while surviving the Church of Florida. Before Hyrum came to San Francisco, she would have had a heart attack trying to deal with someone like Charlie."

Hyrum nodded. "One time, she got super, super mad that I wrote a poem and she thought it was about a boy, but it was just about fog. But now if I said I liked a boy, she'd sigh really loud and then say, 'Well, Hyrum, I hope he's nice to you.' And she doesn't get mad anymore when I wear pink. She used to get *really* mad. So mad that Eli adopted me so I didn't have to put up with her bullshit." His eyes went wide. "I'm sorry. I didn't mean to say that part."

"I think Charlie and Alex softened her quite a bit," Rhys said. "She started visiting more so she could help my sister learn to use her gifts, and she video calls Charlie sometimes with tips from her twin brother."

"She just needed my daddy to die," Hyrum said. "She woulda been nicer without him."

Will finally looked up. "I have a connection to the safe house security cameras. George left a message."

He turned the tablet for everyone to see. There were four panels on the screen showing different spots in the living area; he'd placed a chair on the table, and taped to it was a wrinkled piece of paper with the letters CU@US scrawled across it.

"So he got away," Aisha said. "But what does it mean?"

"See you at Union Square?" Rhys guessed. "What, he's planning on walking? He sent his car away."

"Maybe he called a taxi," Hyrum said.

Will handed the tablet to Rhys, then got up to turn on the monitors wired into security cameras focused on the perimeter of the mountain shelter. "George is resourceful. He'll find a way there."

"Well, then I better get resourceful, too, and make sure I have Grandpa Eli's office on a hot key so I won't fumble next time. Hell. King Eli."

"Stop," Aisha said. "No one is upset when your brain outpaces your tongue. I doubt his Majesty would be any more offended than the Emperor was."

"Maybe," Hyrum said. "He wants to be my daddy but he might want you to go away."

"Damn, dude." Rhys was not offended. "You're mean."

"That's what your mom said."

He thought about it.

"Wait. That didn't work. That's *not* what your mom said. Aw. It was supposed to be funny."

Rhys got up, then bent over to kiss the top of Hyrum's head. "Trust me, it was funny. Thank you for trying to make me laugh."

"She said that, too."

29

"I made a slight change to the power distribution." Rhys spoke barely above a whisper. He didn't want to disturb Hyrum, who was flat on his back inside a sleeping bag and snoring quietly. The odds of waking Hyrum were slim because he'd been helped to sleep with a quick touch to the middle of his forehead, but they kept their voices low, just in case. "We should probably be able to jump a few times now, if necessary."

Why would we need to?

"And I have set perimeter alarms," Will said. "Perhaps this would be a good time to get some sleep."

"I slept last night. But you didn't, so..."

Aisha jumped in to prevent an argument. "That thing you did to Hyrum. Will it work on you?"

"Sometimes," Rhys said. "If I ask him to, my dad will try. The older I get, though, the less it works. I've tried it on him a few times...it's worked maybe once."

"Then we age out of it," Will mused.

"I dunno, maybe. Fortunately, my insomnia isn't as bad as yours. And from what I understand, my dad's is no longer as bad as yours, either. So maybe you age out of that, too."

He needs a sex life for that.

Solo doesn't count.

"You can stop talking now," Will grumbled.

Trust me, pretty soon I'll be gone and you'll wish your Wick would talk to you like this.

"I wish for him to remember that we were companions before he was sent here. I never said I wanted him to mock me with sarcasm and...wit."

You don't get one without the other.

And aren't you glad Rhys translates for me out of reflex?

"I am," Aisha said.

"I could live with fewer personal details," Rhys said. "But, yeah. Even my dad has admitted that he started sleeping better after he and my mom got together. I don't think it's because of sex, though. I think he's just kind of...content."

It's totally the sex.

Whatever insult was about to roll off his tongue, Will bit it back, and then suggested to Rhys that whether he slept or not, he should at least grab a sleeping bag and try. Come morning, we'd pack everything away and jump to the King's office, where there was space to work safely while other people worried about keeping watch. But for tonight, he would keep watch, and wake everyone if they needed to go.

Rhys caved. He handed the jump device over, asked Will to keep it where he could get to it in a hurry, and then scooted over to where Hyrum was sleeping. There was already a sleeping bag waiting for him, and after he slipped in, he took his pillow and gently tucked it into Hyrum's crossed arms.

Hyrum usually sleeps with a stuffed rabbit. Rhys probably thinks the pillow will help.

"Hm. I had a stuffed rabbit when I was a child," Will said.

Same rabbit. But that's a secret. Hyrum doesn't know that and we won't tell him. He found it on his bed after he decided to live with us, and he tells it his secrets. If he knew it had been yours, he would try to give it back, and he needs it.

"Our lips are sealed," Aisha said. "Though I am curious why your Emperor would not save it for his own children."

Rhys was a newborn and didn't need it.

"I am more curious about how he found it. I looked for it when I was twelve or thirteen years old. I don't recall ever finding it. I thought it had been tossed out."

Yeah, well. It went missing for a reason.

"Ah."

You're a thief, Will. Stealing from an innocent child like that.

"I think it's sweet," Aisha offered. "You must have

remembered not being terribly upset by its loss, otherwise you'd have left it alone."

"As I recall, my search was simply one of those 'I haven't seen this in a while, I wonder where it is' things. Its existence in my life no longer carried the importance it had when I was three years old."

Chuckles was damned important to you for most of your childhood. You were just too hormonal to admit you wanted him.

"Hormonal."

Puberty was a bitch.

"I don't recall it being difficult."

Self-circumcision, anyone?

Oddly, he did not repeat that.

You weren't rebellious or anything, I'll give you that. Well, other than portal hopping on your own at fifteen.

"Circumstances required I not engage in typical teenage behavior," he said. "My parents were engaged in understandably—"

"Explain the accent," Aisha said. "You were born in San Francisco. You were raised there. Why do you sound Scottish half the time?"

"My mother is Scottish."

"I'm a teacher, Will. I see kids all the time whose parents have accents but they don't pass those along. The kids have exposure away from home."

"Indeed. But my mother was my teacher, and I rarely spent time with other children after I was seven years old. I spent most of my time with her, listening to her, and far less time with others."

That gave her pause. "Not even with your father?"

"He gave me as much time as he could possibly spare," Will said. "And I have little doubt that some of the time he gave me was stolen."

"Stolen."

"I suspect he portaled back a day or two to make sure I had his attention, then portaled forward to resume his work."

Sometimes that was the only way, Will. He'd give you hours, then go back to just moments after he left.

"He must have been exhausted," Aisha said.

"Knowing what I now know, I am honestly surprised he survived the amount of pressure he was under. Few people across the globe were engaged in the work he had dedicated himself to. For most, the end of everything was simply accepted by way of ignoring its reality. And all the while he did the work to find a way to move that meteor off its destructive path, he formed teams of others to escort people to other Whens."

"Like George."

Will nodded.

"How many did he save, do you think?"

"Not many. There were too many people, too few portals, and so many who didn't believe he could do it."

Twenty thousand, roughly.

"That's it? Out of billions, only twenty thousand were going to make it out alive?" She was incredulous. "If he'd known that from the outset, would he have bothered?"

"He'd have done it if he could have saved only a few. But uppermost in his wishes was finding a way to save everyone and everything."

You're going forward to find him and explain it all, right? Once you get Rhys and Hyrum and me home?

"Indeed."

And even if you don't get us home.

"You're going home, Wick. There has to be a way. I suspect we'll need George again, unless we choose to expose this to more people and utilize the King's pool of science."

He won't do that.

"Probably not."

So you also have to consider what happens if we wind up staying.

There was no doubt that we'd be welcome; there was no doubt that our lives would be spent among people who loved us and treasured us. But he recognized that fundamentally, staying would harm us. We'd live with people who looked like family, and sounded like family, but we'd always know they weren't. We'd always miss them, and never heal because of the constant reminders of what we lost.

"I'll never give up, Wick."

"Wick, he won't give up because he knows if he does, we'll wind up locking horns in an epic custody battle. And no one wants that."

"You'd fight for Rhys."

"Hell, hon, I'll fight for Hyrum, too. I'd want at least fifty-fifty."

"I'm sure we could arrange something. But we're finding a way to get them home. They found their way here, which means there *is* a way back. It's simply a matter of figuring out how they went from When A to When B."

"Occam's Razor," she said.

Who are we shaving this time?

He let out a long breath. "They were on a single bicycle, speeding down a hill that has, in my birth When, a section of the portal tunnel running under it. The logical explanation is that Rhys's transponder somehow picked up on the temporal energy and essentially called up a portal. On the other hand...as far as I know that scenario isn't possible."

"Pretend it is. He's scared, they're out of control, and he opens a portal. Then what?"

"They should have remained in San Francisco. Coming out the other side in Las Vegas is not within the scope of any portal. It has parameters for moving through time, not space. Yet somehow he not only bridged his When to this one, he crossed from there to here."

You know about Finn's paper analogy?

"His tendency to explain time travel using a slip of paper and a pencil?" He explained it to Aisha: roll up one end of a piece of paper, and then use the pencil to represent the traveler. Puncture a hole with the pencil from the top, move it down and around the curled end of the paper back to the spot where you punched a hole. The edge of the hole, the distance between the top part of the paper and the bottom, represented null space. "He also describes it as bouncing off null space, when he actually moves through small part of—"

He stopped, eyebrows knotted, as he imagined it in his head.

"They moved through null space. They didn't bounce off it. They moved *through* it."

She reached over and patted his knee. "And there you go. Another piece of the puzzle. Something you can examine while you're not sleeping and the rest of us are."

"Indeed."

Just don't figure out a way to get us stuck there. Been there, done that, didn't get a t-shirt, and I really, really don't recommend it.

30

The proximity alarm went off at 6 a.m. Hyrum had been awake for over an hour, as was his usual, but it startled Rhys out of sleep he hadn't expected. He sat up ram-rod straight, inhaling sharply, staring straight ahead without really seeing anything but fragments of a dream rapidly fading from view.

He'd barely blinked and Will was already tugging at the sleeping bag to shove it into Rhys's go bag. Aisha had hers wadded up and half in, while Hyrum rolled his methodically. He knew they needed to go quickly, but two years of marching across Midlam taught him that slow is fast, and going too fast can get you into trouble. He had his bag rolled and stowed before Aisha was able to stuff hers down far enough, and he ambled toward the bathroom to pee "on account of who knows when we'll get to again?"

They followed suit. I was last to go, and Hyrum supervised, making sure I didn't fall in and didn't make a mess. The bags were ready and Aisha had hers slung over one shoulder, watching as Rhys strapped the jump device on; Will stood in front of the monitor, keeping track of the four men wandering just outside the hidden door.

They knew we were in here, somehow, but lacking an obvious entry, they scoured the ground for a leaf or snow-covered hatch leading down.

"Where to?" Rhys asked once the device was secure. "King's office?"

Will hesitated. Last night, that had been the destination. Now, he wasn't certain. If the device gave off any kind of electronic or digital signature, the guardians might detect it. The next place they would look—and he was sure they'd already been there multiple times—was San Francisco.

"Where wouldn't they expect him to go?" Aisha asked.

"Outside Pacifica," Will guessed.

"Florida," Hyrum said, though he was not serious and chuckled when he said it. "There's an empty shed in the backyard where I used to hide. It stinks like old people, though."

"Florida," Will repeated.

"Nuh, not really. No one wants to go there."

"No single place is safe," Aisha said. "Just pick somewhere you know we can hide. Anywhere."

Chicago has a lovely abandoned sewer system. I've been there and hated it, but it's a destination.

"Maybe not the sewer, but Chicago is big enough we can probably hide in the open," Rhys said. "There's a park Drew took us to once. We can jump there and get our bearings."

Nodding, Will reached for Hyrum's hand, and Aisha reached for Rhys's while Hyrum just set his on Rhys's arm. A few clicks on the keyboard, a blink, and we jumped.

We forgot about the time of year.

Chicago in November?

It's cold. And snowy.

And Hyrum was still barefoot.

~

We hiked from the park toward city center. Hyrum rode on Will's back, arms around his shoulders and legs around his waist, with no complaint about the lack of dignity in being carted around like a child. Will had a destination in mind—a store less than a mile away, where he could get each of them warmer clothing—and Hyrum decided to make the best of it.

He hitched himself up a few inches higher, grabbed Will's shirt at the shoulders, and flicked his feet in.

"Giddy up. Move it, move it."

"I am giddying as uply as is safe," Will said. "Are you all right? How cold?"

"I'm fine. I can keep myself warm for a little while. Am I too heavy?"

He was not too heavy and he knew it; he'd ridden on Will's back dozens of times, but Hyrum, being polite, felt it important to ask, just in case.

"Can we get breakfast after we get clothes? Or lunch. Just food. Lots of it. Keeping warm is making me super hungry."

We breezed through the department store; I hid under Rhys's shirt while they plucked jackets, sweatshirts, socks and shoes and underwear from shelves and racks, and stayed there until I heard Rhys mutter under his breath that he was being watched. My body created a bulge under his sweatshirt, and he had a feeling that someone would stop him before getting through the exit.

I wiggled my way up until I reached his collar, and poked my head out.

The clerk—or security, I don't know—arched an eyebrow and shook her head slightly. She didn't say anything but the message was clear: pay for your stuff and leave.

At the register, Will reached for his wallet, but Aisha set her hand on his arm and stopped him. Voice low, she said, "Rhys is on that bank account, isn't he? They might be tracking it. Let me get this."

"They might be tracking yours as well."

"Not likely."

Dudes, they're tracking him. *It doesn't matter.*

She won, regardless.

She also paid for breakfast, and I wondered, after seeing Hyrum and Rhys inhale enough food for four, if she regretted that.

I started out in Rhys's sweatshirt, expecting to be fed tiny bites when no one was looking, but the server recognized Will and asked if a highchair would be needed today. I stuck my head out again, and he grinned, promising to cut my meat into tiny bites.

So you've brought me here. I don't remember.

"Before Shazia took the throne, we occasionally met her here for lunch."

Aisha turned in her seat, looking around. "I thought it was familiar. Any chance she'd remember me?"

"We could find out," Rhys said. "She's Midlam's queen, she could hide us, right? I mean, she knows about the portals and all so she'd understand my existence. At least she does in my When."

"She knows."

"Then?"

"This was a diversion jump, Rhys. I'd prefer to not entangle too many people in this, especially a new queen who is still finding her footing."

"Shoot her a text, at least."

No, don't do that. He's right. Leave her alone.

"It's just a text, Wick."

It's an obligation. She'll feel like she has to say yes. She's got royal things to do, and little kids to parent. One of them is a raging asshole right now.

"Drew isn't a...he's not like that," Hyrum said.

"He means Carter," Will said, "who is certainly a little asshole. I fear for the man he'll become."

He'll be one into his twenties, but he gets better. I mean, he hasn't exactly been forgiven for some of the things he did because they were so wrong he belonged in jail, but he tries.

"I like Carter," Hyrum said. "I'm sad that he has to go back to Mars."

"Mars," Will repeated. "I don't recall reading he'd been there. How old is Carter, for you?"

"Forty?" Rhys shrugged. "Maybe a little younger. Drew is, like, thirty-five, so."

"Thirty-seven then."

"Why?"

"Just curious."

"You don't get curious about stuff like that," Rhys said. "So, why?"

Will's eyes flicked toward Hyrum. "No particular reason."

Rhys sat back in the booth, his eyebrows scrunched a bit. It took a minute, but he understood, and nodded. "Okay."

"To answer your question," Will said, looking at Aisha, "yes, she remembers you. She regularly proclaims me an idiot and is upset that I did not have your contact info. Richard has a cousin…"

"She's right, you're an idiot. But Richard's cousin? I like Richard, but…no."

Hyrum cocked his head a touch. "Has anyone met me to his cousin? I don't remember him."

Rhys had not met him. "Yeah, I don't know him, either."

"He lives in Germany. I'm not sure how often he visits," Will said. "Jorge Van Hoff, current mayor of Munich."

"Bullet dodged, then," Aisha said. "I don't see myself in Germany."

"Munich is quite nice—"

"To visit, I'm sure. I'm quite happy living in Pacifica, knowing Jax will be king someday, and King Eli is about as decent and fair as a politician can get."

"Man," Rhys breathed, "you really are an idiot. Balancing on the precipice of convincing her that giving someone else a chance is a good idea."

"I did not—"

"Let's just jump to San Francisco and get it over with," Rhys grumbled. "We need to get home, and you two need…I dunno what you need except maybe glasses."

"Glasses."

"Glasses," he grunted as he started to side out the booth. "You just can't see the bigger picture."

"Oh! If Eli can get me some paper and pencils, I'll draw them a big picture!" Hyrum beamed. "It would have to be big paper, though. But no crayons. If I'm going to draw something you want to keep, I'll need the good pencils."

31

Hyrum sneezed, and the world formed around us from mist and wishes; for a moment, I felt my equilibrium shift. It felt a bit like when the Emperor changed time: that tilt, as if the center of everything had shifted, followed by unsettling quiet. Rhys sucked in a startled breath and spun on his heels, forcing me to dig in with my claws to keep from falling off.

The unsettling mist rose from the pond twenty feet away. There was frost on the grass surrounding it, and the air choked with quiet. We were alone, with no sign of Will and Aisha, and Rhys had no idea where we were.

"What the hell?" he finally uttered.

What were you thinking about when you jumped?

"Nothing! Just…it was time to go. The bracelet should have taken us to San Francisco, but I've never seen this place."

Maybe we went too far forward, or too far back. San Francisco might have looked like this at one time.

"Maybe Golden Gate Park," Rhys mused. "But when?"

Are your coordinates visible? If you missed a digit, that might tell you.

He began tapping at the tiny screen on the bracelet. Hyrum had turned toward the water, staring, and when his hands went to his shirt, fingers twisting fabric, I spoke as quietly in Rhys's ear as I could.

Dude. Something's wrong.

"Hy? What's up?"

Hyrum's breath hiccupped and when he turned back to Rhys, his eyes were wide with a bubbling panic. "We have to get out of here, Rhys. We're in trouble here. Big trouble."

"You know where we are?"

His head bobbed. "I'm not allowed to be here on account of the gators," he said. "Aubrey says there aren't any and that Daddy just said there were to make sure I didn't try to come here by myself, but I dunno. But it's not safe, I know it's not safe."

He tugged at his shirt. "Look. I can't be here in this. Or my jeans. And my hair!" He grabbed at the sides of his head. "It's blue. I can't have blue hair here."

"Why? Where do you think we are?"

"Miller's Pond!"

"I don't know where that is, Hy."

"We have to hide," Hyrum insisted. "We have to hide until we can jump away. We can't stay here, Rhys."

"Where," Rhys asked, trying to be patient, "are we?"

Hyrum's voice was strangled. "Florida," he squeaked. "We're in Florida."

~

Based on the sunlight, the frost on the grass, and mist hovering over the water, Rhys guessed that we'd not just jumped location, but back a few hours. There was little chance of someone wandering into the park and finding us there, but we walked toward the parking lot where Hyrum knew there was a multi-stall restroom. That would be somewhere to hide, he told Rhys, at least for a little bit.

It was cleaner than expected, clean enough that Rhys felt comfortable sitting on the floor with his back to the wall, close to the door. He wanted to be able to see anyone approaching, with enough time to get up and hide in a stall. Hyrum paced, terrified we'd be caught, more so because he was dressed in loud colors which might cause whomever stumbled upon us to call the police, who would call this father, and that would be very, very bad.

"The coordinates were complete," Rhys said after hooking the bracelet to his phone and examining the processes. "We should have landed in King Eli's office. I don't know how we ended up here."

Hyrum dropped into a squat, hands gripping his head. "It's my fault. I bringed us here. Brought us."

"Can't be." Rhys wiggled the makeshift bracelet. "This controls where we go."

"But I was *thinking*. I heard in my brain, 'I'd rather run from the gators than those shiny guys again.' And I sneezed and then we jumped and here we are. This is where the gators are."

Well, probably not.

"But in my brain they are, Wick."

"Jesus." Rhys unhooked his phone and shoved it back into his pocket. "I think I heard that, Hy. Just before you sneezed. I know I heard a whisper about gators and running."

"I'm sorry."

"Not your fault. But how did that override the bracelet?"

Functioning like a portal? The portals take you where your brain says to.

The jump bracelet, even one as rudimentary as his printer-cable concoction, should not have functioned exactly as a portal. It used human physical sensation to steer away from objects, making sure we didn't jump into a wall or in front of a speeding vehicle, but it should have taken us directly to the input coordinates.

You have both the bracelet and portal data in your phone. If a file is corrupted—

He doubted the data could have bled from one file to another, but having no other ideas, admitted I might be right.

"Doesn't matter. We need to jump back."

"Can you do that?" Hy let go of his head and looked up. "Just go back?"

"I can reverse coordinates. That's not the problem. The problem is power, and right now there's not enough." He grunted. "I thought I had that solved. I really thought we could jump a few times."

Hyrum sat down, and extended his index finger. "I can power it up."

"If it were that easy, so could I," Rhys said, sighing. "The power needs to trickle in, and that could take a couple hours. I'm not sure how long we can stay here. The park will open soon."

Well, we can't exactly go anywhere, either. Neither of you fit in, not in Florida.

Rhys looked down at his clothes. "They wear jeans in Florida, right? The men, anyway."

That's not what I meant. And with Hyrum's screaming neon everything, you'll both just...stick out.

"My new jacket that Aisha bought is red and red is okay. I can keep it zipped up."

Your hair, dude. You need a knit cap or something. And then there's the obvious.

Rhys sighed. "Well, I can't just go steal clothes for him. And if there's nothing wrong with mine—"

"You're not white," Hyrum blurted. "That's what Wick means. In this part of Florida you gotta be white. If we went to Miami, you could be not white on account of there are a lot of people whose older people came from Cuba, but not up here. They stay down there on account of reasons."

"You're serious? I'd get it if we landed back in, like, nineteen-fifty, but this is only thirty years ago."

"It's *Florida.*"

Specifically, North Carolina. He would know, Rhys.

"So it's illegal to be anything other than white here? What the hell?"

"I dunno. But I never saw anyone who wasn't until I was older than you. Not even on TV."

Thirty years ago, the Church of Florida still taught that darker skin was a mark of sin. If you were a good person, your children would be born white. Or at least less dark. If they were also good, surely their kids would be white. Some even believed that if you were worthy, you'd personally lighten up until you became white.

"That's messed up."

"That's Florida," Hyrum said.

That will shift when Red takes over the church. So, fifteen years or so. But for us, right now what matters is that we have nowhere to go, and if we stay here, sooner or later someone will find us.

"And do what?" Rhys asked. "Seriously, can we be arrested just for sitting here on a restroom floor?"

"Nuh. We'd be arrested for looking like this. On account of they'd just decide we were up to no good."

Maybe not arrested. But you'd have the authorities up your ass, and they'd probably take you somewhere unpleasant, then say they're holding you until you can cough up a residence or family member.

"Up my ass?" That earned me a tight smile. "Well, then we have to find someplace to hide long enough to charge the bracelet. If it can't be here, then where?"

Start it here. Once the park opens, we leave and find a better spot."

And we would have, too, if the groundskeeper's truck hadn't rolled up to the door.

32

Here's the thing about scrambling...sometimes you go too fast and wind up hiding in the same bathroom stall. They piled in and slammed the door shut before either of them realized what they were doing, and it was too late for one of them to hop to the next stall before the groundskeeper entered the restroom.

Hyrum stood behind Rhys, hand over his mouth to keep from making noise, and we listened as he puttered. I heard the sound of a bag sliding against the metal of the trashcan, a squirt bottle followed by squeaky wiping of a mirror, and broom bristles brushing over the cement floor. I was pretty sure that next he planned on checking the stalls, and the slight increase in the sound of his shoes on the floor made me brace against Rhys's shoulder a bit more, ready to spring onto someone's face if I needed to.

But then Hyrum sneezed again.

The footsteps stopped outside the door, and through the crack I saw him bend over to see which stall had feet visible.

"Y'all can't be in there together," he said finally. "What are you doing here, anyway? Park's not open for another hour."

Rhys turned his head to look at Hyrum; he had no idea what to say.

"Sorry," Hyrum squeaked. "We were out for a walk and tummy things happened so I needed to come in here."

"Uh huh. Together?"

"My nephew is just helping me. I need help sometimes, you know."

"Help."

Rhys nodded, understanding what Hyrum implied. "Yeah,

he's a little older and sometimes has trouble handling everything. I apologize if we're causing trouble for you, but it was this or—"

"I got it," the man said. "You need anything? I've got supplies out here."

Rhys glanced down at the toilet paper roll. "We're good. But we might need a few minutes."

He snickered softly. "I get it. I'll get out of your way for now. I can come back later. But holler if you need anything. I won't be far."

"Nice enough guy," Rhys said once his footsteps faded.

"People here *are* nice," Hyrum said. "It's just the biggy church people, like my daddy. They can be mean. We could even ask regular people for help, if I didn't wear these clothes or if you wouldn't make them upset. I'm really sorry."

"None of this is your fault, Hy. It just sucks that Florida is like this. Like, why should it matter if you like bright colors? Why should it matter if I'm not white?"

"It's just how it is here. Red said that the church didn't used to be so uppity, but when Florida became Florida, they decided to use the worst things about church to make the rules. I forget what he said about learning stuff, but I think he meant that they wanted to keep people stupid, on account of stupid people do what they're told and they think that the important church people know enough. But that's not true. They don't know enough. Except Red."

What began as a proposed gentle theocracy quickly became a plutocratic, oligarchical theocracy; the rich rose in power, using God, the Bible, and the church's own religious texts as the basis for governing the masses—but not for themselves. They reached deep into church history, drawing on dogma founded in the eighteen hundreds, to push out the people they didn't want; if you were a person of color, well educated, or anything other than heteronormative, you weren't welcome to enter Florida before the walls surrounding it were erected. If you were already there and clearly not-white, you'd better bolt for the south where there was a hope of living without constant fear. If you were anything other than straight and wanting marriage and family, your better bet was to flee the country if you wanted to live at all.

"Being gay is a crime," Rhys mused. "I presume that's only if you're not in the hierarchy."

"I don't know what that means, but probably yeah. You gotta get married here, Rhys. Unless you're like me and then you're not allowed. Daddy said that was what Jesus wanted, but Red says that's not true. He says I could get married now, if I wanted to. The church doesn't want people doing kissing things if they're not married, even if it's two boys."

Rhys knew the history of how the United States of America split into five new countries; he was aware it was a decade-long process during which people came and went, searching for a place they belonged, but many simply stayed where they were despite their personal beliefs.

In the early days of Florida, the church was not a single entity, but one of many fundamental Christian sects. One grabbed hold, however, fueled by a system with centuries of expertise in conversion and seizing power. Within fifty years, it was the only religion in the country; anything else was illegal.

Not long before the origin church's sesquicentennial celebration—centuries before the country split—the church began allowing non-white male members to enter the echelon of priesthood-holders; five hundred years later, there was little trace that had ever happened. "If you want to witness life in America had the racists gotten their way," Red once told Will, "visit Florida roughly thirty years after the church took power. You will never see a whiter America."

Rhys held a hand out, turning it over. "By the rules here, my maternal grandfather was sin personified. I'm just a little closer to, what, goodness? Godliness? All because I have less melanin?"

Blow your mind a little more. Here, you're not worthy. But the church sends out missionaries all over the world to convert them. No matter what racial profile those people have.

"Why?"

"To save their souls," Hyrum said. "But it doesn't make sense if they can't go to the highest place in heaven."

It's a numbers game. They want the world to think there are millions of church members. And the more people they convert, the more money they get from tithing. It's all about the money.

"Yeah, we need to get out of Florida," Rhys grumbled.

Peeking out of the restroom, he waited until the groundskeeper was looking elsewhere, and we left the park, heading for the backside of a strip mall that Hyrum was "pretty sure only a little ways up the street" while also acknowledging that he hadn't been there in nearly fifty years.

The mall was a special outing with Red when Hyrum was a small boy. "There was a store that sold lots of different kinds of candy and they had sodas, so when Daddy was gone for church things, he took me there and bought me stuff. The store closed when I was fourteen or maybe fifteen, but I remember it and maybe the place it was in is still there. We can hide behind it."

Strip malls are ubiquitous. If it's not there, another has surely gone up in its place.

Hyrum nearly squealed as we crested a short hill near the area he believed the store had been. The strip was still there; it was likely the same one of his childhood, though now most of the windows were boarded up and there were only a few businesses remaining. Rhys eyed each door and window we passed, looking for signs of cameras and alarms, and possibilities that we could gain entry to one of them.

Hyrum, on the other hand, wanted to venture behind the mall. He'd never been back there, and Red was adamant that he never go, but now, "I'm a grown man and I can do what I want."

Apparently, his long-held desire was to hang out in a back alley. It ran between the strip mall and tall brick retaining wall, tall enough that I had no idea what was on the other side.

In the alley however, it was clear what we saw. Pushed up against both walls were a collection of old, hole-riddled tents along with a disturbing amount of trash. Near the end of the alley there was a mound made of bicycle frames and assorted parts, shopping carts, and crushed cardboard boxes. There was also a significant amount of unidentifiable detritus, and I hoped that we would remain a reasonable distance from it.

Rhys began to back away slowly, not wanting to wake the residents of those tents, but I was quite visible on his shoulder, and the chained-up bulldog just ten feet away decided I was worthy of an announcement.

He began barking his damned head off, and the alley awoke.

33

The dog's name, we learned quickly when her owner yelled at her to be quiet, was Munson. Her owner was Emily, no last name given; Emily crawled from her tent, pulling a sweater over her head as she stood, and apologized for the noise. It was not meant for us, I gathered, but her neighbors.

"You boys want something?" she asked, trying to sound friendly while clearly suspicious. She looked at Hyrum from head to toe, and seemed amused, but she refrained from commentary about his technicolor choices. One eyebrow cocked just slightly at the sight of Rhys, reminding me of the way Will's eyebrow arched when he found something preposterous, but then her focus shifted back to Hyrum. "Lost?"

Hyrum's head bobbed up and down. "Kinda."

"How in God's name are you getting away with…that." She gestured to his clothing. "And where did you get those things in the first place? I've never seen anything like it. Good lord, those pants."

"Christmas presents," he mumbled.

"Well. Of course." With a heavy sigh, she turned toward a metal trash can and peeked to the bottom. "Not out. Good. Want to be helpful? Grab some of that wood over there and stoke the fire."

She pointed to a jumbled mess of broken bits of plywood and tree branches. Rhys gathered as much as he could and set it beside the can, and started to go back for more when she stopped him. That was enough to get the fire going again, and there was no need to leave a pile where someone might trip over it.

The alley was filled with trash, but there was a clear path down the center.

"What's your name, sunshine?" she asked Hyrum.

"Hyrum. What's yours?"

"Emily. And this is my pup, Munson."

"Munson," Rhys repeated.

"Because she's a little bitch," Emily said, laughing. "Fair warning, if you're going to stay here, you won't earn any points if you're one of the faithful. We've all given that up. That church didn't want us, so we sure as shoot don't want it, either."

Hyrum's fingers grasped for his shirt. "They don't want you? Why?"

Emily dragged two milk crates from the tent opposite hers and placed them near her own, then gestured for them to sit. When they did, she sat cross-legged on the ground with her dog wiggling to get onto her lap.

"You think they want *you*?" she asked, pointing at his jeans. She pointed at Rhys then and added, "Or you? At all?"

"No," Rhys said, offering nothing else.

"You spend your life doing everything they tell you. Pay tithing every week, even if it means going without food, because that's what God wants of you. Then your husband dies, and without any other family to help? Too bad. You're a woman, so you can't find work. There's no money coming in. And that church, the one that took twenty per cent of every dime you ever had, shrugs and tells you to figure it out when you ask for help. So good for you, staying away from them."

"How do you get by?" Rhys asked.

"How do you think?"

I'm not sure what Rhys thought, but the volume of the alleyway rose as tent flaps popped open. He watched as a line formed in front of a bent metal door that led into a closed-off store; the lock was long gone and in its place were wads of newspaper and rust. They went in one by one, guarding the door for each other, and every one of them was female.

"All of you," Rhys breathed out. "Lost husbands or fathers?"

"Lost. Or forced out. What's your story? Why are you wandering around the back ways of the dead malls?"

"We just wanna go home." Hyrum was near tears. "I wish we could take all of you with us."

Munson crept closer to Rhys, which made me dig my claws in a little.

"Don't mind her," Emily said. "She's just curious about the cat."

I'm Wick. I'll stay right here so you don't have to worry about me. All right?

Munson let out a tiny woof. "*Good girl.*"

"His name is Wick," Rhys said. "He's not afraid of dogs. As long as she doesn't charge, he'll be fine."

"Used to 'em, eh?"

"I have a dog, too. Thor."

"They're buddies!" Hyrum offered. "Are you okay here? I don't know what to do. We didn't mean to wake you up, we were just looking for a place to sit for a while. Rhys needs to look at stuff on his phone and we saw the mall…"

"Look at stuff," she repeated. "On a phone?"

They have cell phones here, right?

Hyrum scrambled to cover. "It's like a pocket phone. But he's got, uh, what do you call it. Techy stuff. He likes to build things on account of he wants to be a scientist when he grows up. He can look at it and find a way for us to go home."

"That sounds expensive." She nodded at the keyboard strapped to his arm. "Looks trashy, but hey."

Voice even, Rhys said, "It's fairly well useless to anyone who doesn't understand its components. But no, it didn't cost much to build. Just time and quite a bit of swearing when things didn't work."

I heard what Hyrum didn't: *you're not getting it, and if you did, you wouldn't be able to sell it.*

"What's it do?" She leaned forward, trying to get a look at his phone. "It's got a picture screen?"

"It basically steals data from the satellites orbiting earth. This way I can look things up on Midlam's Internet, and find maps. Stuff like that."

"Kid, you can buy a map in any convenience store."

"Well. You need cash for that and I'm broke. So I need to use this, and see if I can figure out where we go next."

"Well, feel free to sit here as long as you need." She got up, and patted the side of her leg to get Munson to heel. "I have a line to wait in."

Rhys disconnected the power pack from the wiring and handed it to Hyrum while he flipped his phone over. The idea was for Hyrum to charge the pack, which was easy to hide since he only needed to place it between his thumb and finger as he slowly fed it electricity. To charge the phone, Rhys needed to remove the back casing, which was a bit more obvious.

"Maybe the phone can wait?" Hyrum asked. "It's got some juice left, right?"

"Battery's about fifty per cent. I can wait until tonight, I guess. But I might chew up a big part of it if I pull up the maps. We might need them to find a safer place to hide."

"This seems safe."

"It's intrusive." He turned the phone over again, pretending to look at the screen. "This is a safe haven for a bunch of displaced women, Hyrum. The last thing they need is to have to worry about a couple of strange men hanging around. We feel safe right now, but I bet a bunch of them don't, and it's not fair for us to do that to them."

Hyrum scrunched his nose. "Why aren't they safe?"

"They are, at least from us. But they likely don't *feel* safe with us here."

"But...why?"

Because some men are like your father, and they punish women for just being women. Whether they know them or not.

"Oh. Okay. Then we should go. I don't want them to think we're like my daddy."

Bracing me with his hand, Rhys stood and reached down to help Hyrum up. There had to be another mall, or something like it, nearby, and we'd find it. Even a spot under a tree away from public view would work, just as long as there was time to get power into that pack.

"With any luck, we'll be back with the Emperor and Aisha in time for lunch. I don't know about you, dude, but I'm already getting hungry."

"Me, too," Hyrum said, shoving the uncoupled power pack into his pocket. "Maybe the Emperor has a couple more energy bars, and…"

He trailed off, causing Rhys to track the spot where Hyrum stared off.

"Dammit," he sputtered. "Police."

"Can we run? If we go the other way? He can't catch us if we run fast."

"He has a gun," Rhys whispered. "I have no idea what to do."

Emily, on the other hand, did. She bounded past us right to the police officer, neither surprised nor upset to see him. Her voice trailed as she called out, "Harley's here!" and then, "Leave the boys alone, Harley. They're not hurting anyone."

Harley didn't care. As the women moved down the alley toward his car—there were boxes on the hood, pink and white donut boxes—he pushed through them to get to us.

"What in—" Confusion blinked in his eyes, but was quickly gone. "It's not Halloween, mister, so you better start explaining."

Voice small, Hyrum said, "I just like bright things."

"I see that. But…why?"

He shrugged.

"And your friend?" Harley nodded toward Rhys, not expecting a word out of him. "Why's he here?"

"I'm his—"

"Wasn't talking to you, boy."

He's from southern Florida. His mom was native. You're his uncle.

"He's my nephew," Hyrum said, still sounding small. "He's just here to see me for a little bit, that's all. He came up from Miami."

Harley finally turned to Rhys. "Cuban?"

"Multiracial," Rhys answered, truthfully. "Is there a problem, officer? We haven't done anything."

He stepped closer, so close I could smell the donuts on his breath. "I don't want you here. These ladies have been through enough, they don't need to worry about some half breed and his deleterious uncle sniffing around."

"Deleterious," Rhys repeated.

"You heard me. It means—"

"I know what it means. I'm not sure you do. But we'll get out of their way, officer. We never intended to be here in the first place."

"Leave 'em alone, Harley," Emily said, licking donut glaze from her fingers. "They're nice guys."

"And they should not be here," he insisted. "It's not appropriate. What would your late husband say, hm?"

"He'd say, 'why the fandango isn't that church helping you find a place to live? And putting food on your table? You know how much money I gave them? Over the years, probably two million, at least.' That's what he would say, Harley. That I didn't need to be here in the first place."

"Em," he groaned.

"They have two hundred *billion* in reserves, Harley. You know that. Would it kill them to build a few safe places for the displaced women of the church? No, it would not. But will they waste money on women too old to breed? No, they will not."

"Why don't they send you to Midlam?" Hyrum asked, sincerely. "They would give you a house and food and stuff."

"We're property, sunshine. The church isn't letting us go that easy."

He leaned toward her and whispered, "There's a giant hole in the wall by the Tennessee border if you can get there. Lots of people get out through it."

Harley heard. "So that's it, that's how you're here. You're not Floridian."

Hyrum squared his shoulders. "I was born right here, in this city."

Harley had enough. "All right. I'm taking you in. We can sort you out later."

"But we haven't done anything," Rhys protested.

"Names," Harley demanded.

Rhys was not about to give him anything, but Hyrum stood as tall as he could, and proudly announced, "My name is Hyrum Charles Munson, and now you can call my other nephew,

Redmond Munson. His daddy is Levi Munson. You can see how he likes it, that you're being mean to his old uncle. I know he won't."

34

Shackled to a seat in a dimly lit office in the police station, Hyrum apologized to Rhys. "I really thought that would work."

"If Red were prophet, it would have. But right now he's just the prophet's oldest son. Was he even a part of the church's hierarchy at this age? He was in his forties when he became the Second Minister."

"I think he was a bishop," Hyrum said.

Does it matter? We need to get out of here. Hy, can you reach the power unit? Maybe stick your hand in your pocket to charge it?

He tried, but lacked enough chain length to get more than a finger into his front pocket. He tried twisting, and turning, anything to get a better reach, but stopped when the door popped open, and blurted, "I'm sorry! My butt itched and I was just trying to scratch."

Harley sighed. "I don't care. But your nephew is here." He bent over and unlocked the hasps on the chains. "Don't move. I'll let him in, but you keep your butts in the chairs. Hear me?"

"Got it," Rhys said. When the door clicked shut behind him, he sneered, "Massa."

"Huh? Is that like a big—Red!" He jumped up when Red entered the room, forgetting that Harley had ordered him to stay in the chair.

Red, somewhere in his mid-thirties, cautiously closed the door behind him. He was not unsupervised; there were windows, and the blinds were open. It was clear we could do nothing to him—not that we would—but we could speak openly with him.

"I'm guessing you're my mysterious Uncle Hyrum," he said, looking at Hy. "You could be. You certainly look like we could be related."

"Except for my hair. I know. Aubrey said it was okay, even though I know she doesn't like it."

He took a step back. "Aubrey."

"Hy," Rhys said, gently, "Don't get ahead of yourself."

"And you are?" Red asked Rhys.

"Rhys Blackshear. And before you ask, yes, of those Blackshears."

Without taking his eyes off us, Red grappled for a nearby chair and pulled it up. When he spoke again, it was quietly. "You know my sister. Are you from Pacifica?"

"In a roundabout way," Rhys answered. "But, yeah, Aubrey is my adopted aunt. My dad is the Emperor."

"You're kidding." He leaned closer. "The Emperor is very... single. So single we thought he was, ah, a confirmed bachelor."

"Gay? He's not. He's just very private. He also respects you, enough that we felt safe asking for you. Hyrum isn't really your uncle, but...he is related to you."

Red leaned back in his chair, regarding all of us carefully. After a long stretch of quiet, he finally said, "All right. I buy that. Now what is it you need from me?"

"A safe place for about three hours," Rhys said. "After that, we'll be out of your hair, and we'll leave Florida. I swear."

Slapping at his thighs, he pushed himself up. "All right then. I don't know why I'm trusting you...something tells me you hear that a lot. But, yes, I'll take you somewhere safe, where you will tell me everything you clearly don't want to say here."

"If you don't trust us..."

"You look like him," Red said. "The Emperor. I can see him in you. And you?" He looked at Hyrum. "You're definitely family. You're a cross between my father and younger brother, Joe. So. I'll offer safe haven until you're ready to go, but you're going to tell me the truth."

~

While Hyrum flailed and kicked at the car windows from the back seat of the car, Red pressed his back to the driver's side door and tilted his head back, eyes closed, and he let out a long, slow breath. Rhys stood nearby, keeping an eye on Hyrum, waiting for the outburst to settle, though he had to admit that this one might take a while.

He'd been fine during the ride from the police station. His face pressed against the window, he named everything we passed, supposedly for Rhys's benefit but really, he was pleased with himself for not forgetting landmarks in the city where he'd grown up. Red was impressed, until he turned the corner to the Munson mansion; Hyrum realized where we were headed, and began sputtering "*no no no no no*" until it became a full-on wail.

"You said safe!" he yelled as Red got out of the car. "Daddy's house isn't safe! Daddy isn't safe!"

After a few silent minutes Red said, "Explain. Why doesn't he think this place is safe? And who is his father?"

"It's a long story," Rhys said. "Let him wind down and we can talk him out of the car, but you'll have to promise that your father isn't home. I'll explain as best I can once he's calmed down."

"You could explain now."

"I could, but..."

"He's like my little brother, isn't he?" Red asked. "He has thirty seconds, and I handle him the same way. He won't like it."

Rhys shrugged. "Go for it."

That surprised Red. "He's my elder, Rhys."

"Chronologically, sure. Look, he trusts you. He trusts you with his life, and once we're not standing in the driveway with god knows who watching us, I'll explain."

I don't think Red believed him, but he yanked the car door open anyway and barked, "Hyrum! Enough! No one is going to hurt you. Now get out of the car."

"But Daddy—"

"My father isn't home, Hyrum. No one is. That's why I brought you here. No one will be home until tomorrow."

Hy sat up straight and wiped tears from his face. "No one? Not even your Hyrum?"

Red twitched back. "My Hyrum? How did you even know...?"

"Long story, chapter one," Rhys said. "It's the prolog you'll want to hear first."

"You can start by explaining how we're related." He helped Hyrum out of the car, and then slammed the door shut. "And honestly, at this point, I'm not sure I'll believe a word coming out of your mouth. You're evasive, out of your element, and frankly... odd."

So much for trust.

Rhys hesitated at the front door, even when Hyrum bounded in. "Look, we can go somewhere else. Hyrum only asked the cop to call you because yours is a name he knows and trusts. The last thing we want to be is an imposition."

"Just go in," Red barked.

The living room was much like I remembered it, but the little room of nightmares was still under the stairs, and Hyrum zipped past it to the kitchen, trying to ignore it. He went straight for the back door, staring out at the yard, breath fogging the glass.

"I forgot how pretty it is," he said, trying to wipe the mist away. "Oh! I can see Lazybones' grave thingy! Only it's still nice and white and when I saw it before it was kinda dirty. Wick and I cleaned it off, but—"

"Hy," Rhys hissed. "Wrong When."

"Oh." He turned around. "I'm sorry. I just got excited."

Red stood on the far side of the dining room table, and I was certain it was to keep a safe distance away.

He doesn't trust us right now. He did, now he doesn't.

"I need explanations. Now," Red said. "You need a safe space for a few hours, I can provide that. But you'll only get that if you tell me what's going on, and who you are."

In a tone I hadn't heard since he was three years old, convincing his mother to put him down so he could get close to George and James, trapped under a lamp post, Rhys said, "You should sit for this."

Red pulled out a chair and sat. He blinked rapidly, trying to understand why he had done what the teenager ordered.

"Like we said before, Hyrum is my uncle, by way of adoption. My father is the Emperor, and Hyrum lives with Aubrey and Jax. That's the truth. The kicker is that I haven't been born yet, and Hyrum? He's your little brother, just thirty years older."

Red eyed the telephone hanging on the wall just past where Rhys stood. He weighed his chances of getting to the phone, and the odds of being able to make a call before Rhys ripped it from his hands. Red's gaze dropped to Rhys's arms, the muscles wrapped in tight skin, veins pushing out like little blue ropes, and decided against it.

There was fear mixed with anger in his eyes, and Rhys saw it.

"I get it, you think I'm full of about six kinds of shit. But it's the truth. Hyrum and I are from the future, and we landed here by mistake. The current Emperor and the woman who will someday be my mother are standing in several inches of Chicago snow, wondering where the hell we disappeared to, and that presumes the people chasing us haven't done anything to them. We're just trying to find a way home, to our own When. I promise, the last thing we wanted was to drag you into this or expose you to our truths. Florida was never a place I intended to land."

He barely blinked, even when Hyrum sat down.

I jumped from Rhys's shoulder to the table, and sat in front of Red.

You helped Aubrey run away when she was fourteen. She left with a boy named Simon, the one Levi was going to force her to marry, but the dude was super gay and they took off to save themselves and avoid destroying each other's lives. You found them but instead of taking her home, you drove him to L.A. and her to San Francisco...and you gave her a lot of money. Money your mom gave you to pass on, because she didn't want Aubrey to come back and suffer the ongoing abuse from your father. We know what happens under the stairs, Red. You were happy she got away.

Strangled in tears he fought to hold in, he uttered, "How?"

Rhys had to think of a way to explain it to him, and he couldn't find a way that didn't sound like fantasy.

We all have gifts. Tell Red about his. Right now, the siblings aren't sharing and don't know they each have one. Except for Hyrum.

"You have an ability," Rhys said, carefully. "A gift. Lightning-fast reflexes. So fast that when your brother David threw a knife at you, you snatched it from the air without so much as blinking."

"Oh!" Hyrum bounced in his chair. "I set Daddy's hair on fire when I was sixteen. But I put it out and he didn't really get hurt."

Red folded his arms, refusing to give any response.

"You two aren't the only ones," Rhys went on. "All your brothers have gifts. So does your mother. I'm not sure about your sisters, other than Aubrey."

At that, Red sat up straight. "My mother."

"She hides it to keep your dad from finding out. She's always coached you to hide it from him, hasn't she? I mean, she still doesn't really talk about it with your sibs, but she visits us a few times a year to help my sister and brother deal with their gifts, especially since my sister has the same one she does."

Red's heart was pounding hard enough that his pulse was visible in the vein on his neck.

"Most of us have gifts. Aubrey's an empath, if you didn't know. And my dad?"

"The Emperor has a gift," Red said, sounding far away.

"A few, actually. But you've seen him on TV? He always has gloves on if he has to touch someone, right?"

"He's known to be a bit of a germaphobe."

"That's not it." Rhys held his hand out. "I share the same gift. I can show you, if you like. But I have to warn you, it's intrusive."

Red stared at Rhys's hand, but didn't move.

"He won't hurt you," Hyrum said. "Rhys would never hurt you. He loves you."

"You speak for the cat," Red murmured.

"Another gift. Hyrum understands him, too."

Red shifted his gaze to Hyrum. "I sometimes thought my little brother understood Lazybones."

"I think I heard words. But I didn't know I was hearing him. I thought I was making it up in my head. But David understands! Wick talked to him when I went to visit him in jail one time."

"David is in jail." He did not sound surprised.

"Well, not anymore. Aubrey made Jax let him go and they took him to another When where he'd be safe. Haley went to live with him and they're really happy there. You'd like him now, Red. He's nice and he prays a lot and he got a job helping people on account of he says he owes that to God."

Got a headache now?

He still didn't believe a thing Rhys said, but reached for his hand anyway.

Ten seconds after they parted, he barfed into the trash can.

~

Without prompting, Hyrum pulled the bag out of the can, replaced it, and took the breakfast-splattered trash outside. He puttered while he was outside; his mother had been gardening before she left with Levi, and Hyrum carefully washed off her tools and placed them in the shed, hanging neatly the way she liked.

Red watched from the door, still looking a little green, until Rhys ducked past him to sit on the back patio. Red followed, and for a while we just sat there and watched Hyrum work; he seemed to be in his element, and quite happy to clean up the odds and ends Valerie Munson had likely not intended to leave. She was, and I knew this from experience, fastidious and hated any sort of mess left behind. It seemed out of place, that she'd left her tools and bags of potting soil out, but Red sighed and said that his father had been in a mood lately, and probably rushed her out.

"In a mood," Rhys snorted. "How can you tell?"

He didn't get an answer.

"Dad's death," Red said. "Is that why he seems so happy?" He nodded toward Hyrum, who stood outside the shed with a broom, carefully sweeping dirt from the path that went from the shed to the yard. "Dad dies and Hyrum is...free?"

"I think it's probably more complicated than that. But I wasn't there, so I can't be sure."

I think he's happy because he lives with Aubrey, and she treats him the way he deserves. Everyone loves him and wants him. He's not afraid all the time now.

"Everyone," Red repeated. "Not one of you has issues with how he is?"

"Why would we?" Rhys asked.

Red reminded him of the tantrum in the car. "That gets exhausting."

"Sometimes," Rhys admitted. "I try to keep in mind that he's just trying to communicate. He doesn't always have the right words, or he's scared out of his mind. But it also doesn't happen a lot, so it's not the big deal it could be."

It used to happen more. The longer he lives with Aubrey and Jax, the less he lashes out. Today, he's really tired and he's afraid, so it's not a surprise.

"And with our father, he's in a constant state of terror." Red let out a heavy sigh. "If they'd just sucked it up and taken him to better doctors when he was a baby. Maybe they could have fixed him."

Anger flashed in Rhys's eyes, but was gone with a blink. "I'm gonna quote my dad here. 'We will not fix him, because he is not broken.' And the damage was prenatal, anyway. There's nothing to fix, not unless we take him to my dad's birth When."

"Then why not—?"

Do you want another Levi Munson? You change Hyrum's brain, and you might change his personality.

"Hy knows it's possible," Rhys said. "He knows that if he makes that decision, my dad will take him. But he also knows that not one of us thinks it's a good idea—Aubrey especially. She believes he is as God intended, however horribly he became Hyrum. The rest of us? He's a fucking light in our lives, Red. Why snuff that out?"

"But to forever be a child…"

"What? He's a grown assed adult."

"One, he really isn't. And two, watch your mouth, Rhys. I'm

tiring of the swearing. I understand the rules are different where you're from, but here we simply do not."

Unless you're Joe.

"Sorry. I'll try to watch it."

"Thank you. Now tell me…if you can stop time, why not just do that long enough to charge your device, and use it? Why the need for a safe space?"

"Because charging takes longer than I'm willing to interfere with the flow of time. I don't know what the fallout is, or how long I can keep everyone else held in a single moment without hosing up the entire world. I'll do it in a pinch, and I try to keep it to under a couple minutes, but I won't risk everyone else to make my life easier."

Red nodded as if he understood. "If only everyone else held to your personal creed. Especially those in power."

"Your dad won't have an iron grip on the church forever, you know. Nor on Hyrum."

"If I could have found a way to protect him…"

"Absent killing your own dad? In your society, what could you have done? Deep down, you know what he would have done to you."

"I could have died for him," Red murmured. "I should have taken that chance. I had the moment and squandered it."

Think it through. Older you did.

If you'd tried and failed, it's not you he would have hurt.

"Hyrum," Red breathed.

Or Joe. Or Spencer. Or all of them, really. He would have cut your heart out without ever touching you.

"And in the end, I got out, and he's stuck until they're dead."

"Maybe. Maybe not." When Hyrum closed the shed door, Rhys called him over. "Tell Red about your jobs, dude."

"Jobs?" Red was surprised.

"Ugh. Do I have to?" Hyrum's nose scrunched. "Jobs are boring talk. But if we don't get home soon, I'm gonna miss finishing all the flow charts for the new Elysium shuttle. And Rocko's dad said that if I wanted, I could watch when they make the parts for the engine. He says there's lots of sparks and white-hot light, and it's really, really big."

"You'll get home in time," Rhys said.

Red was curious; he pressed for more, and he leaned back in his chair to listen as Rhys and Hyrum chattered on about Hyrum's work at Ozoo, and some of the ideas he'd had that came to fruition.

"Drew would be dead without the air system Hyrum came up with," Rhys said proudly. "And a couple years ago he convinced the engineers to add onto it, bringing the tubing down through the entire space suit. It's trippy, but it works."

"I didn't do it by myself." As always, he refused to take all the credit. "Oh! I should check on the battery thingy and your phone. Maybe they're charged all the way now."

He bolted inside, leaving the door open.

"You believe us now?" Rhys ventured.

Red didn't think he had a choice. "How do I deal with your memories floating around in my head? They're beginning to feel like mine."

Rhys held his hand out again. "No worries, this won't hurt and you won't feel nauseated. I'm just going to show you how to create a tiny space in your brain where you can store it all to look at later."

Half a minute later, Red knew what to do, and Hyrum ran out, blurting that everything was charged but there was a new car outside and people were trying to open the door.

We can hide in the shed.

Rhys twitched in that direction, but Red went inside and Hyrum followed him. "I guess we're meeting people," Rhys said. "Watch, with my luck lately, it'll be Levi coming home early."

Oz throat punched him. That's always an option.

His luck held. It was not Levi; it was Darlene, Red's wife, accompanied by a much younger Hyrum. She'd been driving past and saw his car there, and stopped to make sure everything was all right.

We hadn't expected Hyrum to meet himself; the younger bolted into the kitchen with Red's name on his tongue, ready to speed-talk his way through everything he'd done that day, but he skittered on the polished floor and his mouth dropped open.

It only took three seconds. "Red, look! He has blue hair! It's really blue and he has pink pants! Pink! He's a *boy* in pink!"

Darlene nudged him from behind. "Hyrum, don't be rude."

Together, they said, "I'm not rude."

"His name is also Hyrum," Red explained. "They're quite a bit alike."

"Hi, I'm Rhys." He reached out to shake her hand, surprised when she only allowed him to touch her fingers. "We were about to leave. We'll get out of your hair."

Red shook his head. "Not yet. We'll get you on track soon enough." To his wife he said, "They wandered into Florida unintentionally, and I need to get them closer to the border so Rhys can call his father without detection. They clearly can't get there on foot, not with the blue hair."

"And me," Rhys said. "I get it, here I'm a bit of a problem."

Red tried to argue that it wasn't, but Darlene set a hand on his arm to stop him. "Red, sweetheart, don't lie to them. How many black people do you see running around here? He'd be stopped every mile, if not arrested."

Been there, done that already.

"And he won't be, if he's with me."

Rhys shrugged. "I just tell people I'm from Miami. They assume I've got Cuban ancestors."

Young Hyrum was in the kitchen, peeking into the freezer. "Can I have a popsicle? There's blue and that's my favorite. Oh. There's red and that's my favorite, too."

Red told him no. He didn't want their parents to know anyone had been in the house while they were gone. "Mom will know if a popsicle is missing. You know that, Hy."

"But they're mine!"

"And she keeps track of how many you have. We're not supposed to be here, and I really don't want to have to explain to Dad that I was in his house without permission."

He slammed the door closed. "He can't spank you, Red."

Our Hyrum went over to him, and guided him away. "But he can spank *you*," he said gently. "Don't make him want to punish you, okay?"

"Okay. Hey, you want me to meet you to my cat? He's dead but you can still talk to him."

They ran out the back door without another word.

"What's going on?" Darlene asked, looking out the open door.

Rhys gave her a sparse explanation: we'd wandered around, trying to get our bearings, and wound up in an alley with a dozen women. It wasn't long before a police officer showed up, and less than an hour later we were stuck in an office at the station. "Red's name was the only one we could readily cough up. I mean, aside from his dad. So they called him."

"Red, you rescued two men who had just been arrested?"

"Not arrested, just...taken in."

"The cop didn't want us in that alley with a bunch of women, that's all," Rhys said. "I understand that and I agree. I'm not sure what his deal is, though. He rolled up with a bunch of donuts for them and I didn't get the impression he had any problem with them. Just with finding us there."

"Harley," she said under her breath. "That man would feed the world if he could. Of course he took you in. He's very protective of the alley camps. But how did you wind up here, if not from Florida?"

Both Hyrums ran back in, sparing Rhys. The younger blurted, "Red! His name is Hyrum, too! And he had a white cat when he was little, too! And he likes cheeseburgers just like me! Can we go get cheeseburgers? I didn't eat for hours."

"An hour," Darlene sighed. "Hy, how about we stop for ice cream on the way home? We'll have a snack now, and I'll make cheeseburgers for a late lunch."

He bounced on his toes. "Promise? Can I have three of them? And fries? I'll scrape the skin off the potatoes for you." Without an answer, he headed for the front door. "Let's get chocolate!"

He was in the car before Darlene even turned to leave.

"Maybe press upon him that no, he can't dye his hair," Red suggested. "I might be late getting home, so don't wait on me. I really do need to drive them to the border."

"Don't get caught," she said, going up on her toes to kiss him. "I know where you're taking them, Red. It's not safe."

"People leave from there all the time. It's fine."

I'd been to the hole in the wall once, though from the other side. Hyrum began his trek across Midlam from that hole, and Aubrey escaped Florida from the same place. If that's where we were headed, I was worried less about that than the idea that Rhys needed to figure out exactly where that spot was, and calculate new jump coordinates with a less than perfect system.

"We can leave from here," Rhys said when she was gone. "The power pack is ready."

"Or once you're over the border you call the Emperor, tell him where you are, and let him come get you. I'd drive you out to the nearest rest stop, but I don't want to have to explain that if someone reports my trip to my father."

"Just call him." He turned to Hyrum. "Why didn't we think of that?"

"On account of a new When and probably you don't have his phone number."

His number has never changed. He's had the same one since he was seventeen.

Rhys reached for his phone, but Red stopped him. "Don't call from here. If you call up a Pacifican number, we'll have authorities here within minutes, and that's not something I can easily wave away."

"Aren't you like way up there in your church? Can't you just...order them away?"

"I'm just a bishop, Rhys. I have no power here."

"Yeah, well, give it time."

Rhys and Hyrum rode in the back seat, where they could crouch low. I presumed the ride would be nearly silent, just so that it wouldn't appear that Red was driving around talking to himself, but they talked nonstop.

For most of the time it took to get there, Red peppered them with questions about Aubrey. He was clearly aware of the trajectory her life had taken her, but was never given any details and hadn't spoken to her since the day he dropped her off in San Francisco. He left there hating himself because he had no idea how a 14-year-old could possibly make her way in a city that big, having been raised in the church, and was overwhelmed when her engagement to Prince Jackson was announced.

Rhys told her everything he knew, and I filled in as many blanks as I could. She'd landed running, found a place to live and fast-talked her way into school and a job; she worked hard to just survive. She met Jax through the Emperor, when he met her at the coffee shop she worked in, and kept working through the two years they dated, through grad school, and taught fifth grade until Rhys was four years old.

"Even after her children were born?"

That was non-negotiable. And it's where the Emperor stepped up. He was basically their nanny until they were teenagers.

"They're small now, though."

"Pretty small. And I don't even exist. The way things are going, I might never exist here. My potential future parents just cannot get their sh...crap together."

By the time we reached the hole in the wall, Red had a basic understanding of time travel and how changing things possibly created new timelines. He sympathized with Rhys's wish that the Emperor and Aisha just get over themselves already and admit they still had feelings. "I'll pray for that," he said as he got out of the car. "For your peace, as well."

Hyrum latched onto that. "Will you pray with us now? Or me, since Rhys doesn't believe. But my tummy says I need a blessing."

Believer or not, Rhys got a blessing. Red placed a hand on each of their heads and offered a quiet prayer, and ended it with a request that they both find their way, whatever that might be, whenever it might be.

Hyrum threw his arms around Red's waist. "I needed that. I always liked it when you prayed with me and blessed me and really liked it when you played with me and bought toys for me to have at your house, on account of Daddy threw all mine away."

Without letting go, he craned his head back to look at Red's face. "Your Hyrum knows you love him lots. But he's not sure about anyone else."

"I promise, I'll tell him often." He pointed the way to the

wide crack in the wall that surrounded Florida. "Get to the other side, and you can call the Emperor. There's a gas station a bit down the road if you want to walk that far and wait there."

"I know where it is," Hyrum said. "It's kinda far but we can walk that."

"Check the box in your brain later," Rhys suggested. "Lots of info there."

"Ok," Hyrum said as he headed for the wall. "Bye."

"Bye?" Red chuckled.

Rhys took a few steps and then turned back. "They're coming for him," he said. "Hyrum, I mean. There's no way the Emperor will leave him here now, not knowing what your father does to him. King Eli already knows. And when he tells Aubrey? I would expect it before Christmas, so...fair warning and all that. I'm pretty sure the Emperor will hurt anyone who gets in their way."

I rode on Rhys's shoulder, looking back at Red. He leaned against his car and watched as we neared the wall, but I didn't think I should tell either of them that just before we stepped through, Red hit his knees and started to cry.

35

Once past the border, Hyrum stopped to get his bearings. He remembered this place, but not as clearly as he hoped. There was a gas station ahead, but his gut told him it was too far to walk before calling Will. He had a sense that it had taken him longer than it should have, but he couldn't remember why.

You helped a guy with a broken-down car. You pushed it for a long time.

"Oh. Yeah. Well, I think not too far there's a spot we can sit in the shade and wait. It took me a couple of Amazing Graces and a few Christmas songs to get there."

Just to be sure, he sang the entire way. It took half an hour, but as he suspected, there was a small rest area to the side of the road. It looked like any one of dozens he'd used on his trip across Midlam, with a small restroom, two picnic benches, and a few well-canopied trees. That he remembered it was there made me wonder how much of that journey was seared into his mind.

I hoped it was not much at all, especially the last of it.

"What if he doesn't answer, Rhys?" Hyrum asked as they sat on the grass to lean against a tree. "What if the Guardians have him?"

"Then we jump. I'll set it for King Eli's office and hope we don't get shot."

We were not shot.

Will answered before the end of the first ring, and within two minutes had our coordinates as well as a plan to get us. He asked us to sit tight for an hour, and he'd be there with a shuttle.

"A shuttle," Rhys muttered when he clicked off from the call. "Not a car, a shuttle."

"What's that mean?"

"It means he's got access to a high-speed shuttle that can get here in half the time. And that means he's already spoken to Eli. We won't have to jump and risk going off course. The Emperor will deliver us to the king like the hairy, smelly future-forward gifts that we are."

"Do we stink?" Hyrum sniffed at his armpit. "I don't stink."

"It's already been a long, sweaty day. We probably stink a little."

"We can't meet Eli if we stink! That's rude, Rhys! We have to ask Will to take us somewhere we can take a bath or a shower and clean our clothes."

You can ask him, but he won't. And you don't smell bad. I would notice if you did.

"Wick's just being nice. We have to clean up!"

Rhys gestured to the vast emptiness around us. "Where? Find me a shower stall and I'll strip down and use it."

Hyrum stopped just short of rolling his eyes. "There's a bathroom right over there." He leaned forward and pointed to the small building fifteen feet away. "There's probably a sink. And probably paper towels and stuff. We can clean up, kinda. I did it all the time on my walk."

He did not clean up as often or as well as he supposed.

I didn't say that out loud.

By the time the shuttle was in view, they were mostly clean and redressed. Hyrum began waving, both arms making wide swoops, though I wasn't sure if it was a grand hello or more like, "Hey, we're over here, don't miss us!"

The doors popped open just before the shuttle's wheels hit the ground, and Aisha jumped out, racing toward us. She didn't know who to go to first, but Hyrum was closest so he got the first hug.

The Emperor, on the other hand, was more concerned with getting everyone into the shuttle as quickly as possible. "We can talk on the way back. Load up. We may be outside Florida but that doesn't mean we're not in their sights."

"Red was pretty careful," Rhys said as he buckled into the

front passenger seat. "He wouldn't even let me call you until we were on the safe side of the wall."

"How did you wind up here of all places?"

"Operator error, I suppose. At least we landed there and not, like, the middle of the Atlantic."

"But I can swim now," Hyrum blurted. "Me and Drew swim laps a lot. And when I get tired, he says, 'flop over onto your back, Hy. Just float.' And sometimes he makes me do that even if I'm not tired, on account of he wants me to practice so I don't drown."

They were treated to our Florida adventures from Hyrum's viewpoint, an hour of excitement and wonder, and they let him ramble because he got the point across and he seemed happy telling it. Just as we landed, he ended with the tale of meeting himself, and with amazement said, "He was really nice. I loved him. I wish I'd loved me back then."

~

By the time we landed in San Francisco, we were tired and despite the rest stop sponge bath, Rhys admitted his level of body odor was inappropriate for meeting the King. He asked Will if we could head for the lab first, grab a shower and some food, before walking across the street to see King Eli.

The request puzzled Will. There was no lab; the space Rhys thought he could use as refuge was the Emperor's playground, and the level where the lab would eventually be built currently housed rental storage units. Instead, he moved the shuttle to a space across the street from his teenaged apartment, and offered it for the night.

"You kept it." Aisha stared at a window one story up. "Wait. Do you still live there?"

His primary residence was the one-bedroom apartment across the hall from Jax and Aubrey. He moved there to accommodate their child care needs, but bought the old apartment. He wasn't sure why, other than it seemed to be a reasonable investment to a twenty-three-year-old.

"Well, was it?" she asked.

"Not one bit."

It was small and still smelled like sweaty teenagers, but it was clean, there was a bed and a sofa, and most important to Rhys, a shower. He and Hyrum took turns in the bathroom while the Emperor called for pizza, and when they were done they fell asleep on the living room floor, the easiest I'd seen Rhys drop off since he was a little boy.

~

King Eli's office was bright. Open window shades allowed natural light in from a fogless, sunny day, and the overhead lights—thousands of tiny bulbs embedded in the ceiling—twinkled as the sunlight hit them. I squinted and Hyrum audibly groaned at the sudden visual onslaught.

Will, on the other hand, was not bothered by it. He gestured for everyone to remain still, warning that the door might pop open suddenly with an armed guard on the other side, but we'd be fine.

"Eli is expecting us, right?" Rhys said. "He wouldn't send guards."

It was still early in the morning and we'd tripped an alarm. Will expected the first person through that door to be the Officer of the Day, and he would surely be armed.

"Bet he's got legs, too," Hyrum snickered.

The first person through was a middle-aged captain with his hand firmly on the grip of a plasma gun, though it was holstered. He also had both legs, which made Hyrum point and say, "See?"

Right behind him, already dressed for the day, was King Eli. He caught me by surprise as he entered; from his profile, I thought it was Jax. It took a few heartbeats for the thought to form that not only did fifty-something Eli resemble his son, but the Jax at home was older than this King. Eli's hair was fully black; Jax's was flecked with gray.

I was not, however, surprised by his resemblance to the Emperor. There was a strong genetic river flowing through the bloodline, and they tended to have overt similarities. Finn might have been the only exception; he seemed to take after his mother a bit more than his father, with her fairer complexion and slight build. But from Eli to Rhys and his siblings, there was no denying the family ties.

Eli had clearly expected us and began speaking without any acknowledgements. "Yesterday a car parked itself on the other side of the street, just outside the main doors," he started. "Within three hours, it was surrounded by four men in unique tactical suits. None attempted to gain access and disappeared soon after, but we presume they're watching."

He picked a remote off his desk and turned the giant monitor on, calling up security footage.

"Those are the same men," Will said. "I'm surprised it took that long."

"Your friend was able to make contact just before this happened. He was recovered from Denver and is on site." He turned the monitor off. "I don't know how the hell you find these people, Emperor. He managed to worm his way into the safe house security system and accessed a direct line to my office."

"He wrote the program that runs the whole thing," Rhys said. "Probably has a hand in a lot of the software you use. That car is his, too, if you didn't know."

"You came here after sending a decoy," Eli mused. "Why? Was your presumption that they would find the car empty and look elsewhere?"

Rhys shrugged. "Something like that, I guess."

"Do you think it worked?"

The look on Rhys's face suggested he was being talked down to, and he was in no mood for whatever lesson the King wished to impart. "I don't think it matters where I go. They'll find me, one way or the other."

Hyrum leaned toward him and whispered loudly, "You gotta be nice, Rhys. He's being nice to us. He doesn't have to let us be here."

If Eli was offended, he hid it. He directed the guard to activate the security net, and told him we'd be on our way to the quiet side of the war room.

"Sir, the net might not be sufficient," Will said.

"Nothing can get past that net, son."

"All due respect, these are men who are likely armed with technology beyond our ability to comprehend."

"Or they're contemporary-to-Rhys nutjobs just out to kidnap a young royal, Emperor. Their tech doesn't seem any better that what the boy is using. The tactical uniforms could be nothing more than elaborate costumes. With that glow, I'd think so."

"They knew I was displaced," Rhys said.

"You're clearly out of your own When. So are they. That doesn't mean they're who they say they are. Let's just get you down—"

The door popped open a few more inches. Queen Donna, dressed in a t-shirt and running shorts, barefoot, was not quite awake but wanted to know what was going on. Was this why he'd gotten up at the crack of dawn? Something the Emperor had gotten into?

Eli gestured to Rhys and Hyrum, and by extension, me. "This has less to do with the Emperor and more to do with these two. They're his relatives and need help."

"Hm. You said he had family but I had my doubts."

Hyrum waved at her. "Hi."

Rhys set his hand on Hyrum's shoulder, fingers seeking bare skin on his neck. Silently, he reminded Hyrum that this was Donna, Eli's wife, and she did not know who we were, nor should she. And if she asked, my name was Major, not Wick.

She took a step closer and reached toward me, rubbing my head with her pointy finger. "You look just like our cat. Though you seem much quieter."

I kept my mouth shut, lest I destroy the illusion.

"But you." She turned toward Aisha. "I remember you. You crushed him. His heart was so broken—"

"That was entirely my doing, ma'am," Will said. "My heart was simply a casualty of my own stupidity."

"Not now," Eli said. "We need to get you to safety."

With a sigh that clearly meant "you people need to get your

shit together," Donna turned to leave, and Hyrum watched until the door clicked shut behind her. Once she was gone, Eli reached under his desk for a button that caused the bookcase behind it to slide out of the way, revealing another brightly lit room.

"There's another room!" Hyrum blurted. "How come Jax never said there was another room? What's he hiding in there? I bet it's snacks."

"I can't speak for Jax," Eli said, leading the way, "but I only use this space as quick access to the elevator."

"There's an *elevator*?"

Rhys nudged him forward. "There are probably a dozen things in the building we don't know about. Like, I didn't know there was a security net. Why keep that a secret? And if there's a net, why does everyone get so bent when we get close to the roofline or edge of the balcony? It's not like we can fall."

"The net is rarely active," Will answered. "As for the rest, your parents are surely hoping you learn to avoid danger."

"Yeah, well, here we are, so that worked out well."

"You asked," Aisha said lightly.

He was not in the mood. I wanted to remind him he wasn't dealing with his parents at the age he was used to dealing with them; these people were barely more developed than he was. Their brains had only recently finished cooking; it would be a few more years before they had full use.

It occurred to me on the ride down in the elevator that if nothing changed, if Will did not do the things necessary to save Donna, in a year, maybe a little more, Jax would become King after Eli abdicated in a fog of grief. He'd grown up fast then; I didn't want that for this Jax, despite having not met him.

I want to have a conversation with Eli about Donna.

Will and Rhys ignored me. Hyrum started to speak, but closed his mouth when Rhys subtly shook his head.

Fine. You need to have that conversation. Let me be there. I can give details.

"What's the cat want?" Eli asked.

Come on. She doesn't have a lot of time left.

"Sir?"

"The cat. What's Wick want? I know you understand him, Emperor. He clearly wants something."

"A litter box," Will lied.

"Me, too," Hyrum said. "Well, not a litter box. But I'd use it if I had to."

Rhys blew air through his lips. "Dude, you are totally scooping that yourself."

"Nuh. I just gotta pee. I don't even need a box. I could use a sink if that's all there is. Or a plant in the corner. I did that when I was little and my mom always wondered why it stinked all the time." He snorted and added, "One time she decided that it was Lazybones peeing on it. I never did get in trouble for it."

Eli assured him that the war room, as well as the conference room in which we would spend our time, had adequate facilities for a long-term stay.

"Not too long, I hope," Rhys said as the elevator doors slid open.

I'd been in the war room once, a bit over fifteen years in the future. It was loud, a cacophony of voices puncturing the air, with a multiplex of surveillance monitors hanging on the walls, all active and observed by the King's trusted advisors and military staff. Then, Will and Jax sped us through to get Oz, Zed, and Drew to a shuttle that would whisk us away to the Denver safe house. This time, we were able to linger for a moment, allowing Rhys and Hyrum the time to stand a gawk at the enormity of the war room buried deep under their home.

"How?" Rhys uttered. "How is this even possible? We're past the bedrock, right? How hasn't the building collapsed?"

"Magic," Eli said. He beckoned to a soldier waiting near a door twenty feet away, who nodded once and then turned to open it.

I know you, don't I?

Anthony Meyers was as young as I could have possibly remembered him. Here, he was not a general, but a major; I quickly did the math and realized that it would only be a few months before he would accept a temporary assignment to forward a battalion of allied military in Europe. He would lead thousands into battle, a war not of Pacifica's making, but one they would win in defense of Russian encroachment across borders they refused to recognize as valid. They wanted everything as far east as Poland, and were poised for victory until Pacifica and Midlam entered the fray.

It was there he earned his reputation as a steel-nerved and rigid-spined combatant; it was that same courage and determination to do whatever necessary for his King and country that would later help save Prince Andrew's life as he floundered in space, stranded outside of the Elysium station.

Major Meyers was all business; General Meyers was a friend.

As we paused outside the conference room door, I reached out a paw to touch him, hoping he would understand that I liked him. His lips curled up at the corners just a tiny bit, but I didn't think he grasped what I meant. I also didn't think he knew Will understood me, and probably shouldn't, so I didn't ask anyone to translate for me.

Once we get home, remind me to tell Meyers that I think he's pretty okay.

The spacious conference room looked as if it had been hiding underground since the nineteen-seventies. The walls were a depressing sort of gray, there were no windows, either real or imitation, and an odor hanging in the air suggested the room had once been staffed by twenty angry teenagers who had bathed in convenience store cologne. Overhead lighting was dim, though there were several table lamps scattered throughout. Divots in the carpet hinted that the long table with more chairs than I count, currently pushed up against a wall, normally took up most of the central real estate. It had been moved out of the way to accommodate beds now in a neat line along the back wall, a sofa that served as a bit of a privacy break, and bean bag chairs dropped onto the floor.

There was a small bookcase near the sofa, loaded with books, paper, markers, and coloring books. In a box near the bottom shelf were small toy cars, a hand-held video game system, and board games.

No one had asked for those things. Eli grasped Hyrum's needs, and speculated at what he might want to have to pass the time. He may not have guessed that Hyrum's input would be needed as the others worked, but he understood that there was a necessity for childhood distractions.

On the wall across from the displaced table was a small kitchenette, much like the one in Finn's lab. It had a small sink, narrow cabinets, limited counter space, and a small refrigerator. Anthony pointed to the various cabinets, listing what we would find there: ready to eat breakfast foods, bread, and snack bars, and the refrigerator was fully stocked with milk, cheese, lunch meats, and soft drinks. Anything else we needed would be provided upon request, including hot meals we could not prepare for ourselves.

He pointed toward a door near the makeshift bedroom, poised to say that the restroom was there, but it opened and George came out, drying his hands with a paper towel.

"Took you long enough," he grumbled. "Ask a king for help, and what does it get you? Locked in the basement, that's what."

He was neither irritated nor annoyed, and Eli laughed.

"I'll have that info removed from your devices before you leave here," Eli said.

"But he knows it cold," Rhys said. "He wrote—"

Eli meant his personal contact information. He might have elaborated further but Aisha marched over to George and lightly punched him in the shoulder.

"That's for ditching us, you moron. What the hell? Why?"

He'd hoped, as Will presumed, to distract or delay the guardians. If they were dealing with him, they weren't off chasing Rhys and Hyrum. "I wish I could say it worked, but... you disappeared, and so did they. None of them said a word, none of them even looked at one another, or even me. They just vanished."

"And what if they'd stayed? What if they did something to you trying to get information about Rhys?"

"What, like some futuristic alien anal probe? I mean, if they offered me dinner after—"

She slugged him in the shoulder again, harder.

"I didn't know you cared," he said, grinning.

"I care about getting them home, George. I care about not leading those...*people* to them. Tell someone before you pull another stupid stunt like that. Warning might have been nice."

"How could I have warned you? An announcement? 'Plug your ears, guardians, I have shit to say.'"

Eli stood with his arms folded, and while they ramped up, he kept an eye on Hyrum. He stood near the center of the room and had begun tugging at his t-shirt, winding the fabric around his fingers, and he stared at his feet. Slowly, he started to rock from heel to toe. This was just the beginning, and if allowed to go on, would end in a full fledge temper tantrum.

Rhys. Hyrum.

He tore himself away from the fight that was not exactly a fight, and went to his uncle. Gently, he set his hand Hyrum's back, trying to get him to look up. "What's wrong, Hy? Body or feelings?"

Everything was wrong. Aisha was nice to them but mad all the time, and now she was yelling at George. Will wasn't really Will on account of he still needed to grow up, but Hyrum needed him to be a grownup now. "I want to go home, Rhys. I want to see my daddy who loves me and knows who I am, and I want Aisha to love Will and stop being mad, and I just know we're going to miss Christmas and then I won't be able to write a note to Santa to say sorry for breaking my bike, and we're gonna miss Aubrey's birthday and Jax's birthday and I just want to go home."

Rhys moved his hand from Hyrum's back to his neck. Sharply, Hyrum knocked it away, spinning on his feet to face Rhys. "Nuh. Don't do that. You're gonna do what Aubrey always does and try to make me feel better but I don't wanna feel better. I wanna be sad and I wanna be mad."

"All right. I get that. But we'll get home. I promised."

"But you *can't* promise," he wailed. "Just because you're smart and can do stuff, that doesn't mean you can find a way home. I'm not a baby, Rhys, I know some things. Maybe you will but it might take years and years and then I'll be old and you'll be a grownup and we won't fit in anymore and we'll have to hide the whole time."

Rhys could not refute the possibility. "If it were just me, yeah, it would probably take years. But I have Grandpa's data, Hy. And we have this Emperor and this Aisha and George, with all their accumulated knowledge. I have help with the coding and the math. All we have to do is find the place where we jumped from home to here."

Angrily, "That might not be there anymore. You can't go to a place that closed."

"No, but anyplace that was ever there can be opened again."

Why can't we just do what Liam did? Return to the spot where we know time diverged, and get home from there?

"Overlap," Rhys answered. "If we go there and portal home to just before I fix the car, there will be another Rhys and that Hyrum will also go home. There would be two of us, and I'm not sure what the ramifications from that will be."

"You wouldn't just merge?" Aisha asked.

"If I'd gone back early enough to stop myself from fixing the car, probably. Dad's done something like that before, when he had to change something to save Oz's life. But he's pretty clear that any changes have to happen soon after the event, and it's been too long now. Not that I would stop myself to begin with. I won't let them die again." His voice caught. "I can't."

She left George and stepped over to him, wrapping him in a hug. When she let go of him, she turned to Hyrum. "We'll help him keep his promise."

"What about the guardians? They don't want me. They only want Rhys. What if they get him and I'm here all by myself?"

Do not promise him that can't happen.

"We'll still look for a way to get you home, son," Eli said. "And in the meantime, you'll be here and safe, with us."

"But..."

"You will be loved, I promise."

Tears poured down his face. "But what if it takes a long time and I forget my real family? I'm getting old and that might happen."

"You're middle aged at worst," Will said. "And I have everything Rhys and Wick have shared with me. I won't let you forget them, and I swear to you, I will personally escort you home if it comes to that, even if it means I stay there for the rest of my life. But it's rhetorical, because we *will* find a way, and it will be soon."

I think Aisha wanted to kick him in the nuts for that; he had no right to put the hint of a time on that. But Hyrum sniffed and nodded, then asked Eli if he could use the paper and markers, so she let it go.

She glared at Will, though, and if she'd had Hyrum's gifts, he probably would have gone up in a sparky burst of flames.

36

It wasn't over.

Hyrum calmed down for a grand total of 16.75 minutes, long enough for Eli to leave and for Rhys and George to settle at the table with open laptops. Aisha dragged a whiteboard across the floor to a spot near the table while Will counted slips of metal sheeting that Major Meyers had delivered at the Emperor's request. He'd brought those plus a box filled with computer chips, microprocessors unavailable to the public but easily accessible in the bowels of the royal house.

"Hyrum, would you like to help count these?" Will asked, not looking up. "It would help to pair a processor to every two strips—"

"Nuh." Hyrum stood in the center of the room, within reach of the sofa on one side and the book shelf on the other. His arms were folded and his brow furrowed, neck bent so that his chin touched his chest. I recognized that look: *you can't make me, I don't wanna.* When he reached this point, there was no making him do anything, and redirecting him was difficult.

"Problem?"

Without looking up, he nearly growled, "I'm not helping anything. I wanna go outside."

"Can't go outside, Hy," Rhys said without taking his eyes off the computer. "We'd be exposed."

"I don't care. I want to go outside and play or walk to the ferries and get a cheeseburger."

"Dude, when we get home—"

"No!" He finally looked up. His eyes were red from the effort of trying not to cry, and he dropped his arms, clenching hands into tight fists. "I want to go outside *now*."

Everyone but George stopped what they were doing and looked at him, watching as he wound up from merely upset to rage, and it happened faster than they could blink five times.

"Yeah, that won't work with me," Rhys said. "You don't have to help, but we can't go out."

He cleared off the bookshelf first. Picture books and coloring books skittered across the floor. A box of markers exploded across the floor, bouncing and rolling, caps knocked off and pinging left and right. A lamp near the sofa rocketed toward the beds on the far wall. Pillows flew over the back of the sofa, landing on the table, where they slid into George's workspace.

He still didn't look up, but pushed the pillows aside, onto the floor.

Hyrum tore around the room, grabbing and throwing anything he could get his hands on, with the exception of me. That was a line I didn't think he would cross, so I simply ducked when the pillows soared over me and waited for him to get it out of his system.

Neither Will nor Aisha knew what to do, but after Hyrum literally growled, Rhys calmly got up and went to him. Hyrum slapped his hands away and told him to get away, and for good measure shoved Rhys hard enough that he stumbled backward.

"Stop it," Rhys said when it looked as if Hyrum were going to hit him. "Be as mad as you want, but you're not getting what you want."

"You can't send me to my room, Rhys. You're not a grown up and I don't have a room here."

"Then just sit down and suck it up. And when you calm down, clean up the mess you made."

He sat on the floor, legs crossed, and as Rhys made his way back to the table Hyrum muttered under his breath, "You can't make me."

"No, but you're not going to be able to draw pictures or read anything until you do. So you can just sit there, bored out of your mind, or you can clean up and then help us with this. I don't care which you do, but you're damn well not throwing another tantrum."

"I will if I wanna."

Rhys was back in his chair, and he spun it to face Hyrum. "Don't be a jerk. Be mad at me if you want, but don't take it out on them. They don't have to help us, you know. They could just leave us alone and let us run from the guardians by ourselves. We're about as safe as we can be here—"

Tears poured down Hyrum's face. "But there aren't windows, Rhys. There weren't windows in the not-safe place, either. Or after that. We're never gonna see outside again, I just know it."

"We were outside most of yesterday."

"But that's not the same! And it was cloudy and not sunny and we were in Daddy's house a lot. It's not like walking to see the ferries. I was scared. I just want to go out and play for a while. And then get a cheeseburger."

"We'll get—"

"Stop saying that! You can't promise that!" His voice cracked, and he nearly choked on the words. "I'm never gonna get to ride my bike again on account of we're stuck here maybe forever and ever."

Quietly, Will placed the boxes of metal strips and processors on the table, and went to the door. He whispered to the soldier outside as Hyrum's crying got louder; when he was done whispering Hyrum was laying on his side, knees to chest, and he was wailing.

They let him cry. Rhys went back to his work; Aisha was torn between wanting to comfort him and not wanting to give attention to the tantrum. Will waited quietly by the door, watching him, knowing it was just a matter of time before he was cried out.

Several minutes later, as Hyrum wound down, the soldier returned with a large box-shaped light on a platform, followed by another with a long narrow air blower that was set on the floor near the sofa. They plugged both in, nodded at the Emperor, and left without saying a word.

"This," Will said as he turned the light on, "mimics sunlight. And this—" he flipped the switch on the blower "—feels like a gentle breeze. Spend some time sitting in the light and you'll start to feel better, Hyrum. It's not the same as being outside, but I suspect your body needs sunlight right now, and that's why you feel so bad."

Sniffing, Hyrum looked up. "My brain feels itchy."

"You spend quite a bit of time outside every day, don't you?"

"Uh huh. I ride my bike and go see my friends, and I play on the playground with the babies. I even get to go outside and play on my work breaks on account of we have a playground with swings and stuff across the street."

"This is not a substitute for that, but it should help. Give it twenty minutes to half an hour."

"Okay."

"Think about what you want to do when you're done."

With a heavy sigh, Hyrum said, "I'll clean up my mess."

"Are you all right?"

"Am I in big trouble?"

"No. Should you be?"

"You're not mad?"

"I am perplexed, certainly, but I am not angry. I understand the frustration of feeling locked up, Hyrum. My parents' lab was underground, and I spent more hours there every day than I cared to. It's not easy, is it?"

Hyrum shook his head. "Did you have a light, too?"

"Indeed. My mother often held our school sessions sitting on a blanket on her office floor, using the light. She needed it every bit as much as I did."

"Did you ever just lay there and read?"

"I did. I found that time to be quite enjoyable."

"Okay. I'll read and you can count things if you can count high enough."

"I will endeavor to count as high as necessary."

Hyrum plucked a book from the floor and stretched, flipping through the pages to make sure it was something he wanted, as he often said, to spend the minutes on. Minutes weren't forever, and there was no point in wasting any on books that were filled with kissing things or fractions.

"How," Aisha whispered to George, "did you ignore that?"

"I've dated many a diva," he said with a hint of amusement. "Between them and the raging bad-boyfriend bar fights at Rico's? This was nothing."

"The difference," Rhys interrupted, "is that he can't help it. He's generally so controlled that he actually deserves the occasional outburst. If we'd been home, Aubrey would have sent him to his room and let him go at it as long as he needed to."

And he knows it's okay. No one hits him and no one makes him miss dinner because of it.

That gave Rhys pause. "Wait. What? I knew his dad was a dick and hit him but no dinner?"

That wasn't his dad. That was Valerie's choice punishment.

"His mom? Seriously?"

I know you think she's nice because she helps Alex and Charlie, but she had her moments as a horrible parent.

"No, I don't have any illusions about her, but damn. How can you not feed a kid who's always that hungry?"

As Will sat in a chair close to Rhys, he softly said, "Perhaps his hunger isn't merely attributable to his high metabolism."

"We all have kinks," Aisha said.

George snorted. "So tell us about yours."

She admitted she probably had a few but couldn't cough them up on the spot. I had ideas—in the years since Will broke her heart, she had sought comfort wherever she could—but I didn't want to embarrass her.

Not yet, anyway.

If we really did get stuck there, I had plenty of time for that.

~

They worked all day. Food was consumed at the table next to their computers. Hyrum cleaned his mess and then dutifully began helping count and sort materials; his mood was greatly improved, which made me think that Rhys could stand to spend a few minutes under that light, too. Though he tried not to be, he was grouchy and especially irritated with Aisha.

It was almost a relief when, right after Hyrum crawled into bed, he admitted that he was tired, too, and had little doubt that he could sleep.

"Maybe everyone should try tonight." He sighed as he got up. "Brain cells are fried. Numbers on the screen look like Greek. Surely, I'm not the only one."

"I've got another hour left in me, I think," Aisha said. "I'm so close to finishing this. If I get it right, and if my assumptions are correct, you'll have better control over the variables."

"And I'll have this part—" George tapped the partially assembled jump bracelet "—all but sealed up. You'll be able to test it first thing."

No one said the quiet part out loud: this would allow Rhys to jump anywhere, anywhen, but he'd still be stuck in this timeline. Will especially was not going to admit out loud that he was no closer to finding a way for Rhys and Hyrum to travel from one timeline to the other.

Tomorrow someone needs to get root beer in here. Hyrum will be happy if he can get root beer.

"Water is sufficient," Will said, softly so that he wouldn't wake them.

It's not about sufficiency. It's about making someone happy. You remember happy, right?

"You're not happy?" Aisha asked.

How can he be happy with that giant stick up his asterisk?

"Keep it up, Wick," Will said. "I'll stop translating for you."

You miss this, admit it.

He set his tablet aside. "I do miss you, Wick. I look forward to the day you remember more of life before this When. But I reserve the right to complain about the snark."

He was probably going to start complaining right then and there, but Aisha sat up straighter and uttered, "Eureka. I think this will do it." She turned her computer so George could see. "Use the micro-thin processor. It will fit better between the strips and should put off less heat."

"Yeah, none of that looks like math to me," he said. "I'll take your word for it. And I found the parameters that allow for adjustment during a jump."

Her math and his on-the-fly coding meant that Rhys would have the control Aisha wanted: his jumps would not rely solely on the computations in the bracelet itself, but would link to his transponder in an eighth of the time. It was thinner than Will's bracelet, less noticeable, and if he wanted, he could wrap it around his forearm or even his bicep to better conceal it.

"How's this going to affect your future work, Blackshear?" George asked. "If Rhys's father invented it…"

He didn't care. He'd had the idea and had been working on it when not attending to the royal offspring or his duties to the prince. All he cared about was that it functioned as he'd hoped, and with the data he now had, he could spend more time trying to understand it instead of attempting to create it without access to all of his father's research.

"I'm surprised you didn't leave home with it."

"I had what he could give me. When I left, he still had not coalesced the notion of physical transporting while also navigating time. He believed he was only moving people through time, not space, and had no time to explore both."

"So he sent people away, into other points in time, to what?" Aisha asked.

"To save our sorry asses," George said. "Jesus, when he went public with this? We knew there was a potentially planet-ending hunk of rock hurtling our way, yet a whole lot of people thought it was some publicity stunt to loosen political purse strings. Religious nutjobs were screaming about the sacrilege of even the idea of time travel, a very vocal group was screaming about the whole thing being a lie perpetuated to generate fear that would end the way our government functioned, and only a small number bothered to look at the data and admit, yeah, we're fucked."

"He knew that would happen," Will said. "I think the impending chaos is the biggest reason he was willing to let me leave so soon."

He knew who you were by then. I don't think he felt like he had a choice. The Emperor of San Francisco had to exist in this When, not that one. And it nearly broke him.

I was spared further explanation, and any hint of the possible turmoil of his parents' possible separation, by Hyrum. He slipped out of bed, sniffling, and shuffled over to the side of the sofa, where he paused when he realized he didn't know what he wanted.

"Did we wake you, sweety?" Aisha asked. "I'm sorry."

"Nuh. My tummy woke me. It hurts."

She started to get up. "Do you need to eat? I can make you something."

"Not that kind hurt. The sad kinda hurt." It clicked with him, and he went to Will. "Can you cuddle with me? On the sofa? I think that's what my tummy needs."

He was well acquainted with the cuddling of small children; between Oz and Zed, it was a near daily occurrence. I don't think he'd ever been asked to cuddle with a fully grown man before, and I saw the confusion blink in his eyes, but he nodded, said, "I would love to, Hyrum," and got up.

Hyrum threw his arms around Will's waist and hugged hard before taking his hand to lead him to the other side of the sofa.

"You're an idiot, you know," George said quietly, to not be heard over the soft talk coming from the sofa. "Find me another man who would be as gentle and patient."

"You wouldn't?"

"You've met me, right? No, I wouldn't. Neither would James, for that matter."

"James has his moments."

George scooted closer. "James can fuck. Don't conflate that with being gentle and caring. We both know he can be the biggest bitch in the room if it suits him."

"And you think the Emperor can't?"

He hesitated. "I think he can be the biggest *threat* in the room, certainly. He's probably always the most dangerous. But he doesn't need to show it off, and because that's innate, he doesn't worry about perceptions. If he needs to be gentle, he will be. I suspect he wants to be gentle. And don't get me wrong, I've spent every day since kindergarten hating him, so I'm not trying to puff up some old friend. He could spontaneously combust and I'd be fine with it. But I still think you're an idiot."

"But he—"

"You think you're the only one who's ever had their heart broken? Get over it already. It's been what, ten years? Hell, in my twenties I was crushed at least three times. One of those was someone I honestly thought I'd be with for the rest of my life. And he was outright cruel when he ended it. For a few awful weeks, I wanted to die."

"But you never went crawling back to him, did you?"

"Aisha. I'm married to *James*. I've crawled back after he's broken my heart more times than I can count. Definitely more times than is healthy. And hell, so have you, at least once."

"And I have apologized."

"I'm not looking for an apology. I get it, I really do. I'm trying to get you to open your eyes. If you were willing to give a serial cheater another chance, why the hell would you hold a grudge against someone you never even kissed?"

"Because it mattered to me, George. Because he took me from euphorically hopeful to a sobbing mess in under five seconds. Because he destroyed every shred of self-worth I had and it took *years* to get it back."

"Hm. And nothing James did was worse?"

"Nothing hurt me as much."

"Liar," he chortled. "You honestly expect me to believe that right after having a baby, a baby so new the umbilical stump hadn't fallen off yet, it didn't absolutely gut you to walk in and find him with *two* other people. In your own bed."

Defiantly, she folded her arms. "I half expected that. He was honest about the odds of him being monogamous."

"Bullshit. He gut-punched you more times that you can count, and you're still friends with him. You co-parent amazingly well. He doesn't deserve anything from either of us, yet here we are. I keep going back and you keep doing whatever the hell it is you do. So tell me, really, why you're so forgiving to everyone else except the one man with whom you can probably be truly happy."

37

Everyone slept.

Will fell asleep on the sofa with Hyrum nestled against him; Aisha eventually stomped off and slammed herself into the bed farthest away from Rhys, leaving George to take the middle bed. He could have slid into the one next to Rhys, which had previously been claimed by Hyrum; if Hyrum woke up, he would seek out that bed. If Will decided he needed a bed for better sleep, taking the middle left only the one next to Aisha.

I'm not sure what his point was, but I gave him a little bit of credit for trying.

Hyrum woke first, confused to find himself stretched out on top of Will. He carefully slid off and made his way to the tiny kitchenette, where there was a coffeemaker and a giant can of fresh grounds. As quietly as he could—which was not exactly quiet—he went about the task of preparing coffee, the same as he did at home nearly every morning. After that was going, he peeked into the fridge to see what he could make for breakfast, and bounced on his toes when he spotted cans of pre-mixed cinnamon rolls.

"Oh. Wick. These would be a good way to say sorry, right? On account of I wasn't nice yesterday."

I think four out of five people will be very happy with it.

"I've seen Will eat cinnamon rolls before."

Our Will. Who knows about this one.

He sighed. "They're the same person, Wick. Or they used to be, before everything went all wonky. He even cuddles like our Will. It was nice."

You helped him fall asleep. He needed that.

"Really? Good. I wonder how come I can fall asleep all the time but Rhys and Will can't."

Genetics, maybe. But you also burn through so many calories every day you're probably exhausted every night.

Using his pointy finger, he counted out the cinnamon rolls, trying to decide if he needed a third can. "Four each is enough, you think? I'll share mine with you."

If anyone is still hungry they can make toast or something. And I have cans of beefy goodness, so I'm set. It might not be a good idea for me to have sugar first thing.

"It's not good for me, either, but I'm still gonna."

Sweet-tinged aroma seeped into the air pulled them awake, one by one. Will was first, then George, then Aisha. They debated whether to wake Rhys or save breakfast for him; which would he want more, sleep or food, but I knew so I raced across the room and jumped onto the bed, landing on his stomach.

He woke with an *oof*.

And I was right; he wanted food more.

I was also right about Will. He ate one cinnamon roll to be nice, but overly sweet food was not his thing. Aisha only ate two, which made both Rhys and Hyrum very happy, since they got the leftovers. It almost poked through the film of sadness I felt clinging to them. Hyrum still wanted to go outside to play in the sunshine; Rhys just wanted to figure out how to stay ahead of the guardians, and then find a way home.

Will was no closer to an epiphany than he'd been the night before, but George assembled two jump bracelets and proclaimed them ready to test. He volunteered again, but Hyrum snatched a stuffed bear off the toy shelf and asked if it could serve as a tester. "We can make him jump around the room! It'll be funny!"

His sense of humor was not exactly shared, but Rhys didn't see a reason why they couldn't use the bear and it spared George any risk. "We can jump it in here, and into the bathroom. Is there anywhere else we can send it down here? To test at least a little distance with moving it through walls. It doesn't need a transponder for that."

Biff—Hyrum decided he was Biff the Bear—jumped his fuzzy way back and forth across the room, into the bathroom (specifically, to the top of the toilet tank, which made Hyrum giggle) and then, "on account of it might make him scream," Biff jumped to the war room where Major Meyers sat at a control panel.

Hyrum peeked through a 1-inch opening of the door, giggling when Biff appeared near the Major's elbow. He was disappointed by the reaction, though; Meyers' head twitched in the bear's direction, but he didn't startle. He remained focused on his monitor, fingers poised on the keyboard as if he were ready to begin typing out his memoirs, but refused to give us the satisfaction of a reaction.

Will finally went out to retrieve the bear, and he did it without saying a word to Meyers.

"Suffice to say," Will said as he handed the bear to Hyrum, "he will tell this story to anyone with clearance high enough to hear for many years."

"But he didn't jump."

"He's a well-trained soldier, Hyrum. He doesn't react unless ordered to do so. But he absolutely will not forget the day a little red bear magically appeared next to him in the war room. Everyone in that room will talk about it the first chance they get."

Rhys took the bracelet off the bear and wrapped it around his own wrist. "At least we know it works as well as the other one. Now we figure out what's next. How do we use this to get from here to home?"

George lifted the clunky jump device off the table. "I have no idea, but I suggest that for a while, you wear both. Just in case you need a backup."

"The power reserves are better—"

"Even experienced parachutists have a reserve, Rhys. When your life is on the line, especially if more than just yours is on the line, you take precautions. A reserve is a good precaution."

Rhys took the device from him. "Always code a back door, even if you've been told not to."

"Exactly."

"Funny enough, I had this teacher who told us that on day one. Halfway through the term he had us coding this odd little video game and one of the instructions was to not write in a back door. So many freaking people failed the assignment because they went by the written instructions."

"Sounds like a good teacher."

"Yeah, you will be. I mean, Isaac is kinda lukewarm on you, but who the hell wants to take classes with their dad?"

"I seriously clone myself." George sat in the chair by his laptop. "Eh, with my ego, that's not a surprise. And James is all right with it?"

"Isaac calls him 'Odie.' Like, 'O' and 'D' for 'Other Daddy.'"

"And he's older than you."

"By a couple months."

"You two." He pointed at Will and then Aisha. "If you ever decide to start fucking, let me know. Apparently, I need a head start."

Will cleared his throat. "Good to know." He took that as his cue to leave the room, with the excuse that he was heading up a floor to test a jump from there.

"Really, George?" Aisha said.

"Oh, get over it. You and I both know that if he was down for it, you'd fuck him even without a relationship."

She bent over, hands on knees, until her face was inches from his. "And so would you. I don't care how much you hated him, I've seen how you've looked at him, especially when he had his shirt off. You would ride him hard and put him away wet."

Puzzled, Hyrum turned to Rhys. "How do boys do kissing things, anyway?"

Dude, you know how. Think about it.

"Oh." He looked at George. "Don't do that. That hurts."

"Only if you do it wrong, Hy."

Confusion wrapped around Hyrum. "My daddy did it wrong?"

Before George could answer, Aisha crossed the floor and wrapped her arms around him. "Sweetheart, whatever he did to you was wrong. "

"You're very tall," Hyrum mumbled.

"Dude, you've hugged my mom before," Rhys said. "You know how tall she is."

Boobs, bro. He's face first into massive boobs that don't belong to your actual mother.

Voice muffled, Hyrum said, "They're nice boobs. But I shouldn't be touching them. That's a sin."

Amused, she let go and I think was poised to apologize to him, but Will suddenly appeared near the bathroom door.

"So, we can jump for sure," Rhys said. "Here, anyway. But we need access to all of Grandpa's data and we can't get that here. We'd have to go so far forward that we might create fixed points that you won't be able to get around later."

Our Will went forward to tell himself all kinds of things and that didn't create fixed points. It just gave this one new reasons to do what he was always going to do anyway.

"Not worth the risk," Rhys said. I understood why he said that—he didn't want to do anything that would keep Will and Aisha apart, and if they were historically apart 200 years in the future what might that mean for now?—but I thought he was wrong.

Finn might be able to help, even 50 years in the future.

"Old Mint?" Rhys asked. "It's time locked. At the very least we can ask someone from his When to go get him. Pass a note if we need to. Or the data we need might be there already, if he logged it."

It was possible, but we would have to jump just outside the lock and then walk in. Will's concern was knowing we could be followed anywhere outside the building; they were out there, watching, surely.

"You and I get between them and Rhys and Hyrum," Aisha said. "Give the boys a chance to run inside. They can't be followed in there, can they?"

The guardians could enter the Old Mint. But with the time lock in place, they wouldn't be able to remove anyone. A person entering the Old Mint could only leave with the things they'd taken in; if no one had a hand on Rhys going in, they could not take him out. I expected a lengthy explanation on the time lock and how it worked, because George's eyes lit up and he had questions poised to pour out, but Rhys suddenly looked up.

"The net is down," he said. "It just went quiet."

I cocked my head to listen. The annoying background whine was gone.

"We need somewhere to go, and fast," Rhys said.

Aisha thought the Old Mint was still the place to shoot for; if they'd breached the net they were in the building and not outside, which made it feel safe to her. I think Will was about to agree with her, but Hyrum shook his head and grunted, "Nuh."

"No?" she asked.

"We should just go see someone who knows a lot about time stuff. Drew knows more than Finn, I think."

"Andrew is seven years old," Will said.

Sighing, "Not *him*. Old Drew. We go see him a lot. And I met old me, and he told me about Drew's time spaghetti. He uses it to go to spots in time and he whispers things to people to get them to do what they need to do. I think if anyone can figure it out, it's Old Drew."

"That's jumping forward," Will said. "I cannot—"

"Yeah, you really can," Rhys said. "You can go anywhere from here to about forty years from the day you left, because we know time exists to that point. Forget everything your dad told you. If you know the time period exists, you can go."

Just don't take Aisha places like, say, nineteen thirty. She would not be treated well.

They agreed; since Rhys and Hyrum had both visited Drew in his sixties, there was no reason to avoid it. He wouldn't know any of us and might be gutted with grief upon seeing Will, but he would help.

"And this is where we part ways," George said as everyone moved to stand together. "You have everything I can give you and I think from this point I'd just be in the way. Slow you down. I'll keep looking at the data and if something pops out at me, I'll call Aisha."

"George..."

"Someone needs to be home when James comes back with Jaime, Aisha. You know him, the odds of him staying with his parents as long as they planned are slim. If he comes home early…as far as I know, you're using the kid-free time to knock around San Francisco with an old friend. I won't even have to lie."

"Thank you," she said.

"Same," Rhys added. "For everything. And man, I hope to hell you really do become a teacher, because you're my favorite. Seriously."

George might have had more to say, but because Rhys had no idea how much time we had, and to spare anyone an emotional farewell, he tapped his bracelet and we jumped.

38

We landed in Finn's lab. I'd expected to pop up in Drew's office, with the giant windows facing the bay and the Golden Gate Bridge, but we appeared in the middle of the lab's first level. Unchanged over the years, the offices and bathrooms were to our left, the kitchenette to our right, and the computer island was right in front of us. Just behind us was the entry, and I half expected another Will to storm through it with a tiny me perched on his shoulder.

There was no Will here, though. In this When, this far into the future, Will and I had both been gone for a long time.

"This is where Dad's always told me to go if something happens when I portal hop," Rhys explained. "If I'm uncertain or scared, head to Grandpa's lab, because any version of Grandpa will try to help, even if he doesn't know me. And this one won't, because you're not here."

"Doesn't that mess around with fixed points?" Aisha asked.

We jump forward a lot, and Will isn't there. I don't think there's a fixed point.

"We need help, and this is still within the Emperor's potential lifetime. I didn't know where else to go. Drew won't know us and seeing him without warning might really hurt."

Gently, Aisha reminded Rhys that seeing Will might do more than hurt his father.

"Yeah, I know. But he's at least aware of the possibility."

Will moved away from us, wandering the periphery of the room. He marveled at the sameness; it looked like it did when he was a boy, trapped down here to study while his parents worked.

In his adopted When, this level of the lab was filled with storage units for rent, and the wide lanes between them was an ideal spot for parents to bring their children on rainy days, where they learned to ride bikes and balance on roller skates.

"Bikes and skates," Aisha murmured. "So this place is basically, what, early twenty first century?"

"Bicycles exist," Will said with a sigh. "Granted, after age six or so they're not popular. But they exist."

"I ride a bike," Hyrum offered. "I'm not six."

"I stand corrected."

Hyrum gestured to the small table near the refrigerator. "You can sit if you want."

He did not sit.

"I'm not really sure how this will play out," Rhys said. "I mean, he'll help. But when he comes through that door, he'll encounter total strangers. And then there's you."

"I will receive a lecture about traveling forward in time," Will said.

"And you gotta know, right now he's about a hundred years old, but he doesn't really look it. And don't ask about your mom because she may or may not be here. That gets complicated, but it uncomplicates when you don't die."

"You're suggesting my parents' marriage did not survive my death."

"You're not going to die, so it doesn't matter." He reached under the computer island and pressed a button. The sides opened up and the keyboard slid out, turning the system on. When the display lifted from the center if the island, he tapped a few more keys and then stepped away. "If he has this set up the same way, that's all it should take to get him here."

"How can you be sure?" Aisha asked. "If his son isn't alive, why would he keep this as a safe place to land?"

"For the family," Will answered. "For Jax and Aubrey and their children."

"Especially Eli," Rhys said. "I mean, for us he's just eleven years old, but this Finn knows how convoluted his life will become. He's going to have a safe haven for him, if nothing else."

Rhys watched as Hyrum wandered to the pantry and quietly added for Aisha's benefit, "Eli, young Eli, is Finn's father. I don't think Hy knows that, and I'd like to keep it that way."

"Your family tree is just a bunch of knotted branches, isn't it?" Aisha asked. "How the hell do you keep it straight?"

"The Old Mint," Rhys said. At the sound of a crinkle, he turned to Hyrum. "Hy, the rules here might not be the same. Just because Grandpa and Pop Pop don't mind if we eat their food, this Finn might."

He took a bite of the donut anyway. "Finn is Finn. He always has snacks and he shares. Besides, he knows old me so I don't think he'll mind and I'm really hungry even though we had breakfast."

The door creaked and then clicked shut. "By all means," Finn said, "help yourself to anything. There's chocolate milk in the refrigerator, Hyrum. Your favorite brand, even."

Before Hyrum could thank him or even ask how he knew it was his favorite, Finn's eyes flooded with tears as he approached Will. "I told you never to jump forward. What if—?"

"This is not an unknown. Rhys and Hyrum have visited this When many times, so it felt safe."

He had no idea who Rhys was, or even Aisha, but he didn't care. He reached for Will and buried his face against his shoulder as they held on, and they stayed there until Finn could breathe without strangling on the tears. Aisha backed away to give them privacy, but Rhys stayed right there, watching without embarrassment.

I jumped to the island and then to Rhys's shoulder. *Hey. I want a hug, too. Finn hasn't seen me since...well, that day.*

"Wick." My name came out as breath. "Wick, I am so sorry."

It's cool. I'm not going to die, after all. Neither is he.

"Will?"

This was a sit-at-the-table conversation. Hyrum pulled the chocolate milk from the fridge along with water bottles and soft drinks, and quietly went about pouring things into glasses while Will told his father about Rhys and Hyrum's wayward adventure. He promised there would be more later, every detail Rhys had provided about Finn's successes in his own When, but for now the focus was on getting us home.

"I'll have a grandson," Finn marveled.

"Two. And a granddaughter," Rhys said. "Well, you will if these two get their shit together. It doesn't look promising."

"Rhys," Aisha sighed.

Finn was less interested in their potential than he was about, well, everything. And he didn't want to wait; he wanted Will to tell him everything then and there, because not knowing would drive him bat crap crazy.

"Like you're not already," Rhys teased.

Will did what he understood his father wanted. He got up, bent over, and placed a long kiss on his forehead. In a touch, he told him everything he needed to know and much of what he wanted. The room was silent as he did, save the sound of Hyrum blowing bubbles into his chocolate milk through a straw. When Will was done, when the kiss was over, he set his head against Finn's and whispered, "I love you and I've missed you. It won't change anything for you, but I'm jumping forward again, to my birth When, to visit a younger you, so he won't have to wait as long to know the truth. There's no point in waiting. And I will return to you here, as often as I can."

Voice shaky, Finn nodded and said, "Well then. Let's go drag Drew's ass out of bed.

~

This Emperor was largely unaware of how close his predecessor had become with Drew in the last months of his life. The hours spent together as Drew quickly became the Emperor's main caregiver, from the initial days when he realized he was, indeed, time-sick and was going to die sooner rather than later to the days when Drew fed him, bathed him, and carried him from bed to sofa and back, the absolute gentleness that Drew bestowed on him and the long, deep conversations carried on well into the night, were ahead of him if things didn't work out.

For Drew, they were memories. He both cherished and loathed them, and every bright and dark moment flashed across his face the moment he saw the Emperor for the first time in nearly forty years. It was clearly a shock, as well; Will at 30 looked nearly the same as Will at 42, and to this version of Andrew he might as well have been a ghost.

Still, before a word tumbled from his mouth, he raced to grab Will in a hug almost as hard as Finn's, and it took just as long for them to part.

When they did, Drew set his hand on Will's cheek, not caring if he wanted to be touched.

"I've gone forward and watched you as a little boy," he said. "Eli and Finn have been gracious in the amount of time we've spent together, but still...we sometimes go to sit in the shadows and watch you grow. I never would have imagined I'd get to see you again as an adult."

"Are they gonna kiss?" Hyrum whispered Rhys, a bit too loud. "They look like they're going to kiss."

"I'm not kissing him." Drew let go of Will, and turned to Hyrum. "But you? I'm kissing the hell out of you."

Before Hyrum could skitter away, Drew lifted him in a big hug, spinning him around as he planted a kiss on his cheek.

"It's been a long time since you've allowed that." Drew set him down, carefully. "Always telling me to go find one of the babies for that nonsense."

"Why?" He squinted as he considered it. "Oh, your Hyrum is old. I bet it hurts. But it didn't hurt me! That was fun."

"And you two," Drew said as he turned to face Rhys and Aisha. "I wish I knew you, but...I have no memories of meeting you."

"He's my grandson," Finn said. "She's his mother."

"He's what?"

"Rhys is my son," Will said. "Or will be."

With a sigh, knowing it would be a lengthy explanation yet again, Hyrum went to the giant window in Drew's office workspace to watch boats in the bay. He didn't need to hear it again, and there was always something worth seeing near the bridge. I jumped off Rhys's shoulder and went to him, sitting on the floor near his feet.

Is this okay? Just looking out? I don't think we can go outside.

"I really want to, Wick. Look, the playground is still there. The swings look new, too. Those are taller and I bet you can get really, really high."

When we get home, you can ask Drew or Will to replace them with something like that. I bet you're not the only one who would enjoy it.

He sat on the floor next to me, and reached over to rub my head, right between my ears. "I don't think we're going home, Wick. I think I'm gonna be stuck here and Rhys is gonna get arrested by those time guys, and we're gonna miss everything. It's my favorite time of year and we're gonna miss it."

It's too soon to say that, Hyrum.

"Will is super smart and he can't figure it out. If he can't..."

Drew can. Or Rhys will, once he has more data. You said it yourself, Drew knows how to find the whispering places. One of those has to be home.

"Maybe. But if I get stuck here, you know what I'm gonna do? I'm gonna get Will to take me to Florida and I'm doing all the sparky things to scare my daddy so that he lets his Hyrum go live with Aubrey. I'll even tell him I'll set his hair on fire again if he doesn't do it."

That sounds kind of mean, dude.

"I won't really *do* it, Wick. But I'll say I will. Or maybe we'll just jump to his bedroom and sneak him out. I bet they won't even care."

Your mom will.

"I was a lot of work so probably she won't on account of my littlest sisters are still at home and she's tired. But if we get the other Hyrum and he gets to live with Aubrey, at least one of us will be happy."

I wanted to tell him we were going home for sure, but I didn't know that any more than he did. He'd been right before, during his temper tantrum. Rhys's intentions and promises were not a final answer; it could take years to navigate whatever opening in the fabric of time had allowed us to land here. I suspected we'd get home eventually, but Rhys might return as a grown man, and Hyrum might be elderly.

The only one of us who wouldn't change much, if at all, was me, and that felt unfair.

If we get stuck here, even for a little while, I won't leave you behind, Hyrum. If the guardians somehow get their hands on Rhys, I won't leave you.

"What if he needs you?"

He won't. No matter where we are, he's going to grow up and start his adult life. He knows that. But you and me? We'll stick together, okay?

"Rhys won't leave me if we get stuck here, not unless the time people make him."

I'm just saying... We could even visit other Whens if we wanted. Nothing says we have to stay right here if we can't leave this timeline.

He decided that if we were stuck, he wanted to go live in Will's birth When. He didn't think we should stay here, not after rescuing his younger self. Finn would let us use the family apartment. He'd get a job, maybe even with Ozoo, and we'd figure out a way to be happy.

If Rhys could figure out a way to rid himself of the guardians, he would almost certainly want to jump forward. If he remained in this When, his presence might prevent Will and Aisha from having him again. Will would certainly want to care for him, and hold back on efforts to win Aisha over. They'd fight to co-parent a nearly grown man, and I didn't see anything good coming from that.

Forward was a way to find some happiness in a strange yet familiar landscape.

I think he had almost convinced himself when Rhys called out to him. "Hey. Want to see the time spaghetti?"

I glanced at the clock. They'd been talking for over an hour, but I had no idea if Drew had a remote notion of how to get us home. Worse, I was beginning to agree with Hyrum: we needed to consider the possibility that we'd never make our way home, with or without Rhys.

I settled onto his shoulder as we all crammed into Drew's private elevator, angry with myself for accepting the idea, yet I had no idea what else we could do.

~

Right off the bat, they agreed that Drew not knowing Rhys was the final proof that we were, for sure, in a different timeline. This wasn't When-adjacent; it was not the same timeline we were born into and we had not simply jumped into a spot in between known events. Between Aisha's confirmation that her parents were alive and well and Drew having not met Rhys or Aisha before, they declared matter settled.

I thought it already had been, but people rarely consult the cat.

An aura of disappointment bubbled over Rhys when Drew declared that yes, based on the information he had, they were from separate timelines. In some tiny corner of his brain I think Rhys hoped Drew would tell him that despite Aisha's parents being alive, we were all still within the same line, maybe with a stringy loop that amounted to a tiny bump on the timeline, and all he needed to do was hop through a portal to get home. I felt that disappointment roll off him in a static-laden wave, though he only sighed and said, "Yeah, I thought so. If I'd gone back to change it on time, or even at all maybe, this would be the same timeline, but I didn't, so it's not."

He gave Drew a brief explanation of his father's theory, based on his own experiences of changing events in his past. Do it quickly, and it becomes part of your own When and you retain memories of both. Wait, and the things you change spiral off into their own timeline.

"Wait too long to leave," Drew mused, "and you can't even get back to your own When, I imagine."

"I dunno. I think if you stay within a certain time frame, it doesn't matter. Unless it's a major change, then you need to book it back."

"Major, how?" Drew asked.

Go back and save the Queen from dying. That did it once.

I forgot that this Drew could not understand me, but Will translated. As the elevator door slid open, Drew exhaled sharply. "There's a When in which Donna lives. That is major. And now I wonder if someone should tell Eli."

Tell Jax first.

"Eli is still alive?" Hyrum clutched at his shirt. "He met us. I wonder if he remembers. Can we go see him?"

I think Drew was about to tell him that could be arranged, but Rhys shook his head. "Let's not risk it, Hy. I'm still not sure about fixed points and all that."

"That's just on TV, Rhys," Hyrum whined. "Come on."

An argument was about to ensue, but Drew flipped the lights on and all thoughts of visiting King Eli flew out of Hyrum's brain. This room was massive; it went on far enough that I couldn't see the back wall, far enough that it seemed the floor sloped over a horizon I was sure was an optical illusion.

"Dude," Rhys breathed out. "This is like Saint Francis with the program running in the background."

"Saint Francis?"

"Oh. Yeah. It's a simulated future San Francisco. Elves and dragons and a giant cat named Fluffy running around. My grandfather created it adjacent to the lab under Union Square and it's been running longer than I've been alive. But the simulator looks a lot like this when the program isn't active."

Finn shrugged. "I have no clue."

"The Finn coming up behind you will." Rhys wandered further into the room, testing the spring of the floor by bouncing on his toes. "You can run in any direction, can't you? And never hit the walls?"

"Theoretically," Drew said. "It's still quite a bit of conjecture and needs further testing. But this—" he reached for a panel on a wide dais centered between the door and the far wall "—is what you wanted to see."

With the flick of a switch, the overhead lights dimmed and metallic dust rose from the floor a few feet in front of the dais. Rapidly, yet bit by bit, a circular platform lifted, centered itself in front of us, and the air was punctuated with a series of soft clicks and snaps as those computer-driven dust motes linked. Hyrum watched with his mouth hung open; Rhys was wide-eyed and fascinated, arms wrapped across his stomach to hold in the excitement. He knew the significance of this; the Drew of our When was already working on this, building upon his nano-structures, still hoping to perfect the melding of holograms and nanotech.

When the base was complete, three steps up to a round platform with a translucent center, there came new whirring and clicking. Four circular spots, equal in distance from each other, began forming in the same manner, quickly, glowing, until there were four pillars that curved inward at the top. At the same time, from the ceiling descended a thick rope of brightly lit cable, all of it created from interlocking nanobots. At the end of that rope, no more than two feet long, sprouted four smaller lines that curved the same way as did the pillars.

The platform hummed, softly, and the nanobots spun, turned, and became a shimmering pool, liquid yet solid, and when it was done, hanging over it and between the pillars was Drew's massive wad of time spaghetti.

From start to finish it took less than thirty seconds.

"No sauce!" Hyrum gasped. "Old me was right!"

Each one of those lines—each replicated spaghetti noodle—represented a When, timelines Drew knew about and many yet to be explored. The entire mass glowed blue, though there were spots of other colors that seemed to stick to only a few of the lines. Rhys twitched toward it, wanting nothing more than to touch it, and Drew nodded.

"You can step up and touch any of it," he said. "It's all just nanobots and light. Spin it, pull lines apart, hell, massage it or bounce it like a ball. You can't hurt it."

He and Hyrum dashed up the steps to get a closer look, but neither reached out until Drew reminded them it was all right. "You might feel static, but it won't hurt."

Hyrum snorted, and Rhys said without looking at Drew, "Yeah, he's a sparky sponge. He can expel and absorb electricity. It won't hurt one bit."

"And you?" Drew asked.

"It won't hurt me, either, but if it sparks, my inner three-year-old will cry and ask for my mommy." He stood with his nose very nearly pressed against the display, but still clasped his hands behind his back. "Why this? Why jumble all the lines together?"

"I was looking for spots where the lines touched, reasoning that those were places I could move from one When to another, allowing for the possibility of nonlinear time. Tangling the lines in one mass made it easier to visualize."

Hyrum ran his pointy finger over one particular line that curved around the outside of the mass. "What are the little red dots? Are those whispering places? Old me said that you used the spaghetti to go find people and you whisper things to them so they know what to do."

He took a beat. "Something like that. I use this to plot out the points I'd like to visit. The display itself is just that—a display. It has little use beyond allowing me to imagine those connections."

"But you go and no one ever sees you."

"I'd like for the things that I tell them to settle in their brains as thoughts of their own. Physically, I remain here."

"What gave you the idea?" Rhys tilted his head back, trying to take in the entire mass. "I mean, portaling to somewhen, I understand. My dad's gone back to talk to himself several times. I doubt he's considered...this."

"It was just one of those weird ideas you have when things around you are so wrong that you'd do anything to change it."

In the middle of a war with Florida, King Andrew of Midlam had the notion that none of it needed to happen; the war was unwarranted, his mother was broken from the initial attack that started it all, but mostly, he thought the loss of his Emperor was an unnecessary tragedy. He'd never wanted to be king and wanted nothing more than to stay in Pacifica full time with Oz. Something had to be done, and he had time travel to address it. He fought the impulse to use a portal because it had been drummed into him: never go back and interfere with yourself. Never travel back to dabble in changing the things you wish hadn't happened, because you don't know the long-reaching affects.

The world would be better off, though, wouldn't it? Even if the only major things he could change was the Emperor's demise, and the future end of the world.

"But…I had the thought that if I could speak to myself without being seen, making it seem like it was my own idea in the moment, there was no harm. I wasn't time traveling, not really. I was simply sending my thoughts out across time."

"You spoke to your teenaged self and helped save the world."

"More or less. I'd witnessed the Emperor send his father home, and suspected that same tech could be used to push the meteor away from the planet. If that happened, if I managed to get the message through in time, the Emperor might not die. And if he lived, the war would surely not unfold the way it did, and I would not become king. At least not so young."

"Did it work?" Hyrum asked.

"It appears that in your timeline, it did. I have yet to see proof in this one. Things have changed here, regardless. I can see that."

"How?" Rhys asked.

Drew nodded toward Aisha. "While I don't know you and have never met you, I knew of you. In those last months the Emperor spoke of you frequently, with both regret and deep, abiding love. Through all the stories he told, I sometimes had the thought that the closeness the two of you felt for one another was fostered by the loss of your parents."

"My parents were alive," Will pointed out.

"Alive, yes, but lost to you all the same. It was something over which you bonded, one of the things that drew you to her. Without that?" He shrugged. "Who knows?"

Hyrum gripped the line between his fingers and tugged. "It moves!"

"Pull it out," Drew said.

Giggling, Hyrum yanked on it, then stepped back as he freed it from the mass. Once out, it snapped into a straight line that was almost as long as he was tall, hovering in the air in front of him. He pointed at a mark in front of his face and asked, "What's this dot? It's bigger than some of the others."

The line, Drew said, was a representation of his personal prime line. It was spotted with multicolored dots, mostly red, but many were purple, green and orange. "The dots represent major life events. When Oz and I married. When I became king. The orange dots are the births of our children."

I wanted to warn him to not count those dots, but then he would have counted them.

"What about the purple one?"

Drew reached toward the pseudo-spaghetti, splaying his hand, forcing all the lines to straighten. Each timeline became rod-straight, and they lined up in groups of four, extending back into the room as far as I could see. "That one is for my brother. When he died."

"Oh. I'm really sorry. I like Carter."

"Thank you. These lines," he said, plucking out three, "are alternate timelines that I'm somewhat familiar with, and represent time adjacent to my prime line."

"Huh?" Hyrum scrunched his nose.

"General timelines," Drew said. "Not really belonging to anyone else, but not my personal timeline. These are more like... other Whens for other people. Kind of like this one being my When" —he gestured to the line he had designated as his own— "and this one being your When, if you were from this timeline."

He plucked one of the three between his pointy finger and thumb, and brought it forward. "This one is the When coming up behind me, this Emperor's When, and the one in which I am reasonably certain I was able to prod myself to suggest to Finn that he could go back and launch several gates to contain the meteor."

"That happened," Rhys said. "That's exactly what he wound up doing."

You gave the idea to yourself first. Then Finn ran to the Old Mint and found someone from a couple years behind, then went back to help himself work on it. But by then Will was stuck inside the portal. He missed the whole thing.

"The Emperor was *in* the portal?"

He decided to not let me go and went in my place. And got stuck. We think it was because the meteor hit too close to San Francisco, so there was no exit point. If it had hit a few hundred miles away, there would have still been time.

Drew looked at Finn. "Does that mean that in every other When Wick was sent through, he became stuck? Are all those Wicks still there?"

"Possibly. I have no idea how to check and then rescue him if he is."

I probably degraded over time.

"Not if I go back to the moment you entered. And I can do that, Wick. I can save at least one of you."

And start this whole mess all over again? Will that create a new timeline?

Drew angled the lines until one end of each touched, and then double-tapped the line hovering before Hyrum. Tiny threads popped out from it. "Baby timelines. And no, Wick, I'm not certain it would create a new timeline. I think it would simply save the life of that Wick, and return him to his existence."

"Can you place those four lines together, without the rest?" Rhys asked. "And then do that tapping thing to all of them?"

With a circular motion, Drew brought together the four lines he had removed from the floating mass; they had contact points at both ends, and bowed ever so slightly, the space between them glowing. Rhys walked around them, eyes narrow as if he were inspecting them for dirt or lint. After a few minutes, he tapped one the same way Drew had, causing thousands of tiny threads to extrude. Some went nowhere, but others touched adjacent lines. He kept tapping, until the four main lines resembled a single solid one, with hundreds of thousands of smaller lines in widely varied lengths.

"Roots," he finally said.

"Does look like it," Drew said.

"Or blood thingies," Hyrum said, bouncing on his toes. "Rhys, remember when the museum had all the body things? They had this whole box where they showed all the blood things in a body. Oh! And another with nervous stuff."

Rhys nodded. "I remember. It was a display of the human body. Those were entire circulatory and nervous systems that had been removed from dead bodies. You're right, this thing resembles the nervous system."

"Or blood thingies," Hyrum said.

"Or blood vessels."

Will scratched at his beard. "Essentially, time represented as life."

Without asking if it was all right, Rhys went to the dais and began tapping at the keyboard. Red, orange and green dots began popping up throughout the entire 4-line mass hovering in front of us, replicants from Drew's prime line. When he was done with that, he stepped back to the display and tapped at it until the same threads appeared, and then pushed the original four lines back. With the swipe of his hand, mimicking Drew, all of the lines moved back until it was a single wad of spaghetti noodles again.

These lines he replanted did not wrap around the exterior of the mass as they had before. Instead, they implanted near the center and hung lower, until it looked like an animated tree.

That looks like the park in Will's birth When. The room we stayed in had a tree like that.

"Tree of life," Will murmured.

"That's beautiful," Aisha said, "but how does it help?"

"Interconnectivity," Rhys answered. "To see where all the colored spots overlap. Plus...it just looks cool. I don't think it means anything more than I wanted to see what it looked like."

He reached toward the keyboard to clear it, but Drew stopped him. He wanted to know if there was any particular reason Rhys placed the dots where he did; there was a consistency in the pattern and it seemed deliberate. To illustrate, Drew again straightened out every timeline and flung them backwards, so they lined up four at a time, extending well into the darkened parts of the room.

It reminded me of an infinity mirror, with its carefully placed lights designed to look as if they went on forever. They were straight lines that glowed blue, not light bulbs, but it felt the same.

The dots interspaced at the same intervals, though some started higher on their lines than on others, and they multiplied across every When-line I could see. Rhys had placed them as he visually interpreted the first four lines and presumed he had skewed the numbers a bit, but it didn't matter. He just wanted to see what it looked like and if there was any overlap.

"If you view each timeline as a closed loop," Drew said, splaying his fingers to bend each line individually and then connect them from start point to end point, "you can see how each circle has those markings just a little further ahead than on the next line. Which makes sense to me. The more information we have each cycle, the sooner some things occur. Or not at all, as the case may be."

He pulled the original four further away from the mass, but left them as circles.

"Here's my prime." He touched it, and pulled it aside. "Again, just a representation based on logical progression. In the next loop, the mark where Oz and I decided to approach our relationship as just that, a relationship, show it happening a few millimeters ahead of when it did. But the mark where I became king? It's not there at all in the second one. The next similar mark is our marriage, then the birth of our kids."

"The black one is gone," Hyrum said, pointing. "What was that?"

Drew swallowed hard and refused to look away from the display. "That was the day the Emperor died."

Rhys had input a replication of all the marks Drew had made, but allowed for change.

"Okay. But he's not gonna again, right?"

Aisha's hand went to Hyrum's back, rubbing gently. "Sweetheart, these are just guesses, I think. Drew can't predict the future."

"I know the future," Drew said. "What I can't predict with exact certainty is another When. The best I can do there is predict events that remain or fall off the line. I can, however, plug in events Rhys is absolutely sure of and create a model of his personal timeline, then compare and contrast."

She sighed, trying to understand. "But if your prime line is the same as this timeline, where you exist, doesn't it just loop back around? What good will knowing what happens in his timeline? They're not the same."

"They approximate the same," Drew said. "I know, for example, that this mark—" he pointed to the first one on the line "—is my date of birth. If he can come even close to getting the dates right in his own personal events, we can line them side by side, extrapolate the date he left his home, look for a tendril of change, and then bridge the gap."

"How?" Will asked.

Drew tapped the lines, causing the threads to reappear. "He travels along these. Somewhere around the date he fixed her parents' car, there will be a thread. A tendril. That thread became a line of its own, but we can find the start of it and hopefully a place where it touches our own. Plug in the day he and Hyrum jumped, and we can be reasonably certain that's the moment he needs."

"But that tendril *is* your timeline," Rhys said. "Unless…none of the changes really matter until that point of connection."

"Until it makes the connection," Drew said, "it can be reverted."

"I understand the logic," Will said. "I fail to see the method he can use to get there."

Drew finally turned away from the display, and he was grinning. "Simple. I'll teach him to whisper, and from there…he can jump."

39

The temptation to work well into the night was tempered by Hyrum's restlessness. There were no windows in the underground workspace, and the light had been dimmed to allow Rhys and Drew to poke through all the visual lines hanging in the air. Hyrum had played with a few blue lines plucked from the mass for his amusement, but after a bit he tired of them and wanted to do something else.

'Something else' involved lying on the floor on the far side of the dais, where he rolled back and forth, his feet scraping the wall. He kept his arms rigid by his side and rolled from one side of the room to the other, repeating until there was a dark smudge from the floor board six inches up.

Drew noticed, but seemed wholly unbothered. Rhys twitched in Hyrum's direction a few times, but decided it was better to just let him go than to point out he was destroying someone else's property. Aisha had a small child and to her this was just another thing to be cleaned up later, and the Emperor looked once and probably began calculating how much he should offer Drew to get the wall cleaned.

When Hyrum tired of rolling, he co-opted a white board from near the door, and stood off to the side, drawing the Golden Gate Bridge and the playground from memory. There were boats on the water, one surfer, and a giant shark cutting across the bay, headed straight for him.

When he finished that, he sat on the floor and began mumbling quietly to himself. Rhys glanced over his shoulder, trying to figure out what Hyrum was doing. He wasn't praying; for that he would likely stand, hands pressed to his chest. His hands were on his lap, palms up, and every minute or so he swiped a finger across one hand.

"He's pretending to read," Will whispered to Rhys. "Perhaps we should send someone to get physical media to keep him entertained."

Rhys agreed, but Drew declared us done for a few hours and decided we would go to his office, where we could have dinner while looking out over the bay. He sent an intern out for food, and at Will's quiet suggestion, another was sent to find coloring books and crayons, inflatable mattresses and bedding, and a stuffed animal.

The food intern returned with buckets of chicken and an assortment of sides, as well as snacks for later. The other returned with everything requested, and he added a plastic racetrack with half a dozen tiny toy cars. It was the first thing Hyrum reached for, before food and before setting up his bed. Rhys decided to help him instead of poking through his computer, which surprised me.

That was a spot-on choice.

"He knows the Hyrum who lives here," Will said.

Rhys is not exactly happy, you know. He wanted to keep working.

Drew wanted to move to the office while there was still light outside. The setting sun sent beams streaming into the office, and as Hyrum sat by the window putting the track together, he seemed truly relaxed for the first time that day.

Aisha plated food for them; they ate by the window, playing with the cars, and for half an hour Rhys was a typical kid, something rare.

When they were done racing and eating, they slid the track off to the side and sat side by side, gazing out the window. There were people on the playground, many of them Ozoo employees meeting their kids after work, and beyond that several lounged on the beach. In the distance, tourists made their way on the path toward the bridge, and in the bay a small fishing boat bobbed on the water. I knew Hyrum could engross himself in watching the goings-on outside Ozoo, and it was usually followed by marathon drawing and coloring. He was setting an image in his mind, using tips Jay had given him, and I think Rhys finally understood the why of taking a break from the basement workshop.

Hyrum sat with his legs crossed, elbows on his knees, fists supporting his chin. Without looking over, he finally spoke. "What's your brain doing? Mine is painting."

"Thinking about Grandpa."

"Finn's coming back. He had to go do some stuff but he wants to see Will again before he goes home."

"Not this Finn. My actual grandpa. He's been spending a lot of time staring at the bridge and I think I finally get it. It's the towers. He's been focused on the function and placement of time, and I think his brain is trying to understand the support pieces between each set of columns."

"Well, duh. That's so they don't fall over."

It wasn't really the bridge Finn saw. He envisioned timelines and how they might be comprised. Rhys thought he was close to an epiphany, one that could help them get home, if he'd had it before they disappeared.

"You saw how Drew tapped that spaghetti and those other little lines appeared? Some of them touched the timeline next to it. I think Grandpa sees two lines, and the cross pieces are like the little lines."

"Is that like the DNA he was talking about?"

"Maybe. I think he used DNA as a way to describe it. Side by side strands with pieces connecting them. Though DNA..."

He stopped, blinking rapidly as his brain worked. He suddenly spun around and said, to no one in particular, "The prime timelines. They aren't, like, straight lines. They kinda twist, the same way DNA strands do. And then those threads, where changes are made? Those connect *everything*. My timeline to yours. I made the change in my When, which forced that thread to peel off, but I don't think I jumped onto it. I jumped *over* it to the timeline it was touching. It's a bridge, and we jumped its length."

Drew's eyes lit up. He could visualize what Rhys suggested; if the timelines could be characterized in appearance as strands of DNA, and also wound around in the same wad Hyrum decided was spaghetti, extruding threads touching other timelines, it clarified to him how he was able to speak to himself and others throughout time.

It didn't matter which timeline he was in; he was speaking across all of them.

This is going to turn into the great dork-off, isn't it? They're going to start with the technobabble, getting super excited about it, and the rest of us get to watch and listen and not understand anything.

Hyrum chuckled. "That's my life, Wick."

I wasn't wrong, exactly. Rhys went back to the sofa where Drew sat with his laptop, though it wasn't on his lap and instead had been placed on the coffee table. Aisha decided that was a good time to set up the mattresses, and Hyrum helped her. When they were done, she joined him in stretching out on the floor to color, but half-listened because she wanted to understand what was going on.

They'd already explained how Rhys and Hyrum arrived in Las Vegas, but Drew wanted the story again. He wanted all the little details, no matter how unrelated they seemed. How long had they been riding around the city before it happened? What was he thinking about while Hyrum piloted the bike? How many different things were spinning in that crowded brain of his, and what unintended street were they on when they jumped?

Rhys guessed it had been roughly half an hour, maybe forty-five minutes. And it would be easier to list things he hadn't been chewing on. When he and Hyrum weren't talking, his brain popped and crackled with the programs and coding Finn had given him, trying to understand how his grandfather could fail to see the connection between the portal and the transporter, and why it had taken him so long to cough up a working model of the latter when the former had come to him so young. The math wasn't all that different; it was something Finn could do without thinking too hard. Yet, it had taken years for him to accept the exchange of matter from one moment in time to another, and one spot in space to another, and then find a way to fix it.

"I mean, I was probably working out the math when the brake cable broke. And then all I could think about was how fast we were going, how much it was going to hurt when we managed to stop, and then this tiny bubble of a thought about a massive pile of soft sand my mom had mentioned. I figured we could use it right about then."

"You were on California Street?"

"Yeah, a little more than halfway to the part that flattens."

"Where the portal tunnel lies underneath."

Rhys shook his head. "No, that's nearly two hundred years in my future. And even so, the portals are the only functional access points, and as far as I can tell they're held open by dust and fairy wishes."

"But the tunnel *is* there, and may have remnant energy you were able to draw on."

Will wasn't convinced. Had that happened, we would have entered a phantom portal and exited at the same geographical point that we'd entered. The portals, regardless of temporal permanence, moved people through time and not space.

Drew thought about it for a moment, and then got up. He dragged a clear board from across the room and wired his laptop to it. This drew Aisha and Hyrum away from their artistic endeavors; Aisha was curious, and Hyrum hoped to play with the board when Drew was done with it.

"I'm going to put an equation on the board," Drew said as he searched through his files. "Solve it."

The board filled with numbers and symbols. Hyrum scrunched his face as he tried to follow the first few lines, muttering that it wasn't real math, just gobbledygook. Aisha actively tried to solve it, but was only partway through when the answer rolled off Rhys's tongue, sounding much like a foreign language.

"Well?" Drew asked Aisha. "Is he right?"

She didn't know. "I'd need time to solve this," she said. "I'm damned near a math guru and there's no way I could do this without at least an hour or two to consider it."

"He's correct," Drew said. "And yes, it took me quite a while to work through it. Long story short, this is something we hand new hires to test their mettle. Since we started that, I think three out of a thousand have solved it. Most give up after a few days."

"That's mean," Hyrum said. "We don't make anyone do stupid math to get a job. Will just makes them have lots of degrees, or maybe just one if they're a doctor. But not the kind of doctor that gives you shots."

"They already have the job," Drew explained. "Consider this a mild sort of hazing."

"Teasing," Rhys said to Hyrum.

"Well, teasing isn't nice, either. But Rhys got it. Does that mean he's smarter than you?"

"I think that goes without saying," Drew answered with a chuckle. "But it also tells me something I suspected when he said he was doing the math in his head before speeding down California."

"That I'm a loser and need to get a social life?" Rhys said. "Yeah, I hear that from my little brother all the freaking time."

"Sympathies. I got that from my older brother. No, it tells me how you jumped, Rhys. Neither the portals nor the tunnel had anything to do with it. I think *you* moved the three of you, by yourself. And if you did that one way, you can get back the same way."

"Say what?"

"You have the transponder. Your head is filled with all the math, all the coding, every little detail of how both portals and transporters function, and you understand most of it. You have the ability to do complicated math on the fly, and you can do it in your head faster than you can verbally express it. You have everything inside you that a portal does when it moves a person from one When to another...as well as the knowledge of how to transport and exchange matter."

The transponder responds, typically, to the computer controlling the portal tunnel, and by extension, to all the required computations. "It should require the tunnel to bend time, but..."

Will's head snapped up. "He can control time. He can

stop it, and in doing so create a bubble in which he and others of his choosing continue to function. I am unsure what other proclivities with time he might have."

He can re-start time for individuals when everyone else is frozen. He did that for George and James once, when he was three.

"So we know how you landed in front of Aisha. You have control of time, you have all the data stuffed into your brain, and you have a transponder. You also had an abstract idea of something and someone you considered to be a safe place to land. You just missed your exit point and sailed onto the next timeline. But you managed it, so there's no reason you can't do it again."

"We are not speeding down California on a busted bike," Rhys said.

"You shouldn't need one. Rhys, you can do this on your own. Tomorrow, that's what we'll focus on. Moving from one spot in the room to another. Because if you can do that? You can go anywhere, anywhen, any timeline."

40

Two days later, Rhys still had not jumped. The attempts to move from a spot near the office window to a spot near the sofa were met with frustration and a mantra that alternated between "I can do this, I know I can" and "I can't freaking do this, there's no way."

Will attempted to modify one of the jump bracelets, hoping to amplify its connection to Rhys's transponder, despite Rhys's insistent reminders that he hadn't been wearing one when we originally jumped. Will countered with the idea that he'd been near the portal tunnel when screaming down California and was not near a portal now.

"But we are," Rhys said. "One office over, there's a silent portal. In my When, it's my dad's office and he opened one so he and Drew had a place to run in an emergency."

"Not me?" Hyrum asked.

"Dude, their plans always included grabbing you first."

"So why not work in there? That way, if the time people come back, we can use it to go to Saint Francis."

If we were home, that would have been a reasonable option. The simulator didn't exist in this timeline. I didn't want to bring up the notion that there was no portal in that office; the Emperor was long gone in this When, and thusly had not opened it.

Rhys held up his arm, pointing at the jump bracelet. "But we could still run away."

"Oh. Yeah. My brain is tired, Rhys. It needs to go outside and play and get some food and maybe ice cream."

"Outside is not safe," Will reminded him. "The guardians

would have easier access to you, and this is well protected space—"

"You said the same thing about Eli's basement and they got in the building anyway. I just wanna go outside and get a cheeseburger and then go to the playground on account of it has swings and I really wanna swing. Please? I've been good."

"My reluctance has nothing to do with your behavior, Hyrum."

"But it's not fair. I—"

The argument was interrupted by the beeping of a proximity alarm, set up to prevent anyone from entering Drew's office unannounced. He bolted to the monitors near the door, then visibly relaxed. "It's just Oz."

Will twitched toward the door. He had not been prepared to meet the adult Oz; in his world she was a small child, young enough that she hadn't yet run away from home to find cupcakes in Sausalito. Drew was merely a summer presence in her life; they were not yet soulmates, and barely even friends.

She bounded through the door, arms loaded with packages. Drew reached out to help, forgetting that half the people in the room were strangers to her. Will stood in the center of the room, still, unsure what he should do. No one moved, because we all wanted to see her reaction to him.

She would have been there sooner, if not for being halfway around the world, chairing a meeting of the world's environmental protectors.

Once her arms were free from the burdens she carried, she turned to him. "I don't care, I don't care, I don't care," she cried, stepping quickly to Will, arms extended. "Oh my god, you're really here. You're not dead."

He returned her hug as hard as she gave. "Not yet."

"He won't die the next time around," Rhys said. "And now that you've met, you can keep seeing this one."

"This is Rhys," Drew said as she and Will parted. "Future Emperor spawn. Also, Aisha, future mother, and Hyrum. Your uncle."

Hyrum bounced on his toes. "I'm Hyrum! You're really pretty for being old."

"Jesus," Rhys breathed.

"Hyrum. I know you, you know. An hour ago you launched a waffle across the kitchen because, and I quote, 'it's just a squishy flying disk toy.'"

"Oh. I gotta try that."

Oz was getting a hug from him, whether she wanted one or not.

Hello, I'm Wick. Miss me?

"Is that really Wick?"

Rhys plucked me from the arm of the sofa. "In all his furry glory. He wants to know if you miss him."

"He wants to know." She took me from him, planting a kiss on top of my head. "He told you that, hm?"

"He did."

"He's not kidding, Ozzy. The Emperor, Rhys, and Hyrum understand him." Drew gave a light shrug. "Apparently in their timeline, so can I."

She needed no convincing.

"Wick," she said, holding me where we could see each other's faces, "when Finn tells you to step into the portal, just… don't."

Been there, done that, didn't get a t-shirt.

"That's in our past," Rhys said. "I mean, I wasn't there, but I've heard enough about it. He lives, my dad lives, I get born. But this Emperor's Wick could use the advice."

She held onto me for a long time. I curled up on her lap when she sat, and listened to another round of explanations about how we came to be there. Eventually Hyrum tired of it and he went back to the window, hands plastered to the glass as he watched the world outside.

"Is he all right?" Oz asked quietly, once the conversation entered a lull.

"He wants to go outside and play on the swings," Rhys said. "Oh, and go get a cheeseburger and shake."

"Then let's go to the playground."

Drew shook his head. "They're safer here, Ozzy. We have a closed system that would be damned near impossible to bypass."

She waved that off. "Your guards are here. Ozoo's guards are here. Now my guards are here. No one will get near them."

At that, Hyrum turned. "Really? It doesn't have to be for long. Please?"

Will was also poised to list reasons why we could not leave the building, but Aisha stood and declared, "We're taking a chance and going out. We all need fresh air. We need to breathe. Let the guards do their job, and give us a little bit of downtime so we can think clearly when we come back."

I would not mind going out for a bit.

"We'll have a picnic." Oz stood, handing me to Rhys. "I'll call for cheeseburgers and have them delivered to the playground. What else would you like?"

Drew knew better than to argue, and Hyrum eagerly listed the things he'd like for lunch. Will was clearly annoyed, but didn't say anything, not even when Hyrum practically stuck his tongue out at him and said, "See, you have to do it when the queen says so."

She's not the queen, dude.

"Yes, she is. Jax quits and she has to do it. That's how it works."

"Uncle Hyrum, I gave up the throne a few years ago. Pacifica is a social democracy with a President now."

He scrunched his nose. "Why'd you do that?"

Sighing, "Looking back, it was a poor choice, not one I'd make again."

"My Oz isn't queen yet. But I met old Oz and she was queen when she was the same age as my Oz is. So I dunno what's going on with that, but okay."

His sense of time was a little skewed, but I was grateful Rhys didn't correct him. He was less interested in the facts than he was—though you'd never get him to admit it—in going outside for a bit. He and Hyrum were the first ones out the door, just behind the first set of guards, and it took everything in them to not run to the playground.

I dug my claws in, hoping to avoid becoming a skid mark on the street that separated the Ozoo building from the playground.

I enjoyed their glee and thought I might even allow myself to ride with one of them on the swing, but they headed for the merry-go-round and I noped my way right out of that. I leaped off and ran to Will, climbing his leg to get to his shoulder.

Oz walked closely on his left side and Aisha was equally close on his right. It amused Drew, who trailed by a few steps.

Hyrum's giggles cut through the air. He held on tight as Rhys spun him around, hard and fast, and I was pretty sure that if they kept it up everything Hyrum had eaten for the last two days would spray the playground in a sticky, multi-colored wad of chewed up goo. I was close to yelling at them to stop before someone got hurt; if Hyrum let go, he'd hit the ground hard enough something might break.

Hyrum asked him to stop before I could yell. An intern from the office came out bearing gifts of blankets, and he wanted to help spread them out for the picnic. "We gotta be polite," he said to Rhys as they made their way over. "Oz doesn't have to get us cheeseburgers but she's nice so she did."

"For the cheeseburgers," Rhys snickered.

Hyrum stopped, then raised a fist high, and yelled out, "For the cheeseburgers!"

"Come on, Emperor," Oz said. "Join them."

"I will not."

Once the blankets were spread and we were sitting on the ground, Hyrum ran a hand over one and asked, "Aren't these the biohazard covers? I hope they got washed."

"Wonderful," Aisha said under her breath.

They were not, Drew assured us, biohazard covers. They were just blankets, stored in his office for days when the kids were with him, or lately, the grandkids.

Hyrum leaned toward Aisha. "He just doesn't wanna tell us that they were on top of the tank that has cooties floating in it."

"Hyrum, they're not—"

"What kind of cooties?" Rhys asked.

"Hm." Hyrum shrugged. "Probably girl cooties. If they were boy cooties they'd smell like feet."

"Like Charlie's?"

"Nuh. Like your daddy's."

Everyone looked at the Emperor.

"I will not take the bait."

"Says the guy with the stinky feet," Rhys snorted.

He was spared anything further by the arrival of bags filled with cheeseburgers and fries, several milkshakes, and a cooler loaded with soft drinks. Oz handed one bag to Hyrum. She presumed that he enjoyed the same Empty Leg Syndrome as did her Hyrum, and suspected he and Rhys might want more than one burger each.

"I had cheeseburgers with old Hyrum once," he said as he dug into the bag. "He only ate one on account of we also had onion rings and shakes and wanted dessert after. But I bet he had a snack later, too."

"Old Hyrum," Oz mused. "Why 'old'?"

The question seemed to puzzle him. "On account of he's loads older than me."

"It's just a way for us to keep track of which people we're talking about," Rhys said. "Like, my dad takes me forward a lot, and if I'm telling my brother or cousins about it, it's just easier to say, yeah, old Jax said this. Or old Zed did that. That way they know I'm not talking about the people we live with."

"So I'm 'old Oz.'"

Around a mouthful of cheeseburger, Hyrum said, "Well, maybe not today. We're about the same age and I'm not old. I know your Hyrum is older than you, so maybe you can call him old Hyrum sometimes."

"He doesn't seem that old to me," Oz said. "I can barely keep up with him."

"Does he ride a bike a lot? I like to ride my bike every day, and I..." He stared down at the burger in his hand. "I forgot. I'm gonna miss my bike a lot. It got me everywhere, even places Aubrey said not to go to but I did anyway on account of I'm allowed to do what I want."

You'll get a new one.

"I know, Wick. But it'll never be the bike Santa gave me."

Rhys crammed the last bite of his burger into his mouth and stood up. "C'mon. Let's go try the swings. We can eat the extra burger after. I want to see how high we can crank one of those puppies up. I bet we can get it to go over the top."

Hyrum jumped up, bike somewhat forgotten. "Me first!"

I watched them run to the swing set. Hyrum's arms were flung wide, a featherless bird descending toward his perch. Rhys sprinted and got there first, choosing the middle swing for Hyrum.

"The contrasts in those two are fascinating," Will said as Hyrum hopped into the seat. "Equal parts intelligence, wisdom, and childhood bubbling on the cusp."

"I get Hyrum," Drew said. "Maybe because I know the other him so well. But Rhys is a contradiction. He's like an old man fixated on a problem, yet he's also this…kid."

"Says the old man fixated on multiple problems," Oz teased. "Admit it, your entire year has been made by trying to figure this thing out for them."

"Finding the answer will expand my own research," he admitted. "But damn, Oz, this kid? Every gift your family has and then some. I thought Eli was a handful, but Rhys has to juggle so much more."

I already knew about all of the gifts Rhys was aware he had. I also didn't want to sit on the blanket and be grilled about the things he might have not already told them about, nor sit through further explanations of the math and the spaghetti and all the little strings, and it felt like that was next.

I ran to Hyrum and waited for the swing to slow, and then jumped into his lap.

I want to swing. But don't go so high, all right?

"We were gonna try to go over the top," Hyrum said.

Please? It'll still be fun. I only want to ride for a minute or two. They're talking about you over there and I didn't want to get asked a lot of questions.

Rhys pushed gently, so that we only rocked back and forth a bit. "Old people gossip. They think they're being contemplative and concerned, but really, it's gossip."

"People always talk about other people," Hyrum said. "Gossip is mean. They're just kinda talking."

"Gossip isn't always mean. Like, when we got that new P.E. teacher who turned out to be sexist as fuck. Charlie showed up to class in nothing but a pair of sequined gym shorts and a skin-tight t-shirt, and the teacher damn near lost her mind. She marched to the admin office to get him suspended, and all the vice principal did was shrug it off. We talked about that for the rest of the term. It wasn't mean. We just thought Charlie had balls and it was funny."

"Is that gossip?" Hyrum wasn't sure. "Gossip is like my mom telling her friends about someone else at church getting caught sinning, and everyone being judgy about it."

"Well, we were all judgy about the teacher, that's for sure. And after that she hated us. I mean, really hated us. It got to the point where there were no calm colors around her, only a constant fire of hate."

Hyrum leaned forward and looked off toward the blanket. "What colors are they right now?"

Whatever the topic at hand was, they were amused, but there was an undertone of concern.

"And every time Aisha talks to the Emperor, she flashes red. It's not, like, huge and she has a lot of other colors surrounding her, but yeah, she's still angry."

Have you been watching the whole time?

"Most of it, Wick. I know I shouldn't, but...I feel like I need to know. Not just about her being upset with him, but everything. I need to know how they really feel."

"On account of maybe they want to stop helping us?"

"Something like that. I know Oz won't feel like I'm snooping because she can't turn hers off, but I keep thinking Aisha and the Emperor might."

They won't mind.

"It won't matter," Hyrum said. "Aisha's gonna have to go home soon, anyway. And Will has to take her. Maybe we should just use a portal and go to our When, even though we don't belong there."

The Emperor won't abandon you. Even if he has to take Aisha home, he'll come back. He won't leave you until we find a way home.

Rhys was afraid that if he did that, left her in Las Vegas and then came back, they might never reconnect. He would respect her anger, leaving her alone until she decided otherwise, and she would dig her heels in.

Hyrum didn't see the issue. "Maybe we don't get born in every When, anyway. Maybe in this one they don't get married and have babies. That's okay, Rhys."

"I know it's selfish," he said. "But it doesn't bother you even a little that you might not get born in the next When?"

"Nuh. I'm here now. And it would maybe be better if I wasn't born again. I like the idea that there won't be another me that has to live with my daddy. Then when I die, I go to be with Jesus."

You don't think that will happen anyway?

"I dunno. I think that if old Hyrum is me, and I'm me, the next one would be me, and that means we have the same soul."

Or copies of the same soul.

"Possibly," Rhys said. "But I've thought about that, too. Like, we exist, get to the end of our own line, then loop back and do it again. Recycled souls. That's basically all we are, recycled souls. And I know most people are never even aware of it, but...I am, and I don't want to be a one-off."

If we're recycled, how can we exist with ourselves? Drew once said that he worried if we touched our other selves, the world would implode because two versions of a person can't occupy the same space. But then he saw your dad touch himself.

"Dude. No. Don't put that image in my head."

Hyrum giggled. "I touch myself but I lock the door on account of no one wants to see my wiener."

"But you're not one of my parents, so I don't care."

Pervs. You know what I mean. My point is that if we're recycled, teenaged Drew might have been right. But if we're copies, we can interact with ourselves.

"And none of this changes the idea that I don't want to be the only me, ever."

"Okay. So maybe after we get home, we can use a portal and go find them in the When behind us, and make sure they do kissing things."

Will already went back and talked to himself. He planted all the right ideas in his own head.

"And look where that got them." He nodded toward them. "This is the same Emperor he spoke to. She's pissed and he's not ready to fight for what he wants."

"I know it makes your tummy hurt but maybe you gotta just let them figure it out. There are other Whens, Rhys. Maybe other timelines."

"I know, but I can't help—"

In unison, our heads jerked up at the whine that cut through the air. Rhys reached for Hyrum's hand as a pop followed the whine, and just a few feet in front of us stood four guardians. They nearly blazed against the dark backdrop of the Ozoo building, bright enough I squinted against it.

The same guardian we'd encountered outside the tunnel in Denver was forefront, his hand reaching out. Oz's guards were close, but not close enough; they drew arms quickly and rushed toward us, yelling at the guardians to step back. "Rhys, please," the guardian uttered breathlessly. "Just lis—"

He should have spoken faster. I blinked, and we were gone.

41

Hyrum landed on his backside, but he didn't lose his grip on me. He hit the floor with a grunt and an *oof*, then rolled onto his hip so he could get his feet under him, all while carefully cradling me. Rhys turned and ran for the window, hoping to see four men in shiny blue suits on their knees with laser guns held to their heads.

"They're gone," he moaned. "Dammit."

I was still getting my bearings. *Where are we?*

"Drew's office." Hyrum followed Rhys to the window. "Did they see us go? The guards look confused."

Outside, Will pointed toward the building, and they ran.

"Great. I'm not sure if I hate that he noticed where we went and the guardians might have seen that, or I'm relieved that he saw and they'll all be here in a minute."

Hyrum thought that we should back away from the window, just in case. "Those guys haven't caught us yet, so I want Will and Aisha with us. Maybe they're good luck."

"They're something, anyway," Rhys said under his breath.

"It's my fault. I'm sorry. I just really wanted to play for a little while and I wanted a cheeseburger and a shake, and I know I was whining but I'm really sorry."

"It's not your fault," Rhys said. "None of this is your fault. It's their fault. They keep coming after us for no good reason, and if they weren't maybe I could focus better and find a way to get our asses home."

"You made a jump bracelet." Hyrum pointed to Rhys's wrist. "That's pretty big."

"George technically made it."

"But you had to tell him how. He just stuck the pieces together."

Take the win, dude.

He took the win, admitting that if not for his understanding of his grandfather's files and his ability to explain the little details, he'd still have a keyboard attached to his forearm and jumping might be a crapshoot. "The thing is, I didn't even..." he trailed off at the sound of thundering footsteps in the hall.

"Thank god," Aisha breathed when she was through the door. "You disappeared and I had this feeling...it wasn't good."

"I aimed for the office because it seemed safe, for now," Rhys said.

"Pretty quick on the jump," Drew said. "I never saw you move for your bracelet."

The silence hit hard. Will's focus was entirely on Rhys, and Aisha looked back and forth, her expression asking the same thing Drew's did: *you did use it, right?*

"You reached for Hyrum with one hand. The other never moved from the chain on the swing," Will finally said. "How?"

Rhys didn't know. "All I know is I wanted to get away from them, and thought the office was a good buffer. Like, literally, 'we need to get to that office, fast.' Next thing I know, here we were."

"Fascinating. And perhaps we have the missing puzzle piece."

"How so?"

In both instances of travel, Will saw one thing in common: anxiety. Speeding down California with no brakes sent a surge of adrenaline through Rhys, right at the moment he'd been pondering the things his grandfather was doing, and then immediately he considered a place to land. "This jump shares similarities, I believe. You've been working on this, it's a constant in your brain. You know how it all works, you had a safe place in mind, and a flood of adrenaline. In that burst, you jumped."

Drew went to the computer he'd left on the coffee table. "Well, then, with that, all we need is to find an insertion point."

"What if we sent them back to just before he fixed my parents' car?" Aisha blurted. "That's where it all started, right? What would be the effect? Would our timeline just vanish if he changed it?"

"I already said, I'm not doing that," Rhys said. "I'm not saving us at their expense. Don't ask me to. I won't."

"But if we—"

"I met my grandparents," Rhys said, softly. "I met them and I liked them *so* much...even if it hadn't been too long, I just can't. They don't deserve to die again just because I want to go home."

"It's not just you," she said.

I don't want them to die again, either.

"Jesus would be mad," Hyrum added. "Red says sometimes we have to bear crosses that feel too heavy, but we gotta on account of what's good for other people. It's not good to let them die just so we can go home."

She didn't think they had to die. If Rhys could stop himself before he even saw them, couldn't she and Will just do the repair instead? It was their timeline, her parents, and they were alive in her life. Surely if they made the repairs in Rhys's stead, they would go on, and he could go home.

He was tempted, and I thought he was about to agree.

It's been too long, Rhys. You might be able to stop yourself, but to what end? Your worry about winding up with two of you, two of me, and two of Hyrum at home might not be so far-fetched. Because if you stop yourself from fixing the car, there are still two of you there, and you both want to go home. This isn't like when your dad saved Oz...it's been too long for you to merge with yourself.

While they talked, Drew cleared off the coffee table, and with his computer perched on his knees, he tapped at the keyboard. The top of the table began to glow, tiny projectors lifted from its edges, and a small-scale version of the wad of timelines appeared. He picked at them, pushing them away until there were only a few, and then tapped at the display until the tendrils appeared again. He connected two, twisted them, and pushed the rest away.

"All right. Look at the red dots. We need to find proximity of a major event in this line to one in yours."

How? Those aren't actual timelines, Drew. They're just a visual guide to your theories. A demonstration of data. It's not a gateway.

"I'm getting to that," he answered, not looking up.

Will leaned in close, looking at the dots. "What's this one?"

"Finn's birth," Drew said. "Granted, he was born in a different When, but it was significant to me, in mine, so I placed it there. I'd like to find something closer to Rhys's When on his timeline. We have his birth date, and his siblings', but something closer to the day they jumped would be helpful. I'd like to find something near one of these bridges." He touched one of the tendrils. "Those are the key."

"So what?" Rhys asked. "We find a spot in between yours and mine and I go there, hoping I can portal the rest of the way? With that logic I can just shoot for your birthday in both and then portal."

"I'd feel better if your event was your own."

What about something major for me? We could compare the day Finn and Jo arrived in my When with the day they did in yours. But you have to tell us how we're going to do this because right now it all sounds like you're talking out your ass.

"If you're looking for a bridge," Oz guessed, "you'd need an event in which time was changed. That's what creates the bridges. No?"

Tell Rhys how first.

Hyrum's hands went to his shirt. "The whispers."

Drew nodded. "The whispers. If Rhys understands how I can do that, how I did that, then he can surely jump that." He held his hand out to Rhys. "The only way is to invite you in. It's a long, convoluted equation, but I have no doubt you'll not only understand it, you can utilize it. So pick my brain. Literally."

"You can't just pop it up on a monitor? I can memorize it."

Drew pushed his hand a bit closer. "Only if you want to remain here for the time it takes to read through it, probably another month. It took me twenty years to figure out, Rhys. My gut says it will take you fifteen minutes, maybe twenty. And you can soak it up from the source."

The rest of us settled in to wait. Rhys sat on the sofa, his hand resting on Drew's, both of them with closed eyes. Hyrum went to the window "on account of someone needs to keep a watch out," and the rest of us waited in chairs. I moved from person to person, collecting head rubs and kisses, because just sitting and staring at them was like watching white paint dry, and it also felt a bit intrusive.

"I wonder what that feels like," Oz said after a minute. "Having someone else in your head."

"Disconcerting," Aisha grunted. "A little nauseating."

Will reached out, offering Oz his hand. "For a moment, if you wish."

She wished, and I scrambled to her lap so that I could get a paw on the bare skin of her forearm. If she wanted someone in her brain, then maybe an extra visitor would be all right.

He only held her hand for a minute, but in that short burst he showed her glimpses of her early childhood, the days he was currently in the middle of, when he was her babysitter and playmate. The last image he showed her was of a day on the beach, only a few months ago for him, when she filled a bucket with sand, and at Drew's urging, dumped it over the Emperor's head. His pretended anger ended with picking her up and twirling her around, high-pitched giggles cutting through the air. He whispered the truths he wanted her to know.

"I love you, too, Empy," she murmured when he let go. "And yeah, that's disconcerting."

Does it itch? My Aisha says that sometimes it itches.

"Mentally itchy, yes," she said.

Cotton swab in the ear. Push deep. That ought to do it.

The Emperor did not repeat that. I don't know why.

"Empy?" Aisha asked.

"The Emperor nanny," Oz said, amused. "Or really, I just had a hard time forming the word 'emperor.' He didn't seem to mind."

"I didn't mind. I rather enjoy it, to be truthful."

"I know." She reached over and rubbed his arm. "In the last days, you wanted to hear it again."

"He never touched you in the end?" Aisha asked.

"He did, a bit. I think he was too busy fighting to let his thoughts loose. He communicated with Drew that way, though, quite often. But Drew was also his primary carer, and they became especially close."

In my When, they're brothers. I mean, not literally, but they bonded when Drew was only twenty years old.

"How?" Will asked.

Check the brain box. It's there. Look for the trek across Colorado.

"Is that something I should do now?"

Absolutely not. Wait until you're alone. Trust me.

"You're tempting me."

Just wait. And know ahead of time it probably won't happen in your lifetime. As far as we know, it's only happened in our When.

"War," he guessed.

"That was my daddy's fault," Hyrum said, still looking out the window. "I don't know why he did it. But if you stop him, you stop the war and all the other bad things that happened."

Will promised him, again, that he would do everything he could to bring the Hyrum of this When home.

"If you keep the extra bracelet, you can just jump to his bedroom and take him. Daddy won't do anything to find him. He'll just say that Hyrum got out of the house and eat by a gator at Miller's pond."

"My sudden appearance might frighten him horribly. I would prefer to find a way in which he wants to leave Florida."

"Then take Aubrey. I knew who she was even though I didn't see her for years and years except on TV. And if you don't want it to be a secret, tell Daddy you know that Hyrum set his hair on fire once, and that he can do more things. *Sparky* things. Let Aubrey tell Hyrum she wants him to live with her and if he's scared, she should sing 'you are my sunshine' to him. And give him a piece of candy. She used to sneak candy to me. And then she can say to him that if he goes, he'll have toys again, toys he gets to pick out, and his own room with space books and posters, and lots of things to color with. And no one will get mad if he eats his crayons."

He finally turned around. "She should tell him she still remembers when she said she would love him forever. On account of he remembers, too. And that in her house, there's a daddy who will love him, no matter what. He really wants that, Will. He wants a daddy who loves him. Maybe more than anything, even more than the toys and crayons. And promise him he'll never have to eat peas again."

"I swear to you, I will do whatever it takes," Will said, softly.

Rhys let go of Drew's hand and sat back into the sofa cushions, his eyes darting as he absorbed all the details.

"Give him a minute," Drew said. "It was an info dump. He has the full equation, but he needs time to process it."

"He can whisper now?" Hyrum asked.

"He can whisper now. And if I'm right, he can extrapolate the data for that and use it to access the bridge from here to home."

You say that as if there's an actual bridge.

"There is, Wick. It's how the three of you wound up in Las Vegas, thirty years in your Aisha's past, but in this timeline."

"An actual bridge." Oz repeated.

"Eh. Quantum. Metaphysical. Magical." He pointed to the laptop. "It's a stringy thing he can move along."

I liked it better when his vision of time—the old Drew of our When—looked like snowflakes on broken glass. That made more sense to me, and I could picture jumping from one to the next.

"That still could be, as well, Wick. Like you said, this just represents the data. In a singular When, that may be right. But with multiple timelines, they may twist and turn around each other instead of co-existing in straight lines side by side. As we understand time travel now, there is some loop—"

"The hole in the paper looped on one end," Will mused. "My father demonstrated it with a pencil. Through the paper, over the end, to the other side."

"Smart man, your father."

"When he's not on Mars," Hyrum said, chuckling. "How do you go whisper? Do you use a portal? Or a spaceship?"

After a few clicks on the keyboard, Drew turned the laptop so Hyrum could see. "I get into this contraption, hooked up to a really, really, *really* big computer."

"Your nanosuit!" He peered closer. "It's got lots of wires, though. Will Rhys need to wear one? Will I?"

"You got here without one," Drew reminded him. "I use the suit so that I don't have to physically travel. Just whisper."

Why? Why not just leave the info at the Old Mint?

"Because the teenaged me I needed to speak with had no access to the Old Mint."

You could have told Finn.

"He was probably on Mars that day," Hyrum said.

"When is he not?" Rhys sucked in a deep breath. "No, that's not fair. Damn. My brain actually hurts."

"Not used to letting someone in for so long?" Drew asked.

"Not really. Yeah, like, maybe Wick sneaks into my dreams every now and then but I don't tend to just let people wander around in there. Not so intensely, anyway." He twitched back in his seat. "Wait, you have a daughter?"

"Now that is information you weren't supposed to hear."

Rhys swore it wasn't intentional. She was positioned in the forefront of his mind and unavoidable. "I wasn't trying to snoop. But damn. You don't have a daughter in my timeline."

"Yet," Oz snickered.

Hyrum began bouncing on his toes. "What's her name? When is she gonna be born? Does she like me? Are we gonna be friends like me and Rhys or is she just my friend like Marco or—"

"Take a breath, dude," Rhys said. "She might not be born in our When. We don't know what Oz and Drew's plans are."

"No one said she was planned," Drew said.

Hyrum ignored that. "Well, she's gonna. Jesus would want that, right? She'll be born in every When."

I don't think he saw the disappointment that blanketed Rhys. There were no guarantees. He knew that. But he hoped against that, even if it felt selfish.

Drew saw it. "What do you think? Can you do it?"

Hyrum clenched his shirt between his fingers as Rhys considered it.

"It makes sense to me," he finally said. "But Wick, you can't just ride in the hood of my sweatshirt, okay? Not even the pocket. I need to have a hand on you. Same thing, Hyrum. You can't just grab onto my clothes. We need to have skin on skin, just to be safe."

Will reached for me, and flipped me onto my back.

"Your fur is already growing back."

Great. You're gonna shave the kitty again, aren't you?

42

He shaved the kitty.

Every one of my useless nipples was exposed to the air, glaringly bare skin blinked like neon in the middle of the night, and they squinted against the brightness.

All right, fine.

But my naked belly was bright and cold, and my complaints were shoved aside with the news that shirts for cats existed, and when we got home, I was getting one.

They could buy all the little kitty shirts they wanted. That didn't mean I would wear it.

The goodbyes to Oz and Drew were short and laced with gratitude. Rhys extracted a promise from Drew to not let the Emperor return home without contacting Finn again, and after a tight hug, Oz left to call him.

I didn't know who I wanted to say goodbye to first, but Will stepped forward and chucked me under the chin. "Wick, I look forward to the day you remember your life before leaving to live with Jax. While I enjoy the time we currently spend together, I miss our long conversations. Even the snark."

Remove that transponder and reactivate the other. That's how my memories began returning. You took one out to use on Finn's time machine, and when he came back, he activated the other. Do that.

"How exactly did the transponder interfere with your memories?"

The secondary one sent new lines into my brain, but skirted the first set already there. The impulses from the power in it created a roadblock. At least, that's the theory. Will pulled it out and the lines came with it, attached. It didn't hurt, so don't worry about that. Just take it out.

He agreed to do it, and rubbed two fingers between my ears as he focused on Hyrum. "I will miss you, Hyrum, and I very much look forward to meeting you and getting to know you again."

"You won't be the Water Man, though," Hyrum murmured. No one but me understood, and they looked at him with curiosity.

Look in the brain box later. It's there.

"I will endeavor to be whatever he needs me to be."

"Maybe you can be the milkshake man. He likes chocolate. But not with whipped cream. He hates that. Ok?"

"I won't forget."

Rhys's jaw tightened and I heard his teeth click together.

He wanted to leave; he did not want to say goodbye.

"When I received the alert on the bank card," Will started, "I honestly expected I would find your father. I am happy to have been wrong, Rhys. Meeting you and Hyrum has been a highlight of my life, one I will never forget."

"A highlight for me, too," Aisha said. "As confusing as all of this has been, I'm glad it happened and wouldn't trade this week for anything."

"So...maybe I can be a bonding thing," Rhys ventured.

I know Will hoped so. His eyebrow twitched, but he knew better than to say anything.

Aisha leaned in to give Hyrum a kiss on his cheek, and then Rhys. "I am so grateful that I was your safe spot in a crisis. And selfishly, I hope one day you find your way back even if it's just to touch base."

"He can whisper to you," Hyrum said.

"I'll take what I can get."

"As would I," Will added.

They stepped back. Hyrum set his hand on Rhys's bare neck, and I wiggled until my belly had full contact with his hand. His fingers flexed a bit, tense, trying hard to not tremble. I couldn't see his face but I was sure his eyes were closed in concentration; both Will and Aisha looked pained, waiting for us to vanish right before their eyes.

They kept waiting.

"Jesus," Rhys muttered. "I can't do it."

"Give it time," Will said.

A minute later, Aisha marched the five steps between them. "Goddammit, Rhys. You have people waiting at home who need you. You *have* to go."

"I'm trying. I swear."

"You're holding on and you need to let go. Need a reason? We have lives to get back to. As much as we'll miss you, I have a kid at home and he has toddlers to watch after. It's *time*."

I heard him sniff, and was sure he had tears in his eyes. "I know."

She didn't soften. "Look, I know deep inside you have this need to make sure I give up the grudge against him and give him a chance. I know you're screaming inside that you want to be born here, too, but god*damn*, Rhys."

"I just—"

"You want the hard truth? I'm not sure I want to. But I'll make you a deal. You have two minutes to get your ass home. If you leave, I'll take him out to dinner tonight. I'll listen to everything he has to say, and I'll give him an honest shot. A better than honest shot. But if you're still here? I'm going home. I'll get Drew or Finn to take me, and I will never—and I mean this—*never* speak to him again."

Rhys's intake of breath reverberated down his arm.

"Look at me," she went on. "I know you're watching my aura, or whatever the hell you call it. You can see if I'm lying, and you know I'm not." She reached up and set her hand on his cheek, softening. "Sweety, I love you, but I will never speak to—"

"—him...again."

It was cold. Early November in San Francisco often had a snap to the air, with pockets of fog slipping leisurely down streets and alleyways. Union Square was sunny this day, though, and the cold was just a reminder that winter was on its way, and would be, perhaps, 4.5 degrees cooler, with gray skies and periodic breezes.

Basically, like every day from October to February.

Hyrum began bouncing on his toes and let go of Rhys. "You did it! You got us home! Look, the Christmas tree is there and the ice rink, and the bakery!"

Aisha still hadn't taken her hand away from Rhys's face.

"Oh my god," he breathed. "You were touching me."

She finally pulled away.

"Maybe this isn't home," Rhys said. "Maybe it's still your timeline, but I just...hopped to Union Square."

"You know it's not," she said, weakly.

"Rhys, it's your daddy!" Hyrum jumped up and down, waving at Will, who sprinted across the Square, phone in hand.

"I've got them," he said into it as he neared. "They seem fine. Union Square. No, you don't need to report here, we'll sort it out later."

"Dad?"

"Is that a question?" He turned to Aisha, grinning. "Well, hello."

She moved closer to Rhys.

"Dad, that's not—"

"I can see that." He was still grinning. "Hi, my name is Will. I'll be your emperor today."

"Oh my god," Rhys groaned.

She stepped out from the fog of fear and toward Will. "I'll be damned. How is this possible? You don't look much older than I am. And you're what?" She looked at Rhys. "He's close to sixty?"

"Close but not there yet," Will said. "I presume my son pulled you through a portal? Or did you follow along to visit?"

"It's worse than that, Dad," Rhys said.

"We went on an adventure," Hyrum added, though quite a bit less enthusiastically.

Maybe we should get out of the public eye. She really looks young, and since we just kind of popped onto the Square, people might start looking.

Will gestured to the elevator doors, leading down to the lab.

"It's seriously complicated," Rhys said as the doors slid shut. "I mean, astronomically complicated. Like, so complicated we didn't even *use* a portal. Or a bracelet."

We were halfway down to the lab when Will said, "Hands on me." Without questioning, they all reached for him, and a blink later we were in the middle of the living room at home. He held a finger up—don't say a word yet—and went to the front door, poking his head out. The guard assigned to assure that Oz's boys did not escape unnoticed was there, and when asked, he moved down a level, with the orders that no one other than Aisha and the twins were allowed up the stairs.

Only little Eli was at home, and he was old enough to understand the younger Aisha if he wandered across the hallway.

"All right," he said when he turned back. "Explain."
You might want to sit down. This will take a while.

~

Aisha, our Aisha, was already on her way home from work. She'd bolted from the classroom when told her oldest son vanished into thin air, and was halfway home via Royal Guard shuttle when notified that he and Hyrum had been found just a few minutes later halfway across town from where they disappeared.

She wanted an explanation, so she continued on home.

She arrived just minutes later, tossing her bag and jacket onto the sofa without bothering to make sure things landed where intended, and rushed to hug her son. "What the hell? What happened? Where did the two of you go?"

It was then she spotted the other Aisha.

"Ah. Hello. He went to visit...me?" The idea made her laugh.

"I wish that's all it was," she said.

We sat at the table with coffee and soft drinks. Rhys began the long explanation, long enough that Hyrum wandered off to get paper and pencils from Rhys's bedroom, and he stretched out on the floor to color while Rhys and New Aisha explained it all.

"It wasn't intentional," Rhys said. "But yeah, it was my fault. Now Hyrum's without a bike and she's stuck here."

"So we'll take her home," his mother said. "We've taken Jax and Aubrey home more than once."

Will shook his head before she completely finished. "Completely new timeline," he reminded her. "The fact that he traversed it at all is amazing and impressive."

"And means I can take her back," Rhys said.

New Aisha bristled. "You are *not* risking it, not again."

"You have a little kid at home. He's got a shit life ahead of him if you're not there. I mean, George seemed all right but he has a history here, and he will make that boy's life miserable without you there. He'll never be able to become who he really is without you. You know that."

"We'll find a way," Will guessed.

Liam. Call Liam. He's done it before. He jumped back from the new timeline where you saved Donna.

Liam Finnegan, Finn in who knows how many Whens gone by, was otherwise occupied in the future. Will wasn't sure how to contact him, or if he had actually remained there. "He has a habit of jumping around and living entire lifetimes before coming home."

"How?" she asked.

"As near as we can determine, multiple exposures to null

space have significantly increased his lifespan. We don't know how old he truly is, and neither does he."

Guess my age.

"Wick," Will sighed. "Not now."

She reached across the table to tickle my chin. "Rhys explained your age. So I get it."

Fine. So how are we going to scare the shit out of him? Because he needs to be scared to jump. And then he has to be scared to jump back.

"What if that doesn't work again?" Mom-Aisha asked. "He's liable to adjust to the fear. I don't want him to get there and not have a way home."

"I'd be well taken care of, Mom," he said. "It's not like I'd go and then have to figure it all out on my own. The Emperor made it pretty clear that if Hyrum and I had gotten stuck, we had a home. I'd have family."

You just want to make sure she goes out to dinner with him. And then bonks the snot out of him.

"Excuse me?" Will said, eyebrow slightly raised.

"They're, um, not a thing," Rhys said. "Yet. Maybe never. And that might be my fault, too. If I hadn't shown up and used the damned bank card, she'd have another thirteen years to stop hating him."

"I don't hate him," new Aisha said. "But I am angry still."

Aisha reached over and patted the arm of her younger self. "Of course you are. And you will be for quite some time."

"You were pissed at him?" That was news to Rhys.

"Oh, hon. I was mad for a couple of decades. I don't think I stopped being mad until we moved back to San Francisco and Jay became fast friends with Zed."

Rhys glanced at his father.

"I am aware."

"But—"

"Sweetheart." Aisha's voice was gentle. "She has a few years left of being really, truly angry with him. It took hearing endless stories about him from Jay, who practically worshipped him, for me to admit to myself that we weren't the same people we were at twenty. And honestly, sometimes I still get those stabs. I get irrationally upset because we could have had those two decades if he had been honest with me. I knew there was something he wasn't telling me and I invented an entire life story for him to make myself feel better about it."

New Aisha snickered softly.

Aisha looked at herself. "Hon, he does have his reasons, and because my husband traveled back to tell him things he shouldn't have, your Emperor has better reasons. But the truth is that he was a teenager who left home too soon, and just did what his parents asked of him. And trust me, there will be significant anger and resentment over that later, but he felt helpless against it and had no idea he could learn to control his gifts."

"I know the reasons. Yet, still…"

"I know. I didn't soften until enduring the endless stories about the grumpy man who doted on Oz and Zed's friends while trying to make it seem like they annoyed him. Jay showed me video after video taken at parties on the roof…and hon, that man cannot dance. Fair warning."

"Hey. I can dance."

Her eyebrow twitched upward. "Then I went back and looked at videos of him through the years…so attentive to the kids and to Jax and Aubrey, always watching. And it hit me…the gloves. He never touched them without the gloves. Most of the time it was a formal event and the gloves just kind of worked, but I stumbled on one of him rushing to slip a pair on while running to escort Aubrey from a car, which meant it wasn't just me. I saw him go from actively picking up the kids to keeping his distance. But his love for them all was so clear."

It was only a year or two before his 43rd birthday party that she accepted the fact that there was more to him than he had admitted, and that she had never stopped loving him. The hard shell of resentment cracked, and she wanted to reconnect. "Oh, I was so nervous, but when Jay came home and said we'd been invited and he wanted to go? I knew it was then or never. And when that night was over, I regretted every irate minute I had spent."

"Would you change anything?"

"Oh, hell yes," Aisha said, laughing. "So many things. For starters, I'd call Aubrey sooner and beg forgiveness for losing her number and changing mine. If you do nothing else, call her. But knowing what I know now? I'd want him to do what he needed me to do in order to get to Vegas when I did. I'd marry James all over again, even though he's...James."

That made new Aisha chuckle.

"Bilbo." She tapped the back of his hand. "Go get Jay. Tell him to bring the baby. And don't question it, just trust me."

New Aisha's mouth dropped open.

"You've already met one of your future kids. You might as well meet the one you already have and see how he turned out. And I want you to keep this in your head: this wouldn't be possible if Will had not had the nerve to do what he had to do."

"But the way he did it..."

She wanted new Aisha to think about it honestly. She'd shown up on the Square with an entire life plan in her head, when they had never discussed anything beyond a few silly games of what-if. And the Emperor had been honest, in that, at least. It was entirely what-if and his answers were always laced with "if my life were not what it is."

"You dropped all of this on him like a bomb. Your intention to be patient for as long as it took. The relationship, the two-point-five kids and an apartment close to Aubrey and Jax. How badly you wanted to be with him, and only him. But hon...never once did you ask what he wanted. You said you loved him yet you never asked if he felt the same way. And you didn't stop talking long enough for him to get a word in."

New Aisha's face flushed.

"The truth is that he wanted it all. But he couldn't admit to it because doing that might derail the future and prevent his father from saving the world. It was bigger than us, Aisha. It was *billions* of people, and the end of everything. It wasn't a risk he could take."

"Billions," she whispered.

"That man will give it all up for the people he loves. And even for those he's never met, if it's for the greater good."

"That's why Jesus loves him," Hyrum offered.

"Jesus loves everyone, right?" Rhys asked.

"Fine. But he loves Will lots and lots."

"If I could just work past—"

Aisha shook her head, just a tiny bit. "That anger is a choice. It's understandable, but hon, what you do with it is pure choice. You can hold it tight and turn it into a personality trait, or you can loosen your grip on it and examine it hard to figure out why it still matters so much. But it's all choice, just as much as getting up every morning and choosing to love him. That's what we do. Every single day."

"You chose to forgive."

Aisha took a beat to consider. "I don't think forgiveness is something you can just bestow on someone. It takes work from both sides, and if you don't let him in, he can't do the work he needs in order to make that forgiveness complete. I thought I'd forgiven him, but no. We needed to work together to get there."

She had more to say; this had the feel of working up to a sermon, and she was about to impart every tiny thing she had mused about over the years, but New Aisha's attention suddenly shifted.

She heard the baby before Jay was halfway up the stairs. He was babbling, talking Jay's ear off though he had no idea that his son was reminding him that it was past snack o'clock, and he also needed a dry diaper. He wasn't yet fussed about it, but warned he might be, when Jay and Will reached the top step.

Jay came through the door first and she shot to her feet, a small gasp escaping her. Tiny fingers poked at the face she could not take her eyes off, a face dotted with unshaved whiskers from the last three days and lines from lack of sleep.

He grinned widely. "Damn, Mom, you're kind of smokin' hot."

"Still am," his mother said.

That broke new Aisha's reverie. "It really happened for you. You went through the whole thing, all the surgeries."

"Just one." He moved closer, and handed the baby to her. "And that single surgery meant this little shit was possible. We waited a long time to have him, but if not for that…"

Her heart melted. Not in the literal, call emergencies services way, but melted nonetheless. She inhaled the scent of new baby and didn't flinch when a tiny fist slammed into her chin.

"His name is Takar, after Navi's grandfather," Jay said. "We tend to call him Tak. Or Tako, to the rest of the kids. They think it's funny."

"It is," Hyrum said. "Tako kuda."

"Takar," she repeated, softly. "You're a handsome boy, aren't you?" She looked up at Jay. "And so are you. I never could have imagined this. You as a fully grown man."

"How old am I for you? I'd guess you can't even imagine me as a little boy. Oh. Pre-turkey baster, or post?"

"Post." Absently, she dropped kisses onto the baby's head. "We're just starting the process, but we've found a promising doctor."

"Mass. Great doctor. Still my doctor."

"To be fair, he's now the royal physician," Will said. "But yes, see him. Take the Emperor with you. They'll be surprised to see each other."

The next surprise came gushing out of Takar's mouth, all over her shoulder. With one last kiss, she handed him back to Jay, and watched as they left, not taking her eyes off him until he was out of sight.

"That's what's at stake," Aisha said. "For starters."

"And then there's Rhys."

There were two more reasons and they bounded through the door, dressed in karate uniforms, sweaty and half out of breath.

"Ya lose, sucka!" Alex barked at Charlie. "Half a step behind me."

They stopped with the same abruptness they'd entered. It took a second or two to assess the mood in the room and the extra mom, but then Charlie marched forward with his hand out. "Hi, other mom. Nice to meet you."

"I'm Alex," his twin called out.

"I'm Charlie and we're your future weirdlings. In case you didn't know."

"Weirdlings."

He gave a half shrug. "If the shoe fits, wear it, and run away from the guy it belongs to." He turned to Will. "Should we leave? This seems serious. We should leave. We'll go bug Aunt Aubrey for cookies or lunch if it's not too late. Or even if it is. She'll feed us."

"Whirlwind," new Aisha uttered as they left.

"Hence, the weirdlings," Rhys said. "So yeah, I need to take you home so that one day, if you stop being pissed off, they can ruin your life, too."

"You love them," Hyrum said. "Stop being mean."

I hear a whine.

Hyrum sat up. "I'm not whining!"

No. A...metallic whine.

Rhys popped up from his seat at the table and told Hyrum to get up and get behind him. Hy was flanked by both Aishas, one looking confused, the other angry. Will stood shoulder to shoulder with his son, but he had no idea what the problem was, and turned his head to look at Aisha, questioning.

Within three seconds, they were there. This time there were only two, and the closest one began speaking quickly, before Rhys could say anything.

"Rhys. I'm not here to hurt you. Don't jump. Just stop and listen."

"Like hell. Leave me alone. I'm *home*."

The guardian took a step closer, and at the sound of a snap, looked down. "Aw, damn. Hyrum, I'm sorry. I think I broke your pencil."

Hyrum pushed forward. "You know my name?"

"Of course I know your name. I've known you since I was..." He tilted his head back. "Of course."

"Rhys?" Will asked. "These are the people chasing you?"

"A couple of them, yeah."

"Never the same ones, I don't think," new Aisha said. "But this one. We've seen him more than once."

"Outside the safe house in Denver," Rhys said. "Outside the shelter. Outside Ozoo."

The guardian held his hand up as if to say, "Stop."

"Don't put your hand out at me," Rhys snapped. "Fuck off. I'm where I belong and that can't be against any laws. You can't arrest me in my own home, in my own When."

"Arrest?" He blinked rapidly. "I'm not here to arrest you. We were never—"

Rhys was nearly nose to nose with him, so angry that his hands were balled into fists. "Like hell. I'd been displaced for maybe two hours when your first set of freaks popped up out of nowhere and told me I had to go with them because I wasn't where I was supposed to be. I have no idea what they would have done if not for the DNA test."

"Newbies." Sighing, the guardian tapped behind his ear, cocking his head as he did. "First timers. They hosed it up. We're not cops, Rhys. No one was there to arrest you."

"Then why the hell were you there? For shits and giggles?"

He looked puzzled. "We were there to take you home."

When the words punctured the bubble of anger surrounding Rhys, he looked as if he'd been punched and took a step back to keep it from happening again. Will took over; he was just as angry but had his wits about him, and was more willing to listen.

"Explain."

Somewhere in the future, knowing what was coming, Rhys sent members of his own organization, named simply as "the guardians." Their job was to pinpoint Whens in which he was lost, and to bring him home, wherever that might be.

"You sometimes switch time streams," the guardian explained. "You're pretty good about finding your way back, but every now and then you have issues finding the right insertion point. It takes us days, at best, to find and return you. And I'm not certain why the original two did not explain this. They were told it was the first time you'd drifted."

"Drifted," Rhys repeated.

"What do you mean, he switches time streams? How is that different from a timeline?" Will asked.

Something about him poked at my brain. I ran across the room to my hover cart and turned it on, speeding toward him as it rose. I stopped next to Rhys's shoulder and tried to really see the man dressed in blue with light sticks running down his shirt.

I know you, don't I?

"You don't know him, Wick," Rhys said. "He's just blathering on because he's not getting what he wants. Me."

"I'm not here for you, Rhys"

He glanced at Hyrum. Then, dripping with anguish, "Then who?"

The guardian nodded toward new Aisha. "For her."

Will and Rhys both stepped together, blocking him from easy access. I moved the cart until I was directly in front of his face, despite Will's order to move back.

Show me you.

Hyrum repeated it for me.

"Nothing afoul here, Rhys," he said. "We're only here to escort her home."

When he didn't respond, I said it again. *Show me you. I know you. But your face is wrong.*

"I'd forgotten," he said. "The last time I saw you, you knew who I was. But this is the first time ever, isn't it?"

He double-tapped the spot behind his ear, uttered "recalibrating," and tiny pieces of him began to move, flipping and turning, clicking into place, until he was a young man.

Rhys nearly choked on his name.

"Quinn."

44

Aisha, our Aisha, was the first to react. While Rhys stood with his mouth open, she stomped around him, and poked at Quinn's chest. "You. Whatever the hell this is, I swear, I will drag you home by your hair and fling you at your mother's feet. And she'll allow it because this is just...wrong."

Quinn's mouth twitched at one corner as he tried to bite back the smile. "I don't think she's home. The last time I saw her and Dad, they were headed for London. But Hagar is at home, I think. He might agree with you. He's never been a fan of poking about time."

"Mom." Rhys tugged at her shoulder. "This isn't Quinn from now. This is future shit. How far forward?"

"From now? Approximately three hundred twenty-five years. Give or take a dozen."

"I'm still alive three centuries from now?"

"In a roundabout way."

With a heavy sigh that warned of a good spanking on the horizon, something she had never inflicted on any of the kids, Aisha ordered Quinn to sit at the table. Before he complied, though, Will looked to the other guardian and asked who he was. If we knew him.

"Show him your twenty-year old self," Quinn said.

He repeated the sequence Quinn had, and we stood quietly as his faced changed.

Asmonk.

"Dude." Rhys could not believe it. "You fucking hate me. Why would you help him?"

Asmonk shrugged. "I don't hate you, Rhys. I never hated you. I was terrified *of* you, but I did have the grace to finally grow up." He gestured to the sofa. "Mind if I wait there? I doubt I'm the one you want to rake over the proverbial coals."

Quinn sat at the foot of the table, where Aisha directed him. Will took the seat at the head, and everyone else filled in, all eyes on the living, breathing, artificial representation of Rhys's friend. He folded his arms and leaned on the table, very much like teenaged Quinn would do.

"Start from the top," Will said.

"Well, once upon a time there was a teenager who wanted to win a contest by turning an android head into something easy to look at."

"You are fully aware of what I meant."

"But that *is* where this began. All those years ago when Rhys's interest in artificial intelligence was given an academic outlet. If not for that, I never would have become this, and he never would have crafted a way to shorten the amount of time he spends trapped across time streams."

"That." Will pointed at him. "You didn't answer. Streams versus lines. Explain."

Timelines, Quinn said, were contained within the same temporal branch. There was a fine line between Finn's theory of converging lines and Drew's theory that new events created new lines. They were both more right than wrong; individual events created new timelines, but those would be absorbed into the prime line as time progressed.

There could be billions of timelines within a stream. And every now and then, when a change so significant occurred, a line would break off and become its own prime. New prime, new stream. Rhys typically traveled within his own stream, crossing and hopping timelines, but every now and then he wound up in an adjacent stream, and getting home could be tricky.

"It takes you micro-seconds to return within this stream," Quinn said. "But when you cross? Sometimes it takes years. You have the knowledge, but not always the power. The older you get, the more difficult it is."

"Because he's less afraid as he ages," Will mused. "Generating that adrenaline isn't as easy."

Quinn nodded. "Whereas, we need no adrenaline. Only additional power. Sometimes it means crossing the stream and finding him, only to have something—" he glanced at new Aisha "—hold him back. We have to return to base, so to speak, recharge, and then try again."

That's why you didn't immediately return, isn't it? We were gone for a week. How long did it take for you to get here?

"Easily twice as long," Quinn said. "Look, I know this went sideways from the start, and I'm sorry. I tried to tell you who I was outside of the tunnel, but Hyrum's impressively flashy throat punch gave you that single moment you needed to jump. I never had a chance after that."

He didn't blame Rhys. After all, he was being chased by men in oddly conforming and somewhat glowy uniforms, and their lead did not stop to consider his own face. Who would stick around for that?

"Whose idea was that uniform, then?" Rhys asked.

Quinn snorted. "Charlie's. He thought it would get your attention at a distance. Mostly, he just thinks it's funny. But the reflective properties have a purpose if we're caught mid-stream and need to find each other."

Is that like getting stuck in null space?

"No, it's not exactly the same, Wick. We can cross the streams using bridges. Null space is just that. Emptiness. But the bridges do cross null space."

"Bridges he creates when he jumps," Will mused.

"Anyone who can navigate between streams creates a bridge," Quinn said. "I have seen far more than he could create."

Different Rhyses in different Whens. In different timelines.

"Possibly. We're not certain who else has this ability, but if he does it stands to reason there are others. But they're not my job. My job is to find him and bring him home."

Quietly, Aisha asked, "Have you ever failed?"

"If we have, it's because he jumped and we don't know about it."

New Aisha seemed less certain, and asked her other self, "I'm supposed to trust him? How do you know he's who he says?"

He looked at Rhys. "Ask me something only your Quinn would know."

That wasn't foolproof. Anyone imitating Quinn probably, at some point, had access to his memory stores. I knew that; Will and Rhys knew that. But we kept quiet because this *was* Quinn and he could take her home.

Rhys struggled to think of anything. But Hyrum bounced on his seat, eager to help, and asked, "What'd I go to the store for when Rhys was fixing his grandpa's car?"

"Dude, that was three hundred years ago for him," Rhys said.

"Water," Quinn said. "And snacks. But he didn't grasp whose car that was until Wick pointed it out as we walked away."

"But *what* snacks?" Hyrum pressed.

He didn't know.

Hyrum smacked the table with his hand. "That's Quinn! If he was lying he'd have made something up on account of he'd think we weren't sure."

I didn't follow his trail of logic, but new Aisha did, and agreed to let him take her home.

"Fuck it up and I will find out, somehow," Rhys said.

"It's a return trip, Rhys. The bridge is open."

They moved to the living room, and Asmonk got up from the sofa to stand by Quinn, ready to go.

"Wait." Rhys set his hand on new Aisha's arm. "Go back to Drew's office, in your future. The Emperor will still be there. You meant it, right? That if I left, you'd take him out to dinner and give him a chance?"

"I meant it. Can he do that?" She asked Quinn, too. "Can you do that?"

"I can do that."

Desperation tinged Rhys's voice. "I mean, he'll understand, I guess, if you don't want to. But he heard you say it, and he's probably hoping. I know he's hoping. I saw the color swirling around him, and—"

"Rhys. If he's still waiting there, the first thing I'll do is tell him to pick a restaurant, and we're going. I will listen to everything he has to say, whether it relates to us or not. And before you ask, I won't limit his chances to a single meal. I'd like to find a way back to friendship, even if I am still unbelievably pissed off."

She reached out, pulling him into a hug. "I know you think he's my soulmate. But, sweety, soulmates aren't just found. They're made. And that takes time."

"I know it's not fair." His voice cracked. "It's selfish. But I really need you to be my mom again."

"Rhys," Will said, sounding more like a warning.

"I know. I said it's not fair."

"There are likely a billion timelines out there, and in a good number, you might not exist. I might not exist."

"And I might be a one-off, and I need to be okay with that. But I'm not."

"You're not," Quinn said. "Trust me, you're not the only Rhys we chase around. But they're all you, just different Whens. But still you, nonetheless."

"Seriously."

"You're the first. Not the last."

"I hope you're still the first in my timeline," new Aisha said. "I'll give it an honest try, Rhys."

"But you can't promise."

"I'd be lying if I did." She stepped in between Quinn and Asmonk, setting her hand on Quinn's. "All right, boys. Take me to the Emperor. He damn well better be in the mood for a plate full of carbs."

Quinn nodded, but looked at Rhys again. "It should go without saying, but I will anyway. You can't tell me about this. The next time you see me, I know you'll want to, but I'll need my head free of this in order to *become* this. You know where my head is at right now, Rhys. I have to accept the possibility that I'll live out my life in Saint Francis before I can thrive in the environment that will allow me to leave."

"Leave for good?"

"It's home. It will always be home. But I need to leave at some point, which won't happen if I don't do the work first."

I know Rhys had more to say, and a thousand questions he wanted to ask, but before he could draw in a full breath, they blinked away.

PART THREE

45

Christmas morning arrived at 5 a.m. Technically, Hyrum had been awake since 4, but he sat in bed and waited as patiently as he could; his bedroom floor was littered with sleeping teenagers, with the exception of Rhys, who was awake and trying to be as quiet as Hyrum was patient.

When he noticed Hyrum sit up, Rhys crawled from his floor mattress and climbed into bed with his uncle, cuddling until it was time to get up. I jumped onto the bed and wedged my way between them, sucking up their warms.

"You did it, Rhys," Hyrum whispered in the dark. "You promised we'd be home for Christmas and we are."

"Did you doubt me?"

"Yep."

"Jerk," he snickered. "But...no lie. I doubted me, too. I think I would have been more scared if we hadn't met Aisha and the Emperor, though. I mean, I was scared, but not as much as I would have been."

"Do you think she got over being mad and kissed him?"

"I don't know. I hope so. But the truth is that they might have gone out to dinner like she promised, and she might have decided she doesn't want to be friends with him."

"Does that make your tummy hurt?"

"Yeah," he said with a sigh. "If I think about it, it makes my tummy hurt. So I'm trying to not think about it."

"We should think about something else."

What do you think Santa brought you? Think about that.

Hyrum had asked for simple things, as usual. He wanted new pencils to draw with, and new crayons to color with. If he'd been good enough, he hoped to get extra plastic tracks for his toy cars, ones that looped, and if he'd been very, very good, he hoped for a new pair of neon-colored jeans to replace the ones he'd ripped.

I knew all of those things were waiting for him. Some were wrapped and under the tree, others were stacked neatly near his stocking. His stocking was packed with all the usual things; everyone got candy and toothbrushes, the older boys were gifted new razors, and there was an assortment of tiny toys.

Rhys couldn't think of anything he wanted, but there were tools and computer gadgets, all things he could use when he was ready to work on the drone again.

They knew better to ask me. I admitted to seeing Santa, but I was sworn to silence. They'd have to wait, just like everyone else.

"And the parents?" Rhys asked.

Same as always. Lots of little things. Booze, mostly.

"Scotch and Chambrizi," Rhys chuckled.

"How'd Santa get Chambrizi? That's from the future."

No, I meant they got booze for each other. Finn got the Chambrizi. I'm not saying what Santa brought.

"Do you know if Santa got my letter?" Hyrum asked. "I wrote to him to say sorry for breaking my bike. I hope he's not mad."

I didn't ask about that, sorry. All I do is watch.

"Hm."

The bedroom door at the end of the hall creaked open, followed by soft footsteps back and forth across the living room. Alex and Charlie stirred; she stretched, groaning about the air mattress and Charlie's feet—he'd kicked her in the middle of the night, though she was equally unhappy about the smell—and then sat up, waiting, running fingers through her hair in a hopeless attempt to manage the bedhead. Marco did the same, muttering that this tangled mop was going to spur his mother into cutting his hair.

Charlie grunted when he sat up, but he didn't care about what his hair was doing. He scratched at his newby whiskers, three days post-shave, seemingly content with their existence.

"Lay the odds now," he said, voice thick with sleep, "I get a plasma razor this year. I'm shaving *everything* tonight."

"Ew." Alex scrunched her nose. "Gross."

Jax stomped down the hallway, audible permission to get out of bed and greet Christmas morning.

Hyrum sprang from the bed and raced to the bedroom door, but he stopped and turned to make sure the others were up and ready to go, too. No one looked ready for anything; it was a mass of bedhead and rumpled t-shirts and shorts, yawns and rubbed eyes, but they acted eager and happy for his sake.

Christmas morning was for Hyrum and the younger children; in the years between belief and acceptance, the truth about Santa was clear: he existed, because anything else was unacceptable. As long as a single person in the family believed, he was real.

Once Hyrum cracked the door open, I rushed to get ahead of them. I wanted to see the look on his face, expecting it to be every bit like the expression he'd had his first holiday here. Elation and disbelief, colored in highlights of sheer joy.

He raced from his room, and as he had then, stopped cold just before the living room.

It wasn't possible.

It was whole again, shiny bright red, with the basket clipped to the front. All the breaks and bends were mended, with new cables, a new derailleur, and a new chain. Even the wheels and spokes glittered brightly, and he could not quite grasp what he saw.

It took the span of a few heartbeats for him to take it in, and when he did, he bounded into the room with a squeal. There was a tag hanging from the handlebar, dangling from a blue ribbon, with his name written in large, very precise lettering.

"Santa found a bike just like my old one!" he blurted.

Read the tag.

The kids assembled around the red bike, more eager to see that tag than to get to their own gifts. The adults looked at each other, confused, not even trying to pretend that they knew what was going on.

"Hyrum, I could never be angry with you," he read out loud. "You have taken great care of this bicycle for many years. My elves have repaired it to perfect working order, but if you wish to buy yourself a newer, better bike, I won't be offended. I only wish for you to be happy. Thank you for being such a good man, and for taking great care of this for so long. Love, Santa."

He stared at the note for a long, quiet minute, and then turned to Will. "You wrote this, right? This sounds like you."

Will swore that he did not, and Jax looked at Aubrey as if to say, "Well, if not him, then who?"

Rhys set his hand on Hyrum's back. "Santa found your bike, dude. He found it and got it fixed."

"But how? How could he go there?"

"I dunno. Maybe the Santa there knows how to get to here and brought it for ours to give back to you. But it's the same bike, right?"

Hyrum searched the length of the top tube, and set his finger to a tiny spot where he'd used paint to write his initials. "It's my old bike," he murmured. "It says so. HCB."

When he looked up, there were tears in his eyes. "I already bought a new one on account of I said to everyone not to get me one. Should I take it back? I don't want to hurt Santa's feelings."

"You won't hurt his feelings," Aubrey said.

"Seriously," Rhys agreed. "He even says in the note, he won't be offended. If you want, we can hang this one from your bedroom wall, maybe build a frame and add some lights. Turn it into art."

"Really?"

"Really. But you can still ride it, too. We can mount it so you can pull it down easily. Nothing says you can't ride both."

Charlie ran a hand over the seat. "Santa is fucking awesome."

"Charles," Aubrey sighed.

"Sorry."

It would not be the last time he apologized for his language that day, but it was quickly forgotten in the frenzy that followed. Kids poured out of every corner, it seemed, so I jumped into the wood box I had been gifted fifteen years ago, and watched as they tore open their gifts, waiting for the wads of wrapping paper to fly overhead and for Thor to lose his damned mind over all the new balls he hoped he could chase.

Rhys told him to sit, which meant no running across the floor, knocking over teens and pre-teens, though his siblings made sure to toss a few massive chunks of wrapping paper his way. He learned quickly—as he did and then promptly forgot every year—that wrapping paper is not tasty, and no one wanted to touch it again after it had been in his mouth.

I caught a few in the face, but I also managed to slap a few back at whichever kid had thrown it, and on one particular paw strike, I landed a golf-ball sized piece of crumpled paper on Charlie's wet lips. It stuck and hung there until he exhaled sharply, sending it rolling over his chin into his lap.

"Jingle balls," he chuckled.

The aroma of cinnamon rolls drifted through the air, and with it, the flying wads slowed and then stopped, which was fine because I knew it would happen again after they'd eaten.

Will sat on the floor next to me. "There are gifts for you, too. Would you like help opening them?"

Maybe later. I'm chillin' in my box.

"All right. And are you going to tell us who brought the bike in?"

Santa.

"Wick."

It was Santa. That's all I'm saying.

"Not even a hint?"

Santa. Are you having hearing issues? Maybe it's your blood sugar. Go have a cinnamon roll.

His voice dropped to a whisper. "Wick. Someone was in here last night, and we don't know who. That's a security breach. I need to know."

I know who. That's really all you need to know.

He closed his eyes, sighing deeply.

There was no breach. Trust me.

We both knew he wasn't worried about some rando wandering around the royal house; he was upset because something happened under his nose and he'd been unaware.

As far as he knew, it could have been Drew. It could have been the elder Eli. Even Finn. We were all aware of how Hyrum had marked his treasured bicycle; that was proof to Hyrum, not proof itself, and it made Will mentally itchy to not know.

I was okay with that.

Amused, even.

"Who has the money and the know how?" He was thinking out loud, watching the mass of family surrounding the table, waiting their turn to grab one of Aubrey's homemade cinnamon rolls. "Either Jax or Aubrey would have told me ahead of time. Drew wouldn't be able to keep it to himself. Oz? I don't think she's paid that close of attention to his bicycle. Zed would have simply offered him use of his old bike."

Why does this matter so much to you?

"It just does." He reached over the side of the box to scratch between my ears. "You have money. Did you somehow pull this off, Wick? Convince—"

He turned back to the dining room. "Rhys. He did this, didn't he? If any of them, he would do it. He knew that bicycle almost as well as Hyrum and he has the funds to facilitate its replacement. He was here all night. This was his doing, wasn't it?"

Well, look at you, getting all Sherlock Holmes on us.

"Elementary, my dear Wick."

He pushed himself off the floor and headed for the food. It was Christmas, after all, and a little junk food is what Christmas is made for.

46

Whole-family dinners in the royal apartment were no longer possible; there wasn't enough room for everyone, not even with extra tables and chairs set up in the living room. Christmas dinner had been held in the old staff kitchen a floor below the royal apartment for several years. There was more room for the extra tables and chairs, and plenty of floor space for kids to sit and play with new toys. Post-meal, there were comfy chairs for the adults to drop into for a bit of post-prandial drowsiness while the kids cleaned up, and it was then Finn whispered in Rhys's ear: *come to the lab with me. I need your help with something.*

He whispered to Hyrum, too, so I scrambled to climb Rhys's leg, and settled on his shoulder. As soon as we were out the door, Finn reached a hand out, and with a tap on his bracelet, we jumped to the lab, landing near the center, facing the elevator door.

Rhys turned at the sound of feet shuffling behind him, surprised to find Will standing there.

"Wait. You were just..." The lightbulb went off. "How? You're here. How?"

Hyrum practically bounced over to him, throwing his arms around Will's waist. "Emperor! Merry Christmas! I miss you. Is it Christmas for you?"

He hugged back. "Sadly, no. Christmas is over for us. It's late January for me."

"How?" Rhys repeated.

The Emperor lifted his arm. "You left the bracelet. Drew gave me the data he passed on to you. It took a while, but...

there's an open bridge between our Whens, and it can still be traversed."

So you just decided to hop on over and say hi?

"I wanted," he said, reaching under the lab center console, "to play Santa."

He pulled out the stuffed red bear Hyrum had played with in the war room's conference area. "Eli held onto this. He wanted you to have it, Hyrum."

With a surprised gasp, Hyrum reached for it, but then pulled his hands back. "Biff! Wait. What about your Hyrum? Did you go get him? Won't he want it?"

"Our Hyrum," he answered, pushing the bear closer, "is home safe with Aubrey, and he has several stuffed friends. His favorite is called 'Chuckles.'"

"I have a Chuckles! He's a blue rabbit and he just showed up on my bed one day!"

"Imagine that."

"Yeah," Rhys chuckled. "Go figure. But you got him? He's living with Aubrey and Jax now?"

Hyrum bubbled with excitement. "Is he okay? Does he eat crayons? I still do that sometimes. Is he happy? His daddy is still alive, so..."

Will and Aubrey barged their way into the Munson's 700-year-old brick colonial less than a week after we left. The shock of seeing her gave way to Levi Munson's anger, and if not for the Emperor's reputation, he undoubtedly would have resorted to violence to rid himself of the intrusion. He vehemently refused to allow Aubrey to see Hyrum, much less take him, until Valerie confronted him.

"I know things, Levi. Things I can tell the world, and there is proof. You either allow that boy to go with his sister, or I swear to all that is holy, I will hand it over to the Emperor here and now."

"Mom did that? Didn't she want him anymore? Was she mad at me?"

Rhys set his hand on Hyrum's shoulder. "Hy, she wanted him to go because that meant his father could never hurt him again. *Your* mom used to ask you to go home with her because he was dead and she missed you, but if he'd still been alive? Once she knew it was possible, she would have done anything to get you to Aubrey and keep him away from you."

He finally took the bear from Will.

"Tell Eli I'll take care—"

The bathroom door creaked open, and they turned to see who it was.

"Will, I swear to God, this kid is ninety per cent..." Whatever irritation she felt dissolved, and she grinned when she saw them. The baby she held close hiccupped, and by rote she began patting his back.

"You made a baby!" Hyrum blurted. His free hand went to his shirt, clutching the fabric as he forced himself to stay put and not run over.

Aisha made her way to us, turning the baby so we could see his face.

"Is he?" Rhys asked.

"A he? So far, yes," she said.

"How long?" He finally gathered his wits. "It's been a few weeks for us, but clearly longer for you. How old is he?"

"You left us five years ago," Will answered.

"And he's nearly five months old," Aisha added.

"Five years." He immediately looked at their hands, searching for rings that weren't there.

"No, we are not," Will said, understanding what he wanted. "Not yet. But soon."

She'd done exactly as she promised; when Quinn dropped her off in Drew's office, she told Will he was taking her home, where she would shower and change clothes, and then they were going out for dinner. She promised to keep her attitude at a minimum, and would honestly listen to anything else he had to say.

He made no excuses and offered no promises. He also refused to kiss her goodnight, reasoning that this dinner was not a date but an obligation. He wanted to see her again, on her terms, and confirmed that she had his number. Then he left.

"I don't think he was all the way to his car before I texted him."

He made sure she reconnected with Aubrey before

consenting to an actual date; when the time came, she took a shuttle to San Francisco to spend the afternoon wandering the city with him and then had dinner at the cheapest dive-like bar they could find. They stayed until closing, watched the sun rise from a bench on the beach, and she realized she didn't want to leave.

"I went home to get Jimmy, a few personal things, and quit my job," she said. "I never looked back."

"But you had a baby without getting married?" Hyrum blurted.

"Kissing things can do that," Rhys reminded him. "All that matters is that they're happy, right? And look, he's here."

"What if he's not you? What if you can't be born yet?"

"Happiness first," Rhys said. He reached out and touched his pointy finger to the baby's hand, laughing at the spark he received in return. "Can I hold him? I won't drop him."

No one thought he would, but Aisha didn't argue when he insisted on sitting at the table before taking him, and I jumped to the center island before he sat. He cradled the baby on his lap, hand supporting his head, and he looked into eyes as green as his own.

"Hey, little man," he cooed. "I am so happy to meet you. Oh. Yeah, I know."

Tiny feet slammed into his chest.

"I hear you. I bet you have a ton of things to say. It sucks when no one else can understand you. But you should talk to Wick. I think he can."

A soft light gradually enveloped them. It began in the space between them, a tiny fluttering brightness that grew until it bubbled. Rhys didn't seem to notice, and given that neither Will nor Aisha reacted, I assumed it was not new.

"It's all right," Rhys whispered to the baby. "You can go in there. I don't have any secrets from you. Just keep in mind our lives aren't going to be the same."

Aisha leaned into Will. "They can communicate? Does that mean he understands us?

"He understands himself," Will said. "Whatever internal language one has, so does the other."

Or, you know, Rhys is a freaking genius and has been since birth. Which means yours is, too. Life will be fun as you scramble to stay ahead.

"What gift is this?" Hyrum asked in a loud whisper. "I've seen sparky things but not glowy things."

You glow sometimes. When the sparky things happen and you let it out all over, you glow.

This felt different to him.

"Tell you what, little dude," Rhys said, "you don't need to worry. She's not sick. Trust me, it'll be okay. Twins are fun and they'll be your friends."

"Oh *hell* no," Aisha breathed. "Not yet."

"Him?" Rhys went on. "Yeah, you're gonna love him. And he'll help you figure out your gifts. Mine got rolling when I was three, and he taught me how to snuff out the sparks."

"Is that about me?" Hyrum asked. "I remember showing him."

"I think so," Aisha said. "Hy babysits now and then and is so good with him."

They'll be best friends.

"Oh! He's younger than me, too. His knees won't hurt as much when he gets off the floor."

Rhys bent closer to the baby, touching foreheads. "I promise. And you don't need to worry about that. Even if we are just recycled souls, yours gets to go on like everyone else's. What? No. You won't ever be alone. People have your back, little man. So many people, in all the different Whens."

The light began to fade, but not before the door opened and Will, our Will, stepped in. He saw just enough to stop him in his tracks, but recovered quickly, and grinned.

Aisha, on the other hand, took a step toward him and slugged him in the arm.

"That's for telling Will what was going to happen and convincing him to break my heart."

"You're welcome."

The light evaporated, and Rhys stood, carefully, to hand the baby back to his mother.

"He's me, Dad," he said to Will.

"I can see that. He looks just like you did." He brushed a finger across baby Rhys's cheek. "Four months? Five? He became a biter at five, which was fine until his teeth erupted."

"Wonderful," Aisha sighed.

"How did you manage to traverse the time streams?" Will noted the Emperor's jump bracelet. "I imagine that was not enough."

The Emperor explained the bridge and how they accessed it. "It is, as far as we can tell, permanent. If that bridge is, surely others are, as well."

Queen Donna.

"Perhaps, Wick," Will allowed. "But I believe that may be a bridge best left unchecked."

But the one between their world and ours, Rhys wanted to know if that should be left alone as well.

"My parents are there," Aisha said. "They know what happened, and who the boy was who helped them on their way so many years ago. They never forgot him, and they'd like to thank him. Doubly so now that they know what was at stake."

"Perhaps," Will said again.

"They're also open to seeing your wife, and forging a relationship."

At that, he bristled. "That may not be ideal. The pain of seeing and then leaving them there? How could she handle that?"

For the first time since we arrived in the lab, Finn spoke up. "Bullshit. How many of me do you know? You have relationships with all of us."

"I didn't go through the pain of losing you."

"Eh. More bullshit. We were as good as lost to you for twenty-five years. And hell, son, you sat with your mother in another When and held her as she died, and then came home to your own. You've loved us all the same, Dash. Give Aisha the grace of the choice, at least."

"They're her *parents*," Rhys said. "Like, direct-line. The exact people she lost. Not just counterparts from five Whens ago...it's them, just splintered off from here. Thinking she couldn't handle it is like not wanting her to visit if they lived on Mars and weren't planning on returning."

He didn't seem convinced.

"I'll take her if she asks," Rhys said. "You can't expect me to not tell her it's a possibility. It's not your choice."

This was not a battle Will could win. He already knew that Rhys would travel and he would traverse other bridges into other streams of time. He knew he would become lost from time to time, and that Quinn would never stop searching for him.

"I suppose," he allowed, "that practicing with this bridge is as benign as it will get for you."

"He is safe and protected with us," the Emperor said.

Quietly, Hyrum said, "I want to go sometimes, too."

Even if you get stuck?

He nodded. "It's not an adventure if something doesn't go wrong as long as it's lots of fun."

I'll get stuck with you, okay?

"Let's not get stuck," Will sighed. "I'll ask your mother what she thinks, Rhys, but I will also inform her of my concerns. We'll figure it out." He touched a finger to baby Rhys's hand. "At the very least, I hope his existence brings you comfort."

"Little bit, yeah."

"When you were born, we suspected that you weren't tied to any given When. Time would not attempt to pick you apart if you stayed in one place too long. But I never would have imagined..."

"Liam," Rhys said. "He's done it."

"And stayed gone for centuries. He lives out entire lifetimes, Rhys. You likely will not have his longevity."

"But he knows *how* to get himself home, he just chooses to stay where he's at and screw around. I won't make those choices, Dad. I have way too much to do here, and my family is here."

Will's eyes flicked toward the Emperor.

"You're *here*. Not there. I know the difference. And they have their own Rhys. I won't stay lost. And if I take mom there, or take you there, we'll get back. We know the way now."

Will didn't have to say it: for how long? What did it take for future Rhys to feel compelled to organize a virtual army of cybernetic nanobot-enhanced droids as his personal rescue squad? Where was he stuck, and for how long?

His voice broke. "I hate this. I hate that you can do this. If you go through a portal and get lost, I can find you and bring you home. With this I have no way—"

"Carts, horses," Aisha said, gently. "He can cross the bridge from here to our When, we know that. Will and Drew have worked around the need for a burst of adrenaline to get moving. If he has us as a destination, maybe he won't get lost, ever."

"Tell me that in fifteen years, when this one jumps to god knows where," Will said.

She looked at Rhys. "You landed at my feet because of your mother. She gave you a notion of a safe place to fall. Visit, let this baby get to know you, and become *his* safe place." She turned back to Will. "We don't have to like it, but this is what we've got. The lost boys. We just make damn sure they have the image in their head of where to land gently and not get hurt."

Hyrum whispered to Rhys, "Am I a lost boy, too?"

Without a doubt, he was. Years ago, the idea of being one had him choking back tears; now, it excited him.

"If we land on you again, we gotta see Disneyland there," he said to the Emperor. "We go every year here. You should do that with your Hyrum and Rhys. Oh! When we go next month we oughta dress like lost boys!"

"Beats the princess dress Charlie used to try to get me to wear."

"I will not wear tights," Will said dryly before turning to Aisha and the Emperor. "Don't be surprised if we show up soon. With luck, he can time the jump to match the difference between the day we leave and your current calendar. And yes, if my wife wishes to accompany us, I won't try to stop her."

I'd work on convincing him only one parent at a time should go.

Right now, Rhys was happy; he lived on in another When, and the Emperor and Aisha planned on marrying when Jax took the throne. They were waiting until then to be wed by King's decree; Eli was amenable to the idea but agreed that it would mean more if done by King Jackson instead.

Two months more, Aisha said. That was all. Eli had announced his retirement and subsequent plans to travel with his now-healthy queen, and the preparations for Jax's coronation were well under way. A week following that, they would be married on Union Square, with the city invited to attend.

Jax and Aubrey planned on moving into the official royal apartment; the Emperor and his family would move into the newly vacated space, just as Will had so many years ago.

Before they left, the Emperor pulled out his phone and poked his way through a series of photos until he found the ones he wanted Rhys to see.

"George asked that you see these," he explained, turning the phone toward Rhys. "Isaac Denton, now eight months old. He could never get the idea out of his head and realized that perhaps the information you'd shared was something he needed. He and James hired a surrogate to carry his clone."

"I've never seen him so happy," Aisha added.

Rhys flipped through the pictures, smiling. "Tell George he might not want to withhold the info that Isaac is his clone. Our Isaac found out just a few weeks ago and not gonna lie, he's struggling with it. I think he'll be all right, but...yeah. Tell him. And maybe tell him about me, so he knows that he's not George's ego project. That the seed was planted, and he was so damned wanted..."

When they jumped, arms around each other with the baby between them, light swelled around them, then winked out with a tiny pop. We stood silently for a moment, until Rhys sucked in a deep breath. Will turned and set a hand on his shoulder. "Merry Christmas, or...Merry Fucking Christmas?"

"Last one," Rhys said, chuckling.

"But?"

He had to think about it. We jumped home, and he was still thinking. Hyrum didn't want to hang around for the thinking part of things, and went downstairs to figure out a place on his bedroom walls to hang his old bike and then write thank you notes to everyone.

Will promised he'd find a way to get a note to Santa.

"Recycled souls," Rhys said later, when Will and Aisha were sitting together on the sofa. "That's what's picking at me. We visit ourselves in other Whens, people that are both us and not, and my brain has been trying to wrap itself around the idea that we can be individuals apart from ourselves. How can we possibly exist in more than one When simultaneously? Or is it even simultaneous?"

"It's been a conundrum for as long as I've been alive," Will said.

We're all energy, Rhys reminded him. If the seeds of our souls are pure energy, when we die it has to go somewhere. "Maybe some of those seeds stick together and speed back to the starting point, to live all over again. And maybe there are leftover seeds that sprinkle themselves through time, waiting to bloom. I was so fixated on not being the only Rhys, ever, that I overlooked that we're probably *all* the only Rhys, ever. We're all one person...branches of the same plant."

He didn't think it mattered if we ever figured out the composition of time. We could picture it as spaghetti, DNA, roots, or one long strand that looped back along itself like a spring. It didn't matter. There could be timelines or streams of time; it only mattered that we protect it.

"We may have gone too far in trying to protect it," Will said. "We tried so hard that I believe we may have affected when the world was saved."

Rhys nodded. "I know. There are a lot of what-ifs. What if Grandpa never sent Wick into a portal to check out the end of everything? What if he'd sent a drone instead? What if he'd just taken the chance in this When to visit his younger self in that one to compare better notes?"

"Which is why Jax and I eventually went back to interfere in Donna's life. And why I find no fault in your changing the outcome for your grandparents. Timelines will split, and our lives will go on."

"I just wanted…"

"I know. But I think in time you'll come to accept that there will eventually be a When in which you don't exist, and the idea will not seem so overwhelming. There are likely billions of streams of time, and within those, billions of timelines. We exist in many, partially in some, not at all in others. And our lives here go on."

"Then what bothers me so much?"

Dying.

"Wick?"

You don't want to die. If you don't exist in a When you know about, it's proof you can die. Or something like that.

"No one wants to die."

No, but the older you get, the more at peace you become with it. The fear fades.

"You're not afraid of dying."

I'm more afraid of never dying. But now you know, you're going to go back to the start of you, and do it all again. And apparently, you're getting lost along the way…a lot. It sounds fun.

"I don't imagine I'll have, you know, a family. That's not a great way to hold a relationship together. Or fair to kids."

"Don't get ahead of yourself," Aisha warned. "You don't know how old the Rhys was that Quinn began chasing after. You could be like Liam, old as dirt. Or even like Finn, just starting to explore the things that truly interest you after your life's work is settled."

Or you're like your dad, trading days from one When so that you don't outlive your family in this one. Spend a month somewhen, come home for years, and repeat.

He didn't need to figure it out right then and there, but he knew that at some point, he would begin to travel, and he'd get lost, not knowing for how long.

But he'd given Quinn freedom, and for that, Quinn would never stop looking for him.

Everywhere, everywhen.